"*36 Streets* glows bright and hallucinatory as tropical neon, goes down smooth as warm sake, cuts deep as a nano-steel blade. Napper honours classic cyberpunk with fresh perspectives and hot genre recombinations, a nasty new-future gleam, the proverbial new coat of paint. But there are more austere echoes here too, of Graham Greene and Kazuo Ishiguro, of a whole post-colonial literary heritage banging to be let in. In a genre stuffed with facile hero narratives, *36 Streets* consistently chooses something else – messy humanity, grey moral tones and choices, hard-edged geopolitical truth. Raw and raging and passionate, this is cyberpunk literature with a capital fucken L. Get it while it's hot!" **Richard Morgan, author of** *Altered Carbon*

"Brutal, brooding, brilliant . . . an angry vision of violence wrapped around a complex meditation of memory, trauma and hegemony. This is cyberpunk with soul. Street crime and resistance; nihilism and heroism; sinners and saviours; tiny Vietnam and the all-devouring empires that have hounded it; turn this book this way and that and these opposites meld and merge and flash bloody smiles at you, like the edges of a single perfect blade, with Napper's hand on the hilt." **Yudhanjaya Wijeratne, author of** *The Salvage Crew*

"Intimately concerned with the little guy in a world of neon gods, Napper paints a prophetic and uncomfortably believable vision of the future. A fascinating interplay between advancing technology and wish fulfillment, *36 Streets* is ambitious in scope while remaining deeply human." **Tim Hickson,** *Hello Future Me*

"A fun, frenetic journey of neon-blasted streets, sinister underworlds and oodles of brutal tech, rendered in cutthroat prose so tangible you can almost smell the grime and cigarette smoke. T.R. Napper's cyberpunk world is a feral, back-alley brawl of a novel with real blood under its nails." **Jeremy Szal, author of** *Stormblood*

"High-octane, immersive SF at its best. *36 Streets* is sure to become a classic in the field." **Kaaron Warren, Shirley Jackson Award-Winner**

"For his impressive debut novel, rising star of Australian speculative fiction T.R. Napper gives us an engrossing, intriguing action-packed duty tour of a tech-thick, violence-infused, neon-scorched near future gangland Vietnam, where unwinnable games run hot and wild. Highly recommended." **Cat Sparks, author of *Lotus Blue***

"Napper has made a remarkable character in the form of his protagonist Lin Thi Vu, subverting to some degree the conventions of the world of male power and violence. Lin is 'other' in this environment: female, somewhat Australian, not Vietnamese enough, desiring and desired widely. It's a great achievement. The set pieces, the interludes, of performed mastery with weapons and skill, are well poised and set the scene with ritualised violence." **Stephen Teo, author of *Chinese Martial Arts Cinema: The Wuxia Tradition***

"Beautiful, shimmering, ghostly science fiction." **Anna Smith-Spark, author of the *Empires of Dust* trilogy**

36 STREETS

T. R. NAPPER

TITAN BOOKS

36 Streets
Print edition ISBN: 9781789097412
E-book edition ISBN: 9781789097429

Published by Titan Books
A division of Titan Publishing Group Ltd
144 Southwark Street, London SE1 0UP
www.titanbooks.com

First edition: January 2022
10 9 8 7 6 5 4 3 2 1

A CIP catalogue record for this title is available from the British Library.

Printed and bound in the United Kingdom by CPI Group (UK) Ltd, Croydon,
CR0 4YY.

For Sarah, Robert, and Willem. You three: the ground beneath my feet, my sky, my stars.

A Note on Vietnamese Language Usage

By English-language convention, character names do not use diacritics, nor does the country name Vietnam. However, all other Vietnamese words use diacritics to indicate tones, except where a non-Vietnamese speaker is using them. This may sound a little complicated, but I swear you won't even notice.

It was their thirty-eighth fight. This time she fought with the kanabo, a three-foot iron-studded mace. Fights with such were not expected to last long.

They stood twelve feet apart on the tatami mats. Lin Thi Vu held her weapon two-handed, the weight of it already stinging her triceps. Her shihan held his with one, raised above his head, angled so the tip was pointed at her. The third person watched from the shadows, past the edge of her peripheral vision.

Shihan, silent, no war cry, not a breath: whirled, iron flashing, a gyre that tore towards her.

The fight did not last long.

Her arm, broken, was folded behind her. She gasped with pain, vision flowing in and out of focus. Her kanabo lay beyond her fingertips on the white mat, now dotted red with her blood. Probably only a three-mat fight.

Legs astride her, the master held the mace above his head, ready for the last blow.

Bao Nguyen emerged from the shadows at the side of the room. Stood next to her, looking down. Eyes watching always watching, marking now the pain on her face. Her failure. Time and again, her failure.

Bao said: "[The will and the act.]"

Lips swollen, voice blood-slurred, she replied: "The will and the act."

Bao said to the shihan: "[More.]"

With a triumphant cry, the master brought the iron down.

PART ONE
Fat Victory

I'll give you twenty endless years
Twenty years seven thousand nights of artillery
Seven thousand nights of artillery lulling you to sleep
Are you sleeping yet or are you still awake

– Tran Da Tu, *Love Tokens*

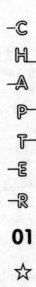

CHAPTER 01 ☆

The problem with heroes was they thought the world owed them tribute before being sent to die. Awed respect. Last requests. Nobility in death. All that bullshit. This hero was no different. Handcuffed to a rusted wall pipe, wrists bloody, looking up at Lin Thi Vu through a sheen of sweat and fear and perverse hope. Dark eyes, lean shoulders, lean face. He said, jaw set: "[Get word to my mother. Tell her what happened.]"

The words came through her on-retina translator, in English. She understood what he was saying, but out of habit read the translation before nodding once.

Uncle Bao had given her the location of the safe house, told her to be careful, only go for the target, call it off if he had accomplices. Do no more than they'd been paid to do. Her thoughts, precisely.

He'd come alone; she'd got him. As usual, she'd made it harder than necessary.

☆

Thirty minutes earlier Lin had been waiting on a plastic chair in the darkest corner of the room, wearing a conical bamboo hat, the rim down over her eyes. Chain smoking to help keep the tremors in her hands under control. The target was late, so the shakes had gotten progressively worse. Lin tapped her foot on the ground in a nervous staccato; her free hand gripping and un-gripping the loose material of her faded blue pants. The pulse pistol rested near her crotch. She picked it up, checked the charge, put it down again. Up, and down again. Battered blue metal, faded Baosteel logo stamped into the rear of the stock.

Lin was down to her last three cigarettes when a key rattled in the lock. She jumped, the pistol clattered to the ground. She bent down to scoop it up, dropped it again as the door opened, a shaft of light splitting the gloom. A shadow outlined in the doorway as Lin, down on one knee, finally grasped the weapon.

"[Who's there?]" asked a voice. Lin could see more clearly now. Clear enough, anyway, to confirm it was her mark: young man, twenty-two, message runner and scout for the Việt Minh in Hoàn Kiêm.

He took one step forward, squinting into the gloom as he reached for something at his belt. She squeezed the trigger, the room lit up, strobe-flash-blue, the boy's eyes wild-wide.

But her aim was off, the blue arc of electricity hitting his shoulder then striking the wall behind him, the shock popping a black-and-white picture of Ho Chi Minh from the wall. The boy shouted at the pain, half turned, legs wobbling. The weapon he was holding – a hook-bladed knife – dropped to the floor. He reached for the doorframe behind, trying to drag himself out.

Lin said: "*Fuck*," and pulled the trigger again. The gun answered *click*. Then repeated itself: *click click click*. She swore again, too strung out to care what the neighbours heard. The shaking in her hands abated, her vision cleared, the adrenalin of imminent failure pumping into her system.

She sprung up, took four steps and swivelled her hips, delivering a high kick to the young man's temple. His head snapped sideways, bounced off the doorframe, and he collapsed at her feet.

Lin dragged him by the arms across the smooth tile floor. Breathing heavily, she handcuffed him to a pipe and gaffer-taped his mouth, just as the shakes started up again. She stagger-stepped towards the couch, slumped backwards into it, missed, slid off the rounded armrest and cracked her temple on the side table as her butt hit the floor. Undeterred, Lin slid the vial out of her pocket and held it up in the thin light.

A sigh escaped from her lips. The viscous yellow liquid glowed as though generating its own light. No drink to mix it with, she pulled the dropper, hands respectfully calm as the chemicals in her body began to change in expectation, already starting to behave as they would post-hit.

Three drops onto her tongue. Bitter, pungent, cat-piss taste and then—

Euphoria.

The glow of the drops spread from her tongue, to her eyeballs, to her earlobes, to her fingernails. So she was glowing, glowing just like the vial. At peace, just like the vial, welcomed, belonging, just like the vial, part of an infinite present, connected via vital luminous threads to all the other vital luminous beings in that web, spread out in space, connected, all connected, all needed, all known, all wanted…

She awoke. Mouth dry. Lips tingling, aftereffect of the drug; she drew her thumb across them, as though to wipe the sensation away. Lin grunted as she pushed herself up. Left arm pins and needles where she'd been lying on it. The timestamp on-retina said: **6:16 pm**

She'd been out twenty minutes. The boy was still there; the tension ebbed in her chest. Wrists bloody, must have woken before she did, one last desperate attempt to flee.

☆

"[Yes, you'll tell her?]" he asked again.

Lin nodded. Even that single gesture heavy, weighed down with the lie. There'd be no back-channel communication, no quiet moment

7

over a kitchen table, Lin's hand on some old woman's, mumbling condolences. Tokenism of that sort could be linked back to Lin. And Lin, well, wasn't much in the mood for being kidnapped by the Việt Minh, then tortured, murdered, filmed, and later broadcast out onto the freewave as an example of what happens to traitors.

"[Promise,]" he said.

Lin pressed her lips together in displeasure at his demand, but replied in Vietnamese: "*Chị hứa*." No point in letting him get all emotional before the authorities arrived.

"[She lives on Chan Cam. Green apartment, third floor,]" he said. "[You know it?]"

Lin nodded. In the thirty-six streets. Of course she knew it.

"[Tell her I died as a patriot, for our country.]"

Lin lit a cigarette and settled back into the sofa. The body buzz from the drugs relaxed her limbs, sharpened her focus. The boy wasn't speaking to her anymore. He was speaking for himself, the words forming heroic images in his mind. The coda of his life's narrative. She blew out a cloud of smoke. Twenty years old, more or less. Pretty short story.

The smoke pooled across the ceiling. Peeling paint, dirty white, no fan. Narrow window, sunset, room darkening. Outside a view of a courtyard, overgrown, a tight square between apartments stacked on top of each other, four, five, six stories high, depending on how much risk the landlord wanted to swallow. Poorly made top-floor apartments were known to lose roofs, contents, even occupants, if the winds got high enough.

This one was solid. Just old, its entrance hidden down one of the alleys in the Old Quarter. Labyrinthine passages, unmarked, slick concrete, shocks of green emerging from cracks, from drains.

She smoked until someone tapped on the door, light. Lin rose to her feet, fluid, knife in her hand. Black moulded grip, long black blade, matching pair each ankle, nano-edged Chinese special forces knives that had found their way onto the Hà Nội street market.

"*Yes?*" she asked, in Vietnamese.

The door creaked open, hesitant; Lin reached, no hesitation, and pulled the person in. It was her street kid, grubby face, eyes round in their sockets. He was too poor to have a memory pin, the room was dim, and the rim of the conical bamboo hat covered half of her face. Still, she grabbed his hair and gently tilted his head until he was looking at the floor.

"[They're here,]" he mumbled.

She sheathed her blade, pulled a wad of yuan from her pocket. A cashless world, they insisted. Against all contrary evidence. Citizens didn't like putting prostitutes on their credit link, for one, no matter the guarantees of anonymity. Everything black market required cold hard.

She handed him a note. He grabbed it, big smile cracking his face. Lin turned him around and pushed him out the door. Increased jamming in the Old Quarter lately had neural links dropping out all the time, so she'd gone analogue, found a street communicator. Better anyway, harder to trace.

Lin closed the door and walked over to the young hero, checked his cuffs, gleaming in the low light, firm around his red wrists. She'd add the price of them to the bill.

He looked up at her. The fear was consuming him now, chasing away the last hints of righteousness. He asked: "[What will they do to me?]"

Torture you. Virtual, physical, until you don't know the difference. Over weeks. Turn you. Turn you against everyone you ever loved. Everything you ever loved. Everyone you ever fought alongside. Make you confess every offence you, or anyone you ever knew committed. Put a bullet in you. Bury you in the jungle in an unmarked grave.

"Don't know," she said.

He nodded. Steeling himself.

She found herself staring at the young man. His thin shirt, sweat-soaked skin, his failing courage. Utterly alone. She wet her lips to say something, but the *thump thump thump* of heavy boots on stairs changed her mind.

Lin Thi Vu left the room quickly, passing the men with her eyes down, conical hat covering her face. Not wanting to be seen, and most of all not wanting to see them and the hard purpose in their eyes.

At the bottom of the stairs she picked up her bamboo pole, baskets on either end holding bananas and lychees and mangosteens and whatever else she could find in the market earlier that day. She stepped out into the darkened alley, into the steaming night air.

Loose pants, traditional tunic, conical hat: at first glance she looked like a young hawker. And hawkers didn't warrant more than a first glance. She walked towards the light and noise. The traffic frenetic, as though in the intensity of nine million glimmer bikes and one million cars the world could be forgotten. The war could be forgotten. The fierce energy of the city hit her as her foot touched the sidewalk, the fury of occupation, of defeat, of a rebellious, quarrelsome, unbreakable city that now lay broken. The fury now directed into white noise, throwing it like a cloak over thought and memory.

Memory most of all. To forget the past, to forget even the present, obscure it with sound and movement; with arguments over the price of produce, fistfights over one bike parked too close to another, stabbings over the outcome of a soccer game.

A whole city pulsating with fear and denial, sweat streaming down its face, in a heat that clogged the throat and clouded the mind.

Lin, bamboo pole balanced on her shoulder, walked through it all unseen. A spectre, part in the city, part elsewhere. The weight of the bamboo bearing down as she stepped between slick, stinking puddles, through the cacophony of blaring horns and street sellers.

Straining under the burden, head bowed, she made her way into the fetid heart of the thirty-six streets.

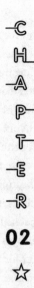

Lin walked up the narrow, uneven staircase. Musky air, moisture on the stone. A hundred years old, a hundred years of soft-soled feet trudging up and down, smoothing the steps, bowing them. The *drip drip drip* of human existence wearing down the rock, wearing it smooth and indifferent.

Three floors up, Lin banged on a blue steel door with her fist. She took a step back and tilted her head upwards, let the nano-cams above – and the people behind them – check her face. Simultaneously, sensors in the door received the pass code from her cochlear implant. Human and technological components of the security system satisfied, the door creaked open.

She stepped into a room filled with smoke, laughter, and the sour smell of masculinity. Maybe half of Bao's men were inside – thirty or so – sitting on knee-high plastic chairs drinking, eating, playing cards and dice.

They yelled *chúc sức khỏe!* [Good health!] as they downed rice whiskey and fresh beer, red-faced, boasting, boisterous. Smoking cheap cigarettes rolled with black-market tobacco for hours on end, day after day in between jobs. Nicotine coated the white blinds in a thin film of yellow, stained the roof. The concrete floor, swept every night by an ancient bent woman in exchange for food, was covered now in peanut shells and spilt beer.

At the table closest to the door, a skinny toe-cutter named Snakehead Tran and a thick-necked southerner called Bull Neck Bui sat with heads craned over a game of Vietnamese chess. Bull glanced up, whacked Snakehead on the shoulder, indicating Lin with his chin.

Bull was a third-generation taxi driver from Sài Gòn, now a head enforcer for the gang. She never quite knew where she stood with him. Technically, she was above him in the hierarchy, but neither he nor anyone else acted as though this was the case.

She lowered her pole and fruit baskets to the ground with a sigh.

Tran smiled, Bull burst into laughter, "*Bah hah hah!*" pointing a shot glass at her clothes. "[Hey! Silent One! Make me some phở!]"

A man at a nearby table joined in: "[Little sister! Off to work in the fields?]" And another: "[Little sister, some fucking doughnuts!]"

Lin glanced at the translation of the comments on-retina and replied: "*Đụ má!*"

The men fell about laughing. Lin could never quite get the accent right, even when using words she always used, like *motherfucker*. The men always found it hilarious. Red-eyed, sheen of sweat on their skin, missing teeth. Ugly men, violent men, crude, uneducated, loyal, tough. Better than most. As good as it got, in this city.

Lin walked past the smoke and insults, pushing through a cheap wooden door at the other end of the room. The door swung closed and she leaned against it. Alone in her tiny, dark office, shutting her eyes for just a few moments. She sighed, yanked off her hat, chucked it into a corner, and nudged her way around her desk. Standing, she opened the top drawer, pulled out a bottle of green-labelled sake and a white ceramic cup. Filled it, took a shot, filled it again, got the glowing dropper out, gave it one.

Lin turned to the window, cup in hand. Lights across the city now, the crackle of gunfire somewhere in the distance, raucous laughter of the men coming from behind. The violet neon of a gin bar gleaming down below. She sipped her sake and ice-seven.

A crack of light, as the other door to her office popped open.

A voice, quiet but not soft, said in Vietnamese: "[How are you, little sister?]"

"Fine, Uncle," she said in English.

"*Fine*," he repeated, using the English word, then waited.

Lin sighed again. "No more of those jobs."

"[Why?]" Curiosity in the voice.

She turned. Bao Nguyen stood in the doorway. Full white hair, black moustache, watchful eyes, always watching, never missed a thing. She made to say something, then changed her mind.

"[Bring the bottle,]" he said, and disappeared from sight.

Lin closed the door and was reaching for her sake when the throbbing pain in her temple made itself known.

It'd been there all along, under the buzz of the drugs and the dulling guilt. She winced as she touched it and drew away her hand, spots of blood on her fingertips. She went over to her cooler unit – a small black box sitting on the floor against the wall – removed the ice tray, popped some cubes out onto the floor. Sifted through the shelves until she found one of her singlets, wrapped it around the ice, and pressed it to her temple.

Holding the sake with the other hand, she went through to the next room.

Bao sat behind his desk, the fauxwood surface battered and scratched, flexiscreen to one side, half-bottle of brandy and a plate of sunflower seeds sitting in front of him. Bao was simply dressed. Worn cloth jacket, shirt with drooping collar. Like always, nothing to give his status away as the most influential gangster in Hà Nội.

She sat across from him and poured herself a drink while he watched. Bao had a habit of looking at someone for too long before taking his turn to speak. Lin was never sure if he was thinking about what he wanted to say, or was trying to see something in the person he was talking to. Lin sometimes wondered another thing, related to those rumours that followed him around. Whether he actually wasn't interested in what was being said, his mind's eye, somewhere else, back in the jungle.

Lin put down the ice pack for a moment so she could light a cigarette, snapping closed her steel lighter before chucking it onto the table in front of her. Ice pack in one hand, sake and cigarette in the other, she was set.

Bao smiled wryly and lifted his small, red-coloured glass. He said: "[Good health,]" she replied: "*Chúc sức khỏe*," and they downed their drinks.

Bao always seemed calm, reserved, with just the occasional glimpse of dry humour. She'd only seen him violent once in the five years she'd known him. Though that one time. Well.

"[You got the job done,]" he said. Not a question.

"Yeah."

"[That is what matters.]"

Lin said nothing to that, taking a drag on her cigarette instead.

"[How old are you now, Lin?]" he asked.

Lin raised an eyebrow at him. "Does it matter?"

"[Yes,]" he replied, and waited.

"Twenty-four."

"[Hm. Your spirit is older than that. But still, you have the naïvety of the young.]"

"Fuck. Uncle. I've been a gangster since I was nineteen. With you."

"[Yes. But when you are young it is still possible to believe in something.]"

14

Lin downed her drink. As she poured another she said: "That's all you got, Uncle: don't be naïve? You're young, you don't know what you're talking about?"

He stared at her for a few moments. "[Well. Yes. It works with everyone else.]" He smiled. "[They nod respectfully and then pour my brandy.]"

"Ha. Pour your own fucken brandy." The glow from the ice-seven was spreading. One drop, just enough to relax her body, focus her mind, shift her conscience to neutral. Bao was the only one she was comfortable speaking English with, other than her family. Nearly nine years returned, she could understand pretty much everything that was spoken to her in Vietnamese. But she found it useful to double-check unfamiliar words on-retina, make sure the meaning she got was straight.

She had a few strong suits. A couple, anyway. Language wasn't one of them. Hated the laughter every time she foundered on a tone, self-conscious with new words, she fell back into silence. Perfectionist, acutely self-conscious, proud: the unholy trinity when it came to learning a language. So she never talked much. Switching between English and Vietnamese, embarrassed at using either, at the impurity of her identity.

Her reluctance to talk earned her the gang name Silent One. They called her Mouse at the start, but after she broke the knee of Laughing Man Tran and pushed his face into a pan filled with deep-frying tofu, well – they decided the Mouse didn't quite fit. The Laughing Man had called her a foreign dog. Probably the last coherent thing he did say. Lips melted, nose halfway down his face, a slurring horror show that no one wanted to look at.

Bao condoned the fight; she fought exactly as he'd taught her. After Laughing Man got out of hospital he didn't want to hang around. Packed his bags and was gone. Rumour it was for the underground freak fights down in Đà Nẵng.

She'd fought him in silence. Took the abuse, then unmanned him. It didn't take much to make it as a gangster: you just had to be smarter, tougher, and meaner than anyone else in the room.

Bao cracked sunflower seeds between his fingernails, popping them into his mouth, discarding the husks. Watching her, always watching.

"[It's war,]" he finally said.

"Yeah," she replied, settling back into her chair. Bao had comfortable chairs. Cloth hand-sewn, padded armrests. She tilted her head back until it rested against the back, her face pointed at the ceiling. Moisture ran in lines across the surface above, warping, bubbling the off-white paint. It was cool in Bao's room. No point in being the boss if it didn't come with air conditioning.

Lin smoked, cold pack still pressed against her temple, and watched the water seep across the ceiling. Listened to the *crick crick crick*, as Bao broke open sunflower pods; clatter of dice and beer glasses on tables from the room behind lulled her, drew her back to that first time.

CHAPTER

03

☆

Nineteen, drunk, lost. No language, too scared to ask where she was, no credit for a taxi. Every dollar spent on fresh beer. Empty stomach, regretting not having bought some fried tofu. Boiled peanuts. Anything.

Paved alleyway, close on all sides, the Old Quarter. The men at the bia hơi she'd just left watched her go, sullen, red-eyed. The heat beating down, worse than usual, night but still unbearable, air thick. Tempers on edge, the aftermath of a Chinese crackdown the week before. A prism grenade thrown into a high-end restaurant popular with Chinese military; two dead officers, two dead waiters, a dozen injured. Not the most notable of attacks, except one of the dead officers was a general. So there were raids and arrests and bodies turning up, young men and young women, tortured and aired out and worse. Everyone an informant, everyone Việt Minh, no one able to talk or trust.

She lurch-stepped down the alley. The Thirty-Six Streets they called it. Maybe it was, maybe once, when the Old Quarter was built. Thirty-

six streets for the thirty-six guilds that existed seven hundred years before, for the artisans in silk or silver or wood or cloth or bamboo or herbal medicine.

Whatever the past, now there were myriad streets, and alleys, and lanes, and dead ends, and hidden entrances, and backways of smooth brick and deep shadow. Signs torn down to confuse the Chinese. Lin was in the labyrinth now, unsure of the way home, back to that narrow, frightened space she lived in with Kylie and Phuong. She aimed herself towards the far end of the alley, herd of glimmer bikes droning past; she'd figure it once she got to the street. Stagger along until she found a landmark.

"[Little sister, where are you going?]" Men in the shadows, three, sitting near their battered scooters. Two playing Vietnamese chess while the third watched; all looking at her now.

She ignored them, kept walking, her head down.

"[Little sister, join us for a drink,]" said the man.

She glanced over. The speaker was shirtless, the other two had their singlets rolled up, bellies exposed. Shirtless had a shaved head and a bottle of cheap rice whiskey in his hand.

Large drops of rain, splashes the size of her palm, fell infrequently. Splash – step – splash – step – splash.

Lin picked up her pace, wanting to be away from the sickly heat of their attention, slipped in a puddle, righted herself, slipped again and ended up pitching forward.

The men laughed. Lin winced, trying to rise quickly, embarrassed, slipping again.

A hand appeared near her face. "[Let me help.]"

Lin batted the arm away, rose unsteadily to her feet. A badly pockmarked face was suddenly close to hers, whiskey and decay on his breath as he asked: "[Do you have a boyfriend?]"

Adrenalin pushed her senses through the drink haze. Aware now of how dark it was here, a partial blackout perhaps. The bia hơi thirty metres back down the alley had forgotten her. An old woman sat out the

*front of her home a few feet away. Weathered, silver hair parted down
the middle, a dark-skinned highlander sitting on a six-inch bamboo
stool washing dishes in a large plastic bowl. She wasn't watching. Lot of
things happened in these streets people made sure not to watch.*

*Lin was aware of her body now. Shoulders bare, just wearing a black
singlet, tight jeans, plastic thongs on her feet. The heat and the fat drops
of water made her top stick to her skin. The man – around the same
height as Lin – let his eyes range over her, linger on her breasts.*

"Leave me alone," she said. In English.

The man's face hardened. "[What?]"

She pressed her lips together.

"[What?]" he asked again. "[Are you Vietnamese?]"

The next part happened fast.

She tried to push past—

—he slammed her in the stomach with whiskey bottle and fist—

*—she doubled over and threw up on his feet. Bare feet, plastic
sandals.*

*Lin groaned, hands on her stomach, the taste of bile in her mouth.
The man jumped back and called her bitch.*

*"[Hey! Leave her alone!]" someone yelled. A woman, the old woman,
nearby, deciding to see.*

"[Eat shit, bitch,]" the man said.

"[Small dick!]"

"[You are black like a dog's shit.]"

A pause, and then angrily: "[I'll get my son!]"

*The shirtless man pulled a knife from his belt, the blade small and
scratched, and showed it to the old woman. "[Go inside.]"*

The woman said nothing.

He waved it at her again. "[I'll cut your neck!]"

*She stood up. "[Your dick is like that knife! I'm going to call my son!]"
She stormed inside, leaving the dishes on concrete.*

His attention returned to Lin. "[Fat lips. Cock-sucking lips.]"

One of the other men said: "[Spicy hot.]"

The last, indifferent, was still looking at the board, figuring his next move.

A lesson Lin had learned hard, growing up: if you were going to commit to a course of action, commit fully. No half-measures.

She rammed the heel of her palm into the nose of shirtless. Bone crunched and he staggered back, his bottle shattering on the stone.

Lin's head snapped sideways. White flash of pain and she was falling, her palms scraping on slick stones.

Someone called her a bitch again and kicked her in the stomach. Lin's eyes popped, she gasped, rolling in the wet. A second man had joined the first. Blindsided her with a punch. She got onto her back, instinct kicking in, legs coiled and ready to lash out when they got too close.

Fear clarifying, she saw and heard and smelled them, watched the two move, arranging themselves around her.

Fear clarifying, against their dark intent.

Fear, primal, clarified.

She rammed her heel into the balls of the first man who stepped up; he groaned, hands on crotch, mincing backwards. Pockmarked face stepped in, she lashed out, he tore off her thong trying to grab her foot and she kicked again. He laughed and stepped back. Blood on his top lip and chin, his nose broken. Still, he smiled. Teeth gleaming, enjoying himself. He stepped towards her, knife flashing in his hand. She pushed away, still on her back, until her head was against the gutter. The duo positioned themselves near her legs. The pockmarked leader with his blade and broken nose, the second holding his groin, the third over at the game, still contemplating his next move.

Shirtless said: "[A drink would have been easier.]"

"Not if it involved smelling the open sewer of your mouth."

"[We can teach you how to behave like a Vietnamese.]"

"I reckon I'm nailing it."

They moved closer, she lashed out again, hitting the same guy in the groin. He collapsed backwards; Lin couldn't help but smile. Hard to beat the satisfaction of a good clean heel to the nuts, twice.

Her smile lasted a good half-second. Until shirtless laid his foot into her. She cried out, then he was down close, hand over her mouth, eyes gleaming.

His fingers dug into the side of her jaw as he said: "[You don't belong here.]"

He let an errant finger near her mouth, she bit down, something gleeful and rabid rising in her. It was his turn to scream, high-pitched; as he tried to yank his finger out, she bit down harder, blood spurting into her mouth. Something struck her face, that only locked her jaw; he struck her face again, back of her head hitting pavement and—

—the lights blinded her. Lin gagged, coughing out blood and fingertip, and rolled away as the man pulled his weight from her. Lin held a hand up against the glare, scooter lights, alley alight.

Silhouettes, three.

"[Small dick!]" The old woman's voice, somewhere behind Lin's head. "[My son is here!]"

The three new humans walked down the alley; the two who'd attacked Lin backed away slowly. Lights from the other direction, more scooters. More men. Lin rose to her knees, her feet.

The lights lit up the obvious leader of the new arrivals. Thick grey hair, cigarette hanging from his lips, his eyes watching, quiet, unwavering. Near his shoulder, a dark-skinned man followed, eyes popping with anger.

"[Uncle Bao,]" said the pockmarked one, clutching his bleeding fingertip. "[I didn't—I didn't realise. I didn't know you...]"

"[Beehive Hung,]" said the white-haired newcomer. "[I do know you. You spend your wife's salary on whiskey and boxing bets.]"

"[I apologise, Uncle.]"

"[Ten point three million dong owed to me. Three days overdue.]"

Beehive Hung looked at his feet.

"[Fifteen million now.]"

Beehive looked up, but said nothing.

"[Pay to Aunty Be,]" said Bao, indicating the old woman nearby, "[for the insult.]"

Beehive made a couple of different shapes with his mouth, then nodded, eyes back down.

"[Now,]" said Bao, with a well-timed exhalation of smoke, "[fuck off.]"

They fucked off. Beehive Hung had a hard time starting his scooter with his bloodied hand, but started it. The idle game-player sighed and helped the pale-faced, groin-hobbled second man onto the back of his bike, and they disappeared as well.

Bao walked over to Lin. She stood her ground, fists clenched.

He looked her up and down. One of her eyes was closing up. Adrenalin, post facto, made her legs shake.

Bao waited for a few seconds longer than necessary, then said: "[You're Phuong's sister. The bad one.]"

"How did…?" Lin started, then stopped. The man had this way, this presence, that stopped a lot of talk around it. A bullshit filter, an Australian would say. Something stronger, actually, that shut it down all together. Those eyes, his eyes, held a promise. There wasn't any compromise in that promise.

Bao and Lin stood in silence for a few moments more, while he considered it all, and he decided he wanted to talk again.

"[First thing,]" he said, "[is to teach you how to fight.]"

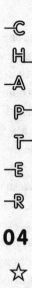

CHAPTER

04

☆

Lips dry, she stretched her shoulders. Something itched on her face. A sunflower seed came away in her hand, several more sat in her lap.

"The fuck, Bao?"

He held another black sunflower seed between his fingers up next to his ear, ready to throw. "[Most of my men pretend everything I say has the weight of the law, and the wisdom of the ages.]"

Lin grunted, shifted upright.

"[You just fall asleep.]"

She patted pockets vaguely for her cigarettes. "Sorry, Uncle."

"[No you're not.]"

Lin found her smokes, hesitated, rested the pack on her lap. She sighed. "I am, Bao. I just—I just don't like working for the fucken Chinese."

Something stilled in Bao. Smoke idled from his cigarette. He said: "[No one does. This work I take on—]" He exhaled a cloud of white smoke. "[—is for precise reasons.]" She waited for him to elaborate.

Instead she got: "[Get out of here, clean yourself up. I have a new job for you.]"

She raised an eyebrow.

"[At the Metropole, this evening.]"

She lit her cigarette, inhaled, savoured it.

"[Little sister, you want a change from your regular job. This is a change.]"

"Yeah?"

"[Westerner, very wealthy. Imagines we are private detectives.]"

She smiled, sardonic. "How'd he get that idea?"

"[Sandfly Ha works the bar there. Helps the clientele access things they legally cannot access.]"

"Legality?"

"[Appearances must be kept, even during a war.]"

"The war is why the rich come here. They can do whatever they want."

"[The rich can do whatever they want anywhere. But decorum needs to be maintained at all times. People like Sandfly help them play these games.]" Bao took a drag on his cigarette, spark in his eye. "[So this man. English, or something European. Was asking around about private investigators. Sandfly said yes, no problem, we have private investigators in Vietnam. Very good, very cheap. No problem. The Westerner says he had something 'most vexatious' to be sorted and they had to send their best man. Sandfly checked the meaning of vexatious first, then tells the man yes, no problem, we'll send our best man. Very best. Fixes vexatious all the time.]"

Lin smiled. "Private fucken eye?"

"[Maybe he likes old movies.]"

"I don't think I've seen any of those movies."

"[I have,]" said Bao. He looked at her, and for a few moments she wondered if he wanted her to say something. But then he added: "[This is not much different from what you do already. Working contacts, lookouts, informants. Tracking people down who do not wish to be found.]"

"If you say so."

"[Drinking too much, like a private detective.]" His eyes flicked over towards the gash on her temple. "[Getting beat up.]"

"I fell."

"[Drugged out, asleep in the boss's office. Snoring.]"

"I don't snore."

"[Single. Snores like a drunken cat. No close relationships.]"

"I get laid all the time."

He paused and smoked. "[No family. No stability.]"

The sting floated up from somewhere beneath the buzz. "Don't start, Bao."

He watched.

Lin smoked and thought about another drop of ice-seven.

"[Your sister was in the news again.]"

Lin finished her drink, smoothing her face. She stood, grabbing her bottle.

He said: "[The case. The Metropole, tonight, seven-thirty.]"

"Why me?"

"[I told you why.]"

"Why else?"

"[You are more comfortable around them.]"

Her lips tightened. "That's not true."

"[Perhaps. But you understand them better. They trust you.]"

"What are you trying to say?"

"[You speak English.]" She thought he was going to add something to that, but instead he said: "[You wanted a different kind of job. This is the job. You will take it.]"

Lin bent down, scooped up her singlet. Cool in her hand, water dripping on the floor. She sighed. "Yes, Uncle."

"[And, little sister.]"

She turned back to him. "Yeah?"

"[This man.]"

"Yeah?"

"[Make sure you take all his money.]"

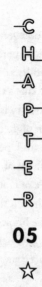

CHAPTER

05

☆

Lin paused outside her apartment door to listen to Barry sing. She smiled, a wry one. The trilling stopped as soon as she thumbed the lock.

Barry the yellow songbird was hanging in his bamboo cage at the open window, facing towards the courtyard. A handful of the other residents had the same habit: their songbirds – blue and black and red – singing to each other in the tall closed space between apartments, deep courtyard hemmed in on all four sides. Lush green overgrown space below, peeling concrete walls above, the air in between filled with *trill-trilling*.

The man she'd bought the songbird from had insisted it was flesh and bone. Genetically bred to be resistant to the bird flu that had killed three per cent of the people and all the birds in Hà Nội twenty years before. It was probably just a repurposed drone, uploaded with a limited AI and a *tweet-tweet* soundtrack. But Lin wasn't about to slice him open to find out.

"You ever going to sing for me, fucker?" she asked the bird.

Barry corkscrewed his little head at her, the way birds do, and refused to answer. She took out his seed tray, refilled it, paused. "You realise that's the deal, Barry? Food for song? Like your mates out there."

Barry twisted his head the other way, but still said nothing, waiting.

Lin sighed and slotted the tray back in. Barry hopped along his perch and pecked at his seed. She glanced around her small dim apartment absently as she shucked off the urchin attire. Lin picked a change of clothes up from the floor and dressed, pulling on her jacket last. She felt the inside pocket to confirm the presence of her cigarettes and the book.

"Okay, Barry." She sighed. "I gotta go to this fucking job."

Barry started singing as soon as she'd clicked the door behind her.

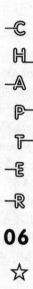

CHAPTER 06 ☆

Lin's third time downstairs at the Metropole. Third time feeling the anger in the pit of her stomach. At the yellow gold, the shimmering crystal, at the white-jacketed waiters carrying thousand-yuan cocktails. At the diamond and tuxedo-clad patrons washing down blacklisted food with champagne like it was nothing out of the ordinary.

Like food shortages, starvation, pyres of the burning dead were all on another planet.

Lin stood in the foyer as the clientele swirled past. Ignoring her. Actively ignoring her. As requested by Bao, she'd worn her best clothes: denim jeans, shiny dark blue bomber jacket, short hair combed back. She'd walked out of her apartment feeling overdressed.

Next to the tailored suits and gleaming silk cheongsams, her best looked vagrant. If she was lucky they'd think it was post-materialist peasant chic.

Probably not, from the looks she was getting. More disdain, like she was a rodent.

Two young Chinese women walked past, giggling, hands over mouths. One was wearing a Mao suit and gold-glitter eyeliner, the other was walking a shaved cat on a diamond-sparkling leash.

Yeah. This was another planet.

A Vietnamese man wearing an impeccable dark suit, silver name badge, and too-straight back approached her.

"[Miz Vu, from Nguyen Investigations?]" he asked, eyes flicking over her attire.

Lin nodded.

"[Follow me,]" he said, turning on his polished boot.

When they got to the elevator he said: "[Herbert Molayson is a valued client.]"

She said nothing as he pressed the button for the second-to-top floor.

"[We know who you're with. We don't want any of that business coming into the Metropole.]"

The door pinged and still she'd said nothing. The concierge made a tight line with his mouth. "[The Metropole is backed by the Chinese military. That gang makes your gang—]"

Lin put a finger to his lips and whispered: "*Shhhhh.*" Red crept into his features as she left the elevator.

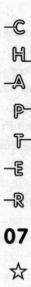

Herbert Molayson was posed against the bar when she entered his suite. Grey pinstriped pants, matching vest, pressed white shirt, one ankle crossed over the other. Grey hair, curly, high forehead, small square beard hanging off the end of his chin, bow tie, plump, fifty-five. Glass of alcohol dangling at the end of soft white fingers. Looking at her with the gleaming, empty eyes of old money.

Lin stopped a few metres away, taking in the room: real hard wood, dark, was everywhere; the coffee table near a dark leather couch, the bar top, the concertina doors that led to the bedroom. White rug, thick; gold curtains, the smell of flowers and wood oil; red-framed pictures on the walls – of an old Chinese pagoda, of golden carp circling in a pond, of waterlilies. Through the door to the next room, a glimpse of a bed with snow-white sheets, and green-hooded bedside lamps.

"Miz Vu, I believe," he said in a rich English accent.

She looked at him in a way that said *yeah. Obviously.*

"Herbert Molayson," he said, dry English smile. "It's a pleasure to meet you."

When she still didn't say anything he said, unflustered: "Would you like a drink, young lady?"

"Juyondai."

He furrowed his brow theatrically, said: "Hmm," and looked towards the wet bar. "You know I'm not sure they have sake here. Terribly embarrassing. Can I get a man to bring up a bottle?"

Lin pointed with her chin. "Bourbon."

"Of course," he said. He gave her a generous pour, then refilled his own from a separate bottle. Grappa.

He closed the space between them, limping slightly, and handed her a half-full crystal glass.

Herbert held up his drink. "I find the beginning of any relationship mostly about pretending to listen and holding in farts. Usually things go downhill after that. I hope ours, my dear, is far more productive. Cheers."

Lin popped a brief, involuntary *who is this guy* smile and took a long chug from her drink. She made her way over to the couch and settled into it, pulling a pack of Double Happiness from her pocket.

"So, thank you for coming," he said, taking the couch across the coffee table from her.

She lit her cigarette, took a long drag.

"I'm sure you're terribly busy."

She finished her drink.

"Yours is a war-proof business, I would imagine."

"Nice seat," said Lin, sliding down until her head rested on the soft leather.

He cleared his throat. "Ah yes. This establishment is finely apportioned, with a storied history to match. It withstood US bombing during the American War, more than a hundred years ago. All variety of journalists, activists, celebrities stayed here singing songs, humping like rabbits." His curls shook as he said: "War is the great aphrodisiac."

"Your bourbon is good. So I could sit here all day waiting for you to get to the point."

"Ha. Well. Your English is excellent, at least. Your man at the bar didn't lie about that."

Lin moved her shoulders a little, working herself into the comfortable seat.

"Your manner is more local, though."

Lin raised an eyebrow and smoked.

"Sorry to be precious, young lady, but, ah, I'm not sure you can smoke in the suite."

"Could fuck a goat in here, if you wanted."

"Hm. And why would that be?"

"War may be an aphrodisiac, but it sucks for tourism."

"Ah, of course."

"But you know this already."

"Do I?"

"You've stayed here before."

"Have I?" he asked, quizzical look on his face.

"Yeah."

"Ah. Well then: allow me to join you." He pulled a silver case from his vest pocket. Popped the lid, slid out a white rolled cigarette, snapped it closed. He lit, inhaled exhaled. Pungent, earthy smell. Marijuana, not tobacco.

"Yes. Quite," he agreed, more to himself than her. He took a second, longer drag on his spliff, closing his eyes as he did so. When he opened them again they were a little bloodshot.

"Well, it's a ghastly business. Ghastly. An old friend of mine, all the way back to Eton actually, came here to Hanoi. Poor chap." Herbert shook his head, curls shaking with it. "A joint venture proposal came about, very promising, very lucrative. As you well know, war is a time of great opportunity."

Lin kept her face smooth. She'd become very good at it. Lin had been told some time back that her facial expressions were 'westernised' after fifteen years in Australia. At first she hadn't been sure what they meant, until she'd met a Japanese woman who'd grown up in the US. She did all the things Lin must have once done – scowling, wide-eyed, nose-wrinkling, over-the-top, crass – and she looked ridiculous. Lin worked hard from that point not to show anything on her face, to keep it carefully blank. It wasn't like she was going to try copying Vietnamese expressions, which were just as varied of course, if a bit more nuanced. Lin was too embarrassed to take either cultural side, so she tamped down on it all. Tried to give nothing away. The ice-seven helped. Gave her complete detachment, dulled her emotions.

Not that the fat Englishman was taking any notice. He just wanted to speak, mouth wide, filling the air. For some Westerners, silence was subordination. They sought to dominate with loud voices, determined opinion. Even though that mob were just yelling into the wind tunnel now, no one in the world listening anymore.

Shoulders unsquared, Herbert Molayson contemplated the roof momentarily. "Now. Where was I? Ah yes, lucrative deals. So Raymond Chang was a programmer. Spent some years in Silicon Valley until he received a better offer from Zhongguancun. While he was there, in his spare time he developed a game called Fat Victory. Have you heard of it?"

Lin opened her palm, bringing the same shoulder up: *of course* she'd heard of it.

She knew next to nothing about PoV games or on-retina services in general. Didn't understand the attraction. How people could walk around with games or conversations or concerts or ball games or roulette or you-name-it on-retina, up in the corners of their vision, every waking minute of the day. The constant distraction, buzzing at the edge of consciousness, overwhelming.

Lin kept her visuals uncluttered as a rule. Sometimes when she was high she'd cue up an endless white sand Australian beach, walk down it. Untouched, unspoiled. The Australians didn't appreciate the rarity of the things they had. Isolated on those eternal sands, silent save the waves and the gulls, alone and at peace. The opposite of life in Hà Nội.

The program was stored in the cochlear-glyph implant behind her left ear. She didn't stream anything; hardly anyone in her business did. Even if she'd had the inclination, and even if reliable streaming was somehow available in the Old Quarter, being wired up to the freewave all day and night was inadvisable. Eventually some group would peer down that line – government, mega-corporation, organised crime – and see what you were doing, who you were meeting with, what you were saying. The c-casts in a warzone were compromised every which way, unregulated. Gangsters – serious gangsters, anyway – had the freewave node in their neural implant fried, replaced with a local web, encrypted, shared with the gang for comms and little else.

Yet, despite all this, Lin had heard of Fat Victory. Everyone played it, every newscast had mentioned it the previous year. Everyone in Vietnam staring into the action against the black of their eyelids. In their rooms, on their chairs at bia hơi, riding pillion on a scooter, they played Fat Victory. The game was from the perspective of a US soldier during the American War. The whole life – deployment, stifling comradeship in the base, patrols, and, inevitably, death at the hand of a Viet Cong or North Vietnamese soldier. Every. Single. Time.

Lin couldn't see much point in an unwinnable game, especially if it meant a Vietnamese player were in the role of an American, where every single mission ended in a bloody and horrific death. Sometimes tortured by Viet Cong; sometimes limbs blown off; sometimes screaming, for hours, dragging entrails through the mud and mosquitos. The game – like many PoVs – tended to trick the brain, make the body think these things were happening to it, depending on the settings.

The settings on Fat Victory had been intense, apparently. News ran hot a while back on players experiencing side effects. Bad dreams, depression, violent outbursts. Like a lot of heavy PoV users, reality and the virtual started to blur.

Eventually it had been banned, though black-market versions were everywhere. Bao had sold them for a while, until one of the men had coaxed him into playing. Six hours later, ashen-faced, Bao had opened his eyes and told the man to delete all the copies. Prohibited the Bình Xuyên from playing it, banned anyone else selling it in the thirty-six streets. Said it in that way that made it final, so it was final, and no one mentioned it again.

"I couldn't quite understand *why* it was so popular," said Molayson, in sync with her line of thought. "But it was, stupendously. We rode a hot streak of fortune on that one. Though, I suppose, not so much for Raymond or Hermann, by the end."

"Hermann?"

"Hebb. A second programmer brought on to the project."

"I'm dry," said Lin, pushing herself from her seat. Herbert's mouth showed a hint of annoyance, which she ignored completely. Her back to him as she stood at the bar, she snuck a small drop of ice-seven into her bourbon. Returned with the bottle, set it down as she sat.

"So, Raymond is dead and Hermann is missing," she said.

"Hmm," said Herbert. "I don't recall saying – how did you know?"

Lin drank more, settled back into the seat. She talked around her cigarette as she lit it: "You spoke about your mate Raymond in the past tense. You told Sandfly Ha that you wanted help finding someone."

"Astute."

"Sherlock fucken Holmes."

Herbert pursed his lips, then wet them with some grappa.

"What did they do?" she asked.

"Programmers, primarily."

"You were the money."

He nodded.

"Did well," said Lin. Not a question.

"Well," said Herbert, swirling his drink. "I'm not here to discuss such unseemly aspects. But yes: a roaring success, Fat Victory, far beyond any of our expectations. I suppose the popularity came from the Vietnamese being able to win something for a change. Making the invaders suffer horribly and at length. Transported from plastic chairs next to a stinking gutter in an occupied city, to a place where they were winning. Raymond hypothesised the players fantasised that they were killing Chinese, not Americans. Hermann went ahead and tweaked the programming so some of the US troops even looked Chinese. Quite intoxicating, I suppose, from a certain perspective."

"No," said Lin. "That's not it. Not all of it, anyway."

He waited. When she didn't continue, he tilted his chin a little higher and said: "Really, darling? Well." He leaned forward and said, in a manner both self-deprecating and utterly self-assured: "Don't sit there enigmatic and taciturn, young lady, edify this louche old soul."

"Nihilism."

"Hmm." He pursed his lips. "What a word. Now where did that come from?"

Lin took a drag on her smoke, one eye on the Englishman. "It's a Vietnamese thing. You wouldn't understand."

Herbert laughed, quite genuine, curls bouncing. "Young lady, I hark from a country that once ruled the world, where the sun never set on its empire. That same country, my dear England, is now a small, despotic island sitting off the coast of Europe. Drabness and rain and truncheons, every day of the year. Nihilism, I understand perfectly."

"Then I don't need to explain anything."

Herbert inclined his head in agreement and lit a second joint. Holding it again between his two middle fingers. His eyes reddening like the sunset.

"How," she asked, "did Raymond Chang die?"

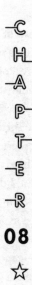

CHAPTER

08

☆

Herbert Molayson finished the last of his grappa, hesitated, then said: "Beaten. To a bloody pulp. Then shot in the stomach. I found the body, I…" He took a long drag on his joint. His shoulders settled a little and he said: "I knew something was wrong. Just knew it, when he hadn't been contactable for a few days. I went to his hotel room."

"I guess the police said it was a robbery gone bad."

"Yes."

"And I suppose the hotel called the police?"

His hand shook a little, until he took another hard drag on his joint. "I suppose. Yes. Yes, now I think about it, I told them to and they did."

"Strange a cleaner didn't find him."

"He wasn't staying in the Metropole, my dear. Nothing like it."

"Why?"

"It's a long story. Raymond Chang was a talented man. But, ah, he was a down-and-outer, by nature. He began his tenure in Hanoi with the best, of course – over at the Oriental. He moved to steadily less salubrious places over time."

"I reckon the police found the criminal, hey? A petty street thug, full confession. Told you he was going to be executed."

"You're quite good at this guessing game."

She shrugged. "It's Hà Nội."

Herbert carefully placed the stub of his finished joint on the edge of the hard wood tabletop. "Your insinuation is correct. I didn't believe any of it. I don't know how, Miz Vu, I don't know why I am so certain of this. But I know damn well that little man they brought out and showed me didn't do it. I know damn well it has something to do with Fat Victory. Pour me some of that bourbon, will you?"

He leaned forward with glass in hand. She poured him one, another for herself.

"Okay," said Lin. "That's Raymond Chang. Now: Hermann."

Herbert cleared his throat. "Yes. Hermann Hebb. A distinguished programmer we brought on to the project some weeks in. Hermann had run into some trouble back home. Fell in with the wrong crowd, you know how it is." His eyes sparkled as he said this, looking at Lin. "You might say he was eager for a change of scenery. Dear Raymond was having difficulty with the workload, and Hermann was an alum of our university, though two years behind."

"Why not a local talent?"

"A question I asked myself. Strange. Our other investors insisted on someone from England. In any case, the core of our project became a trio." He sighed. "Now I find myself the only one still at liberty. I don't know why, Miz Vu. Raymond Chang was murdered, deliberately, pre-meditated. Hermann Hebb, well, I fear the worst. I fear he, too, has been killed. It is as though he simply vanished into thin air. I put a huge reward out, bribed all the right police. Nothing. Not a murmur. Not a trace." Herbert gave the depths of his drink a long, red-eyed gaze.

An addict. Herbert was an addict, like her. Not having a bad day. Not just louche, not simply the idle rich. An addict. Grappa and dope just the appetisers. If she looked around she'd probably find some prescription opiates, or ice-seven, or ice-nine. She never quite understood why soft men with soft lives became addicts, though maybe it was precisely those reasons. We're not meant to live easy. It runs against our nature. If peril doesn't fall on us from without, then we find a way to bring it from within.

Lin said: "You got a file you can send me, pictures, conversations, all that?"

He drew himself away from bottom-of-the-glass contemplation and blinked a few times. "Ah, yes. Yes of course. Dates they arrived in-country, all the relevant accommodation and expenditure information."

"Sounds like data."

"Yes."

"I want some visuals."

"I'm sure a selection could be arranged."

"Fuck." Lin sipped her bourbon and ice-seven.

"Yes?"

"I don't suppose you'll transfer your memory file from that period?"

"Well." He sipped on his bourbon, as though thinking it over. He said *no* a few seconds after Lin saw it coming, then added: "Commercial-in-confidence reasons of course, I can't simply go around memory-dumping my business dealings."

"It would save a lot of time."

"Come now, darling." He smiled. "Have you ever known anyone who'd hand over weeks or months of memory? Would you?"

Lin leaned back into the couch.

"No, you wouldn't," he continued. "I've downloaded two of the most expensive exo-memory assistants money can buy and had them trawl through my memory feed. The exo-mas provided no possible suspects, no clues. Nothing." He gave her a pursed-lipped smile. "And besides – I wouldn't want you to know where I hid all those dead prostitutes." When she didn't react, he sighed and drank his drink.

She put a fingertip to the cool steel of her cochlear implant and whispered a command, pinging him. "Here's my code," she said. "I'm not on the freewave. This is a local intrafeed number. Direct access to me."

Herbert made a little O with his mouth. "Oooh, the gangster net. I've heard about this. You know I..." He trailed off when he saw the look on her face. "Well then, here." His eyes drifted off to the middle-distance left as he looked over something on-retina.

Her cochlear-glyph beeped softly inside her ear, a sound only she could hear. She opened the file. It showed the man she assumed was Raymond Chang sitting at a desk, green-glowing flexiscreens spread out in front of him. Chinese heritage, skinny, unkempt black hair, expensive blue shirt stained and wrinkled; absorbed in the work before him, a bottle of Lagavulin on the table, glass near his hand.

A second figure was standing towards the back of the room, in shadow. Large man, tracksuit, yellow-tinted glasses, features not discernible.

"That's Hermann at the back?" said Lin. "Barely see him. This the best you've got?"

"Apparently, yes. It's rather strange, but I only met him once, in general we never spoke face to face, rather over c-vision."

"So he wasn't a friend."

"Ah. No. Just vaguely, as I said, through the same university."

"Met him once. Yet you had a falling out."

Herbert swirled the bourbon in his glass, watching her. "You're far more perceptive than you look. Are you running some sort of micro-expression reader on-retina; deductive non-linear algorithm of some kind?"

"No," replied Lin, and waited.

"Well, the falling out," said Herbert, unflustered, joint paused two inches from his lips. "The same thing all disagreements are over, I suppose."

"Money."

His eyes drifted from smoking tip over to Lin. "Indeed. Far smarter than you look."

"How do I look, Herbert?"

"Like an angry young woman with a chip on her shoulder."

"That so?"

"Quite fetching though, in those jeans and gangster jacket. I'm sure you're the belle of the ball down in the local bia hoi."

Lin clenched, unclenched her fists. "You spend a lot of time in Hà Nội, Bert?"

"Well, it's hard to say. Yes, I suppose—"

"Then you should know by now it's bad idea to piss off a Vietnamese woman with a chip on her shoulder."

"Hmm. Yes. A Vietnamese woman with a strong Australian accent. I suppose that's the chip."

Lin quieted her face, dead calm, then her chest, her hands. She decided to finish her bourbon rather than break his nose.

"Money," she said, as though the words he'd just put into the air had never existed.

Herbert smoothed his vest. "Hermann felt his share of the profits was insufficient. Messaged me constantly about the issue."

She waited for the speech. It didn't come. "That's it?"

Arch. "What more can one say?"

"Everything."

"Such as?"

"He wanted more money from you – okay, I get it. But you're not going to disappear him. Certainly not hire someone to find him if you had. So: did he have any enemies? Did he fuck the wrong woman? A man? Ladyboy? Did he cross undesirables?"

"Yes."

"Yes? Which one?"

Herbert inhaled a preparatory breath through his nose. "Hermann was a rougher type, you might say, that had a taste for a rougher crowd. I heard he had a woman he met at a club, but I don't know the woman, or the club. I do know he spent a lot of money on her, but that didn't stop her procuring more clients. There was a disagreement with one of her other customers I believe, and shots were fired. Hermann was injured, slightly, but on the positive side, his lusts were well and truly cured."

"Right. Who told you all this?"

"Oh." He drew his eyebrows together, thinking. "You know, I can't quite remember. Perhaps it was Raymond."

"So Raymond had a gambling problem, Hermann had a woman problem." Lin leaned back into her seat, eyes over Herbert's head. "Hmm."

"Yes," he said. "Indeed."

"One thing I don't understand."

"Just one?"

"Why you so keen to find Hermann? Raymond I get, but Hermann and you barely knew each other."

"I suppose I feel it is all connected. That finding Hermann will lead to Raymond's killer. I just can't—just can't shift this sentiment, much as I can't accept Raymond's death was random."

Lin blew some smoke at the ceiling, nodded to herself. "Okay. This will do for now."

He inclined his head.

"One more thing."

"Payment," he suggested, through a knowing smile.

"Payment."

"Of course."

She doubled the figure Bao had suggested. "Yuan. Twelve thousand a day. Plus expenses."

"Seems reasonable," said Herbert. No blink. No surprise.

Lin dropped her cigarette butt in her empty glass and stood up to leave.

"One more thing," said Herbert.

Lin raised an eyebrow.

"Could you organise a goat for my room."

Lin half smiled, despite herself.

"White, fluffy, shampooed. Female, obviously. When in Rome, as they say." He said it all with a straight face, cheeks rosy, eyes red. No guile, no humour that she could see.

Her half-smile faded. "Don't fuck with me, Herbert."

"No," he said, the humour seeping from his features. "And for two thousand pounds a day, you better not *fuck* with me, either, Miz Vu."

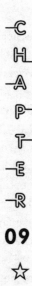

CHAPTER
09
☆

Lin was two blocks from Hà Nội Towers when the wild-haired madman with a meat cleaver ran screaming out onto the street. The first victim was a skinny old bloke pushing a bicycle. Surprised, unmoving, as the cleaver bit into his forehead. It was only after the old man fell backwards, over his bike, blood spurting, that the street reacted. A woman screamed and held her child, a group of youths backed away, a scooter swerved and crashed into another, the taxi behind shuddering to a halt.

Eight in the evening, the night was just starting. One side of the street was a tangle of storefronts, glimmer bikes on the pavement alongside shop owners and residents cooking dinner on gas stoves. The other, a long brick wall behind which stood a large Hà Nội government office. Hit with a nova shell, now a blackened husk no locals dared go near, for the ghosts that roamed and cried within it.

Lin backed away. Best not get involved. Hands and shoulders jostled her, a dozen people crowding out of a narrow bar. Traffic backed up quickly, horns blaring, drivers hanging heads out of windows. Scooters at the front, trying to push away from the cleaver man, ignorant riders and drivers at the back pushing forward.

The madman tore his shirt off, cheap plastic buttons popping, and started waving it over his head. Eyes up to the black as black night sky, he yelled: "[Here! Here! I'm here!]"

Two security guards in cheap blue uniforms approached, pulse rods crackling blue at the tip. Minimum wage wasn't worth dying for, in her opinion. Maybe they were bored. Lin gave up trying to push back through the crowd, deciding it was getting interesting.

The guards got close and the cleaver man was oblivious, his thin body coated in sweat, eyes boggling. The younger guard circled; the older one rammed his pulse rod into the small of the madman's back, and the nutter did the jitterbug, shirt falling from his hand as his back arced.

But he didn't fall. He roared, jumped forward, and slashed at the younger guard. The young man managed to catch the blow on the arm, pulse rod dropping, soft cloth cap flying as he jerked his head back. The guard turned and ran into the crowd.

The growing audience, caught between spectacle and imminent danger, backed away again, some slipping and falling. Mad eyes gleaming, the nutter kept coming forward, propelled by the old man's shock stick, Lin right in his path, bodies against her back, taxi bumper against her thigh.

Panic all around her, pushing, bodies standing on bodies, bodies tipping scooters, bodies denting bonnets. The madman buried his cleaver into the back of a man spreadeagled over the front of the taxi, right beside Lin.

She sighed.

Lin kicked low, side of the madman's knee. He gargle-wobbled, hand going to his damaged leg on instinct, before returning his attention to yanking the cleaver from the man on the taxi – who screamed and tried to twist away. The wild man's halo of hair bobbed as he yanked, sinews in his shoulders tight.

She stepped-kicked down on his other knee, deeper this time. The wild man gargled some more and twisted, bloody cleaver flashing at her, she raised her arm on instinct, something bit, bee sting pain. She three-four stepped back and he tried to follow, jibber-jabber rage, but his legs gave way and he pitched forward onto the road.

Lin two-three stepped forward and kicked him in the face. Nose broken, eyes glazing, not mad anymore, dancing with consciousness. She kicked again, her hardened boot making his jawbone snap loud. He quieted. Blood patterned the road near the man's head. Skinny man, poor, sallow skin that hadn't seen much daylight. She stared down at him, the world stilled in the silence that followed all of her fights. Lips tingling, aftereffect of the ice-seven, she drew her thumb across them.

Lin stayed like that, head bowed, until her senses crept out from the tunnel vision of hand-to-hand combat. Panic around her subsiding, replaced by the hum of conversation and boiling vegetable oil and passing scooter. Someone yelled: "[*Move that crazy fuck off the road*,]" and life in Hà Nội went on.

Belatedly, the older security gentleman skittered up and stuck his pulse rod into the madman's back. The prone man convulsed, but did not awaken.

"*Great work*," said Lin, in Vietnamese.

The old guard missed the sarcasm and nodded vigorously.

She took a deep breath and found a spot for herself on the concrete gutter. She pulled a pack of Double Happiness from her pocket and tapped out a cigarette. Her hands shook. The nicotine took the edge off. A couple of men with beer eyes came past to compliment her knee-breaking. Lin just nodded, not wanting to speak. The dead old bicycle rider and the half-dead bloke in the cheap suit were carted to the side of the street by more blue-suited security guards, suddenly everywhere. Used to idle days of guarding glimmer bikes or alleyways or side entrances to shattered buildings, it was easily the most work they'd had in weeks.

Lin smoked. A baby nearby cooed. Couple of stabbings, barely worth mentioning. Nothing compared to the hollow thump of a grenade attack, the *bratatat* of a machine gun as Chinese troops chased down Việt Minh. To the bodies, tongues missing eyes missing, the burgeoning business in orphanages, the immolated monks, the swarms of black rats around it all, like the punctuation marks of tragedy.

The traffic washed by, as did the conversation. Kids yelled and ran up and down the sidewalk. A man on a bamboo ladder nearby worked on a section of cables, on part of the thousands upon thousands of kilometres of thick black electrical wires, often thirty or more cables bundled together, legal and illegal, twisted around trees and poles like some noxious invasive species trying to strangle the life out of its competitors.

The smell of beer and fish sauce and sewer and chili filled the air. Bicycles fitted with small speaker systems rode past, blaring exhortations to report dissidents, to appreciate the prosperity and stability bought by the Chinese, to obey traffic signals, to not use car and bike horns. The kind of things routinely ignored.

The Old Quarter hadn't changed in decades. Longer. Outside, Hà Nội grew, evolved, recreated itself. Slowed, stopped for a while, in the first few years of the invasion, but the Chinese money poured in after Hà Nội was taken; the reward for a quiescent new regime in the North, in the new Chinese province of Jiaozhi.

So the city rebuilt, from the flooding after China had bombed the lees that held back the rising river waters; from the firestorms that had blacked the military buildings; from the craters drones had made of dissidents. So the city crept outwards as shanty towns and bamboo villages added themselves to the periphery; crept vertical, as mammoth yellow cranes raised buildings into towering apartment complexes; and spanned the air, as replacement bridges were built across the Red

River. Hà Nội the capital of the pacified zone, they said, a harmonious neighbour all the way down to the 17th parallel.

The new Vietnamese leadership had recognised the cultural and scientific superiority of their big brother to the north, and agreed to live in harmony within the rightful world order. Their puppet, President Nguyen Van Huong, travelled to Beijing to acknowledge China as the nation that had saved the world from climate change, shutting down every coal-fired power station and closing every coal mine, at a savage cost to its own people. China, the country that brought stability to the global system after the collapse of the Western economies. But more than anything, to assure Beijing that the peaceful southern land recognised its privileged historical position within the Chinese realm. Jiaozhi was the southernmost province for nine hundred years, until Vietnam rebelled. Now it had returned to the fold, its manifest destiny as part of the Middle Kingdom.

The Chinese news outlets had broadcast the speech, again and again and again. Kept broadcasting until the President dared not appear in public anymore, whether for fear or shame no one was sure. Not just the President speaking. Not always. Sometimes regular people appeared, echoed his words. Different though, these ones. They looked sincere, nothing forced. Their eyes sad, mothers would speak of sons and daughters fighting down in the jungle, giving their lives away for nothing. Peaceful coexistence was far better than an unwinnable war. Vietnam would still be independent, was still independent, just in a larger realm. The North was happy now that it had submitted, and prosperity returned. They looked like they believed. Whether memory wipes, or genuine conviction, Lin wasn't sure. Pretty much the same thing, anyway.

Outside the thirty-six streets, Hà Nội had transformed. The Transit Elevated Buses, the glimmer cars, solar passive apartment blocks, men in shiny suits making shiny deals; air-conditioned shopping centres with stores for Fujian Original & Dolce and Gabbana and Yiqing Yin, with Tesla showrooms and Chinese fast-food franchises and organic coffee stands.

The thirty-six streets were a time warp. The Chinese, after years of bloodshed and ruin and a local stubbornness that bordered on the nihilistic, had decided on a policy of containment built on an uneasy truce. Chinese patrols broke off when they got to the edge of the labyrinth; if they went in it was only with considerable force, and then only rarely.

Inside the thirty-six streets, surveillance drones – small hummingbird cousins of the mile-high bomb throwers – were shot down, and jamming devices were everywhere. Lin had no idea how they got away with it. Jamming tech could be tracked, the punishment for using it a jungle gulag.

So the Chinese used human assets instead. Like Bao Nguyen and his Bình Xuyên gang.

Blood trickled down her arm. Just a shallow cut, a couple of inches long. Good excuse to turn around and go home. It'd been weeks since she'd turned up at a Sunday roast, they wouldn't be expecting her. Sweat pooled in the base of her throat, tickled.

She put a hand against her jacket, felt for the shape of the book in the inside pocket. Make sure it hadn't fallen out in the commotion. Yes. Still there. A gift from Bao, a lifetime ago. The battered, precious paperback – called *The Sorrow of War* – she'd read time and again, sheathed safely in a shimmer smooth spideriron cover. Protect it from the elements. Protect her heart as well, from a bullet, or a blade.

Lin sighed a thick cloud of smoke, hand dropping away, and got to her feet. She flicked her cigarette away and slouched towards an old home.

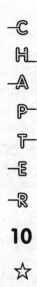
"Holy shit, I don't believe it," said Phuong Lashley as Lin walked through the door. Raised eyebrow, cigarette vertical between two fingers. "You lost?"

"Shut up," said Lin.

Across in the kitchen, Kylie Lashley looked happy, then tried to hide the happiness. Playing with her apron, not sure how to react, never sure what to say around Lin.

Phuong smiled, beaming. Lin found herself mirroring it. Phuong strode up and hugged her fiercely. Lin closed her eyes for a few moments, resting her cheek against her sister's. The restlessness in her quieted. Lin's act, well-worn and comfortable after years of practice – so much so she'd forgotten putting it on – fell away whenever her sister was around.

Phuong pushed Lin away and made a big show of looking her up and down.

"Let me see. Uncombed, red-eyed, sweaty. Smells like cigarettes and fish sauce. Oh, and dripping blood onto the carpet. Sister, don't you ever change."

Lin glanced down. The cut on her arm shed a slow red tear. "Oh. I thought it had stopped."

"Where's the first aid, Mum?" asked Phuong.

"The bathroom, honey. Oh Lin, what have you done to yourself?"

Lin folded her arms. "I'm fine."

From the bathroom, Phuong said: "Mum, don't you have a nano-spray?"

"Oh. I can't afford one of those, darling."

"Huh. That's embarrassing. Is this your way of asking for a pay rise?"

Kylie reddened. "Oh no, I'm just happy to help."

Phuong rustled around in the bathroom. Kylie and Lin waited for her to come back, unused to being in the same room alone. Lin breathed an inward sigh of relief when Phuong returned, and allowed her to stick a wide Band-Aid over the cut.

"Did you collect some debts on the way here?" asked Phuong, cigarette upright.

"Shut up."

She gave her a single-shoulder shrug. "Fine with me, sis. So long as you make a donation." She held out her hand, eyebrow raised.

Lin shook her head. Phuong. Her identical twin, yet they had nothing in common. Lin was the *before* picture, Phuong the *after*. Phuong wore stylish clothes and makeup that accentuated her unusually full hips and lips – today it was designer jeans, sleeveless white blouse, pale pink lipstick and matching eyeshadow – where Lin tried to hide both attributes. Phuong's hair was shiny and healthy, cut medium length in line with contemporary fashion, where Lin's was short and uncombed. Everything Phuong did seemed *effortless*. The way she interacted, the way she dressed. The way she won friends and the confidence of strangers. The way she learned the language and customs, and then ignored them when it suited her.

Phuong was a loud personality: eager to question, to be fascinated by the person she was talking to, whomever it was. Unlike Lin she'd never bothered to quiet her expressions, to adjust them for the local context. Phuong laughed with her whole body – arms, chest, face, her back bent in glee.

Yet she was accepted completely, utterly, back into Vietnam. Started a non-government organisation to support war widows and widowers, provided small loans to local businesses, grants to relieve debt, free healthy breakfasts for poor kids before school. She cultivated support and funding from wealthy locals and, after a time, the Chinese government. For that last sin, a normal person would be accused of being a traitor, could expect a midnight visit from lean, angry men, eyes gleaming with revenge. But not Phuong. The community loved her, and word was the Việt Minh had made her and the charity off-limits.

Compelling, free-spirited, impossible not to love. Fucking Phuong.

Lin ignored her sister's outstretched hand and moved towards the kitchen. "Got anything to drink in this place?"

"I didn't know you would be coming," said Kylie. "There's beer."

Phuong said: "Don't apologise, Mum."

"Beer is fine," said Lin.

Kylie made to move to the fridge and Lin said *I'll get it* far sharper than required. Kylie stopped, making apologetic noises, while Lin fumed at herself and at the woman's weakness. She grabbed a gold-coloured can of Bia Hà Nội from the fridge and took a long drink, washing down her anger.

"You drink like a miner," said Phuong.

Lin said: "I gotta piss."

She walked down the short corridor to the bathroom. Kylie Lashley had a simple serviced apartment: bedroom, double bed, view of a swimming pool below and the other tower across; lounge room with a large older model tai screen; kitchen nook with chrome finish; bathroom-laundry combination. Hardwood floors scratched and worn, faded green curtains; fresh-cut yellow flowers in a vase that Kylie likely placed there herself.

Surly door staff, slow elevators, green plastic plants coated in dust in the foyer. Faded luxury, once populated by wealthy Euros. Long time past.

A work desk was pressed into a corner of the lounge room, topped with pictures of Kylie, Lin, and Phuong together when they were young. Two little Vietnamese girls and a white woman on an endless beach, turquoise water, squinting against the sun. All happy then, when they didn't know any better. Lin had glimpsed the picture once, several visits back. Made sure never to look at it again.

Lin looked at herself in the bathroom mirror. Bruise at her temple from her last job, eyes red courtesy of four early evening bourbons at the Metropole, part of a stray noodle in the hair above her ear. She couldn't remember eating noodles.

"Jesus, Lin," she whispered to herself. Wry smile as she rested her beer on the sink and picked the food from her hair. She gave the beer a drop of ice-seven, held the vial up after and shook it; just a couple drops of the glowing liquid remained. She slid it back into the pocket of her jeans and took another long chug of beer, finishing it and crumpling the can.

Lin closed her eyes as the glow spread. Touched the endings of her anxieties, the beginnings of her hates. She walked back out, took another beer from the fridge, and planted herself on the couch. Kylie busied herself in the kitchen, Phuong gave her a raised eyebrow and said: "My, you look relaxed all of a sudden."

Lin ignored her sister and allowed herself to actually look at Kylie.

Dark, curly hair, fifty, hadn't lost her figure. The echo of freckles across her face, a smile always hovering, nervously, on the edge of coming out. Eyes with depth, but also a reluctance to see too much. She wore denim pants and a simple blouse. She'd taken to wearing

Vietnamese garments, but had reverted after Lin had mocked her during a dinner some years back.

Lin tapped out a cigarette. Sake was her drink, but damn, cigarettes and beer were a hard combination to beat.

"What's cooking, Kylie?" she asked.

"Oh, you know. Sunday. A roast. Phuong likes it."

"Like it?" said Phuong. "Mum, your roast is *the bomb*. You invite a man over here for that roast and he'll be bringing a ring to the next visit."

"Oh, Phuong," said Kylie, reddening, smiling. "I'm too old for that."

"Your body doesn't think so. You look *fine*, Mother."

"Phuong."

"It's true."

"Still trying to cook Vietnamese?" asked Lin.

"Oh sometimes." Kylie paused her slicing. "I was never very good at it."

"Mum," said Phuong. "Nonsense. Your phở is spectacular."

Kylie smiled. "You're very good to me, darling."

"Remember the first time you tried to make it in the other place?"

"Lin," sighed Phuong.

"The house smelled like dirty socks for a week."

"Don't listen to her, Mum," said Phuong. "She's being a bitch."

"Oh, she's right. It was a disaster." Kylie was still red, though not smiling anymore.

"That was the time the neighbour was over, the one you liked. Tuan, right? He insisted on eating the whole bowl, despite the stench. Excused himself right after dinner, looked like he was going to puke. Never saw him again."

"He left," said Phuong, voice tight, "because you were ridiculing Mum, and he was embarrassed for her."

"Pretty sure it was the phở."

Kylie had been clenching and unclenching the tea towel in her hands. She placed it carefully on the kitchen counter. "Excuse me for a moment," she said, and walked erect from the room.

Phuong watched, sympathetic and sad, as her mother left. When she turned to Lin both expressions were gone. "Is this why you came over?"

Lin smoked.

"It's a serious question, Lin: is this why you came over – to hurt your mother? Haven't you done that enough, already? A whole fucken lifetime's worth."

"She's not my mother."

Phuong breathed out in disgust. "*You ungrateful bitch.*"

Lin sipped her beer. The anxiety the ice-seven had banished was returning, a knot gathering right below her heart. She needed another drop, needed that distance, to *keep* that distance.

"Why are you here, Lin?"

Lin sighed out a cloud of smoke. "I don't know."

"You don't know. Well, she was delighted you turned up. She asks after you all the time."

Lin's eyes stayed on the ceiling. "And look at where that gets her."

"You're right about that. She'll be in her room, ashamed."

"She blunders around trying to be a part of a culture that isn't hers. It's embarrassing."

Phuong stubbed her cigarette out in an ashtray at the corner of the kitchen bench. She put her hands on her hips. "At least she is curious. At least she cares. I'm glad she's not some soft-handed foreigner. The type that's too scared to ask a question, thinking it a sign of weakness. Terrified of being thought of as ignorant on anything. I like curiosity. I love her *blundering attempts*. Our mother is a humble woman with calloused hands. I'm proud her."

"You make a virtue of her ignorance."

"*You're* judging her? You, who didn't even finish fucking high school? You listen." She jabbed a finger at Lin. "She lives here, in our country, during a war. In a place the complete opposite of a small country town. Fucken Hà Nội, Lin. Scared. Alone in this apartment.

One daughter won't even talk to her. Our mother is *brave*. It takes *courage* to live in this world."

"She's a creature of habit, Phuong. We all are."

Phuong wet her bottom lip. "*You* are fucking ignorant. We choose our habits, sister. Our mother's habits include two daughters that she loves unconditionally."

Lin was silent.

"You forget what she did. You forget where we came—"

"*Enough*," hissed Lin. "*I know where I came from.*"

Phuong lit a new cigarette. She laughed without humour, eyes on the orange tip. "Yeah. Got us out of that hellhole. Do you know what happened to the other kids in that place? The lives they endure? Fuck."

"She took us on out of pity. Arrogant pity. Our saviour."

"Fuck, Lin. What sort of person thinks like this? Arrogant? She struggled her whole life. Never asked for anything, never got a damn thing. There's nothing complicated. There's no hidden agenda; she's simply a good person. There are people like that in the world. You might have forgotten that, given where you live."

"Where I live helps me to think clearly."

"Ha. With sake and ice-seven a permanent fixture in your bloodstream. You haven't been sober since you left home."

"Well, we can't all marry up, sister."

Phuong pursed her lips. "That has nothing to do with where I am."

"Young Chinese officer. Party connections. Yeah. Sure. Not a fucken thing."

"What does that mean?"

"I mean all this talk of respecting Vietnam, and you *married* one of the invaders."

Phuong crossed her arms. "You're criticising *my* patriotism?" she asked and her voice was quiet. "The Bình Xuyên is known for many things, sister. Patriotism is not one of them."

Lin clenched her jaw, her drug calm punctured like a balloon.

"Now," said Phuong, pointing again with her cigarette. "When our mother comes back out, you will drink her beer, eat her food, and you will tell her how nice—"

"We're not her daughters. We're just cute little china dolls a lonely, barren white woman brought home to play with."

A shocked pause, cigarette wavering, eyes wide, and then Phuong strode over to where Lin was sitting and slapped her.

Lin put a hand to her stinging cheek, mouth popped open in surprise.

Phuong said: "Ungrateful bitch. Get the fuck out of this house."

Lin curled her hands into fists and stood, jaw set, glaring.

"What you going to do, Lin?" asked Phuong, unrepentant. "Beat me like a strung-out ice-addict with overdue debts? Do it." Phuong mirrored her sister's stance. "Do it. Put that last nail in the coffin of your heart."

Lin swallowed her words, knuckles cracking.

Instead she left.

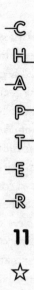
Lin woke with a hangover, splitting. She let out a groan, and put the back of her hand to her face. Half to caress her headache, half to block out the light. She lay like that for a few minutes, contemplating how dry her mouth was, how much her eyes hurt, and how much she needed to pee. Eventually she dragged herself to the toilet. In the bathroom she discovered a variety of injuries she had no recollection of receiving. Bruised knuckles, another huge bruise on her thigh, long red scratch in her cheek, blisters on each of her big toes.

Blisters. She sighed. If she'd danced she must have been truly wasted. If any Bình Xuyên had seen her she'd never hear the end of it.

The water tower barely had a cup's worth gurgling in the bottom, she downed half, still parched, cursing herself for not ordering a replacement earlier. Shuffled over to Barry's cage, took out his water, and replaced it with the last of hers. The yellow songbird waited until she'd closed the little wire door before hopping over and pecking at the fresh drink. She watched the bird, bleary eyed. He steadfastly ignored her.

The flexiscreen on her coffee table pulsed a slow green. She thumbed it and a message popped up: **Didn't want to wake you. Seemed like you needed some rest.**

Lin didn't remember Nanh coming over at all. Atypical note, as well. First because she left one at all, second because she almost sounded concerned.

She spent an eternal ten minutes trying to find her cigarettes. They were crammed into one of her boots. Of course. Where else. She lay on her back on the thin rug, next to her scuffed boots, and blew smoke at the ceiling, trying to recall the night she had after leaving Kylie's.

Scored ice-seven from the Shivering Kid, yeah. Argued with a taxi driver over the route he took – a gold Buddha, mini cognac bottle, sports car stuck to his dashboard. Bourbon at the Stray Dogs bar, alone, watching the street. Beers at a corner bia hơi, unsure what street, with Saigon Thanh and Bull Neck Bui. Later, smoked-filled neon bars, a rocking Filipino cover band, her tongue deep in the glass as she downed the booze / strobe flash / flesh on flesh.

No. The session with Bull and Thạnh was last week. They'd gone to the fights afterwards, bet big against a middleweight with Bình Xuyên connections and blown the winnings on Australian red wine and French cuisine at La Badiane.

She could always call it up on-retina. Hell, she could tell the AI that ran her exo-memory program to give her the selected highlights of the evening.

But something held her back. Something she didn't want to see. It didn't matter, anyway. All these nights became a blur, merging into one another. The same faces, the same drinks, the same bars, same conversations. The gangster life she signed up for, never knowing quite why. She'd just nodded yes when Bao said he was going to teach her how to fight and one year later she was breaking kneecaps on the shore of Hoàn Kiêm Lake pre-dawn, thinking only about the next ice-seven and, after, a warm bed.

The only parts from all those nights that stayed crystal were the fights. Those she remembered. The victories, that moment when hope drained from her opponent's eyes. That eternal moment, when she stood over them, and they were broken and she was complete. In that victory was the final argument. No debate, no more contradiction. Just a line of truth, unbroken. She was complete, physically, emotionally, only in that moment. Honing herself, as she'd been taught: *the will and the act*, as one.

The defeats, those she remembered as well. Moreso. Played them over on-retina, at night, again and again. Analysing, shaming herself, making sure they were never repeated. Turning it off, closing her eyes and dreaming of each defeat instead. Eating that pain again and again, asleep and awake. If the fight had been a particularly bad one, she would have to change the outcome, just so she could sleep again. Like Fat Boy Danh, who'd caught her twenty beers in at a bia hơi, and given her a beating with a retractable baton. She'd tracked him down, two weeks later, and jammed his face into a sewer grate with her boot heel, over and over, until his jaw popped. Then her truth was all that mattered. Then she was whole and unbroken.

Only then could she sleep.

Lin finished her cigarettes there, on the floor. Room slowly heating as the day advanced, motes dancing in shafts of light. She watched the smoke pool above.

As the on-retina timer clicked over to 11:30 am, someone knocked at the door.

"*Who?*" she asked in Vietnamese, trying to remember where she'd put her pulse pistol.

"[Mosquito Brother. With your order.]"

The AI cross-checked the voice print and gave her a green: **Authenticated** on-retina. She stretched her back, winced her way standing, and opened the front door.

Her nostrils flared. Food.

Not just any food, but a *bánh mì* filled with vat-grown pork sausage, plus two hard-boiled eggs, six hash browns, a croissant, water for the tower, two glasses of *cafe nâu đá*, two packs of Double Happiness, and a skinned pineapple.

Mosquito Brother passed her the tray. The nervous type, he never looked anyone in the eye, especially Lin. Skinny, short, likely a malnourished childhood. Toddler at the wrong time, during the famine, the outbreak of hostilities with China fifteen-sixteen years back. One drooping eyelid, an old injury, never explained. Hung around Lin a lot, quiet, good with a blade. The boy heaved the large plastic bottle of water by his feet, red-faced, neck straining, then quick-stepped inside and set it in the tower.

She didn't remember ordering any of it – probably a five-in-the-morning demand – but she wet her lips, hungry, as she laid it out on the coffee table.

All except the pineapple, which she picked up and said: "The fuck?"

"[You messaged this morning, elder sister. You wanted a pineapple.]"

Lin grunted. She hated fruit. She signalled him over, dumped the pineapple in his arms, peeled off a couple of notes from her roll and stuffed it in his hand. He smiled and nodded and slouched over to Barry's cage. Stuck his little finger through the bamboo slats. The songbird hopped over to peck then nuzzle the square centimetre of flesh.

Lin glared, then cleared her throat, and finally swore. At the last, Mosquito Brother got the message to piss off. He pissed off.

Lin sat down on the couch. She poured hot sauce on the *bánh mì*, hash browns, and boiled eggs, and demolished them. Washed it all down with a long glass of water and whispered: *"Fuck yes."*

She burped, wiped her mouth, and leaned back on her couch, iced Vietnamese coffee in hand. The late-morning sun burned through the venetian blinds, painting the room black-red-black-red. She had a cigarette with her coffee and enjoyed that space between this job and the next, between the sublimity of a post-ice-binge hangover breakfast and the rest of the miserable day, between the soft edges of daydream and the hard face of the street.

Lin was the only one in her block to live alone; two whole rooms to herself. Neo-Confucianism was coming back into vogue, making a sin of independent youth. The rest of the building gossiped about her, judged her for not living with family, a husband; they watched the delivery boys that came and went, swaying with beer and sake bottles and midnight noodles; they caught the scent of her cooking, the rare times she did, as they passed her room; they watched wide-eyed when her lover turned up and then commented on that, as well.

They didn't quite know how to take her, how to respond to her peculiarities. She was and was not of the country. A stranger, yet embedded in the underbelly of the city. The only thing they agreed on was they couldn't trust her, this young gangster woman, living by herself on the third floor. Boy, were they right about that.

Lin picked up her precious novel, *The Sorrow of War*, from the coffee table and found her place: "*My life seems little different from that of a sampan pushed upstream towards the past. The future lied to us, there so long ago in the past. There is no new life, no new era, nor is it hope for a beautiful future that now drives me on, but rather the opposite. The hope is contained in the beautiful pre-war past.*

"*The tragedies of the war years have bequeathed to my soul the spiritual strength that allows me to escape the infinite present. The little...*"

Her c-glyph bleeped, drawing her attention. A message – from herself – popped up on-retina: **Midday. Time to go to work, fucker.**

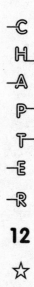

CHAPTER 12 ☆

The first time they fought, shihan broke both her legs. The second leg after she was already down, gasping, one hand up in surrender.

The eighth time they fought, he shattered her jaw with a flying knee. Lin was yanked from unconsciousness when he pulled her arm behind her back and snapped her wrist. She had liquid dinners for three days, sucking them through a hole in the translucent cast that covered her lower face.

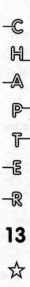

CHAPTER 13 ☆

It took two aspirin, the rest of her coffee, and a shot of sake to get Lin's head straight. Well, to tone down the pounding. For whatever reason – and the reason was usually post-binge self-disgust – she held off on the ice-seven. She'd lost days to that nirvana glow before, and Bao wasn't going to let her walk on another offence.

Lin had her exo-ma bring up the picture of Raymond Chang and Hermann Hebb.

Raymond Chang at a desk, looking at a brace of flexiscreens. Expensive blue shirt stained and wrinkled; bottle of Lagavulin on the table, glass near his hand. Sallow skin, eyes burning with technological fervour, or dope.

"Enhance the area on the table, I wanna see what he's looking at."

The voice of the AI, emotion-free and metronome, replied: "Yes, Miz Vu."

The image closed in on dirty fingernails, fingertips stained purple. Backwash green highlights from the flexiscreen. On one of Raymond's screens, hovering symbols and ideograms; on the other a set of numbers, vaguely familiar.

"That shit on the screens – what is it? Code?"

A pause, and then: "A betting algorithm and gambling markets. Horse racing in Hong Kong, Muay Thai in Chang Mai, weather patterns in Sichuan province."

Ha. Lin took a drag on her smoke. White clouds drifted above the coffee table, glowing in the shafts of light. Special kind of dumb fuck right there. Horses and fights can be fixed, that's one thing. But no one can fix the fucken weather.

The second figure was standing towards the back: large man, tracksuit, sunglasses, white. Hermann Hebb in shadow, at the back of the room, features not discernible. Spot of orange, cigarette in his mouth.

The room itself was nothing fancy. Neat enough, clean white walls, air con, generic girl-with-bamboo-hat-in-rice fields picture on the wall. But cheap. White fauxwood furnishings, narrow space, a washed-out look. The idea of a hotel room, fading from disuse.

"I want to see that man, up the back. Can you give me any more detail?"

"Not under my current programming, Miz Vu."

"Why?"

"The picture is filtered; my encryption protocols are unable to penetrate."

"Filtered?"

"Correct."

"So the memory feed isn't giving a correct image?"

"No, Miz Vu."

"Motherfucker."

"Miz Vu?"

"Shut up. I'm thinking."

Lin smoked and thought.

"Which end is the filter on?"

"Miz Vu?"

"Is it on the viewer's end, or is Hermann wearing one?"

A pause, and then: "I cannot ascertain that, Miz Vu."

"Well ain't you fucken useless."

"On occasion."

She grunted to her feet, grabbed a bottle of sake and cup from the kitchen bench, and returned to the couch.

"Miz Vu?"

"What?" she asked, ceramic cup in hand.

"There are a variety of Baosteel decryption applications I could suggest, or even full exo-ma upgrades, that could quite possibly suit your present needs."

"Listen, dickhead."

"Yes, Miz Vu?"

"Try to upsell me one more time and I'll delete your program and buy something less chatty from Chinalco."

"It will never happen again."

"Also."

"Yes."

"Your name is now 'Fuckchops'."

"Wonderful."

"Fuckchops."

"Yes. Miz Vu?"

"Send this picture to Blue Point Pham, tell him to decrypt the filter."

"Yes, Miz Vu."

"And one more thing."

"Yes?"

"Send a message to the boss, encrypted. Tell him I need a gun."

CHAPTER

14

☆

The Hotel Pale Flower on Hàng Buồm was a glorified flop house. Two years away from the first floor being turned into a karaoke joint and every other room being rented out by the hour.

Lin paid the dead-eyed desk manager five hundred yuan to take her to the room Raymond Chang had been murdered in. He looked at her a couple of moments too long when she asked him in English, but the money bought his deference. He led her to the third floor, room 304.

The young man stood on the inside of the door as she entered, maybe waiting for another tip, maybe just bored.

Lin said: "Know who I'm with?"

The young man shrugged a *yes* with his thin shoulders.

"Fuck with me, I'll break your elbows."

He swallowed.

"*Understand?*" she said, in Vietnamese.

"[I understand,]" he replied.

He made to leave, she pointed at him to stay.

Lin paced the room. She overlaid the image from the picture on-retina and took up position where Herbert had been standing when he took the shot. The overlay was close to perfect.

"This room been used since?"

His eyes unfocussed as he looked up the answer on-retina. Back on her, he said: "[No.]"

"Why?"

Shrug. "[The war.]"

Lin searched everything. Under the bed, the drawers beside the bed and in the desk. The cupboards, pulled the sheets from the mattress, the cover from the old-school air con. She stepped out onto the small balcony, thick heat slamming into her. Rusted iron railing, slick with rain, bare. Just beyond her fingertips, the rain poured, deafening, crashing down on roof and stone. Rivulets of water spearing off the roof.

Lin closed the door behind her, wiping the rain spray from her face with her sleeve. She put a finger to the cool steel of the implant behind her ear and subvocalised: *Give me a DNA overlay, Fuckchops.*

"Yes, Miz Vu."

Her vision filmed over with a pale blue layer. She did a slow turn. Neon red highlights on-retina picked out her spoor – a couple of points where a strand of her hair had fallen, or her palm had touched a surface – and nothing else.

Lin tapped a cigarette out of the soft pack, eyes on the desk boy (who was teeming with DNA). He fidgeted as she lit her cigarette, and smoked it, and watched him. Pressed his lips together, looked at the ground, tapped his foot. White shirt with grime around the neck, scuffed shoes, fore-fingernail nearly an inch long.

Lin had once asked the cleaning lady at the Bình Xuyên headquarters why some men had the single long fingernail – taxi drivers mainly, but the occasional desk man and security guard as well. The old woman had replied: "[Because they're lazy and have nothing better to do. Never marry a man with long nails.]"

Lin was halfway through her cigarette when the desk boy said: "[Elder sister, I need to get back to the—]"

"Drugs?"

He stopped scratching at his arm.

"*You want drugs?*" she asked, in Vietnamese.

He wet his lips, looked up looked down.

Lin pulled three notes from her roll. She held the money up between two fingers. "Who, the fuck, cleaned this room?"

His eyes darted around the space. "[Cleaned?]"

She tipped the money one way. "Fifteen hundred yuan." Then the other. "Broken elbows."

"[Men.]"

"*Police* men?"

"[No.]"

Lin sat down on the chair at the desk, threw the money on it, and continued smoking.

The young man wet his lips. "[Vietnamese.]"

Cloud of smoke. "Who?"

"[I don't know who.]"

"*Who?*"

"[I don't know, elder sister. Two Vietnamese and a white man. I don't know them.]"

"The on-retina."

He scratched at his arm. "[They took my memory pin.]"

She sighed the last of her smoke, stubbed it out on the desk. "Description."

"[I can't remember.]"

"Old, young, rich, poor?"

"[I can't…]" The young man was sweating, itching, foot-tapping, eyes returning to the money sitting on the desk. Decent natural memory was rare these days, especially among drug addicts. "[Oh. The white man was big. Huge.]"

Lin got to her feet. "Get a replacement pin?"

He shook his head.

"Let me see."

He turned his head to one side as she approached, showing the smooth steel neural implant, the c-glyph, behind his left ear. Like all, it had a control jack and a memory hole. Each hole the approximate width and depth of a pin. The control jack normally had an exo-ma – an AI that helped sort artificial memories, connect to the freewave, communicate with others, all that. The memory hole held a memory pin that, via nano-transmitters, attached to the optic nerves and inner ear, kept perfect back-up memory.

Well, technically back-up memory: for most people it became the primary recall mechanism for everything seen and heard. The head of the desk boy's memory pin was absent, the hole empty.

Lin nodded and left the room. As she did, she heard him scrambling for the notes.

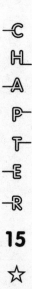

CHAPTER 15 ☆

The eighteenth time they fought, shihan cracked her in the temple with the pommel of his katana. Then he cut off her little finger. He kept the finger in a small stasis unit on the dojo floor. He didn't let her reattach it until she learned the katana forms he'd designed specifically for her. That was three weeks later, in time for their twentieth fight.

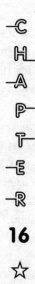

CHAPTER 16

☆

Seventeen Cowboys was the loudest, liveliest, and dodgiest bar in the Old Quarter. Two storeys, mezzanine above, all stained dark fauxwood. A stage underlit with blue glass tiles, Filipino cover band belting out any song, Vietnamese or Western, you'd care to name. The stage draped with red and blue neon, the drummer in a plasglass cage to one side.

Only women worked the bar. All hot, thin, boots with six-inch heels, midriffs exposed. Wearing cowboy hats with a felt cowboy face sewed onto the front. Black-faced cowboy, yellow eyes that seemed to follow you around.

The bar was set right in front of the stage, like a compressed horseshoe, side-on. The walls were covered with culturally inappropriate representations of American Indians. A large, cross-armed, stony-faced cigar store Indian stood by the door; the railing around the mezzanine had several of the same stern-faced Indian stuck to it, wearing traditional headdresses. Cowboy hats stuck to the wall, the floor marinated with liquor shots and beer. It was a place for the lowdown, the drunk, the lonely, the wild. Seventeen Cowboys was a fauxwood cage of raucous rock, bourbon shots, disco pussy, and cigarette smoke.

It was Lin's favourite place in the whole damn town.

She sat in her booth up behind the bar, watching the show. The waitresses knew her, served her, sat on her lap, flirted. Lin let her hands linger on their thighs, made sure to tip them all. They laughed, practised their English, took her money, and told her Nanh would be in later.

Three booths over a group of street-level guys from the Bình Xuyên yelled *chúc sức khỏe!* and pulled waitresses into their laps. They'd quieted when she walked in, indicated for her to join them. She ignored them and took a booth to herself. Distance, always distance.

So she leaned back and waited. Drinking, wincing a little at the pain in her hand. Mystery fight from the night before. Smoking, enjoying the sting of it on her lungs. She worked through the bottle of sake while the band wailed. Hidden in the dark and smoke, Lin smiled and sank into the music.

Two hours later Nanh sashayed up to the table. Tall, slender, her milky-pale waist exposed for Vietnamese gangsters and glazed-eyed old white men alike. Small-breasted, sexy, dirty. Long hair, pointed shoulders, always lipstick though never red. Played dumb for the men in the bar, but wasn't dumb. She was a hustler, like everyone who wanted to survive a war without starving or killing.

Nanh stood real close. Tonight her lipstick was blue. Lin put her hand on her waist. Flesh soft, yielding. "Get another bottle and join me."

Nanh whispered: "[Glad you're feeling better.]"

Lin raised an eyebrow.

"[Oh. You know. The other night…]"

"*I'm fine,*" she said, in Vietnamese.

Nanh shrugged, sentiment immediately forgotten. "[I'll get that bottle. Anything else?]"

"Cigarettes, peanuts, that arse."

Nanh smiled. Broad, genuine. God, she was cute. "[Sake and ass coming right up, Silent One.]"

A third of the way through the bottle, the band taking a break between sets, Lin said: "Need to find someone."

"[I'm not enough?]"

Lin ran her eyes over Nanh. "You tick most of the boxes."

Eyes wide, mock disappointment. "[Most?]"

"Still waiting for ice-seven to flow out of your pussy."

Nanh's eyes flicked over the translation on-retina, then slapped Lin on the arm, laughing. "[How can you say these things?]"

Lin tapped her implant. "I'm sending you a picture. Send this picture to the girls here now. Ask if anyone knows him. Big tip if they can tell me a story."

"[If it's Seventeen Cowboys, I should know him.]"

"I want a wider net. All the girls here work in two or three different bars."

She shrugged a *yes* and unfocussed while she sent the picture around.

A couple girls tried it on, offering up any random white guy. Lin gave them *don't fuck with me* glares and no tip.

Nanh leaned in close. "[She gave you feed access, Lin.]"

"Huh?"

She drew a fingertip to the implant behind her ear. "[One of the girls, to me.]"

"Which one?"

Nanh batted her eyelashes. "[She wants to keep it a secret.]"

Made sense. Wouldn't want to get a rep for kissing-and-telling.

Lin held up her empty glass. Nanh filled it, face carefully docile; Lin leaned back in her chair and closed her eyes.

"Send me the clip."

Dark club, younger crowd, spinning lights, polished chrome bar top. Vietnamese girls in sailor costumes, or shimmer-gold halter tops, or skin-tight Mao suits, or pink miniskirts. Red lipstick. Chinese men, young, off-duty soldiers, good skin – officers perhaps; Vietnamese men with slick hair and shirts, top three buttons undone. An expensive joint, somewhere outside the Old Quarter.

The woman walked past dancers, drinkers, and eye-glazed feed junkies. She caught the old white guy in her middle vision, alone up the back above the dance floor, sitting at a single high-stool at a small circular table, spliff between second and third fingers, watching the room.

She reached out, touched the man's shoulder. Voice, flirtatious, light. "Hi."

Herbert Molayson looked at her with bloodshot eyes and a dry smile. "Well, hello young lady."

"[Can I get you anything?]"

Herbert said: "Hmm, excellent question." *He inhaled through his nose as he mentally prepared his answer.* "My dear, I quite sincerely want to sodomise one of the bar girls, and you would fit that particular bill to perfection. But to do so would take six months of dinners, presents, and my listening to interminable stories about the latest purchases at some gauche local store. Which, quite frankly, is far too much time to waste on simple buggery. As such, in answer to your question: what I want is to smoke this marijuana cigarette and watch these pretty young things get rowdy. Preferably while you lean against me as you pour my drinks, and later, massage my shoulders when I say I'm tired. So, my dear – what is your name?"

She told him, though the sound was muted. The woman who passed it on to Nanh must have put a block in on her name.

Herbert said: "Ah, a lovely name. So you may do all this, (muted), confident in the knowledge that I'm good for a very big tip."

The woman said nothing for a moment, before squeezing his shoulder. "[You're so big.]" *Presumably she had a routine set of responses* for the tediously predictable banter of her clientele. Herbert was talking outside the box, so she simply moved to step two.

"True," he replied, glancing up at her for a moment before returning his gaze to the crowd. "The consequence of an appreciation for salty snacks, in particular after I've blown some smoke into the air. Combined with little inclination for outdoor activity, and voila." He spread his hands wide.

Step three. "[Handsome.]"

"My dear," he said, with a self-deprecating smile. "I'm no such thing. Distinguished would be a far better adjective. Honestly I expect a higher class of lie for my money. Now, (muted), give it your best shot, lest I be obliged to ask one of the other girls over for an audition."

The woman slow-blinked a couple times. Then she bent in closer, running her hand down his muted silver vest. "[Distinguished, and rich.]"

He bobbled his eyebrows. "Getting better. Easy, once you try."

"[Generous.]"

"Possibly."

"[And...]" She leaned in close to his ear, and said in English: "I like it in the arse."

He laughed uproariously at that, curls bouncing. "You'll do fine; you'll do just fine. Now bring me some extremely expensive grappa, and two glasses."

"Stop." Lin leaned back.

Nanh was there, watching her.

Lin lit a cigarette. Around it, she said: "Nothing."

Nanh waited until the song was over, sipping her drink, smiling at a group of young Vietnamese businessmen as they walked past the booth. Lin, hidden in the shadows, bopped her head to the beat, clenching her eyes shut when the Filipino singer nailed the high notes. Hunger gnawed at her stomach; she hadn't eaten since breakfast. Seventeen Cowboys wasn't known for its cuisine. Lin saluted the band with her sake as the song finished, sucked it down.

Lin said: "Kiss me on the mouth."

Nanh glanced around, long eyelashes backlit by the stage.

"Don't worry," said Lin. "It'll only add to your popularity."

Nanh smiled and leaned in.

It was good, like always.

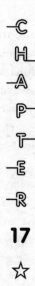

They were waiting for her when she got home.

Lin hadn't eaten on the way back. Sake, bourbon, and beer roiling in her empty stomach, mouth like an ashtray, Nanh had bundled her into the taxi. Her regular cab, message runner for the Bình Xuyên, serving as Lin's driver when required. Nanh wanted to stop for noodles but Lin grunted: "*No.*" She had ice-seven hidden back in the apartment, which would settle her stomach and put her to sleep; in the narrowness of her drunkenness, she'd become fixated on the gold-glowing vial.

Lin staggered down the slick alley, Nanh shepherding. At the base of the stairs Lin stopped, held up a finger, and threw up volubly. Nanh rubbed her back. Up the stairs, leaning on the bar girl. Bleary eyed, fumbling keys, she finally got the door open. Caught the scuff of feet and a whispered command a half-second too late; Lin's jaw crunched, her head snapped sideways.

Nanh screamed and lights flicked on, blinding; Lin on the ground with one arm up, trying to ward it away.

On-retina a message from her AI blipped:

Possible concussion. Laceration inside mouth. Drink a glass of water, take an anti-inflammatory. Have someone drive you to the medical clinic on Tràng Thi for full scans. Shall I send them the details of your injuries in advance?

Lin's combat upgrades were above average. Supplied, over time, from Bao, as she rose through the ranks. Adrenalin spur, clottocyte injection good for six months, hardened bones. The adrenalin spur linked to a Chinese military type-14 combat system. A superseded model, but still made her faster than just about anyone in the Old Quarter.

Rolling drunk wasn't so good for the reflexes, though. Concussion not great for her speed.

She spat blood and half a tooth onto the floor. Pushed herself unsteadily to her knees.

Nanh was straining, twisting against the grasp of a Vietnamese thug in a black singlet. He grinned, a metallic glint coming from his teeth. A second man, also Vietnamese, short dark hair, black t-shirt with a Tsingtao brand logo in white. Cigarette dangling from his mouth, rubbing his knuckles. He looked vaguely familiar. Both men wore black baseball caps pulled low.

But they didn't draw Lin's attention.

That was held by the third man. White, six foot six. Cream-coloured homburg. Pure muscle, arms bare, shining with sweat. Combat vest, black, with a spideriron sheen. Strapped to his back, a *dadao*, its foot-long handle visible over his shoulder, intricate swirls of light and dark metallic brown. Around his neck a thin metal chain connected to a slender silver tube. A nova grenade, white hot screaming death. His jewellery.

He took off his hat, smooth, his movements clipped, precise, and dropped it on the coffee table. Looked like he had a high-grade endoskeleton humming underneath all that.

Shaved head, heavy jaw, the centre of his throat a flat silver circle – for reasons she couldn't figure he was wearing a voice modulator. His pale blue eyes were concerned, even soft, as he looked down on her.

A concerned giant with a sword as tall as Lin strapped to his back. Fear coiled in her heart.

Her combat system was jacking her up with endorphins and adrenalin. The pain in her jaw ebbing, her vision clearing. But there was a thin, ragged edge to her senses. Her hands shook.

The white man said: "Cut her, slice her, just a little. Cut her, make her scream."

They weren't carrying firearms. Beer shirt had a knife strapped to his belt; shiny teeth had a pulse pistol and a dull metal telescopic baton.

Beer shirt walked over, knife in hand. Lin looked at him slack-jawed, eyes glazed. He grasped her chin, tilted it up, his groin close to her face. He smiled down at her.

She hit him in the dick.

Half-cry half-groan from deep in his throat as he doubled over, cigarette falling from his mouth. Lin rose simultaneously, knee to his face. His head jerked back and she moved on, the second man pushing Nanh away as he fumbled for his baton.

She fly-kicked, his hand came up, head snapping back and he staggered against the wall. She bent, one-two punched his groin, lifted with her elbow. Miscued off his forehead, pain shuddering through her arm.

Blood on his face, he yanked the pulse pistol out of his belt.

She kicked it aside and straight-fingered him in the throat. On target this time. He choked, she scooped his pistol from the floor, and whirled to face the huge white man, half staggering as she did so. Light-headed dizzy, adrenalin juicing her empty stomach.

The man's hand was wrapped around Nanh's throat. One huge hand, circling it completely. Chin pushed up, Nanh's eyes wild with fear.

"Snap, snap," he said, American accent. "Snap snap, goes the neck."

"You've just started a war with the Bình Xuyên," she said between hard breaths, "you dumb motherfucker."

"Drop the gun, little lady, or snap goes the neck."

"Listen, you vanilla fucking gorilla: she's got nothing to do with this."

"Snap snap. *Snap snap.*"

Lin took a step back so she could see the other two men. Both were still down, one groaning, one unconscious. Behind her was the kitchen bench, in front of her ten feet of hard floor, then coffee table, Nanh, white man, couch, low shelves underneath the window.

"The fuck are you?" The gun shook in her hand.

His expression didn't change as he spoke. Just that unaccountable look of concern. "No questions, little girl, just answer, just listen. Last warning, little girl." He squeezed his hand, Nanh's face was turning purple. "Snick the little bone."

Lin pursed her lips. The pistol clattered on the floor.

He nodded; Nanh's face went from purple back to red. He said: "Fat man, English man. He doesn't want the answer. The answer he'll hate. Tell him another one."

Lin backed up a little more. She didn't quite follow. "Okay," she said anyway, opening her hands. "Okay. You've given your warning."

"No. Not yet. Oh no." He flung Nanh to one side like she was a paper cup. She bounced off the wall and laid still as he strode towards Lin.

Lin set her hands up, flat, guard. Raised herself to the balls of her feet. Tried to calm her breathing, slow down time, to watch his neck and top of his chest, make sure she saw the blows coming.

They came.

Jab / jab / right / jab / left hook.

Fast. A boxer.

She found the rhythm, duck dodge, head-body-feet moving. His fists snapped the air. One hit would take her down. One hit would shatter her.

He changed stance, rolled into a side kick: Lin rode the blow, turned it into a backflip, hands grabbing the edge of the bench, somersaulting to the other side.

Kick boxer, then.

He smiled, didn't bother going for the Chinese greatsword strapped to his back.

Lin eased her hands down, eyes fixed on the man, to the long-bladed daggers at each ankle. And flowed: one knife hurled, following it over the bench as it hit the man in the chest, second knife in her other hand.

The knife, stuck in his armoured vest, clattered loose as she slashed and slashed back-handed. He backed up two steps three steps, inside forearm sliced and bleeding.

She flowed into kick / slash / kick, aiming for his neck, for knees. Too big, too strong, weak points the only way to take him down. He batted away her kicks, slid away from her blade.

Lin feinted, blade driving for his throat, and he twisted, hand up, sharpened edge meeting the flesh of his palm. No hesitation he struck upwards with his other hand, hitting her wrist. The blade flew from her hand and she gasped, two-stepped backwards.

They stood apart, a moment of calm. Silence in the room, save each of them breathing heavy, and the soft cries from Nanh. The white giant's head shone with sweat. Boxing stance, his eyes flicked to his left fist, blood dripping from it to the floor.

Lin took the opening. All in: running step, leapt high, fly kick aimed at his face; he swivelled, iron hand around her ankle, and flung her into the wall behind. She balled as she hit the wall, air exploding from her lungs, and took the shelves with her as she crashed to the ground. Arms shaking, trying to push herself up and suddenly she was up, dangling at the end of his arm, hard fingers grasping the collar of her denim jacket.

Eyes calm, he tilted his head to one side, and thrust her into the ceiling. *Crunch*, plaster falling, an involuntary scream from her lips.

And again, and again; she stopped screaming with the third collision, her arms limp, senses going out of focus.

He dropped her onto the floor, a tangle of limbs. Somewhere, someone was crying softly.

His kind eyes bore into hers as he pulled her up by the collar. Sweat dripped from his forehead, onto her face. His other fist, clenched and bloody, hovered above her. He unclenched it and slapped her instead.

She gasped, sharp *noisepain* grew in her head.

He slapped her again, and again, and Lin lost count. Head spinning, world spinning, pain overriding any combat response she had left, the medical warnings flashing on-retina rode her into the dark. The noise rose in her ears, the roar of the ocean, the white noise of unconsciousness.

Tough fingers gently moved her, put her upright. She coughed up water, one eye popped open. Only one would open.

The white giant took a knee in front of her, cup of water in his hand. His eyes soft, concerned.

A voice came into the room, metallic, not from him, but from the gleaming modulator at his throat. The big man moved his lips, but the voice was from someone else. In Mandarin, it said: "[About time. I thought you'd be tougher, Silent One. Now. Pay attention.]"

The giant stood and walked over to Nanh, who tried to resist. He slapped her and she stopped. He straightened her leg, moved it to one side, and drew his *dadao*. It hummed as it slid from the scabbard, making a single high note that hung in the air.

He touched the tip of the blade to Nanh's ankle and looked at Lin. The voice said: "[*This* is your warning.]"

Lin croaked: "*No.*"

The big man brought the sword down.

Nanh screamed and screamed.

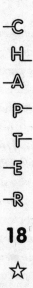

CHAPTER 18 ☆

The injuries he inflicted were always precise. Bones broken, flesh slashed, yes, but never an organ pierced or ruptured: too expensive to replace, too time consuming to recover. Still, he inflicted all variety of grievous. The twenty-first time they fought he pinned both her feet to the ground with long-bladed daggers. She screamed until she passed out.

Every time he won, the Japanese master would look to Bao. Bao would say: "More," and the master would hurt her again. Afterwards, the days of recovery: translucent casts, nanomeds, the occasional surgery, and, when it all became too much, ice-seven smuggled in by Mosquito Brother with her meals. Just to help her get through, he said, smiling shyly as he palmed it to her. He was right, it got her through. More. The new drug perfect. A pain relief that encompassed everything: physical and emotional and spiritual.

Then the hours of practice and weights and running. The days of study, and correct diet, and proper stance, and how to breathe, and know-thy-enemy, and harden-the-fuck-up, and take-this-stone-from-my-hand, and all that bullshit.

No particular school of martial arts, he replied, when she asked him what they were learning. Shihan knew them all, courtesy of memory downloads and decades of doing nothing else but learn and teach. The spaces of his life that were superfluous wiped and copied over with more texts and training memories.

Men and women like him were not unknown. Obsessed, or made to be obsessed by others, devoted themselves to every form. Travelling the world as masters. Every day was lived for the fight. Combat as philosophy, a way of life, as essence, as the sum total of existence.

So they fought.

Bao would watch.

Lin would lose.

Bao would say: "More."

Shihan would do more.

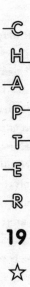

Lin limped in on Bao giving a bribe to a stout Chinese lieutenant named Zhu. Lin paused, Bao signalled her to come in and close the door.

Bao's other office, just outside the edge of the thirty-six streets. A small room up the back of the Drunken Angel on Tràng Tiên. Lots of foot traffic, including Chinese military: one more officer wouldn't stand out. Clean and neat, second storey, looking down on the buzzing Hà Nội street life. On the walls, generic pictures of paddy fields and young women in *áo dài*, a tai screen playing a 24-hour Chinese news channel. On the desk: a flexiscreen unfurled, light pens neatly positioned to one side.

An accountant's office, if you didn't know any better.

Lin walked over to a side cabinet and popped it open while the men made small talk. Or Lieutenant Zhu did, to be precise. Always talking, always looking out for the envelope or the drink or the cigarette, then talking right through receiving them. Animated, telling dirty jokes, a sparkle in his eye. They were sharing rice whiskey at that moment, and sitting next to the bottle on the table, the brown envelope.

She poured herself some sake, downed it, then took the second cup with her to a seat in the corner. She moved slowly, eased herself gently into the chair.

The nanomeds had hastened her recovery. A cheekbone fracture, couple of broken ribs, concussion, cuts and bruises: walk in the park. Nanh, on the other hand. Lin pressed her lips together, tried to concentrate on something else.

Zhu was still talking in Mandarin: "[But the best hot pot is at The Blue Lamp. Fresh-cut chilis, vat-grown beef just like the real thing – better than the real thing, better. The waitresses – oh spicy hot, I'm in love, comrade, I'm going to move here permanently once the war is over.]"

Bao was doing a believable job of looking interested. He replied, in Vietnamese: "[If the war was over you'd have to work for a living.]"

Zhu laughed, red-faced, jolly and knowing and still not caring. "[True, true, but a few more years of this and I won't have to work again.]" When he said *this*, he picked up the brown envelope.

Bao kept his face carefully blank.

Zhu stood, still smiling, and finished his whiskey. "[Speaking of work, I must do my rounds. All the gangs here, comrade – Sheesh! – and all their stupid names: dragon this, blade that, thirteen fingers, feet of blades, the sword of toes, the flaming dragon penis – I can barely remember them all.]"

"[Well, Lieutenant, they all must pay respect to the number one gangster.]"

Zhu slapped the brown envelope across his other palm. "[Occupation, comrade: the biggest protection racket in history.]"

Lin said in Vietnamese, over a swollen lip: "*You must be proud.*"

Zhu turned, all surprised that she'd spoken. Then he nodded in enthusiastic agreement. "[Yes, little sister, yes – to get rich is glorious.]"

He turned back to Bao, nodded goodbye, and made to leave, humming to himself as he did so.

Bao stood, showing more deference than he would to anyone in the Old Quarter.

As Zhu was about to step through the door, the jollity in his face dropped. Just so Lin could see it. A hard face, a street face, eyes on her. Then he was gone.

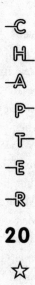

The door shut. Bao stared at Lin as she sat down. He took a drag on his cigarette and said: "[How are you?]"

"Fine."

"[I heard about your visitors.]"

"Good if you heard a little earlier next time."

Bao stared at her until she dropped her eyes.

"[Who was it?]" he asked.

"You tell me, Uncle."

Bao opened a drawer, put away the whiskey, and pulled out a bag of sunflower seeds. "[Big white man, two others. Vietnamese.]" He poured the seeds into a black ceramic bowl and put the bag back in the drawer. "[The Westerner has been seen around the city recently. As have the other two, though none of them in the Old Quarter.]" He placed a second ceramic bowl next to the first, then a half-bottle of brandy and a small red glass tumbler next to the seeds. "[The white giant was seen getting into an armoured glimmer limousine at the edge of the Old Quarter, twenty minutes after leaving your apartment.]"

He shucked a sunflower seed, popped it in his mouth, and put the shell in the empty bowl. "[This is all I know.]"

"Then you know more than me."

"[We would know more if you had sent me the pictures of them.]"

Lin sighed, thinking of Nanh in the hospital, face turned away from her. Refusing to speak. "The intrafeed was down again."

"[What did these men want?]"

"Me to stop investigating."

"Hmm." He popped a sunflower seed into his mouth. She waited for something more, but instead he said: "[Give me the on-retinas, little sister.]"

She did so, wincing as she moved her elbow.

"Bao," she started.

He held up his hand, unlit cigarette between the first two fingers. "[We will take care of this woman. Nanh.]"

"Her foot."

Bao lit the cigarette, eyes on her. He blew out a cloud of smoke. "[She will receive a new one.]"

"Something good. Kawasaki."

The smoke trailed upwards from the tip of his cigarette. "[Something good,]" he agreed.

"The adjustment takes months, even with the best," she said. "It will never be the same." Bitterness crept into her voice at the last sentence.

He looked at her for longer than necessary. "[I am aware.]"

"I want these motherfuckers to pay."

"[As the call, so the echo.]"

Bao's expression didn't change, but she believed him.

A medical alert was flashing at her on-retina, her AI wrote: **Bed rest required, Miz Vu.** She ignored it and pinged Bao the images. He pulled a red fine-woven bamboo scroll case from his drawer, and slid a flexiscreen from it.

Lin hobbled over to the cabinet and poured another sake; by the time she got back an image was floating above the flexiscreen, colour, three dimensions, rotating slowly. The two Vietnamese men who'd attacked her.

Bao looked over the symbols scrolling down the side of the screen and said: "[Rabbit Pham and Three Clouds Thinh. Mid-level enforcers for the Green Dragon.]"

"The Green Dragon? After what you did to…" She let the sentence drift away.

Bao said nothing, concentrating on the flexiscreen. An image of the white man appeared; information streamed down one side of the screen again.

"What are those files?"

"[Police records for Shanghai and…]"

"And?"

"Macau."

That seemed to mean something to Bao, but she let it go.

Bao said: "Passaic Powell. [An American from Passaic, in the New Jersey Protectorate. Hired as cheap muscle five years ago by the Way of Tranquillity and Purity gang in Shanghai. Worked his way up from low-level thug to thug number one. Rewarded with a Baosteel endoskeleton a year ago. He served a short sentence for assault and damage to public property at the start of his career. Since then, he has been a suspect in several cases: murder, torture, extortion, and operating a fruit stand without a licence. The charges were all dropped.]" Bao paused. "[One year ago he was also hired out to the— To the Macau Syndicate.]"

"Right."

Bao drank his brandy.

"You say *Macau Syndicate* like someone just shat in your sunflowers."

"[This is a good description.]"

"Trouble?"

"[Yes.]"

"This Passaic."

"[Yes?]"

"He had a voice modulator."

Bao smoked.

"Someone else's voice spoke through it."

Bao raised an eyebrow, poured himself another brandy. "[Someone higher up, riding on Passaic's feed.]"

Lin grimaced at the thought of someone else inside her head, watching what she was watching, using her voice box to speak. "That's disgusting."

"[Playing puppet for his boss. It happens a lot in less enlightened gangs.]"

She raised an eyebrow. "Oh?"

"[We here in the Bình Xuyên are committed to diverse employment opportunities. We even take Australians.]"

Bao was joking, but still, she winced inwardly. Knew he accepted her, understood she'd risen to number two, overtaking more experienced and older men. Knew she was one of them. But all that knowledge was surface friction; her gut still hated the joke. She tapped a cigarette out of her pack, annoyed at herself. She was hurting, all over. Back aching, her face still swollen. Feet sore from pounding them against a giant with nanocarbon and titanium alloy bones.

Bao didn't like her taking ice-seven. Not in front of him, anyway. She smoked and thought about that moment, just a few minutes from now, when she'd walk across the street, find a bar, and give herself two drops from the vial in her pocket. She ran a thumb across her lips in anticipation.

"Yeah, well," she said. "The Green Dragon learned a fucken hard lesson. Idiots coming back for more."

He looked at a point over her shoulder. "[A year ago, now. Memories always fade.]"

"Yeah. Sure. But they could just pull it up from their feed."

"[This is not how it works, little sister.]"

"No?"

"[No. Not in our world. Here, memories are a weakness. Better to have what was done to their leader wiped from the minds of those who witnessed. Better to simply have the fear fade over time, so the Green Dragon may eventually deal with us, or partner with us, or betray us, as suits their purpose. Without the prejudice of memory.]"

Smoke rose from their cigarettes and swirled slowly in the air conditioning. She said: "But they need to know their enemy."

"[Not the ones that attacked you. Not the soldiers. Those – those are the same as soldiers anywhere. The Chinese invaders return to their homes from the battlefield here, broken. Their bodies can be fixed, easily enough, but minds need more precision. The best Omissioners in China working as the sun comes up, after it goes down, day after day, on those soldiers. Wiping memories, taking away the worst things they have seen. And done. Then they are ready again, to go back to central Vietnam. To the gene-scrambled crops and the heat that melts the lungs, the wet heat that never lets up, makes the skin leprous. Back to the pyres of burning dead on a long brown horizon. To the starving children, with their hollow eyes and jutting bones. To a land haunted by ghosts of the aggrieved dead. Send them back to cycle through the horror, unburdened by pasts, no longer laden with regret and fear and weakness. Then recycle them again, when the past returns.]"

"You never had me wiped," she said.

"[I've never had anyone wiped, except when they needed an alibi.]" He took a long drag on his cigarette. "[I am not the Chinese, Lin. I am not the Green Dragon. I lead men and women, not Escher Men and Jonny Mnemonics. My people keep the gift of horror.]"

She didn't understand, made to press the question, but he changed the path of their dialogue: "[What I did to Nam Cam brought us time with the Green Dragon. But these people are always looking for weakness, or in this case, allying with strength. They have that now, with the iron backing of the Macau Syndicate. They will come. They will come hard. There will be war in these thirty-six streets.]"

"Even if I drop the case?"

"[This would be the worst option. If we bow to them after one beating, then they will certainly come for us.]"

Lin's thoughts went to Nanh. Not just one beating. She pursed her lips. Nanh didn't count; didn't figure in this. Just a hustler with a missing foot. She sighed out: "So?" with a cloud of smoke.

"[So you can't come into the thirty-six streets and crap on my desk.]"

"So?"

"[So solve the case. I'll deal with the Green Dragon and the white puppet.]"

He opened his desk drawer again and pulled out something palm-sized, wrapped in displacement cloth. It made a heavy clunk as he put it down.

Lin leaned forward and peeled back the slippery material. Underneath, a dull gun-metal sheen. She pulled the revolver from the cloth, and tested the weight in her hand. Type-62 blunt nose (the Chinese had the banal tradition of numbering their tech, rather than naming it).

"Could've used this yesterday."

"[You asked for it the day before. How did you know?]"

"A feeling."

Bao waited.

"A feeling about the Englishman. Herbert Molayson. He knows more than he's telling me. Something's not right about this case."

Bao said: "[This is clear.]"

"Yeah, well. He acts like he's unfamiliar with Hà Nội. Then last night I watched an on-retina of him in a nightclub here, acting like an old pro. Wants me to solve this case, while giving me only half the story."

He smoked and listened.

"Why the fuck is the Macau Syndicate involved with this?" she asked. "I don't understand the angle. All Herbert was involved with was that stupid computer game."

Bao stopped smoking. "[Which game?]"

"That one you hate."

"[*Which game?*]"

Lin looked up from her drink, surprised at the anger in his voice. "Fat Victory." She paused and then: "Bao? Uncle?"

Bao leaned back in his chair, eyes gone.

"Uncle?"

"[Bull Neck Bui and Mosquito Brother will be with you from now on.]"

She raised an eyebrow. "I don't need fucken bodyguards."

"[You want to keep the case? Bodyguards.]"

His glare stopped her from replying. Her back ached. She needed to take her last nanomed shot and lie down for the afternoon. Give her bones a few more hours to knit, her muscles time to heal.

"What's with the game, Uncle?" she asked, finally.

"[This is not just a game.]"

"Okay. Then what is it?"

He stopped thinking, or staring, or remembering, or whatever it was the fuck he was doing and finally brought his attention back to her. He stubbed out the last of his cigarette, exhaling the smoke through his nose.

"[I shall give you my copy. Play this game, Lin.]"

"Why?"

"[Because the answer is there.]"

"Uncle. Why don't you just tell me?" She didn't ask hard. Lin was tired, hurting. She asked the question like it was a sigh.

Bao rubbed his forehead with three fingers. When he spoke, all he had was: "[Play the game, little sister. Set a limit – no more than two hours, immersive. Play the game, tend to your wounds, and then we shall talk.]"

"[Motherfuckers,]" said Bull Neck Bui as he looked over the wreckage of Lin's apartment. The ceiling crater where Lin's back had been rammed into it, shelves split and collapsed, broken glass, arterial spray of brown dried blood up one wall, pool of the same on the floor. A trail of it out the door, where Lin, half-conscious, had carried Nanh out and down the stairs, screaming for help.

Lin collapsed on the couch, disturbing the fine layer of plaster dust covering the surface. The dust resettled, sticking to the sweat-coated skin of her arms and face. Barry's cage was the only thing untouched. The songbird ignored the mess, choosing to look out the window instead.

Mosquito Brother and Bull stood uncomfortably in the centre of the room. Bull waiting for an order, Mosquito Brother trying not to look at her. She said: "Fuck off."

"[One of us will be outside the door, charming one,]" said Bull. "[Ping us if there's a problem.]"

Lin rubbed her eyes with her fingers. They moved to leave.

"Wait," said Lin, pointing. "Sake."

Mosquito Brother grabbed the bottle from the kitchen table, righted the coffee table, and placed it on top.

"Now fuck off."

Mosquito Brother nodded respectfully; Bull gave her a hard look. They left.

When the door closed, Lin pulled out the vial of ice-seven.

Barry was looking at Lin. Head cocked, little black songbird eye staring right at her.

"What?" she asked, sharply.

Barry stared.

Lin averted her eyes and dripped three drops straight into her mouth, washing it down with sake.

She drifted off into a golden oblivion, into a body glow so thick she dreamed of nothing. Nothing, save a hard face with soft concerned eyes, looking down at her while she slept.

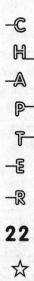

CHAPTER
22
☆

Lin had a feeling the knocking had been going for a while by the time it woke her up. She opened one eye, squinting against the light. Noticed for the first time that the front door had been replaced. No longer a shitty fauxwood; now a dark blue cleansteel.

"The fuck?" she croaked.

"[It's Mosquito Brother.]" It sounded like his voice, hesitant, apologetic.

Fuckchops, she subvocalised.

Yes, Miz Vu, replied the AI.

Is it him?

Voice analyser confirms.

Then let him the fuck in.

A beep, the sound of heavy bolts unshucking, and he came the fuck in, tray of food in his hands. His droop eye pointed at the ground, good eye on the tray.

Irritated, she said: "I was sleeping."

"[Sorry, elder sister. You told me to bring your breakfast in at midday.]"

Her on-retina timestamp read: 12:02 pm.

Lin pushed herself up, stretching her back, her neck. The pain lessened now. Lips tingling, she drew her thumb across them, looking over what he'd brought in.

A *bánh mì* filled with vat-grown pork sausage. Two *café nâu đá*, some hash browns with hot dipping sauce, a fluffy croissant, large orange juice, and a packet of Double Happiness. She felt her hunger returning.

"[It's your favourite breakfast, isn't it?]"

She waved him away. The corners of his mouth twitched in disappointment, and he left, heavy door clacking behind him.

Lin devoured the *bánh mì*, beating her chest with her fist at one point to force it down. Then the hash browns, just as quick. She burped with pleasure and leaned back into the sofa, taking a coffee and croissant with her. Three drops of hot sauce on her jeans. The midday sun filtered through the venetian blinds, striping the room black-grey-black.

She dipped the croissant in the coffee and took a bite.

A green dot blipped at the corner of her vision on-retina. From Phuong. She sighed and opened the message.

That was horrible. We can't keep doing it. I miss you so much, you bitch. Call me.

Lin read it three times before deleting.

She lay down and smoked a cigarette, trying to ignore the gnawing feeling, just below her heart. Pushing back down on the memories forcing their way to the front of her mind. Of white sand beaches and laughter and an endless belonging.

She said: "*Fuck*," as she exhaled a cloud of smoke. Shoved her fingers into the pocket of her denim jeans until she found the pin Bao had given her, held stable in a translucent glassteel vial.

Lin held the vial up to the light. The rays from an overcast sky gleamed dully in her hand, refracting through the glass.

"*Fuck*," she said again, popped the vial, and inserted the pin.

Fat Victory   01

☆

Lin was there. The American War.

The dark heart of the jungle, verdant, unending. Superimposed, the words Fat Victory *in red, flowing script.*

The title faded and the introduction started, a voice-over, pertinent facts repeated on-retina.

"The year 1968 was the height of the American War in Vietnam. Courageous North Vietnamese soldiers and stoic Viet Cong fought the imperial aggression of the United States.

"Yet, the American foot-soldiers were dupes. Mostly poor, conscripted into a war they did not understand, to die for a cause ignoble. These soldiers, on the orders of a venal US regime, marched out to die. They faced the implacable, emotionless Vietnamese soldier, who would stop at nothing to destroy them.

"The American foot-soldier was oblivious to the fleeting relevance of their civilisation. A blink of an eye next to the grandeur of East Asian

history, which held the centre of moral and scientific progress for millennia after millennia. It is said that those who do not know their history are like a tree without a root, a brook without a source. So these foreign soldiers – rootless and lost in this strange, hostile land – marched to their deaths."

Behind the words, aerial footage, black and white. Villages explosively napalmed, cut to: helicopter over a paddy field, cut to: US soldiers carrying an injured comrade into a waiting helicopter, cut to: soldiers on patrol in the jungle, covered in sweat, dragging—

Lin said: "Skip introduction."

The screen said: Welcome Bao Nguyen. Usual settings?

"Yes."

Time limit?

Lin shrugged. "Ah. Nah."

Words and images faded, replaced slowly by a person looking into a mirror. A cinematic transition, the blurry new image resolving itself.

A man, looking back at her. Caucasian, tanned, with a hint of East Asian around the eyes. Grubby face, long nose, feminine lips. But a strong face, a resolute one. All except the eyes. Haunted. The whites around the dark irises glowed, somehow, with the horrors of what they'd seen. Lin knew this intrinsically. She also knew her name, rank, and character history. Some memory insertion protocol embodied in the game. Such protocols, even though they provided simple surface memories, had long been banned.

"Sergeant Duncan."

I – Lin – Duncan – turned. "Yes…" *the other man's title glowed at the corner of the screen,* "Lieutenant Muzzy." *Muzzy was a too-young lieutenant who was never quite able to hide the fear behind his eyes. Tall, well-built. Chin too small; forehead too long. He always gave orders with a hint of hesitation, like he expected them to be ignored.*

"New orders," *said Muzzy.* "Patrol, thirty minutes. Gather the men. Meet me at the East gate."

"Yes sir."

I slung my carbine and backpack, put on my helmet, and stepped out of my darkened square tent into the blazing sun. Wincing, I held up a hand against the white light, bearing down on me from a clear blue sky. Wouldn't be clear for long. The humidity would build and build until I thought I couldn't breathe, then the late-afternoon rain would come. Thunderously. Unlike anything back home in the US; dumping down, pouring off the fat green leaves in spears of water. Visibility close to zero, nothing in my ears bar the rain.

When it was over, the heat would return, just as bad. No cool, no respite. Just the drip drip drip from long green leaves and the croak of frogs, and the heat. Always the dark heat. Sapping morale and sanity.

I headed over to the rec hall. Brown earth piled up the sides, sandbags covering the roof, thick wooden frame inside, most of the furnishings just more sandbags. My platoon was more or less there, in the stifling half-light. Smoking cigarettes, drinking Larue beer, playing or watching ping pong; a poker game going in one corner, Mah-Jong in the other. Silver radio, crackle-playing: "…it ain't me, it ain't me, I ain't no senator's…"

"Alright, apes." (The program put up suggested lines at the bottom of the screen, rating them by aggressiveness. Lin decided to go for the highest.) "Hands off cocks onto socks; get your gear, carpet-munchers. We're moving out."

The men grumbled, downed beers, flicked cigarette butts.

"Where are we going?" asked one of the soldiers. Private Washington, the system informed me. Skinny, black, prominent cheekbones.

"Get a manicure, faggot. What else would we be doing in the front line of a war zone?"

Some of the men smiled, a darkling shadow of anger passed Washington's face before he moved to get his equipment.

"Stop right there. You eyeballing me, mister?"

"No Sergeant," he replied, stilled.

I walked over while the rest of the men gathered their gear and shut the fuck up. I parked my nose an inch from his. "I didn't hear you, Private."

"No Sergeant," he said, louder this time, back straight, eyes a middle-distance stare.

"You got somewhere else to be, Private?"

"No Sergeant."

"Sucking dicks behind the toilet block again?"

The other men tried not to look, or smile, or have any response whatever, lest I come after them.

"No Sergeant!"

"Why are you in this man's army, Private?"

Washington paused, and said, "To defend the world against godless communism, Sergeant."

I slapped him. The sound was loud in the humid dusk of the room. He turned his face back to me slowly, eyes wide.

I said, angry, "Don't you lie to me, faggot. You'd only care about communism if it had a fat dick you could wrap your lips around. Why are you in my army, Private?"

"To serve my country, Sergeant!"

I slapped him again. He stepped back with the blow, then resumed his stance, jaw tightening, anger flaring in his eyes.

I yelled, "You tell me one more lie and you'll be on point duty for the rest of the tour, cocksucker." My teeth were bared, face right in his. "Why are you in this man's army?"

Washington swallowed, took a deep breath. He looked at me. "I was conscripted."

"You're god damn right you were! And what do you want more than anything?"

He replied quietly, "To go home."

"You're god damn right you do. That's the first thing to come out of your mouth that wasn't a lie or another man's balls. And how are you going to get home, Private?"

A pause, eyes still on me. "Follow orders, Sergeant."

"YER GODDAM RIGHT THAT'S HOW. Now. Private Washington."

"Yes sir!"

"You're on point."

"Yes sir!"

☆

We marched out under the gathering clouds, faces dripping sweat. Through the paddy fields to the north, empty, save an old woman who stood and watched us pass. Heading out on a mission that made me want to throw punches, after the lieutenant had explained it.

Washington was on point, the barrel of his M-16 only halfway up, ghetto strut in his walk. Jimmy Chen was in front of me, eyes all around, nearly at the end of his tour, no way he was going to buy it now. Jeb Green three metres behind, singing a blues number quietly and perfectly.

The men stretched in a long line, nine of them, plus the lieutenant made ten, plus the South Vietnamese interpreter, eleven. The lieutenant was two men ahead, not knowing what the fuck he was doing. As close to the radio man – a stout Texan called Five Times Freddy – as possible, so he could scream for air support the second a shot was fired from the jungle screen.

The interpreter moved up the line to talk to the lieutenant. A short, shifty-eyed marine from the South Vietnamese army who went by the name of Binh Pham. The locals in the villages near the base didn't like him, glaring in open contempt whenever he spoke to them. He often argued with the villagers at length, and when the lieutenant asked what was said, he'd simply say, 'they haven't seen any Viet Cong,' or 'they're welcoming us to the village,' or some obvious bullshit.

Now, up ahead, Pham had his words and the lieutenant signalled the platoon in the direction of a hamlet further down the valley. Smoke from cooking fires hanging above it, a screen of verdant green jungle behind. I was relatively calm about the patrol, as far as wandering pointlessly in a war zone goes. This area north of the firebase was 'pacified', according to the generals. *Which was another way of saying all the young men of fighting age were absent, and that the villages were poorly maintained, silent, miserable places filled with half-starved, dead-eyed old people and young children.*

The air didn't move as we headed down, nothing did save the mosquitos buzzing by my ears and the men trudging between glistening rice fields. I felt the sweat trickle down my brow – and Lin couldn't help but marvel at how real the game felt. She could barely breathe as the platoon approached the hamlet, the heat, the sweat-blurred vision, slapping away insects. Every colour, every tactile feeling, my brain perfectly deceived.

Jeb Green's singing was still there, like a soundtrack, as we entered the hamlet.

He fills his chamber up with lead
And takes his pain to town
Only pleasure he gets out of life
Is bringing another man down

Unusually, a crowd was there, just down past the red dirt outskirts. I pushed through with Washington, clearing the way for the lieutenant. The peasants were standing around a pond, maybe twenty metres across. It was a perfect circle, perhaps a crater from a Mark 84.

"Here it is," said Pham.

The lieutenant turned to me and nodded.

I said to the men, "Alright, cock-jockeys, lock and load!"

The men, quizzical, clack-clacked their weapons.

"Now, gentlemen, we are going to pacify this pond."

The men looked at each other until Corporal Chen said, "Sergeant?"

"Did I not speak clearly, maggot?"

"Uh." Chen swallowed, looked at the other soldiers, the pond, then back at me.

I puffed out my chest. "This pond is a strategic objective that needs
to be pacified, by order of the legitimate government of South Vietnam.
What part of that confuses you, Corporal?"

"I don't—" he started, then stopped himself. Smart. There was no
possible correct answer.

I clenched my jaw. "You dumb motherfuckers."

Rifle slung, hands behind my back, I positioned myself at the edge of
the pond, facing the men.

"A magical fish lives in this pond, you slack-jawed pussy-grabbers.
It is well known, in this region, that a carpenter's mute child was healed
by drinking this water – a miracle. A woman unable to get pregnant
conceived twins after she drank this water." I jabbed a finger at the pond
behind as I said this water. "Another miracle. A soldier blinded by a
nova blast washed his face here, and had his sight restored. Another
GODDAM MIRACLE."

The men blinked at me, smart enough not to ask any questions. The
villagers still hadn't left, forty or fifty of them gathered a few metres
back, watching us with sullen eyes.

"Now you tell me something, Private Yang. What is wrong with this
story?" Bernie Yang was a stocky Californian who spent most of his time
keeping to himself on his bunk, staring at a picture of his family back home.

"Um." Yang was a courageous man, but it still took him a few
moments to work up the balls to say, "It's crazy, Sergeant."

"Yer GODDAM RIGHT it is fucking crazy! And why is that, Private?"

Yang paused, thinking, then swallowed and said, "Because only
Jesus performs miracles."

I stormed over to him and screamed in his face. "You are a
goddam genius, Private. You are the smartest ape in this platoon. I am
recommending you for corporal, Yang. Man like you needs to be leading
men, not hiding in his goddam bunk."

I looked over the men. "Miracles are real, but only those performed
by our lord and saviour Jesus Christ. Everything else is the superstition

of devil-worshippers, sodomites, and the goddam Catholics. They are certainly not performed by magical fish in buttfuck Vietnam!"

The men were wilting under the heat and abuse.

"Right?!"

"Yes Sergeant!"

I resumed my position, hands behind my back, in front of the pond. "Now, the legitimate government of South Vietnam, fearing an outbreak of this goddam superstition, has ordered the fish to be captured and or killed. The Army of the Republic of Vietnam have tried to dynamite this pond, to no avail. The Army of the Republic of Vietnam have tried to drag it with a net, but the enemy fish got away. So the Vietnamese government have decided to call on the professionals. They decided to get the finest fighting men on this green Earth to deal with the scourge of superstition."

I scanned the men in front of me. "Any of you here have a problem with that?"

"No Sergeant."

"You pussy-lipped faggots, I asked you a question. Do you have a problem with that?"

"No Sergeant!"

"Good. Now clear away these civilians."

The men moved into the crowd, jamming rifle stocks into ribs, yelling insults. The villagers, usually acquiescent in this part of the country, only did so reluctantly. An old woman even took to arguing with the men, until one of boys knocked her on her arse.

A yellow-robed Buddhist monk separated himself from the villagers and approached the lieutenant, and our adviser Pham. The monk smiled as Pham moved to stop him, but Lieutenant Muzzy said, "Let him through."

The monk, shaved head, smile lines on his forehead, hands hidden each in the opposite sleeves of his robe, bowed slightly and said something in Vietnamese.

"Pham?" asked Muzzy.

Pham answered, scorn in his voice, "It's not Vietnam language. China language. I don't speak."

The Buddhist bowed again and spoke in lightly-accented, perfect English, "I said, wishing the blessings of Buddha on you all. The fish you seek, I have seen it."

"Is that so?" said the lieutenant, feigning interest. I had a feeling this wasn't going to end well for the monk.

The monk, oblivious, said, "The fish has a black back; its belly is yellow. It is an Indo-Chinese carp and its name is Eminent Master Immortal Fish Bodhisattva Dragon King."

"I see," said Muzzy. "Obviously."

"It has the power to materialise and de-materialise. This is why the attempts to destroy it have been futile."

"Amazing," said Muzzy.

The monk signalled the horizon with his eyes. "I travel through this war-torn land, urging all to respect tradition and the spirit world. A curse would fall on you and your men if you were to kill it."

"So this fish performs miracles?" asked Muzzy.

"I haven't said this."

"Yet you're telling us to respect superstition."

"Not superstition, merely the universe."

"The universe." Muzzy looked over at the pond. "A bomb crater filled with unsanitary water."

"Yet it changes lives," said the monk, still with that quiet smile. "Such is the wonder of the universe. A small, unremarkable place that yet gives hope in this blighted land. We must respect the tradition of wonder. We must respect the spirit of place. Without it, the people are like a tree without roots, a river without a source."

The lieutenant looked over at Pham. "This Chinaman is saying you don't respect your own traditions."

Pham said nothing, just grinned ugly at the monk, hand resting on the grip of his .45.

"Remove this deranged vagrant," said Muzzy. "With extreme prejudice."

The monk opened his mouth to reply just as Pham hit him with his pistol. He staggered back, arms grasping at something no one could see, the mark of Cain on his forehead.

The monk fell. Pham pressed his pistol against the man's temple. He flicked the safety with his thumb.

I said, "Wait." Pham looked up, irritated. To Muzzy I said, "Killing a monk in front of an entire village ain't gonna make the local area any more partial to our being here, sir. Might even spark the kinda problems we had a few months back."

Muzzy's eyes were shaded under the brim of his helmet. Insects buzzed around us. "It's hot," was his reply. "Let's pacify this damn pond and be done with it."

I signalled the men over. To Pham I said, "You heard the lieutenant, motherfucker – let that orange windbag have his nap." Pham did as he was told. But slowly, with a look I didn't much like at all.

I gave the order.

The men opened up, laughing, as their guns spat metal. The water jumped to meet the fire. Pham joined in, emptying his .45, and even the lieutenant started shooting. A kind of madness gripped the platoon, drenched in sweat and enervating heat. All the while the villagers watched, without reaction. I stood, smoking a cigarette, as my boys subdued a pond.

The afternoon rains broke, roaring as the guns roared. The skies drenched us, but did not cool the rage, nor our heat madness, nor the blind anger at this implacable alien land. One of the boys yelled, "Fire in the hole," and threw a grenade into the pond. The men flattened themselves on the ground and the pond responded with a thud-boom-splash, and we were sprayed with more water from that, as well.

"Cease fire, faggots!" I yelled, walking over towards the pond so they could see me. "Cease fire."

I knelt next to the pond, now slick with mud. The rain eased off to a pitter-patter. The men gathered around, watching. They looked drained, by the heat, by the visceral thrill of howling metal. Drained by something else too, maybe just the madness of their orders. Maybe another thing.

Something strange was happening with the light. Like the hues all around us were brighter, even though the sun had not come out from behind the clouds. Everything clearer, somehow: every line of dirt on our faces, every crease in our uniforms, the patterning of the rain on the water, the smell of fecund vegetation, the sound of cricket and mosquito and frog, the murmuring of the villagers, distant. My every sense lit with a clarity I hadn't experienced for a long time.

Someone said, "Look."

I looked, and there it was. The long yellow belly of a fish, exposed to the sky. Must have been two metres long, floating in the pond. No one said anything. Nothing else said anything, either: not the insects or the earth. They were silent, as well. An ancient dread settled on us all there, at that pool. Grim sweat on our faces.

I looked around and the villagers were gone. The monk was gone too. Deserted, this place, like no one had lived there for years.

I opened my mouth to order the platoon to ship out. But no words came.

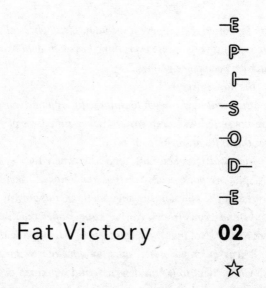

Fat Victory   **02**

☆

"She's the sweetest pussy in Saigon," said Five Times Freddy. "Hot damn, that little lady comes like a machine gun."

"Huh? Like a machine gun?" asked Washington.

"I don't know what that means," said Yang, genuinely.

"Did, like, juice shoot out of her pussy?" asked Green.

"Was she yelling RATATATAT when she came?" asked Washington. "'Cause I don't think that's a real orgasm, brother."

The three men, faces lit by the moon, sat listening to Freddy's Texas drawl as he detailed his exploits in the brothels of Saigon. The three sharing smiles Freddy didn't catch the meaning of.

"Sheee-it," said Freddy, "what I mean is—"

"Alright, maggots," I said, voice soft. "Stop talking about Freddy's pin dick. That pecker is going to be a bona-fide scientific curiosity when this man gets home. They will wonder how something so small can harbour so many different diseases. Every newspaper will talk about the man with the rotted cock, marvelling that he is still physically able to jam that diseased little organ into everything he can find: hookers, Catholics, the crack between fence palings."

The men snickered.

"But right now you got to shut the fuck up and sentry this camp. I'm sure the squad will sleep easier knowing the likes of you are watching over them. Right, men?"

They said, "Yes Sergeant," and went where they were meant to go.

I put my back against a tree and smoked, angled so I could see the rest of the platoon, snoring quietly or slapping at mosquitos. I ate franks-and-beans from a can, so hungry after the day's march I didn't even taste it. Not that there was taste in it to begin with.

It was quiet, all quiet, after we had our victory over the pond. The village next to it had deserted, and remained deserted. The other villages near the firebase no longer sold us anything: food or women or rice whiskey. Said they were all out and watched us with faces of stone as we left. Regular patrols came back in, saying they'd seen nothing. Nothing at all. The jungle empty of animals and people.

So we'd been ordered out on a long patrol, to secure a hilltop fifteen miles away, and set it up as a forward operating base so we could push the lines of the Viet Cong deeper into the jungle. The lieutenant had even got to saying our pond operation had destroyed enemy morale, that maybe more of our missions should set out to destroy symbols of their superstition and backwardness. I'd heard him holding forth in the officer's mess when I'd gone to give him a message. The other officers looked at him like he knew what the fuck he was talking about, desperate to grasp any strategy that might help them win the war, no matter how criminally stupid.

For me, I drank Larue beer, smoked cheap cigarettes, and thought about the white sand beaches of home. My sister and my mother running along the shoreline, laughing and belonging, like the world didn't matter and the truth didn't matter. Me, Sergeant Douglas Duncan, lying on the bunk in my tiny tent, listening to the armed forces radio service.

Martha and the Vandellas and the Beach Boys and James Brown and the Supremes. That's all I fucking did.

Lin did masturbate once, out of curiosity. It was kinda cool, then really messy, and after she felt grossed out with herself. But that was the only time she broke character.

I didn't try to buddy with my men or play poker with the other sergeants. Didn't take my R&R in Saigon to fuck prostitutes, like Five Times Freddy, or get drunk like Washington; or both, like the rest of the men. I couldn't be a friend to these men. I had to seem moulded by iron, impervious and resolute. I could not be a friend to these men because they already had friends and they did not need any more. What they didn't have was order in this chaos, a sense of purpose in the madness. If I kept my distance they would not question me and they could not imagine me weak. From a distance, I was made of iron. When they died and they left me, as all before had left me, the sting of their passing would fade that much quicker. Eventually, I would feel nothing at all. Distance was the key, always distance.

The tour was getting to me in ways I didn't understand. Getting under my skin. I started smoking hand-rolled tobacco cigarettes, sprinkling mary jane in them. A lot back at camp, just a little on patrol, to take the edge off. Make me a little less jumpy at loud noises, a little less likely to slap a new recruit for no good reason, help cut down, just a little, on those fever dreams that woke me at night unable to breathe.

Footsteps, approaching. I grabbed my carbine, held it up to my shoulder.

My finger twitched when I saw the Asian face, relaxed when I saw the US fatigues.

Chen knelt close by. "Sergeant. There's a village nearby. I saw two men with guns, carrying something."

"Just two men?"

"Yes Sergeant."

I removed my helmet, wiped the sweat from my forehead with the crook of my elbow. "Okay, get Yang, Freddy, and Washington. I'll wake up the lieutenant and report. Tell Washington and Freddy to stay here and keep their fucking eyes peeled. You'll take Yang and me to the village."

He whispered a, "Yes Sergeant."

We followed Chen through the jungle. Deep as we were, there was enough moonlight to see where my feet were going. Sweating, even in the depth of night, on edge. We twisted this way and that at each jungle sigh, or rustle of leaf; each time imaging a charging Viet Cong, bayonet affixed, screaming as they drove it into our intestines.

It was a long, long five minutes to the redoubt above the village. Our position was far closer than I would have liked, overlooking a six-hut hamlet below, well-hidden in a mass of undergrowth. Torches had been lit, making everything that happened in the dirt village square utterly clear. Unforgettably clear.

Two men had a dead orangutan, laid out on the dirt with its arms stretched out, its head to one side, eyes open, lips slightly parted.

Other villagers had gathered to watch. Perhaps thirty. Probably the whole village.

The resolution changed, somehow, and everything seemed one shade brighter, as though lit by an internal light. The hushed conversation of the villagers drifted up to me, crystal clear, as did the sawing of the knife through the animal's hide. Chen, next to me, sucking in his breath, the bead of sweat that sat at the end of my nose, itching. Every sense was clarified, pure.

Oh god and so when I watched them skin that orangutan every detail imprinted in my neural pathways, oh god when they pulled the animal fur back it looked like a fat woman with ulcerous skin, and the woman's eyes moved in the orbits wildly. Until they came to rest on us.

Yang screamed.

Chen threw up.

I backed away, eyeballs popping, the carbine slipping from my fingers.

The villagers looked up and saw us. The two hunters grabbed their guns. "Run!" I yelled, and turned back into the jungle. I'd taken two steps before the jungle roared with gunfire, orange flashes in the darkness, all around, bullets whizzing by and I dived off the path, into the darkness, stumble-running and the firing did not let up, branches striking my face ankle twisting I staggered, arms out, crashing face-first into mud and root.

I turned onto my side, gasping for breath in the stifling, airless night. A shadow loomed over me, rifle pointed at my face. Hands up, I turned my face away.

"Come on, Sergeant." A hand reached out to me, a strained voice. "They're coming."

Relief flowed through me as my brain registered the language. I breathed out long and hard and grasped the proffered hand. Chen – at the end of his tour and now in the middle of this – pulled me up. Wordlessly, we continued together. I hobbled on my ankle, but kept pace. Bullets still whizzed nearby, orange spouts of flame lit up small windows of the jungle, but increasingly behind us.

We continued like that for I'm not sure how long. Adrenalin pumping, terrified we were going to stumble into the midst of thirty Viet Cong, faceless, only their eyes showing, bodies wrapped in black. We were terrified to stop moving as well, lest they were still behind us, every echo every broken twig telling us, yes: they were there, just there.

Chen made the decision for us; swaying, highlighted by a shaft of moonlight, he collapsed. I dropped to my knees beside him, eyes all around, looking for the enemy. I couldn't see anything, but that didn't mean much.

Chen groaned. I looked down and noticed for the first time his hands were pressed against his side. His fatigues were slick. "Shit," I whispered, and dragged him deeper into the undergrowth, resting his back against a thick tree. Chen closed his eyes against the pain, his teeth gritted.

"Let me see, soldier," I said, pulling apart his hands. The thin moonlight seeped through the foliage, enough to show me the mess. I shucked off my backpack and found some gauze, placed the white square over the wound, and pressed his hands back down over it. "Keep a firm pressure."

He winced and did as he was told.

I gave him some water from my canteen, which he gulped down. I did the same, emptying it. I leaned back on the tree next to him and took a couple of minutes to get my breathing back under control, the fear back into the cage where it lived, right under my heart.

The firing continued, in the distance. No orange flashes. Just the thin moonlight and Chen's laboured breathing.

He said, "I'm sick of this war."

"Yeah," I sighed.

"I just want to be with my family. My wife and girls." Chen clenched his teeth against the pain, pearly whites shining in the moonlight. "So beautiful. Two and four. Baozhai, the four-year old, she dotes on her little sister. Reads her—" He grimaced. "—stories from picture books, even though she can't read herself. Just makes them up."

He laughed to himself at the thought, but the laughter stopped abruptly, replaced with him sucking in his breath through clenched teeth.

I pulled a squashed soft pack of Double Happiness cigarettes from my pocket, propped one in Chen's mouth, and lit it. He raised a set of bloodied fingers to pull it from his mouth and exhale a cloud of smoke. I lit another for myself.

Chen continued, "It's just our generals, and their generals, that want this war. It won't make a difference to anything. To the Vietnamese here, or to Americans back home. Not a damn thing. We should just lay down our arms and get on with our lives."

I had no reply to that.

"We'll never defeat them," he said, after another drag on his cigarette. "To the Vietnamese, people are disposable. The Viet Cong run barefoot over minefields in their suicide attacks. They don't even have lives to lose."

Chen started coughing, doubled over. I gently eased him back up against the tree.

"If the South ever win, they'll just be slaves," he said. His eyes gleamed in the moonlight, as did the blood on his stomach. "That despotic regime cares even less for their people than the Americans. I'd rather the fighting just stopped." He coughed. "Peace. Stability. Let the generals have a knife-fight over the spoils if they want it so bad. But they won't. They don't care. They have no skin in this game. The sons of generals, the rich businessmen, all escaped to Paris. You know what they call the flight to France?"

"Noah's Ark," I replied.

Chen smiled, bitterly, and there was blood in it. "But not two of every species. Just the same species. The corrupt. The wealthy. Two by two by two."

He was silent, and I thought he'd said his piece. But he winced again and spoke, not to me, but at a place I couldn't see. "While I die here. And my girls wait."

He turned his eyes up to the thin sliver of moonlight shining through the treetops. His breathing became more laboured. I smoked three more cigarettes as I waited for Chen to die.

When he did I closed his eyes, took his M-16, and headed back in the direction of the gunfire.

Fat Victory　　**03**

☆

Hands and knees, through the undergrowth. The Viet Cong all around me. I never saw them, but I was close enough to hear them loading their guns. Nearby, the firing had ebbed. In the distance shots still rang out, echoing through the hot, still jungle.

Thorns scratched my skin, sweat stung the wounds. My fatigues and face were coated in mud, my backpack long gone, discarded when I became too tired to carry it. I kept only the compass from it. That, Chen's M-16, the knife at my belt, and the helmet on my head were all the equipment I had left.

Voices drifted from up ahead. I flattened myself on the ground and inched forward, towards the sounds; they weren't speaking English. I pushed a long frond aside—

—and was dragged forward by the collar, a hand clamped down over my mouth, knife at my throat, white eyes gleaming at me down in the darkness. I flailed my arms around, the blade pressed hard

against my throat and a voice said, "Shhhhhh."

I stopped struggling. The hand grasped around my mouth eased away.

I turned. Muzzy, Pham and Washington were huddled within the long fronds of an old fern. Washington held one hand up, easing himself away from me, and used the point of his blade to show me what to look at. I swallowed, trying to still my heart as it slammed against the cage of my chest, and looked where he was pointing. Through the undergrowth was a clearing, lit up by the moonlight. The sky a shade lighter, too. Dawn was coming.

It was the clearing we'd set up camp in. Some of the men had not moved from where they'd slept. Bullet-riddled. No thought, as they collapsed into an exhausted sleep, that it would be their last. Just thinking on the blister on their heel, or their bunk back at camp, or a cool beer Larue in an air-conditioned neon bar in Saigon.

Not of the abyss. Not of their body in a casket, draped in an American flag.

Yang, the stocky, smart Californian, was alive. He was the only one. On his knees. Blood smeared on his face. The blank indifference of resignation in his eyes.

The Viet Cong were there, all around him. A dozen perhaps, clad in black pyjamas, AK-47s in hand, their lower faces covered with a black strip of material, like bandits. Just the eyes showing. One of the insurgents was barking at Yang in Vietnamese and broken English.

They were asking him where the rest of the platoon were. Yang wasn't talking. The interrogator pressed the barrel of his rifle against Yang's forehead. He yelled, "How many?"

Yang continued staring at a place far away.

There was a swish of branches near me and Pham was out in the clearing, hands raised in surrender, speaking rapid-fire Vietnamese. Startled, the Viet Cong raised their weapons. Pham went to his knees, arms still in the air, voice urgent.

Three things happened in quick succession.

Yang looked at Pham and said, "Motherfucker."

Our interpreter half turned and pointed back at the undergrowth, where we were hiding.

I raised my M-16 and put three rounds in Pham's back. He jerked, stood up, stutter-stepped, and fell on his face.

The Viet Cong raised their AK-47s and fired, I raked my M-16 across them, but it jammed after one shot and I was already down, grabbing earth, bullets tearing chunks from the trees above me. I turned my head to see the lieutenant, screaming, in a foetal position on the ground.

"Lieutenant!" I yelled, but couldn't even hear myself over the gunfire.

I crawled over to him, grabbed him by his pants and tried to drag his attention to me. His eyes were like a wild horse's, insane in their orbits. Shots chewed up the earth, sprayed it in my eyes. I swore and crawled away, dirt in my mouth, ears full of fire.

I crawled and then staggered, then rolled down sudden slopes. Dragged myself along for I don't know how long, roots scraping against my chest, my helmet gone and I don't know when. Gasping, I staggered into another run, no senses reporting in anymore, just the thudding of my heart in my ears and my laboured breathing. I cried out as I twisted my bad ankle on a rock, and fell forward, heavily.

I didn't even try to push myself up, chest heaving. Right then, at that moment, I didn't care about the prospect of a gun barrel pressed against the back of my head. I welcomed it, even.

At some point I realised my arms were submerged in water.

Slowly, I got to my knees. I was at the edge of a reed-filled swamp. Right across from me, at the opposite edge a mile or more away, orange flames flashed from the top foliage and long, frenzied roars crossed the murky water to where I knelt. Tracers marked the darkness, and the space across from me looked like a royal city, ablaze with lights. Flares dropped slowly from the sky, lighting the ground in a quavering, spectral glare.

The US army was somewhere across that swamp, fighting. My men. My brothers. Dying in the mud and mosquitos.

The sub-blue light of pre-dawn turned to the purple of true dawn. The water quivered with the pounding of artillery. I felt for the compass. Gone. I breathed a sigh of relief when I found my cigarettes. Three left, bent. I popped one in my mouth and reached for my lighter. Unable to find it, I pulled my pockets inside out with increasing anger.

"Fuck." I tore the cigarette from my mouth. "Fuck."

Soaked in sweat and mud, my mouth was yet dry. The fear slowly went, only to be replaced by thirst. I cupped the water with my hand and drank, or tried to, coughing up the brackish liquid. I got more down the second time, but not much more, my stomach cramping. To the left and right I saw no end to the swamp, no point where it curved back around to the firefight in the distance. I sighed.

I groaned to my feet, wiped the sweat and muck from my eyes, and walked out into the water. The reeds were high and I was hidden up to my chest. Now and then my boots slid off the trampled stems and muddy water rose up to my thighs.

I'm not sure how long it took me to cross. It felt like forever. Forever. It felt like every memory I ever had went no further than slogging through the reed and mud. My whole history was the sucking sound as I yanked my foot from the water and took another step, the silent weeping, the hard buzz of mosquitos swarming.

The heat visibly distorted everything around me. Endless rows of reeds, waving in the heat. Insects feasted on me. At the start I'd pulled the leeches from my arms, but soon gave up. No energy even for that. Just a narrowing vision, down to a metre in front of me, at the point where I put my next step. And the next. And the next.

Sometime later, in the far distant future, the splashing would stop and my feet hit something firm. That was my dream. That was the dream I had, it ended with me laying down for a long and restful sleep.

☆

I woke up on hard ground, in darkness. Crickets chirping. No footsteps. No orange gunfire. No artillery. Just the ghosts.

I groaned, my body awareness creeping back. The ache in my legs, the pounding in my head, my lips cracked and stuck together. I tried to run my tongue over them, but it felt swollen in my mouth.

Water. I had to find drinkable water. And head south. Head south and never stop. Not until Saigon, and not then, either. From there back home, to my family.

I looked myself over. A sprained ankle, torn pants, leeches, a few dozen scratches. Not enough. I needed something more serious to Purple Heart myself out of this godforsaken place. Self-inflicted, if worse came to worst.

Back home. To those white sand beaches. To a sister that loved me, understood me. To a place untouched by the dead hand of war, the dead hand that stilled all progress, for a nation, and for the human heart.

Sunrise on my left, I limped on through forest blackened by fire, still smouldering. No bodies, no wind, thin tendrils of smoke rising lazily from blackened tree trunks. It took me a few minutes to realise that I liked that. I found a rock to sit on, pulled my second-last cigarette from my pocket, and pressed the tip on the embers. Half a tonne of napalm dropped on an empty forest. At least I was putting it to good use.

I smoked, burning the leeches off my legs with the tip of my cigarette. The thought of home had given me a second wind.

I walked south. Deep into the night, I slept in the blackened forest.

Or tried to sleep. I'd just gone under when the sound of someone crying woke me, abrupt, combat knife in my hand. It was near dawn, light enough to show stands of bamboo nearby oozing red, like they were bleeding. I'd walked most of the night and desperately wanted to sleep. But there, in that broken place, faint sobbing and whispers carried on the wind. I shook my head, fearing for my sanity, but the cries persisted.

I stumbled into the dawn.

The next morning I found a river. I fell face forward into it, slurping down the water, choking on it. It headed more or less south, so I took it. I began sleeping during the day, during the worst of the heat, and walking at night. Covered in ash and mud, like I'd become a ghost, as well. Days and nights, like this.

Eventually, I know not how many days later, I hit an area infected with craters. Large and small, trees torn off at the base, earth and mud flung up in piles. There was an eerie silence, no animal talked. I thought I saw a bridge in the distance. It was strange, as the river by then had thinned to a trickle, though the ground all around had been turned to mud. Starving, I hurried over, hoping the bridge was near a town or hamlet. Somewhere with food.

There was a bridge. But the supports on either side were gone. I didn't understand, didn't understand how it was hanging there, in the air. It took me some time, staring at it, as the centipedes crawled past my feet, for me to see the shadows under the bridge. Solid shadows. People, bodies and bodies piled up on top of each other, wedged under the bridge, holding it up in the air. The Americans had blown a dam up somewhere, miles back.

The flies were everywhere, everywhere. Swarms of big black flies. I backed away as they came at me, waving my arms weakly. Too big, these flies, as big as a dime. As I staggered away one went into my mouth. Crawled and buzzed on my tongue, trying to force its way down my throat. I fell to my knees and retched, my body trying to vomit it out.

Nothing came out. Just a thin line of bile, clinging to my bottom lip.

I staggered away, I'm not sure how long for. Until the maddening buzzing stopped. Until I passed out.

☆

The next morning I found the village, set among paddy fields. It was a smoking ruin, but it didn't matter. To me it looked like a plentiful oasis. There would be food there, hidden away, even if only a few scraps. There would be food.

As I walked into the dirt village, I had this strange feeling. Like I was entering a burnt-out town in a western. A breeze, finally, the first one in days, washed smoke in thin streams across my vision. I expected a man in a black hat to walk out from stage right, high noon.

Faintly, just there at the tip of my hearing, music. I turned this way and that, trying to find the source. Not imagining it, yes it was there, but somehow from inside my own head. Not Western music, not Ennio Morricone, but slow, thin strands of classical.

I didn't care. I went from hut to hut as the music became clearer. Pounded my feet on dirt floors, listening for hollow spaces. I plunged my hands into ash, looking for rice hidden at the heart, smashing empty ceramic jugs. Two huts, three, desperate, sweat soaking my shirt. My hands shook.

In the fourth hut I found Washington. Lying on the earth.

I stood in the doorway, not believing my eyes. Private Washington lay on the ground, his chest rising and falling gently. Sleeping. His face was like a skull, skin stretched back over it, but alive. On his chest was a ceramic bowl, half-filled with rice, and a mango.

Salivating instantly, I fell to all fours, like a dog. I crept over, reached out—

—and Washington's hand was clamped on my wrist. Like iron. The whites of his eyes shining in the gloom of the hut.

I yanked at my arm, but it wouldn't budge. Washington sat up slowly, carefully repositioning the food on his lap.

"Food," I croaked.

"No."

"What? Washington, it's me."

The expression on his face did not change. Just a skull, with staring white eyes. "No. Sergeant."

"I'm starving."

Eyes on me, unblinking, he took some rice between thumb and forefinger of his other hand, and ate.

"No," I begged.

He ate another mouthful.

I pulled my combat knife and slashed the inside of his wrist.

Washington didn't understand what I'd done. I didn't understand it either. Arterial spray from the wound coated his lap, the rice bowl. He went for another mouthful, and saw the rice was now red.

Those dark irises looked back at me. "Motherfucker." He lashed out with his foot and I felt the bone in my nose crunch. Then I was on my back, looking at a thatched roof. Washington stood over me, I put my arms out weakly. He stomped on my stomach. The wind was knocked from my lungs, and it felt like the last of my strength went with it. He stomped on my face. Another bone broke. I passed out.

When I woke, Washington was dead.

Lying next to me on his chest, his face two feet from mine, the whites of his eyes still boring into me. There was blood on his face, on his uniform, pooled on the bamboo mat. Bled out, on the dirt floor of a nameless village, in a country he'd never heard of until America decided it existed.

I tried to push myself upright. I got there on the third attempt. I found the bowl of rice tipped on its side. With trembling fingers I scooped up the blood-soaked rice and shoved it into my mouth. I cried out in pain. My jaw wouldn't work. Broken. Swollen.

I laughed, sounding like a wounded animal. I'd got my Purple Heart. And my food. The hunger overrode the pain. I choked down the rice, then tore apart the mango with my fingers, moaning with pleasure as the succulent flesh slid down my throat.

The music started again, right as I heard the chopper. My fingers stopped their frenetic dance over the fruit. I stumbled out into the light, mouth open, the mango seed tumbled from my hand.

Dubadubadubaduba

The green angel appeared in the sky, over the rice fields. "Here," I croaked. Feet dragging on the dirt, I staggered towards it.

Dubadubadubaduba

Still half a mile away. It might not have seen me. It had to see me. With mango-slick hands I tore off my shirt and waved it above my head.

"Here," *I yelled, voice finding strength,* "HERE."

Dubadubadubaduba

It sailed towards me. The wind picked up, flattening the stalks in the paddy field. I ran out of the village, on the raised path between the fields. The helicopter seemed to hesitate, turning on its side so the open door faced me. I could make out a helmeted head, visor down, looking at me.

A huge smile broke on my face. I waved the shirt above my head, feeling dizzy with relief, with malnutrition, with three fingers of madness sloshing around my brain.

The green angel circled slowly, then hovered above the village. Above the dirt square, perfect space for the chopper to land.

I'd taken one step back towards the village when the rocket-propelled grenade hit the tail of the green angel. It swung around in huge loops, smoke trailing from a stilled tail rotor.

"No," *I whispered, as the music rose in my ears.* "No," *again, as I fell to my knees and the helicopter took one more wild loop and pitched sideways into a paddy field.*

The heavy splash-thump *was accompanied by the blades snapping, flinging themselves away from the crash, pinwheeling across the top of the muddy waters. A fire started in the cockpit, smoke billowing out. No one tried to escape.*

Palms open, resting on my thighs, I said for the last time, "No."

The music stopped.

A songbird trilled, somewhere far away.

I was feeling for my last cigarette when the spectres rose from the water around me. The Viet Cong, soaking, black strip of material covering their lower faces. All looking at me with the black, depthless eyes of the rattlesnake.

They screamed a war cry.

My heart fear-fluttering, I rose to my feet and turned to run—

—and stepped into a bayonet. Right up the hilt, in my stomach, affixed to the end of an AK-47. I couldn't see the man holding it. Just his hands, knuckles white, gripping the weapon. I yanked it from my body, screaming as blood gushed, and fell backwards into the water.

Up, gasping for breath, something slammed into my shoulder and I was underwater again. I thrashed my arms, strength coming from I don't know where, then got to my knees, gasping for air again. Something hit me high on the back, knocking me forward a step.

I was a little surprised to look down and see the tip of a blade sticking out of my body, at the point between chest and shoulder. I stared, lips parted, as bright red blood stained my fatigues.

I put the tip of my finger to the point, not quite believing it was real. Another blow hit me in the back, and another. And another.

The music swelled again. No mistaking this time, no hallucination, rising powerful in my ears.

My strength gone, my hands dropped into the water.

But my body wouldn't. I was suspended, by I-don't-know-how-many blades in my back. I looked down at the water, longingly. It lapped gently against me, shimmering in the sunlight. Gently, unlike everything else in this war. Gently, unlike the last bayonet that tore into my throat, and laid my miserable story to rest.

As the final notes of Barber's Adagio for Strings echoed across the paddy fields, the darkness came.

CHAPTER

23

☆

Shaking her, someone shaking her. Lin gasped for breath, flailed her arms, knocking the hands away. A voice talking to her.

Mosquito Brother was leaning over her, Bull standing behind him. Mosquito Brother was saying, over and over: "[It's okay, elder sister, it's okay.]"

She ran her hands over her body, her neck, at her wounds. Nothing. Still on the couch in her apartment. Soaked in sweat, black singlet sticking to her skin. She pushed herself to a sitting position.

Bull Neck Bui passed her a glass of water. She sucked it down in one long gulp, gasping. She asked: "How long was I playing?"

"[Did you stop at all?]" asked Mosquito Brother, droop-eyed, concerned.

"Stop?"

"[You started yesterday.]"

"Jesus."

Bull grunted: "[Fat Victory is worse than the worst drug. You need a time limit.]"

Lin blinked away the afterimage of her bloodied hands, of dead-eyed Viet Cong stuffing blades into her body. She cleared her throat. "Sake."

Mosquito Brother quickly poured her one.

"[Got some ice-seven?]" asked Bull.

Lin nodded, mind still elsewhere.

"[Give yourself a drop.]"

Lin felt around, hands working on auto. Found the vial, pulled the dropper, one in the sake. She drank.

The drug-glow pushed down at the black fear of the id. Lin looked up at Bull Neck Bui. "You played?"

Bull was wearing his standard tough-fibre army pants and a black shirt. His thick neck red with the heat of the day. He shook his head, as though to himself. "[Once. Saw the bottle marked *poison*, and drank it anyway.]"

She shivered. "The fuck? You were already in the war."

"[Yeah.]"

"The fuck would you go back?" she spat, angrier than she would have liked.

He said nothing, withdrawing from her anger. Mosquito Brother fussed, getting her some more water.

Lin leaned back in the couch and ran a hand through her hair. Half-dried with sweat. "Fucked up."

As he handed her more water, Mosquito Brother said: "[The versions now are all the final cut, I heard. The safety protocols removed.]"

"The fuck do people want to put themselves through that nightmare?"

Bull pointed at the gold-glowing vial of ice-seven in her hand. "[Same reason as this.]"

"This," she held it up, "makes you feel good."

"[So does horror.]"

"The fuck?"

"[The body craves it, little sister. It is an experience unlike any other. Gets so life without the horror becomes unbearable.]"

Lin took a deep breath and downed another sake. She didn't quite know what he meant, but somewhere deep down she saw the shape of it. The kind of knowledge that a veteran or a street walker would understand. An orphan and petty crook, well, she maybe could see a sliver of that truth.

Her nerves strummed softer now with the sake and drug, new chemical constellations saying: *don't worry, it's just a game, relax*, to her muscles, to her fingertips, her mind.

She grunted at Mosquito Brother: "Barry'll be hungry."

Mosquito Brother nodded, went about changing the songbird's seed tray.

Barry hopped up and down his bamboo perch, excited, watching the wiry Vietnamese man work.

Lin sat back in her seat, feeling for her cigarettes. She paused, packet in her hand. "What stinks?"

Bull grunted, indicated her lap with his eyes and a small smile.

Mosquito Brother went red.

Lin looked down. She'd pissed herself. "Fuck," she said, quietly. She looked at them, chin up, eyebrow raised. "Well. It's just piss. Three or four blokes are covered in urine and puke back at the clubhouse every other bloody night."

Bull grunted a laugh. "[On a good night.]"

Mosquito Brother averted his gaze.

"I need a fucking shower." She stood up. "Come back with lunch in thirty minutes, Mosquito Brother."

"[And then?]" asked Bull.

"Then we go talk to a fat Englishman."

Bull Neck Bui nodded. The two of them left.

Lin waited until the door clacked shut before she took three stutter-steps and gripped the edge of the kitchen bench desperately, her legs weak. One drop of ice-seven not enough. She held on for as long as she needed, then walked with deliberate slowness to the bathroom. Stripped off her singlet; her jeans proved too much. Water scalding, steam making the windows opaque, she sat on the floor of the shower, hugging her knees. Staring into space as flashbacks came in and out of her mind, unbidden – three-four seconds of smell and sight in perfect clarity. A black man stomping on her face, a skinned orangutan that looked like an old woman, a bridge held up with bodies, a dead fish belly-up.

Lin closed her eyes, water streaming down her back, face pressed into her soaking jeans. She didn't notice when the hot water ran out.

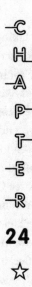

Lin insisted on walking to the Metropole. She needed fresh air. She needed the feel of reality again, to jam it up against that other reality trying to demarcate a place for itself in her memory. She needed to feel the muscles in her legs, the hard road against the bottom of her boots, the frenetic energy of the Old Quarter as it washed over her.

She didn't say any of this to the boys. Just: "We're walking."

It helped. Hà Nội roared in on her. A million scooter drivers leaning on their horns, vendors imploring her to eat this or have that fixed or shined, the smell of incense on the breeze, the violent colours of fruit and silk and signage. She drank it all in.

Which is probably why she noticed the guy following them. The glint of metal on his teeth. First outside her apartment, and second when she and the boys sat on low plastic stools on the sidewalk, under an awning, drank ice coffees and smoked cigarettes. The guy seemed to be taking a deep interest in Chinese army-issue brass cigarette lighters across the street. She did a quiet on-retina comparison, asking for her match. Softly, in her ear, her implant said: *Ninety-seven per cent likelihood it is the same person.*

She leaned in to the table. "Behind me."

Bull said: "[Pretending to buy a lighter?]"

"Been following us."

Bull studied the end of his cigarette. "[Yeah.]"

"Three Clouds Thinh. Visited my place."

"[Accounts for the bruises on his face.]"

Lin blew a long cloud of smoke, Bull casually wiped the sweat from his brow, Mosquito Brother kept his droop eye and good eye fixed on his coffee, hesitant to look anywhere else.

Bull said: "[Three Clouds is not the one to worry about.]"

Lin smoked and waited for the next line.

"[Woman on the glimmer bike, a red Spratly. Visor down. Sitting a hundred metres up the road.]"

"Observant," said Lin, "for someone who can barely turn his head."

Bull rubbed his thick neck. "[A sign of virility.]"

"[I thought that was feet,]" said Mosquito Brother.

Lin looked carefully at the men's feet. "Mosquito Brother has bigger feet than you, Bull."

Mosquito Brother went red, Bull laughed.

Bull tapped the side of his head with his forefinger. "[I'm running a surveillance program – Continental Operating System. Tells me this stuff.]"

Lin glanced at the reflection of Three Clouds in the glass frontage of the coffee shop. He was staring intently at lighters laid out on a wooden board. Along the street, the woman was looking down at her side mirror, waiting.

Mosquito Brother asked: "[So what do we do?]"

Lin said: "Đinh Liệt. Have a chat."

Bull nodded. Mosquito Brother fidgeted. Lin threw too much yuan on the plastic table and stood up. The serving girl thanked them profusely as they left.

They hurried down to Đinh Liệt street, opening up a bit of time between themselves and their followers. The only trouble they had clearing the street came in the form of two fat Euros. Being all authentic and eating phở at a sidewalk stall. Both men wearing pastel shirts, one with shiny hair neatly parted, the other with a bovine dullness to his chin and eyes.

Lin said in English: "Leave."

Hairdo looked up from his bowl, surprised. The other's dull gleam made it unclear whether he understood what she'd said.

Hairdo answered in English: "Sorry? We do not want to leave." He said it with one of those nondescript Euro accents. German or Dutch, some bullshit. An epithet formed in the curl of Lin's lip: *faggot*. An old word she'd only ever heard spoken aloud in a video game. She bit down before she had a chance to spit it out, the red heat of her anger flowing into confusion.

Bull Neck Bui moved up next to Lin, slapping an iron pipe in the palm of his hand.

The main Euro held his mouth in a way that looked like fear. He said: "Come on, honey," to the other one, adding a curt, "*Now,*" when his partner took too long. They rose and left, with as much dignity as two overweight war tourists in a city full of the skinny defeated can muster.

Bull watched them go. Lin cleared her throat and said: "Get everyone into position."

They waited in the shadows. Doorway, alley mouth, behind crates in front of a convenience store. Bull had pinged ahead, made sure the street was filled only with gang members, relatives of gang members, and people they owned.

The glimmer hummed down it, solar particles scintillating, even under an overcast sky. Three Clouds Thinh nowhere to be seen. The scooter slowed, the driver's head scanning to the left and right as she weaved past street sellers and pedestrians.

Right into the metal pipe swung by Bull.

Her visor shattered and she fell backwards off the scooter. Lin was on her as the rider hit the road, bringing her heel down on stomach, hard. The woman grunted, arms weak, trying to cover up. Lin pulled her pulse pistol and shot the woman in the face. A full charge, point blank, was usually good enough to short a cochlear implant, make sure the victim couldn't send out a signal for help.

Five seconds, no more, from pipe hitting visor to an arc of electricity popping a fuse in the woman's head.

The scooter glided onwards, straight line, until a fetch boy for the Bình Xuyên ran alongside and hopped on. The front wheel wobbled, straightened back out, and the bike continued on down the street, as though everything was right in the world. Bull flung the rider over his shoulder. Lin scanned the alley. She said to Mosquito Brother, loitering nearby: "Find Three Clouds. Follow. See where he's going."

He nodded and took off down the alley.

Lin followed Bull to the stairs. Up into the darkness. Outside, the street life resumed. Merchants complaining about food, or why the neighbour's daughter was still unmarried, or a lack of customers. Switching memory feeds back on. A nondescript day, just like so many others, should they ever look back on it. A day when nothing happened. Because nothing had happened.

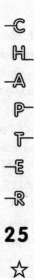

The rider was wearing jeans, leather boots, a thin green jacket, scarf wrapped twice around her neck. Bull pulled the helmet from her head. Bloody gash on her cheek. Oval face, light unblemished skin. Wide mouth, lips slightly parted. Purple mohawk, a little bent from the helmet, but still striking.

Lin looked down at the unconscious woman. Hot. Damn hot. Not a standard gangster tail, not at all.

Bull dumped a bucket of water on the woman's head. She coughed, legs kicking, and sat upright.

They were in a sparse concrete room on the second storey of the apartment block. Thin mattress on the floor, threadbare curtains. Small ancestor shrine next to the door, no offerings on it. The woman looked around. Something in the way she did it reminded Lin of a cat.

Bull said: "[You're with the Green Dragon gang, little sister.]" It wasn't a question. He said it in an avuncular way, adult to a beloved yet misbehaving child.

She shook her head *no*. Casually, still the uncle, Bull slapped her. She cried out, in pain and surprise.

"I love your hair," said Lin.

The young woman held a hand to her cheek, eyes flicking from Lin back to Bull.

Lin held her soft pack of smokes up.

The girl, too scared to blink, shook her head *no*.

Lin lit one for herself while Bui said: "[You're with the Green Dragon, little sister.]"

The girl nodded *yes*.

Lin cleared her throat. "You're new to the gang. Probably been there a year. I don't think you were a hooker first; your skin is too soft." Lin reached out and plucked up her hand, turned it over. Ran her forefinger over the palm. It tingled. "Little rough here though, maybe you were a serving girl, good restaurant in the city. Green Dragon people would go there, throw money around, live that glamorous spectacle the gangster is meant to live. One of them took a liking to you. His moll for a while, until he realised you were smart, maybe had something else to offer for the gang. Pretty girl can get into places a lot of other people can't. Right?"

She swallowed. Whispered: "[Yes.]"

Nice eyes. Gentle features. Lin reached out and ran her fingertip along her chin. "What's your name?"

"Ly."

"They chose well, Ly. Dumb fucks though, sending you out into the Old Quarter. You weren't ready."

Ly said nothing.

Lin gestured at her with the tip of her cigarette. "Your memory feed is shorted. No one'll be able to play it back, see you talked to us. So when you get back, you tell them you were ambushed, knocked off your bike by some bastard. But you ran away, escaped the Old Quarter on foot. We'll have someone here, within fifteen minutes, to reset your memory stream so it looks like it starts again right after the crash. We'll even have some boys chase you out, waving sticks or whatever, so random witnesses can corroborate your feed."

Lin rose and settled herself on a chair in front of Ly. Bull stood also, found a spot for himself against the wall, just out of Ly's field of vision.

"Problem is," said Lin, "if we torture you, they'll *know* you talked. All those burn marks – cigarettes, hot oil. Missing toes and fingers, and depending on how long you hold out, maybe an eye as well. You're not valuable enough to the Green Dragons to be getting prosthetic fingers or eyes, or have a new stretch of skin grown. You're pretty, but Ly—" Lin leaned forward, elbows on knees. " —there're a lot of pretty girls in the world. Even if you got someone in the gang all intoxicated by your muff, someone who's also powerful enough to make that sort of outlay, do you think they'll do it after they know you've talked?"

The girl was listening, her eyes widening as she read the translation on-retina. Skin glistening with water, a small trickle of blood from the cut on her face. Watching, vulnerable, too scared to hide her vulnerability.

"Yeah," said Lin, and blew out a slow cloud of smoke. "Nah. They'll kill you. If they're merciful. If not, you'll end up a street walker for the Green Dragon, servicing pigs who want a freak fuck. Drunken gang bangs, egging each other on as they take turns with you, the monster. Friday after work, all the boys together in their expensive suits, slick hair, let's go down the Old Quarter, fuck that freak with the melted face. Bonding exercise for the boys down at the bank."

Lin stretched, back still sore from the encounter with the white giant. "So," she asked, already seeing the answer in the woman's face. "You going to talk?"

Ly's eyes welled. "[I'll talk.]"

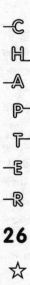

She talked. It felt like the truth to Lin, and Bull said the program he had running in his head didn't pick up any lies.

The reveal: Ly was told to follow Lin. If Lin met with Herbert again, she'd report immediately. If Lin went drinking, Ly was to approach her, flirt. Sleep with her if she had to.

Lin smiled at this. "Shame you fucked up the tail. Could have had fun."

Ly looked uncomfortable, in a way that told Lin that Ly didn't much like girls. But she kept squawking: if she slept with Lin, she was to record everything Lin said on her memory feed and hand that over to the gang. They'd given her some ice-seven to offer to the Silent One; when she was high she wasn't so silent, they told her. Ly didn't know who her boss, Big Circle, was working for. She'd seen the big white guy, but didn't know his name. She'd seen Big Circle getting into an armoured limo out the front of their club, The Bad Sleep Well, in Hai Bà Trưng district. The white guy had been standing next to the limo, holding the door. She didn't know who Herbert Molayson was, and she'd never heard of Raymond Chang.

Footsteps on the stairs, Lin drew the revolver from the small of her back.

Tap tap, followed by an: "[*It's me,*]" that Fuckchops verified as being Mosquito Brother's voice.

She walked over to the door, and Bull took her place on the chair opposite Ly. Mosquito Brother was out of breath, a long V of sweat down the front of his shirt. "[I couldn't find him.]"

"You lost him?"

"[Sorry, elder sister.]"

"Shit."

Lin thought for a moment, glancing back at Ly as she did so. "Listen," she said to Mosquito Brother, keeping her voice low. "Take this—" She pulled her pulse pistol from her belt and handed it to him. "—and a fetch boy, go to the hospital, and watch over Nanh."

"Nanh?" he asked.

"Don't give me your droop-eyed sad bastard routine. Get the fuck over to the hospital. I'll sort it with Bao."

He looked at his feet as he mumbled acquiescence.

She walked back over to Ly, squatted behind her, and put her mouth close to the girl's ear. "Now, cutie, we're going to have a tech come over and iron out your timeline. Until he gets here, we're going to set out the story you're going to have spliced into your feed, the one you're going to tell Big Circle. Make sure you get it right in the retelling." She opened her palm, right next to Ly's bloody cheek. "I believe you have some ice-seven for me."

Ly found it in one of her jacket pockets, placed it gently in Lin's palm, too scared to look at her.

"Good girl." Lin pocketed the vial. "Now. You ready to learn your story?"

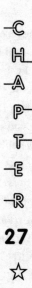

CHAPTER 27 ☆

The tech, Blue Point Pham, reset Ly's memory stream without even looking at her, staring instead at a battery of portable tai screens he set up in the safe house. Red-tipped hair in a modern cut, pallid skin, silver earrings, black t-shirt with the word *YES* printed on it, forefinger nail an inch long.

Pham nodded to Lin when he was done. Bull escorted Ly from the room. The young woman looked back from the doorway before leaving, her eyes red and blank. The look of someone who'd just woken up from being knocked unconscious, whose first words will always be: *where am I?*

Lin said: "Remember the old boss. Nam Cam. Share the memory."

The last thing they'd done to Ly was give her the full unedited account of what Bao Nguyen had done to the previous Green Dragon boss. And what happened to the body, afterwards. It was good for the enemy soldier to know a little fear.

The tech said to Bull: "[Say the code word when you get her on the street. Pull the string, get the doll moving.]"

If Ly understood anything that had been said, her face didn't register it. Bull nodded and guided her out of the room.

When the door closed the tech said: "[I couldn't crack the filter image you sent me, elder sister.]"

"Why?"

He was focussed on collapsing the tai screens down into six-inch black rods. "[Military-grade encryption. Couldn't get a glimpse of the image behind it. All I could see was some of the code.]"

She thought on that. "Which military?"

"[The only one worth mentioning.]"

"Why?"

"[Why Chinese military?]" he asked.

Lin nodded.

"[That's the big question. Why would an English tourist have a military-grade filter set up on-retina?]"

"Yeah," said Lin.

"[Lots there, as well.]"

"What?"

"[Lots of filtering.]"

Lin put her hands on her hips. "Put that shit down, motherfucker."

The tech paused, half-rolled flexiscreen in his hand, and looked up at her. "Huh?"

She was on him and Blue Point Pham didn't have time to blink. Just found himself on his back, her boot pressed against his throat. "I'm the number two of the Bình Xuyên."

Red-faced, one hand on her boot, he choked on his apology. She eased the pressure and he said, round-eyed: "[Sorry, elder sister.]"

"Explain."

Pham took a moment to right himself and catch his breath. "[Well—]" He coughed to get his voice working. "[Well it's not just something small, like skin colour. Or hairstyle. Or clothing. It's—it's much more comprehensive. That's the other thing I could tell. The encryption on the filter, and an idea of the extent.]"

"So Herbert's memory of Hermann has been significantly altered?"

"[Yes.]"

"Important piece of information."

"[Yes, elder sister.]"

"Anything else?"

"Um."

"*Motherfucker.*"

"[I was going to tell you,]" he said quickly, his hands raised, making a calming motion. "[Some of the boys asked around, and I did a feed and freewave search – there's no sign of Hermann Hebb ever staying in the Old Quarter.]"

"*What?*"

"[Or having a meal, or a drink, or a massage, or a walk down any of the streets. He's a ghost, elder sister.]"

Lin let out a long breath. "The fuck?" She ran a hand through her hair, looking at the point where Ly had been sitting. "The fuck is going on?"

After an uncomfortable silence, Blue Point Pham had started to carefully pack his equipment when she asked: "You ever play Fat Victory?"

He stopped what he was doing, hands in his lap. "[No.]"

"Why?"

"[I didn't want to end up in a psych-ward.]"

She gestured for him to continue.

He shrugged. "[I heard from people in the industry that there were problems with it. Violating safety protocols, maybe even seeding false memory during sleep, infecting c-glyphs with viruses. Bad stuff.]"

"And?"

"[Well, Fat Victory was withdrawn from sale, Celestial Entertainment saying it was because there was some bugs that needed fixing. Then black-market versions started appearing all over the place, like always happens when a popular game is taken off-feed. Look, getting shit like that – memory viruses and so forth – it's not uncommon. I've known a few gamers who ended up at the Omissioner's after risking it with the black market.]"

"What if the viruses were there, at release?"

He looked a bit surprised at the suggestion. "[Sounds like a bad business model.]"

"Could they have hidden it?"

"[I mean. Sure. But what's the percentage in it?]"

Lin tapped out a cigarette, lit it, blew a cloud of smoke over Pham's red-tipped hair. "So, the viruses, they're pretty advanced?"

He shrugged. "[As far as that goes.]"

She gestured for him to continue with her cigarette.

"[Elder sister.]" He settled back on his short black stool. "[The memory viruses, the reality protocols – that's not the hard part. The big companies all know how it's done, and these things are more or less the variations of the same formula. Advances slowed when the Chinese government made it illegal and started disappearing top programmers into the camps. Look – the Chinese military is probably doing advanced stuff in a secret lab somewhere, perfecting something they can unleash on the population undetected. Lot of theories on the forums about that. But it's not the hardest part. The toughest bit has always been creating a world believable enough to make these things stick. The details have to be perfect. Better than perfect. Hyperreal, we name it.]

"[The best reality comes direct from those who've been through it, boss. So, in this case, you'd take the most powerful memories from ex-soldiers and program it into the narrative. The Chinese government is excising huge chunks of this trauma from their soldiers all the time, so they've got good material. But even then, even when you have the bloodiest truths, making it feel authentic is damn hard. Getting it right is art.]" He leaned forward. "[I've heard the people who made Fat Victory were true artists.]"

Blue Point Pham wore a glazed-eye indifference when he had first arrived to do the job on Ly. That look was long gone. Now he was nostril-flared intense, words tumbling out, excited.

He continued: "[The bit that makes it all illegal – the virus that seeds itself into the memory feed, and later into natural memory – that's just some code you attach to the story. It sits inside the story you're telling. The Trojan. Like in the myth: a giant wooden horse filled with men with swords.]" He waved his hands, dismissive. "[A dull story, really, the same as all the others: violent men, warriors in a blood rage, swarming out, cutting down their enemies. Boring. Elder sister, the horse is the *most interesting thing*. It's the only part remembered of the myth, the big story. *That's* why Fat Victory was so perfect. Even if you're of the Red Aristocracy, and you have all the best feed screens and memory purifiers, a story that powerful will still get through.]"

Lin thought over his words, working through her cigarette. "Art. Okay. But Fat Victory – I'm not sure art is magical fucking fish, ulcerous apes, giant fucking flies, bleeding bamboo, it's – it's not believable."

"[Yes yes, elder sister. *That's* what makes it so good. The creator hasn't attempted social realism. The good programmers go hyperreal, like I said. Surreal head trips *are* the reality of the battlefield. Seeing shit, dream-like sequences, slow motion or all sped up, your heart banging in your ears; self-mutilation, ghosts, weapon worship, these crystal-clear, yet incoherent fever dreams.]"

Lin said: "You fought," like she didn't believe it.

"[Oh no.]" He shook his head, like the notion was silly. "[I just watch soldier testimonials, some PoV black-feeds from those who've spent a lot of time in occupied villages and the like. Other stuff. You know, for inspiration.]"

"Inspiration?"

"[In my art.]"

"Art."

He nodded.

"You're talking about programming a fucking game. An action sequence."

He reddened at the expression on her face. "[It's my job, elder sister.]"

"Get the fuck out of my sight, worm," she said, angry enough that he stuffed the rest of his equipment into his bags, sweating, without another word. He hurried out with a half-mumbled apology, Lin silent.

She'd forgotten him before the door was closed. She sat, staring at the wall. In her mind's eye, a dead fish floated to the surface of a stagnant rural pond.

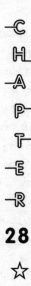

It was their twenty-fifth fight. She wasn't going to lose.

Shihan could have been thirty-five, or fifty-five. Lin couldn't tell. Smooth features, short dark hair, crisp moustache. Not big, not small, preternaturally composed, except when he was into his sake. On the dojo floor, he was a serene presence as he gave instruction, as he watched her response, as he drove his fist into her stomach, as he stomped on her wrist to snap it. Features alive, only ever alive, on the winning strike.

A small, six-tatami-mat room. Crossed-legged, they put down their ceramic sake cups on the low table between them. Her shihan rose first and left the room. Lin followed.

A ninety-mat room. White floor, tatami mats intersected every six feet by brown wood slats. The room was two storeys high, rough off-white plascrete pillars, pale and grey wood inlays on the second floor. Weapon racks. Swords and knives and stick and ropes and spears, and bow and arrows, and all variety of blunt and edged weapons. On the ground floor, a picture of a devastated landscape in black and white: a tori gate left standing, nothing else. Underneath, one word: Hiroshima.

The blood-splattered tatami were replaced between bouts. Mosquito Brother mentioned it to her once, when he was giving her a meal in the medical clinic attached to the dojo. The soiled white tatami mats discarded and burned, replaced with new. She asked for, and so he gave, the number of mats burned after each duel. Lin rated the fight she put up by the number burned: a two-mat fight was poor, four about average. Once she'd given him a twelve-mat fight. All the blood had been hers, but still, she'd sliced open his white gi along the length of his sleeve. Lin liked to imagine his anger at having his karate uniform ruined. She had to imagine it; he gave no indication what he was thinking.

They always fought at night. Dojo closed and locked, lights low. Shihan held classes during the day – one-on-one for Chinese officers, small groups for Chinese special forces – like the man didn't fucking sleep. Lin was given a small room across the alley from the dojo, hidden on the third floor. Her private recovery room. Clean, but the scuff marks on the floor and the scratches on the chrome told Lin she wasn't the first person who'd stayed there.

So much money poured into her training. And when she was injured she was off-line. Not working the streets, not collecting cash for the gang. Instead draining profits to the most sought-after martial artist in Hà Nội.

When she'd asked Bao why he'd said: "We need you to understand the way," and said it in a way that she didn't ask the obvious follow up.

There were no weapons for the twenty-fifth fight.

They faced off, twelve feet apart.

Bao stood in a corner, deep in shadow.

Lin breathed. Watched that spot between chin and bottom of neck. Breathed. Tried to find something in his eyes. And breathed. She watched that—

—he was on her, a blur—

She jumped back, side-stepping, ducking blows, blocking if there was no choice.

Circled, in retreat; he didn't let up, on her on her, no time for a counterstrike, not fast enough—

He high kicked, she part deflected, her body twisting with the impact, which she turned into a flip—

—he was on her on her, ribs crunched, winded, she threw her hands up as she stumbled into the wall.

Legs swept out from under her, she hit the mats heavily, gasping. Forearm up, waiting for a heel kick to the face. It didn't come. After ten seconds she could breathe again. She rolled to one side and the master was back in the centre of the dojo, waiting.

Going to be one of those, then.

She spat out a clot of blood onto the white mat, and got slowly to her feet.

All she could see of Bao was his cigarette. An orange point of light in the corner.

In the second exchange he blocked her kick with one of his own, making her shin bleed.

In the third exchange he opened up her cheek just under her eye, with a punch that didn't quite hit squarely.

In the fourth exchange he took out her knee with a kick that hit just fine.

Bao said: "More."

She hopped to the centre of the room, teeth clenched against the pain, the humiliation.

In the last exchange he took out her other knee. Crawling, gasping, she heard Bao say: "More." The master stomped on her back, then the back of her head. She blacked out.

She wasn't sure for how long. She blink-blinked, raised her head from the mat; the bloody imprint of her face looked back at her. A one-eyed red mask, unblinking.

Lin looked around, her vision blurred, medical alert bleeping on-retina. She cried out as she tried to move a leg, stopped moving it.

Shihan was gone. Bao walked over in silence and kneeled next to her. He waited until she focussed on him, then said: "The will and the act."

Lin replied: "I'm going to kill that motherfucker."

Bao smiled. "Good."

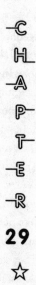

CHAPTER

29

☆

They ascended in the Metropole elevator, caged by its gleaming gold and mirrors. Just Bull and Lin.

Lin sighed, watching the holotype floor numbers tick over on the display over the doors.

Bull said: "[I've never heard you string more than four words together, Silent One. Then you go talk at that girl until she breaks.]"

Lin ignored him.

"[I always thought you were quiet because you were dumb,]" he said, with a gleam in his eye that indicated he believed no such thing. "[But maybe not so. Maybe you should use that big mouth of yours a little more often.]"

She bit down on the obvious reply, eyes still on the numbers.

Bull shrugged to himself. "[As for the related problem: send her to Sài Gòn.]"

"Who?"

"Nanh."

Lin finally looked at him. "Not easy."

"[Not impossible.]"

The doors pinged open. Lin stepped out onto the plush red carpet, checked no one was around, and faced Bull. *How hard is it?* she asked, in Vietnamese.

"[Just money, little sister.]"

"That's it?"

"[We're the hardest gang in occupied Vietnam. If we don't know how to move people, then no one does.]"

"Bao never talked about it."

Bull grunted. The kind that said: *of course not.*

"They say he served in the Glorious Twenty-Seventh. That you were there with him, at the battle of Khe Sanh."

Bull's face turned to stone.

"I saw the news footage," she continued. "Bodies piled up on top of each other, the defenders using them as sandbags. Chinese attack helicopters spiralling down through the air, trailing flame and smoke, like falling angels." She gasped a little, through parted lips. "Oh to have been a witness to that beauty."

Bull took a step away, his chin raised.

Lin noticed him then. Noticed herself. She pushed her hair back from her face. "Forget it," she said. "Fuck. Forget it. That fucking game. It rewired something in my head, fucken babble coming out of my mouth."

"[I have family in Sài Gòn,]" said Bull, gliding on by her horror lust. "[Two daughters, around her age. If Nanh needs it, she can stay with them.]"

Lin took out her cigarettes; Bull took the one she offered. She lit his, then her own, and said: "Thanks."

Bull grunted. "[Don't make it sound so painful, little sister. And no problem.]"

She pursed her lips.

"[You might want to send your family there, as well.]"

Lin smoothed her face. "They have nothing to do with this."

"[Just like Nanh.]"

"No one knows I have a family."

Old knowledge gleamed in Bull's eyes. "[War's about to start with the Green Dragon. The best way to fight a war is unencumbered.]"

Lin cocked her head in the direction of a door at the end of the corridor, ignoring him. "Let's go talk to this English motherfucker."

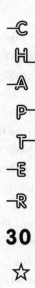

CHAPTER

30

☆

The white door swung open after the third ring on the bell. Lin and Bull entered watchfully. Herbert Molayson was in the same position as she'd first met him, posed against the bar. Same grey pinstriped suit pants, matching vest, pressed white shirt, same ankle crossed over the other. Glass of alcohol dangling at the end of soft white fingers, a joint wedged between fingers of the same hand, idling smoke.

Lin stopped a few metres away. Bull took in the opulence. The hardwood furniture and thick white rug, the gold curtains, the smell of flowers and wood oil.

"Miz Vu, I believe," he said in a rich English accent.

She looked at him in a way that said *yeah. Obviously.*

He looked at Bull. "And you would be—

"[An associate,]" Bull replied.

"Herbert Molayson," he said, unflustered, with his dry English smile. "It's a pleasure to meet you both."

Lin raised an eyebrow.

"Would you like a drink, young lady?"

"You don't have sake here," she said.

"Ah." He looked back over his shoulder at the bar. "No, actually, how-oh…" He furrowed his brow, looking down at a spot two metres from his feet, as though the memory were to be found there. He started to speak, stopped again. Lin waited. Eventually he stumbled into: "Oh, I'm jolly well embarrassed, Miz Vu. We went through this last time, didn't we? Ghastly memory lately – I just haven't been sleeping. Barely a wink."

"Bring us a bottle of your best bourbon and a cool tinnie of Larue, Herbert," she said. "We need to talk."

Lin and Herbert sat facing each other across the table. Lin finished the Larue in one hit, burped in satisfaction.

Herbert's eyes twinkled with a one-liner, but the look Lin gave him kept the words in his cheeks. Instead he poured himself some grappa, and Lin a generous double of the Pappy Van Winkle's. Lin took a sip, widened her eyes in response. Herbert said: "Indeed. The one thing the Americans still know how to do."

Bull was up at the bar, a bottle of dark Beer Lao in his hand, out of Herbert's line of vision.

Late afternoon, the sky clear after a heavy downpour. The last of the day's sunlight shining at an acute angle through the gaps in the curtains. The smoke Lin exhaled from her cigarette instantly full-bodied as it hit the light stream.

"You working with the Chinese?" she asked.

Herbert took a moment before he smiled, but when he did it was quite believable. "What a wonderful opening gambit." When she didn't add anything, he said: "Well, no, not anymore."

"But you did?"

"Of course. I mean, Fat Victory was owned by Celestial Entertainment. They bought the rights from me and Raymond Chang, kept us on as consultants, of course."

"Of course."

"We discussed this, I thought. And you're aware that the gaming company who purchased the rights is ultimately owned by Chinalco, yes?"

"Yes."

"Then why ask?"

"I just want to know what you know, Bert."

"I see," he said, furrowing his brow in a way that said he didn't see at all.

"I'm starting to wonder if you not telling us, well, isn't a matter of choice."

"Indeed," he said, curls bobbing. "Please continue."

Lin drank some more of the smooth bourbon. "I thought you were lying to me, when we first met. About how long you've been in Vietnam, how much you knew about your missing friends, the video game. Whether you could find your arse with both hands. But I'm not so sure, anymore."

Herbert took a drag on his joint, eyes bloodshot. Shutting up for once, and for once listening.

"I think if you review your memory feed, whole slabs will be missing or won't match up."

"And how do you come to that conclusion, Miz Vu?"

"See it sometimes, in this business. People don't know what day it is. Don't know what they did the day before, that morning, five fucken minutes ago. The people they've met, where they've been, who their friends are, their enemies. All sorts of reasons: they've wiped things they want to hide from the cops, maybe a little too often; did jobs for the wrong people, who said they'd make only such-and-such changes to their minds, but did a whole bunch more; sometimes those with too much money – high-class hookers, senior government collaborators – get addicted to wiping away the unpleasantries of day-to-day life. The ugly little details."

Lin wet her lips with the bourbon. "Thing is, those little details are the threads of the spider web of your life. You don't want to pull on too many of those, mate. Whole thing falls apart."

Herbert smiled. Lin couldn't find a whole lot of respect in it. "A wonderful metaphor. But I'm not collaborating with the Chinese. I'm not trying to edit out sections of my life."

"You did it right, you wouldn't know."

"Ha." He conceded with an incline of the head. "Well, I feel like these are just the preliminaries. Lead me down the winding path of your investigation, Miz Vu."

"Why do you have a filter on your memory feed?"

"I beg your pardon?"

"You heard me."

"I don't—"

"Don't bullshit me."

Herbert blinked a couple of times.

"Shit." Lin eyed him. "You don't even know you have a filter on your feed? Maybe it's real time as well. What do I look like to you?"

Without hesitation, he replied: "A pert young woman with shapely hips she can't hide, and a burning anger in her eyes that she can't turn off, no matter how hard she tries."

Behind him, Bull shrugged in agreement.

Lin narrowed her eyes. "You're very good at this role you're playing." She leaned forward, tapped her cigarette into a hardwood ashtray shaped like a lotus leaf. "The image you sent me of Hermann Hebb was filtered."

"Oh."

"So he doesn't look like that."

"Ah."

"So you're paying me to find some personal fucken hallucination."

"I see." Herbert drank his grappa. "I see. I take it you had someone try to decrypt the filter?"

She nodded.

"Unsuccessful, though they saw it was of Chinese origin."

"Didn't know who I was when I walked in the door. Didn't know you had a filter. How the fuck do you know all that?"

Herbert crossed his legs, slowly, like a man careful not to strain anything doing so. "Well, it is my business."

"I thought you were an investor."

"Dilettante, would be a better word. But I've known Raymond Chang my whole life because we studied programming together. I'm actually quite good at it, Miz Vu. Raymond just happened to be far better at it than I."

Lin smoked her Double Happiness. Turned it all over. There was something she wasn't getting in the Herbert – Hermann – Raymond triangle. Something big.

"Raymond Chang had a gambling problem."

Herbert made a pained expression. "A taste for the reckless."

"He was in debt."

"Undoubtedly. He lived in the demi-monde: engaged in all the activities one would expect down there, in the shadows. Debt, indubitably, was a portion of his experience."

Lin poured herself more bourbon. "Little more nuanced than that, old bean, especially if Raymond owed money to the Green Dragon."

"Hmm," said Herbert, thinking. "I'm not sure I know who he owed money to, but that name – Green Dragon you say? – that does have a passing familiarity."

"That man they pinned the Raymond murder on – he didn't have any Green Dragon affiliations, did he?"

"Dearest Raymond," said Herbert. He thought at the floor for a while before looking up at her. "You know, there may have well been a mention of that gang when I spoke with the police."

"I'll check the report," said Lin. "But here's the thing: this whole motherfucking country is in the *demi-monde*, mate. Not much light filters through, down here."

"I see."

"So don't scrimp on the details."

"I shan't."

"Again, you really don't have much of a choice." Lin ran a thumbnail across her bottom lip. The string-pull of addiction starting on her thoughts, on her gut. "Here's what I reckon: you know the whereabouts of Hermann Hebb. I also think you know who killed your friend Raymond Chang. The mysteries of your little trio are all there, in your head, waiting to be revealed. The problem with me pounding the pavement, knocking on doors, asking questions, is that it attracts attention. I keep doing it, it's going to get me killed, and you're not paying me enough for that. The easier way is right here, in this hotel suite."

Herbert took another drag on his joint. He considered the ceiling. Through the double-glazed windows, the faint buzzing of the traffic below. Herbert said: "You do make some good points, Miz Vu. The contrary one is this: if it is true that someone with connections to the Chinese military has had access to my memory stream, I hardly think allowing Vietnamese gangsters in afterwards will remedy the situation." He sipped at his grappa. "Yes, in answer to that question twitching your eyebrow, I do of course know you're with the Bình Xuyên gang. Playing the fool doesn't always mean being one."

Bull didn't give anything anyway, sitting at the bar, up behind Herbert's shoulder. Lin wouldn't have to tell him what to do, if the need came. He'd just act.

She returned her attention to Herbert.

"You're thinking about threatening me," he said.

"I did."

"And?"

"And." She pulled the soft pack of Double Happiness from her top pocket, tapped a new one out, and lit it. She let the smoke sting her lungs, stay the pull of that other string of her addiction. "Seems a bit counter-intuitive."

"Quite."

"Money. You want to do this the hard way, that direction takes more money."

He thought it over. "I could always relinquish your services, Miz Vu."

"Yeah, well. Too late for that."

"That so?"

"We missed that train."

"When did that occur?"

When a giant white puppet speaking with someone's else voice cut the foot off my woman. "When men turned up in my apartment and told me to drop the case. Bad men. Connected men."

"Oh."

"Yeah. Oh."

"I assure you I'm mortified, Miz Vu."

"That doesn't assure me."

"Why don't you let me look over the data your man has gathered."

"We may be just gangsters, Herbert, but our tech guy is the best in Hà Nội."

"Oh I'm sure the talent pool here is scintillating," said Herbert, archly, still trying to act the part.

Lin smoked and waited.

"In any case," he said, undeterred, "let me look at the information, I insist. The field of encryption and filtering is something of a hobby of mine. Give me a few hours and I'll get back to you?"

She glanced up at Bull. He shrugged again: *sure.*

Lin stubbed out the butt of her cigarette, put a finger to the cool steel of her cochlear implant, and pinged him the files. As she did so, something flickered in her memory, strands seemingly unconnected, tied together by an act of imagination.

"You told me Hermann Hebb had worked for some undesirables in the UK. That coming out here to Vietnam was a way to leave those troubles behind, start afresh. Any chance he brought some of those troubles with him? Any chance that maybe he helped indulge your mate Raymond in those vices of his?"

Herbert Molayson had just refilled his glass, and had it halfway to his lips when she asked the question. He froze. Knuckles whitened, a crack, a cry of surprise, and Herbert was looking at his bloody hand.

"I…" His lips twitched. He made a fist, blood seeped through his fingers. Darkness fell across his features.

Bull had gone upright on his bar stool. Lin put down her glass, the sentiment in the room suddenly altered.

"I don't know what you're talking about." He wasn't looking at Lin. Wasn't looking at anything.

Lin raised an eyebrow. "Yeah. Right."

A growl came from Herbert's throat. "Enough with the fucking mouth."

Bull slid off the bar stool. Lin leaned into her feet, ready to rise.

Instead, Herbert gasped and opened his hand. Blood dripped onto the thick cream carpet. "Oh. Indeed. Indeed I think you're right, Miz Vu." He looked up at her, the anger drained from his features. He just looked tired, eyes bloodshot. "Something has been going on in my memory stream, it's true. Something invidious. I will run a full diagnostic on my feed. Send to you any anomalies."

Lin smoked.

"Hermann Hebb was just an acquaintance. The precise details of his past are simply not available to me. But Raymond, well, was a dear friend. I feel, I suppose it's gauche to articulate it in such clichés, but his death cannot go unresolved, unremarked by the discourse of justice. Find out who did this, Miz Vu."

Lin stood, looked over at Bull. He was ready to leave. Two empty bottles of Beer Lao sat atop the bar.

She looked back down at Herbert. He was contemplating the gash on the palm of his hand.

"You're not safe."

Herbert took a second to look up at her. "Oh?"

"I'm going to leave Bull here, make sure you don't turn up gut shot, or beaten to death."

"The security here at the Metropole is quite sound."

"It's half-owned by the Chinese military, like just about every other profitable business in occupied Vietnam. You're upsetting their interests."

"Oh. Should I even stay?"

"No. Don't send anything compromising over the freewave. Don't talk to the police, or hotel management, or to yourself when you're having a shower. Don't mention this conversation to anyone. In fact, go ahead and delete it from your memory feed. Just stay here, get room service, and have Bull teach you Vietnamese chess."

Herbert looked over his shoulder, then nodded slowly as he turned his head back to Lin. "Yes. I see."

Lin said to Bull: "Tonight. Three am. We'll set up a distraction out front. You get him to the other place."

Bull nodded.

"And where are you going?" asked Herbert.

Lin said: "To solve your fucking case."

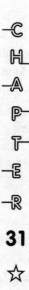
Lin ascended the narrow, uneven staircase. Musky air, moisture on the stone. A hundred years old, a hundred years of soft-soled feet trudging up and down, smoothing the steps, bowing them. Five years of her feet doing the same.

She paused, a flight down from the clubhouse, and took the gold-glowing vial from her pocket. One *drip* was all she allowed herself. To calm the shakes. To focus her mind. Not all she needed, but all she took.

Calmed, her body buzz spreading, the blue steel door clanked shut behind her. The long room was close to empty. Three low-level grunts, playing a game of cards. Two pistols lay on the low table, an AK-47 propped against the wall next to the young woman observing the game.

The fourth man in the room was Snakehead Tran. Sitting on a low stool in the shadows in the corner to her right. The skinny southerner nodded at her as she entered, a long dagger shining in his hand. He'd found a good spot. She hadn't seen him at first, not for that split-second it would take for someone barging into the room.

Lin walked across the peanut shell strewn floor, knocked on Bao's office door, and entered.

The half-bottle of brandy, small red glass tumbler, and plate with sunflower seeds on Bao's desk were the same as always. The compact machine gun with a blocky, drab olive stock – that she hadn't seen before. His usual plain cloth jacket was gone, replaced with a close-fitting, long-sleeved shirt and a shimmering black spideriron vest. She hadn't seen that before, either.

Bao was still as he watched her enter, the blinds closed, a single lightbulb overhead. His wavy, full, white hair caught the light, his eyes cast in shadow, cigarette smoke pooling in the space above his head. Like a white-haired devil, oozing sulphur.

She indicated the room behind her with her head. "Quiet."

"[The men have been mobilised. The field of battle set.]"

"I can see," she said, eyeing his vest. She sat down, patting her pockets for cigarettes.

Bao waited, watching as she lit her cigarette and added to the smoke in the room.

He said: "[Mosquito Brother is at the hospital.]"

"Oh. Yeah."

"[Ignoring my calls.]"

Lin winced inwardly.

"[I know it is your fault. You're the only person he would disobey me for.]"

Lin pushed her hair back from her forehead. "They could use her against me. I'm being strategic."

"[Strategic.]" He cracked a sunflower seed between his fingernails. "[Strategic,]" he repeated, as though talking to the seed. He popped it in his mouth, stared at Lin, just the whites of his eyes visible, the orbits in shadow.

She shifted in her seat.

"[Are you going to marry this girl?]"

Lin blushed, despite herself. "Nanh? No. God no."

"[Are you planning to live together?]"

She shook her head.

"[Yet you are taking men off the street for her. Good men.]"

"Well, because—" she started, before realising there was no place for the sentence to go. No justification she could give for someone who wasn't family or going to be family.

Bao was a step ahead, as always. "[I'd worry about your real family, little sister.]"

Lin was glad of the ice-seven. Enough of a cushion to help her keep rein on her temper. She smoothed her face. "You handled my identity change. No background check will say I am anyone other than Lin Thi Vu. I rarely see my family, and when I do it's in the thirty-six streets. I'm never followed."

"[Your twin sister is on the freewave a lot.]"

Lin took a long drag on her cigarette.

"[The weight of chance and circumstance now bends towards someone asking the question: why does Phuong Lashley look exactly the same as Lin Thi Vu?]"

"Let me worry about my family."

Bao stared at her until she averted her eyes.

"I played Fat Victory," she said.

Bao leaned back in his chair, small red glass of brandy in his hand. The change in angle took his face out of shadow. "[And?]"

"It was all wrong."

He motioned for her to continue.

"A lot of my platoon looked Chinese. They all seem to have something bad to say about the South. The Chinese didn't fight with the Americans during the American War, did they?"

"[No. The US was a multicultural empire, so some Chinese-Americans would have fought. But not nearly as many as the game suggests.]"

"The Vietnamese soldiers, they…"

"[Yes?]"

"They were like automatons. Heartless. Relentless."

He listened.

"Completely different from *The Sorrow of War*." She patted the breast of her denim jacket, where the book sat, inside pocket.

He waited.

"That bloke in the novel – he's… He's destroyed by his experience. Alcoholic, insomniac, prone to ultraviolence. Classic PTSD. The Vietnamese in the game weren't – they weren't even human."

Bao nodded. "[That was the American propaganda during the American War, over one hundred years ago. Today, it is the same propaganda, used by China for the Chinese War. On the surface, this dogma seems contrary to the logic of the aggressor: after all, depicting the opponent as an implacable killing machine is hardly a way to inspire the invader.]" Bao's eyes shone as he drew on his cigarette. "[On the surface. The deeper reasoning is obvious. It dehumanises. In every war, ever, each side shall dehumanise the other. Doing so makes everything permissible: every bombing of a civilian population, every mass grave, every outrage. Fat Victory does this in a way that is audacious: it dehumanises us to our own people. Hundreds of thousands of Vietnamese – more – addicted to a game that embeds the idea that their own people do not feel, and that only the other side suffers. Our side are faceless and remorseless; the other fearful and confused.]"

He placed his glass carefully on the table. "[So tell me: why?]"

"So we'll empathise with the invaders."

"[Yes. And?]"

"So the occupied will see South Vietnam as corrupt, maybe wonder if it is better to be Jiaozhi, China's southernmost province. That fighting back is futile, and hey – maybe it's not so bad to accept a peace deal. Harmonious region, economic prosperity, all that bullshit."

"[Yes. Fat Victory is an exercise in psychological warfare, little sister.]"

Lin sighed. "Why didn't you just tell me, Uncle? These things, these images, keep coming back to me. There was this woman in a village, they— They skinned her. Fuck." Lin closed her eyes as she took a drag on her cigarette. She blew a long cloud of smoke at the ceiling and said: "The thing is, they stole the scene from *The Sorrow of War*. I know that it is fake – not just a fake memory, but taken from fiction. Don't they reckon people will notice?"

"[When was the last time you met a person who had ever read a book?]"

Lin rubbed her forehead with her fingertips. "But that orangutan, that old woman, whatever it is. I still— It still feels real. It feels— It's hard to explain. More potent than my other memories. More real."

After a long pause, Bao said: "[This is the official reason the game was banned. It went too far in integrating game memory into natural memory. This violates all sorts of regulations.]"

"The *official* reason?"

"[Well, the Chinese military usually are not swayed by regulation. This is merely a civilian concern. I do not know why they killed the game, but my suspicion is this: it was a limited test that went out of control. The psychological warfare embedded in the game worked sometimes, other times the players were so traumatised they committed violent acts. Against family, friends, strangers, even Chinese troops. Chaos, Lin. Harmonious society is difficult to attain with a population so erratic. The black market doubled down on this, seeding the game with viruses, compounding the worst elements.]"

Lin thought for a moment. "You still have the game experience in your memory?"

He paused, attention back on her. "[Yes.]"

"Why?"

"[Because I did not know.]" He drew on his cigarette, exhaled slowly. "[I have been there, in the jungle, fighting, in real life. So I did not know what was real, what was from Fat Victory. Memories from the game burrow into your past, into your real timeline, and find places to live and grow. I saw an Omissioner for a fix. He said the game memories had seeded themselves in unrelated neural clumps.]"

"Why not just wipe it all?"

"[I told you. I was not sure what was from the game and what was real.]"

Lin paused. "No. I mean the real memories, as well. Why not get them wiped. With what you said about—"

Bao's eyes went riverbed stone smooth, hard enough to stop her sentence.

He said: "[*I am not an automaton*. I am not the stoic, remorseless Viet Cong of a Chinese video game. I am human. I embrace all my pain. That pain has made me. Ruined me, broke me, pulled me to pieces. I rebuilt all those pieces, and became the man I am now. I embrace it. I live it, and relive it.]"

Lin finished her drink. Uncomfortable. To her, Bao *was* stoic and remorseless. She had drawn strength from that. He had seemed so *unencumbered*.

She said: "I don't reckon Herbert knew what that game was doing."

He listened.

"I don't think Raymond Chang knew either."

"[That leaves the third man,]" Bao said. "[The one with the similar-sounding name.]"

"Hermann."

"[Yes. I never quite understood his role.]"

She ran a hand through her hair. "Yeah. There's a reason for that."

He waited.

She said: "Hermann Hebb doesn't exist."

Bao opened his drawer, retrieved another small red tumbler and a half-bottle of sake. The good stuff. He poured her drink and slid it carefully across the table.

He settled back into his chair and said: "[Explain, detective.]"

Lin eyed her drink. "Hermann exists only in Herbert's head."

Bao waited.

She lit a cigarette, added more smoke to Bao's, circling above them. "First, there've been no sightings of Hermann in the Old Quarter. Not one. Hasn't popped up in one of our gang's feed, not in security footage, nor informants, our drones, nothing. Impossible. Nah. It's impossible for a white man to go unnoticed, for weeks, in our patch." She gestured with her cigarette. "Second, the filtering was on Herbert's end. Strange. Not just a case of Hermann using an illegal filter to distort his image in someone else's memory feed. No. This was Herbert, having a filter for Hermann, and no one else. It doesn't make any sense." She raised an eyebrow. "Unless you suppose it isn't just filtering. Unless the image he's seeing is one hundred per cent generated. A whole, fake, person. Someone – the Chinese military, the Green Dragon, Chinalco, fucken Buddha, I don't know – but someone wanted Herbert to hallucinate this third party."

Bao asked: "[Why?]"

"I don't fucking know. I don't—" Lin stopped and stared again at her drink. She stood up with it, downed it in one hit. "Unless." She paced over to the window, empty glass and cigarette in hand, cracked the blinds, and looked out without seeing the rain pouring down outside. Nor the violet neon glow of the gin bar down across the street, or the pedestrians hurrying to cover, heads bent against the water.

She turned and looked down at Bao. "Unless Hermann and Herbert are the same person."

Bao's thick white eyebrows bent, quizzical. "[Again: why?]"

Lin walked slowly back to her seat, running the bottom of her glass along the tabletop. "Why," she repeated. "I'm not quite sure, Uncle. But I can feel it. I know Herbert's had his fair share of wipes. There are large holes in his history. He's staring at the abyss of Alzheimer's, this close to falling into it. Then there's this Hermann character, who doesn't make any sense. He's got Raymond Chang, the troubled genius and addict. That makes sense. Raymond's back story with Herbert has the shape of being true. But Hermann – why hire him? Celestial Entertainment has the best people in the business. When I asked Herbert the same question, he couldn't remember the reason."

Bao kept looking at her and she said: "Yeah, yeah, I know: why? Let's say someone implanted a second personality in Herbert – what's the percentage in it?" Glass in hand, she pointed at Bao. "Unless they needed a temporary body to do the illegal coding. Stick the viruses in, the shit that splices real memory and fake, the code that makes it bypass all the reality protocols, then wipe it. Keep it in-house. Use someone with intimate game knowledge." Lin sat back down, placing the empty glass back on the table. "What they tried to do with Fat Victory was a war crime. I mean, these pricks tried to mind-fuck an entire population, turn them against the country of their birth. Not even China can get away with this – it's against every mnemonic law on the fucken..." The image of Washington, dead, empty eyes staring at the ceiling came to her unbidden. And the relish she felt, at the blood-soaked rice in her mouth.

She shook her head, as though the motion would erase the images. "Those motherfuckers—"

Lin stopped herself, aware of the heat rising on her cheeks, first the anger, then the embarrassment of the anger in front of Bao.

"[Pour another drink, little sister,]" he said, watching.

She did.

He said: "[If what you say is true, then Herbert is the missing piece of the puzzle. I have played the game and I know what the Chinese are capable of on the battlefield. But even I thought Fat Victory became so potent only after being corrupted by the black market. I did not contemplate the idea that the side effects of the game were the very point of the game – some elaborate conspiracy.]" He smoked a little. "[And I am still not sure.]"

Lin leaned forward. "Uncle. This puts the conspiracy into a cul-de-sac. They killed Raymond Chang, who was addicted to everything worth getting addicted to, and was a liability. They create, then kill off, Hermann Hebb. Noone in Celestial Entertainment has touched the illegal part of the game, except whatever untouchable from the Red Aristocracy is running the whole scheme. This way, the information has nowhere to go. Herbert Molayson goes back to England, the creator, producer, and public face of Fat Victory. No one suspects an Englishman of being part of a conspiracy to erode Vietnamese morale through a weaponised mnemonic virus stuck in a computer game about the American War. *Not even the Englishman in question.* It's too fantastical."

"[Yes,]" said Bao. "[Though in the detective movies there is usually evidence.]"

"Yeah, well."

"[In this, all the evidence is in the mind of Mister Molayson.]"

"Yeah, and he ain't letting us in."

Bao smiled without humour. "[It's long past that, little sister.]"

"Oh?"

"[Oh, we will tear it out of his skull.]"

Lin found herself troubled by that, and surprised she was.

"[Where is he?]"

"Metropole. I left Bull with him. Was going to set up something after midnight. Grenade at a police car, something like that. Get him out in the confusion."

Bao closed his eyes. Lin smoked.

When he opened them, he said: "[I have sent twenty men over. They will be there, on the street, to ensure he exits the premises safely. You and Mosquito Brother keep working the case.]" He blew a slow cloud of smoke, his eyes shining. "[For the rest of us: the enemy has declared their war. Yet we shall not lash out. No, we shall choose wisely the field of battle, and the blood language of our reply.]"

She said: "The will and the act."

Bao's eyes shone. "[The will and the act.]"

PART TWO
Straw Dogs

Heaven and Earth are heartless / treating
creatures like straw dogs.

– Tao Te Ching

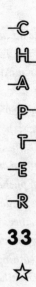

It was their forty-second fight. The weapon was the wakizashi, a short Japanese sword sixty centimetres long.

They stood twelve feet apart on the tatami mats. She held her sword raised over her head, pointed at her shihan, her other hand extended, palm out, forefinger raised. Shihan mirrored her pose. Bao was somewhere behind, out of her line of sight.

The master, silent, no war cry not a breath, tore towards her, his steel flashing; she side-stepped, blades rang out. Twelve feet apart, again.

Again he came, and the blades rang their metallic cry, E-flat hung the air, slow fade.

He flew across the mats, she blocked and flowed into a backside kick, foot swooshing through empty air, her shihan already eight feet away. She turned her motion into a forward attack, still flowing, war cry; he side-stepped / parried easily.

But still.

She'd made him parry. A smile touched the corners of her eyes.

He punished her pride immediately.

The master swept in, Lin hesitated, stepped back as he feint / strike / feinted and was past her. Lin looked down, surprised at the blood appearing on her forearm, a perfectly straight cut, wrist to elbow. Didn't feel the strike.

The injured arm dropped to her side as he came again, his blade sang / a woman cried out, spinning staggering and she was down to a knee.

Lin pushed herself up again.

He made three more passes, blurs of blade and blood and Lin sank to her knees and stayed there this time, her wakizashi now a cane that bit deep into the tatami.

Breathing hard, blood splatters all around, red on white.

Her shihan walked over to her, blade pointed at her head. Slow. Taking his time. Savouring. As she knew he would.

He glanced over at Bao, as she knew he would.

Lin clenched her teeth. Bao was saying: "[More,]" the last part of the word touching the old Vietnamese man's lips, when she jerked up and drove her blade clean through the bare foot of her master.

He grunted – the only indication he'd just had his foot pinned to the floor – and slashed her arm with a quick clean stroke.

Deep. Maybe chipping bone. Lin exhaled a lungful of pain, held her arm to her chest, and sat back on her butt.

Her master reversed his sword and raised it above his head, eyes blazing.

"[Enough.]"

His sword wavered. Her shihan blinked, as though he'd forgotten someone else was in the room.

"[Enough!]"

He lowered his sword and bowed, waiting. Bao Nguyen emerged from the shadows. Stood next to her, looking down. His eyes watching always watching, marking now the clenched pain-triumph on her face.

She grinned up at him through the pain haze. "A twenty-mat fight."

Bao contemplated the room, took the cigarette from his mouth, and exhaled a thick cloud of smoke. "[At least.]"

Ragged, she said: "The will and the act."

"[The will and the act,]" he replied. To her shihan he said: "[Enough.]"

The master hesitated only slightly, only in such a way that someone who'd fought with him two score times would see. But hesitate he did, eyes flicking once between her and Bao, before he bowed, deeply, and slid Lin's blade from his foot.

She laughed as she watched him limping from the room. Laughed, blood-loss dizzy, and fainted.

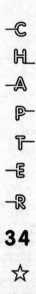

Herbert Molayson's voice came belting from the bathroom: "Do you hear the people sing, singing a song of angry men! It is a music of a people who will not be slaves again!"

Lin waited on the couch smoking a cigarette, looking out at the view over Hà Nội. Dusk. Orange glow over dilapidated rooftops. Thick wires hung between buildings, black lines against the setting sun. Billboards in the distance, giant holotypes glowing fiercely. The blare of horns drifted up and through the third-storey window, neon lights flicking on as the city welcomed the coming darkness. When the real business and life of the city began.

The door to the bathroom popped open, Herbert stopping halfway out, eyebrows raised, when he saw Lin was in the room. "Oh. Terribly sorry, Miz Vu. I didn't realise anyone was here." He patted his hands against his impressive stomach. "I do like to sing after a particularly good bowel movement."

Lin said nothing, blew smoke into the air. Like listening to someone singing a show tune from a musical, post crap, was just part of the job.

He rubbed his hands together. "Can I offer you something? The accommodations are somewhat rustic, but I believe some food and beverage was provided."

Two rooms, decent beds, air conditioning, an old comfortable couch. Down a long and narrow alleyway, back from the bar district. Better than Lin's apartment.

"Larue," she said. A beer she never much enjoyed, but had a real hankering for of late.

Herbert flourished a finger, vertical. "At once!"

He set the gold can of beer Larue in front of her and lowered himself carefully to the other end of the couch, right-angled to Lin. Herbert poured himself a deep glass of red wine, lit a spliff, and settled into his comfortable seat, content.

"Ah. Rustic charm indeed."

Sound came from the tai screen, the smack of leather on willow, a crowd cheering, singing, clapping. Herbert noticed she'd turned it on.

"Ah the cricket. Wonderful. Now that looks like the English team. Who are we playing – is that Pakistan?"

Lin sipped her beer, cool can in the same hand as her cigarette. She motioned towards the screen. "There's women in the crowd and you can see their faces. So no. Not Pakistan. Looks like Sri Lanka."

"Ah wonderful. How are we doing?"

"We? I'm going for Sri Lanka."

"Is that so?" He shifted in his seat so he could look over at her. "Why is that?"

"Because fuck England, that's why."

Herbert laughed, curls bobbing. "Of course. Sometimes I forget that you're Australian."

Lin watched the rest of the over, enjoying her beer and cigarette. A tall man storming in towards the crease, blond hair bouncing as he ran, red-faced, slinging the ball down the pitch. Hypnotic. Sometimes, on her rare days off, she'd have the cricket playing in the background while she lay on her couch nursing a hangover. The dulcet tones of the commentators, explaining abstruse technical details, or statistics, or the history, of a game five hundred years old. She took solace, somehow, in the history. In this silly game played under clear blue skies, outliving war and famines and the daily horrors of a world gone mad. It made all the bitterness of these mean streets seem small somehow. Insignificant. All this would pass, yet the game would live on.

She sighed and muted the broadcast with a verbal command.

"How'd you get the American War so right?"

He shuffled around on his seat, so he was facing her again. "Well," he said, without missing a beat. "I stole everything."

"I noticed. But still."

"I do have a certain flair for storytelling, I suppose. But Raymond was really the master of pulling the narrative together. And Hermann, well, he constructed a lot of the quotidian elements."

Lin let that slide. She had unpleasant news for him already, no need to rub it in with the revelation his friend was imaginary.

When he saw she was waiting for more, he took a deep breath and set down his glass of wine.

"Listen. Let me tell you a story, young woman. It's a true story." He ran the palm of his hand down the small square beard hanging off the end of his chin. "A good friend of mine, Tony Monk, lived in Papua New Guinea. He was an advisor to their Treasury department – this was before the six-year war, of course, and the restoration of order under Chinese administrators. Anyway, Tony developed what appeared to be cold sores near his lips. Quite a proliferation of the blasted things, you might say. His wife, Lucy, was quite taken aback, and understandably wanted to know what the hell he'd been up to. Poor Tony, small fellow, softly spoken, gentle, well, he just couldn't figure it. Got various unguents to treat the sores, but they were quite persistent."

Herbert picked up his glass of wine, wet his lips, preparing himself for the rest of the tale.

"One day, Tony came home early to his apartment in the compound. He'd taken ill after a bad salad at the Yacht Club, and wanted a lie down. Anyway, as he opens the front door the illness hits him. Beastly affliction. So, he rushes to the bathroom, but stops short. Shocked, instead, to find his haus Mary – the term they use for maid – in the bathroom, skirt hitched up, no undergarments, one foot up on the sink. That's not all." Herbert leaned forward, eyes twinkling. "She was shaving her lady parts with Tony's razor."

Lin wrinkled her brow. "What? Gross."

"Indeed. And, evidently, not cleaning the razor afterwards. Thus, when Tony shaved in the morning, his face was getting infected with herpes or whatever the young woman's vagina was teeming with. He fired the haus Mary on the spot, and had the scandalously unhygienic lady removed from the compound. Livid, he was. When he told his wife, she was shocked, for she quite liked the young maid, though she was understanding of her husband's ignominious plight."

Lin looked at the cricket score and sipped her beer. "Great story, Bert."

"Isn't it," he agreed, patting his pockets, looking for and finding a joint. He lit it, giving off an indifferent air. But something in his posture made Lin think he was waiting for something.

She looked back at the cricket, not watching.

"Oh," she said.

"Hmmmm?"

"It's not true."

"Good lord, of course not." He shuddered at the thought. "I mean, it's true I had a friend called Tony in PNG. It's true he got these terrible cold sores. But Tony's problem wasn't an unsanitary haus Mary; Tony's problem was an addiction to cunnilingus. The old boy was running around town, burying his face in whatever crotch he could find. Mild-mannered Tony Monk, vagina fiend." Herbert shook his head, thinking back on it.

He looked back at Lin. "To this day, only I know the truth, and his wife still believes the tale. Two weeks from now, Miz Vu, when you think back on the story, the only image in your mind will be of a Papua New Guinean woman, leg hoiked up on a white porcelain sink, razor in hand. *That's* why I'm so good I what I do: the powerful image can sell the most unconscionable lie."

"Ah," she said. "Canny motherfucker."

He inclined his head in thanks.

She finished the Larue, crushed the can, and placed it on the coffee table. "You're leaving Hà Nội."

"Is that so?"

"You're a liability. Sài Gòn, first, then a third country."

"What would be in this for me?"

"Not dying."

His bloodshot eyes were glazed, unfocussed as he thought it over. "Ah. And for you?"

"You got something we want. We honour our deals."

"Not a common sentiment among the criminal class, I would have thought."

"Or the aristocrats, or the finance capitalists, or presidents, or the fucken generals. But we're a better class of people than those low-life grubs."

Herbert smiled. "You may well have a point." He leaned deep into his seat, contemplating the swirls of smoke snaking across the ceiling. "It begs the question, though."

She smoked and waited.

"What deal, exactly, is this?"

"The deal," she said, "where we take what we want from your memory stream. About Chinalco, and the Green Dragon, and whatever else we want. We take it, and we send you on your way."

His eyes found their way back to her. "Usually deals require both parties' consent, Miz Vu."

"You pulled us into your problems. Got people hurt. Started a gang war. You owe."

"And if I refuse?"

"We're way past that, Bert."

"What assurance do I have—"

"None," she interrupted. She leaned forward, dropped her cigarette butt into her beer can. "Snakehead Tran's coming now, to babysit. Our tech guy as well, to extract what we want from your memory stream. I'm going downstairs for a feed."

She stood as Herbert babbled objections.

"Shut up. We could've killed you, pulled your memory pin, taken what we wanted. Sold your organs on the black market, your hair and bones to the artisans on Hàng Nón.

"We could've tortured you first, made you transfer the bulk of your wealth to us."

He swallowed.

"The others wanted it. I said: nah. He's a client. And I like his bourbon. Give him one chance to make good."

There was a knock at the door.

"That'll be them. You ready to make good, Bert?"

He nodded, quickly, for once short of a word.

Lin Thi Vu turned and left.

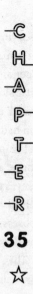

CHAPTER

35

☆

Lin pushed her way through the front doors, out of the breathless night air and perpetual arias of the scooter horns, into the cool of Tadioto. Small, local bar. Tiny wooden tables jammed together, white-shirted staff that always got the food orders wrong; best whiskey sours in the thirty-six streets. They gave Lin a single table in the back, towards the bar, eyeline to the front door.

Cigarette smoke, drunken chatter, clinking glass, all Vietnamese except a table of four Indians laughing and eating olives.

Lin said to the waiter, in Vietnamese: "*Phở. Whiskey Sour. Beer Larue. Ashtray.*"

He stared blankly, like he may or may not have heard the order, and wandered back to the bar to start chatting with the girl there. Relaxed vibe, clean smiling faces, courtesy of an understanding with the Bình Xuyên. Some deal between Bao and the owner, to the details of which even Lin wasn't privy.

Speaking of, the laughter and chatting quieted. Lin looked up to see an old man, trimmed grey beard, thick black eyeglasses, white open collar shirt, mustard silk scarf wrapped once around his neck, cigarette stuck to his bottom lip. The owner, Qui. He looked around at the crowd, eyes twinkling, nodded at the different groups.

Qui had sat with her, a few weeks back. Shared some good whisky. He just wanted to talk about the world outside Vietnam. London, his old home, and to press Lin about Australia. He'd said to her at one point, eyes glazed with the single malt: "There are two kinds of exiles, Lin. Those who insist on the illusions of the new country, and those who obsess over what was left behind."

She'd wanted to say she was neither, but hesitated, unsure of the truth. Then the moment passed, and she just drank his booze instead.

Now, the old man sat on a tall pale wood chair near the front windows of the bar, facing his audience. He cleared his throat and spoke in perfect, clear, educated English. Close your eyes and you'd think it was a British radio host, discussing the arts.

"I have an old poem I would like to recite for you." He smiled, small and knowing. "I'm an old man, you see, and thus disposed to believing everything was better in the past, and unwilling to look too closely at the present, lest I be proved wrong. The poem is called *Love Tokens*."

His gaze moved away from the people in the room. He spoke it soft and clear:

"I'll give you a roll of barbwire
A vine for this modern epoch
Climbing all over our souls
That's our love, take it, don't ask

I'll give you a car bomb
A car bomb exploding on a crowded street

202

On a crowded street exploding flesh and bones
That's our festival, don't you understand

I'll give you twenty endless years
Twenty years seven thousand nights of artillery
Seven thousand nights of artillery lulling you to sleep
Are you sleeping yet or are you still awake

On a hammock swinging between two smashed poles
White hair and whiskers covering up fifteen years
A river stinking of blood drowning the full moon
Where no sun could ever hope to rise

I'm still here, sweetie, so many love tokens
Metal handcuffs to wear, sacks of sand for pillows
Punji sticks to scratch your back, fire hoses to wash your face
How do we know which gift to send each other
And for how long until we get sated

Lastly, I'll give you a tear gas grenade
A tear gland for this modern epoch
A type of tear neither sad nor happy
Drenching my face as I wait."

The room was stilled, save the smoke idling from many cigarettes.
The silence continued, for several seconds, until one person began
clapping and the rest joined in. Not the sort of poem about which you
could be too enthusiastic, in the aftermath, unseemly. So the applause
faded quickly and the silence crept back, each table not quite sure how
to re-start the conversations, or recall what they were talking about.

The poet, Qui, smiled softly as he got down from his chair. He
nodded to Lin, mouthing the words *good to see you*. She nodded back.

The old poet left the room, slowly and deliberately, through the door behind the bar.

Lin had just started her phở – which had been late enough for her to have two rounds of sours and Larue – slurping down the first spoon of the delicious broth, when an alert blipped on-retina.

Snakehead Tran

That was it. His name, glowing red. No message or other data. He'd been injured, badly. His cochlear implant sent an auto-distress to any nearby Bình Xuyên. Lin looked down at the phở, took a last inhalation of the aroma, sighed, and dropped the ceramic spoon into the spun bamboo bowl.

The bar staff didn't even notice as she bolted out the front door.

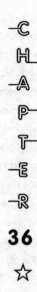

Smooth and swift down the corridor. Pistol drawn, horizontal, both her hands on the grip. Outside the safe room, Lin breathed in-out carefully, listening. No sounds, nothing, save a baby crying somewhere on a floor below. This level had four apartments. The safe house, and three others inhabited by low-level Bình Xuyên members, apparently none at home.

The door, thick plasteel, was slightly ajar.

Breathe in / breathe out.

She kicked the door open, came in low, pistol swinging left-right.

The smell of blood and bowel and fear assailed her senses. She winced, hand over her mouth, pistol steady, eyes loop-looping around the main room.

Trashed. The tai screen smashed, fritzing, couch upturned, one of the wide windowpanes overlooking the city a spider web of cracks. Blood splatters, like an abstract art installation, floor walls windows ceiling. Blue Point Pham's equipment smashed, hurled about the space. As was Pham.

His head had been neatly placed on its side atop the kitchen bench, facing into the living room. Part of the spinal column was still attached. She couldn't see his body. Pham's eyes were open, shining, still registering surprise.

Snakehead Tran was face down in the centre of the space. Taking the big sleep in a pool of blood. She stepped carefully, avoiding equipment and the blood, silent. Listened, again. The combat system had upped her sensory intake: light enhanced, like a yellow film over her eyes that made everything one shade brighter; the soft press of her boots on the thin carpet audible – not loud, but clear.

She searched the rest of the apartment knowing it was empty, feeling the space was now dead.

Back in the lounge, Lin let out a long breath and crouched by Snakehead Tran, pistol resting across her thigh. She turned him over, gently. His eyes were closed – swollen, grotesquely – by the beating he'd received. One arm was bent the wrong way, bone jutting from the elbow. A large, bloodied hole above his belt, the grey sheen of intestine in the wound.

Lin Thi Vu clenched her jaw, looking down at the ruin of the thin man.

Remembering how it ended for him, imagining his last bloodied fevered moments. She pushed her hair out of her eyes. Blue Point Pham's equipment had taken the most damage. The guts pulled out of two small black boxes he always used. Some parts could be missing; she wasn't sure. His flexiscreens had large bullet holes. The neural jacks she'd watched him use on the Green Dragon woman, Ly, were connected to the black boxes, though their connection pins had been torn off.

She subvocalised a message to her AI and sent it to Bao.

Safe house on Đinh Liệt compromised. Snakehead Tran and Blue Point Pham beaten to death. Herbert Molayson missing.

Bao replied almost straight away: Another escalation.

Yeah.

This is not right. They found him too quickly.

Yeah. I–

Yes?

I don't know where this goes next, Bao.

There is only one way.

I mean the investigation. We needed his memories. It looks like Blue Point may have started the procedure.

I shall send someone.

Tell him to bring a mop and bucket.

Oh?

She pulled up an image from her exo-memory of the room, the view just as she'd entered, and sent it through to Bao.

After several seconds he responded. As the call, so the echo.

She nodded, to herself, eyes on Snakehead Tran. Trying to work through the Chinalco – Green Dragon – Fat Victory – Herbert Molayson story.

She subvocalised: We're gangsters.

Correct. Detective.

We don't need hard evidence before we act.

True.

Green Dragon, and someone from the Macau Syndicate, came to my place. Told me to stop talking to Herbert.

Yes.

So we know these bastards are working together to try to cover something up in the game, Fat Victory.

Go on.

Chinalco makes the game. Maybe this story goes right to the top of the Chinese government. Maybe it's an autonomous corporate department working with a psych warfare unit in the military.

The last part is sketchy, even for gangsters.

She nodded, even though Bao couldn't see her. Okay, backing up. They didn't want us to talk to Herbert. We talk to Herbert. They turn up at the safe house while we are doing an invasive exo-memory download, kill the men there, and take Herbert. Despite this, they gotta figure we know their secrets now, that they were transmitted or backed-up, off-site. They can't risk giving us the benefit of the doubt.

A pause and then a Yes from Bao's end.

So let's drop the investigation. Our paycheque's been kidnapped. The war's starting. I don't know where to go next, but maybe it doesn't matter. Let's just air out some motherfuckers from the Green Dragon.

A longer pause, and then No.

Lin pursed her lips. No?

The game matters.

The fuck it does.

The game matters. Find Herbert.

I—

That is an order.

Lin fumed. Turned a chair the right way up, sat down and lit a cigarette. Footfalls and voices from the bottom of the staircase. Reinforcements, finally arriving.

Same as before, little sister. Solve the case.

There is no case, Uncle.

Go home. Wait. We'll have something pulled from a security feed, or from Blue Point's equipment, that'll tell us what we need to do next. Detective work takes patience.

Yeah, well. I'm a soldier, not a detective.

If you were a soldier you'd follow orders.

Ha.

She smoked her cigarette, deadening her sense of smell against the stench of the room. Looked out the window, rather than the carnage inside it. Rain washed across the cityscape. She stood as two men came to the door. They lowered their guns when they saw her standing there, eyes widening at the room's tableau.

Okay, Uncle.

Don't go looking for revenge. Don't leave the thirty-six streets.

She hesitated. Sure.

You wonder why we do not move on our enemies.

Lin said nothing.

All is being set in place, for the Green Dragon. When we hit them, it will not be a half-measure. When we strike, it will be for all time.

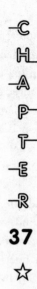

Lin Thi Vu opened the door to her apartment on her sister, Phuong, and Bull Neck Bui laughing and drinking beers. Lin's beers. Phuong on Lin's comfortable couch, legs crossed, leaning towards Bull, on a chair, leaning in as well, like old friends catching up.

"The fuck you doing here?" snapped Lin.

Phuong and Bull glanced up her, unapologetic, blank annoyance on their faces at the interruption. Bull fished around in his pocket, produced a gangster roll of yuan, and held it out to Phuong. "[Take this, elder sister. For the widows.]"

Lin pursed her lips, annoyed that her twin got *elder* sister, while he still gave Lin *little*.

Phuong held up her hands, replying in perfect Vietnamese: "*I didn't come here for work, Bull.*"

He held the roll steady, his face softening. "[My wife died in the second battle of Hà Nội. My girls live with their grandparents in Sài Gòn.]"

Phuong said nothing in response, putting both hands on Bull's outstretched hand, instead. Elegant and natural. Phuong, who did everything perfectly, including sympathy for the secret sorrow of a hard-edged gangster. Phuong held his hands in hers and said: "*Oh, big brother. Come past the centre. Join us for dinner, soon.*"

He nodded. "[I will.]"

Lin hadn't known about Bull's wife; she'd known the man for five years. As far as she knew, this was the first time he'd met Phuong.

Bull Neck Bui stood and left the room, closing the blue steel door behind him. He said nothing to Lin, didn't even look at her as he left. His mind somewhere else.

Lin stood in the middle of her own apartment, yet embarrassed at her interruption. Phuong looked at her, eyebrow raised, cigarette vertical. Lin's lips tingled. She got herself a Larue, ceramic cup, bottle of sake, and sat down where Bull had been. Hunger gnawed at her stomach, mind flicking back to the bowl of phở at Tadioto. She cracked open her beer and sipped it, instead.

"I love what you've done with this place," said Phuong, eyeing the room. Lin had carefully stacked the books that had scattered onto the floor, but otherwise the room was much as it was after the visit of Passaic Powell: ceiling crater, shattered shelves, chunks of wood not even swept.

"What're you doing here?" Lin asked, more tired than angry.

"Visiting my sister."

"You shouldn't be here."

"Don't blame Bull. It's usually reasonable to assume a sibling is welcome in her sister's home."

Lin downed her sake, refilled the cup. "I don't mean that. I mean it's not safe here."

Phuong let her eyes range over the mess of the room. "I can believe that."

Barry watched both of them from his cage, head sideways, one eye switching from sister to sister.

Phuong nodded at the bird. "Didn't we have one like that when we were kids?"

Lin ran a hand through her hair. "Things are getting tense in the thirty-six streets. People gonna notice if my twin starts walking around."

"Bao and Bull are the only ones that know. No one's going to think we're twins, babe."

Lin finished another sake and looked over her sister. Phuong was wearing a western-style business skirt and jacket. Skirt to her knees, jacket long-sleeved, both dark red. Black shirt underneath. Fine cut, tailored outfit; her hair long and conditioned, sunglasses propped on the top of her head. Sometimes Lin forgot regular people had day jobs that required dressing up.

Lin, opposite, in her faded jeans, black singlet, and black boots she hadn't bothered removing when she'd entered the room. Sweat trickling down her neck, shakes starting in her fingertips, whether from withdrawal or the blood visions of a gangster massacre, she wasn't sure.

"You're right about that." Lin lit a cigarette, blew out a lungful of smoke in a long sigh.

Phuong pointed at the coffee table with her chin. "Someone broke your toys." Lin's daggers sat on the top, both snapped. Courtesy of the white giant after his visit. "Are you going to be okay, sister?" Phuong asked, letting her levity drop, finally. "I'm starting to worry."

"I can handle myself."

Phuong formed a retort, then changed her mind, her face softening. Instead, she said: "You need to see Mum."

"I'm not going to apologise."

"God, Lin. Do you even know her? She doesn't want an apology."

"That's because she's weak."

Phuong's eyes flashed. Again, she changed her mind. "No. You're not going to provoke me." She took a drag on her cigarette. "We're too old for this. For all these resentments, kept for so long we can't remember the reason, anymore. You keep that ache for too long, sis, it becomes familiar. It soothes, in its own perverse way. Do you even remember why you're angry?"

Lin swallowed. It was all there. But she didn't want to look at it. That pain.

"You don't have to be alone," Phuong said, and her voice caught.

Lin couldn't look at her. "I'm not alone."

"You are," replied Phuong, her eyes shining with tears, and then the words came tumbling out. Like something she'd be thinking on for some time. "You're all alone. You keep yourself apart from everyone and everything. You deny any connection." She leaned forward. "We have to connect, Lin. The friends we have, the place we choose to live in: they become part of us, and we become part of them. You're diminished without all this, babe. I'm diminished. Our childhoods are so intertwined I can't separate them. I can't imagine myself without you. I can't. We'd sneak into each other's beds in the orphanage, and later, back home in Australia. Pressed together, holding onto each other for dear fucking life." Her voice broke. "Fuck, Lin. That's what it means: it's the parts of yourself you can't separate from another, it's not knowing where you end and the other begins."

Lin's throat felt thick, and so she said nothing. The silence dragged out.

"You have a family," said Phuong, plaintive.

Finally, Lin replied: "I'm where I belong."

CHAPTER

38

☆

Lin looked at the closed door, thinking about getting a fetch boy to bring her dinner. Thinking how much better the food would be at Kylie's. How easy it would be to join them. Week in, week out. And how hard. Phuong was her mirror. Her sister dealt with her past by becoming part of everyone's life, intrinsic, so it was impossible for her to ever be abandoned again.

Instead, Lin took a seat and smoked a cigarette among the wreck of her apartment.

"Fuckchops?"

"Yes," her implant answered, voice even.

"Lights out."

The room dimmed. The only light came through the windows, a weak neon glow, the moon behind thick cloud. She pulled the ice-seven vial from her pocket, held it up. Radiant golden liquid, inner light, all its own. She was working her thumb against the stopper when her on-retina pinged.

Blue Point Pham. Intercession Update. Bao has been notified.

Lin tilted her head, taking a moment to process why she was getting a message from a dead man. "Oh," she said, after a moment. Automated.

She sighed, closed her eyes, and let the message run.

First person point of view: *Bar, modern façade, steel, blue neon. Nod from a burly doorman, dark, strobe light, music blaring.*

Lin turned the sound down.

Up a stairwell underlit with more blue light, past another floor, trance music, to the third floor above. Another doorman, a steel door opening to a large open space. The centre of the space was dominated by an octagon, of a type used by mixed martial arts fighters, and of a quality reserved only for the premium c-casts. Shining brown wood base, black metal wire, white leather pads wrapped around the corners and railing emblazed with vivid blue Baosteel logos. Blood splatters on the white canvas floor kept to a minimum.

Two men – Vietnamese, one short and one tall, both heavyset – were sparring, expelling air through their noses as they punched / kicked / moved. Lin assessed, in the few moments the vision was trained on the men. She assessed and dismissed. Too big, too slow, muscles cumbersome, not balanced out by skill, or the canniness of age, or a really fucking expensive endoskeleton.

On three sides of the ring were bleachers, barely visible in the wash of light from the octagon. On the fourth wall a long bar, backlit in blue, showcasing shining bottles of booze, resplendent – perfect formations of gin whiskey brandy bourbon. Lin thought about pouring herself another drink.

Silence in the room, other than the smack of leather glove on skin and house music pounding away, distantly, through the floor dub dub dub dub.

"[Hey. Sweetie.]"

The vision turned towards the voice, passing over gangster tableaux. The first few rows of the stands, right near the entrance:

Passaic Powell, pale homburg standing out in the gloom, his huge hand wrapped around a tumbler of alcohol. Whatever it was, he was having a triple. A woman pressed against the American, scantily clad Vietnamese; he ignored her completely. Watching intently the men fighting.

Two more men, shiny suits, the women on their arms not being ignored. These men grinning and groping, those women laughing heads back, like they were having the time of their lives. Doing a great job, giving that impression. Purpose-built small tables, set into the stands near the group, had all the gangster accoutrements: lines of white powder, bottles of beer, a crystal decanter, half-empty, muted light refracting through the brown shimmer of the booze.

Passed over quickly, the vision settling soon on a fat Vietnamese man. Red-faced, snub nose, glint of gold teeth in the low light.

"[Big Circle,]" said Ly.

Oh. Her boyfriend was the Green Dragon boss.

"[Come here.]"

She moved as directed, taking a seat right beside, pressing herself in close, hand playing with one of the undone buttons at the top of his white shirt. The fingertips shook.

"[How'd it go?]"

"[Fine,]" said Ly and Lin winced. The woman's voice broke a little, betrayed her anxiety.

Big Circle seemed not to notice, snuffling his snout in around her neck.

"[Good girl. That Australian bitch take the bait?]"

"[There was a problem, but I got out of it.]"

The snuffling stopped. "[What problem?]"

"[Some kids knocked me from my bike and stole it. I managed to get away.]"

Big Circle's ugly face returned to the centre of her vision, he reached out. She flinched. He held her face, probably her chin.

"[You're injured,]" he said.

"[It's nothing,]" she replied and Lin clenched her jaw. Ly's voice quavered, and even a truffle pig like Circle would eventually figure something wasn't straight.

"[What happened?]" he asked, again. And a voice, silk smooth, repeated: "[Yes, what really happened?]"

The vision panned again. Ly was looking directly at two people playing some sort of board game – black and white stones spread out over a grid of intersecting lines. Lin hadn't seen the game players when Ly had entered. In a nook to the right of the bar, raised a half-metre, enough room for a single table, blue-hooded lamp over the board. A slender woman – no, a slender man – powdered face, red lipstick, looking directly at her. Black slacks, white silk shirt with stiff mandarin collar. Opposite him, not looking at her, a man in a grey rumpled suit one size too big. Korean perhaps, sweat on his brow, looking at the game, trying not to look at the girls, Ly, the fight, anything.

The lips of the slender man shone. He had that way of looking, but not-looking. A distance in the eyes, part of the mind somewhere else, somewhere more important.

"[I told you,]" said Ly, and whatever reserve she had was already failing. Something about the thin man made her voice croak.

He stood and walked over. Someone – presumably Big Circle – whispered in her ear: "[What's going on, bitch?]"

She didn't have time to answer. The thin man was there, shining faraway eyes settling on her.

"[Nothing. I was scared. I had to run through the Old Quarter, make sure I avoided Bao's men. I came straight here. I'm just scared.]"

She sounded more believable now, getting a hold of herself. Lin swallowed.

"[Dumb bitch,]" said Big Circle.

"[Sorry, babe.]" She was looking at the man's round face now. She placed her hand on his cheek.

"[She's telling the truth, I'm sure,]" said the thin man, from behind her, in Mandarin.

She turned back to him and her relief was evident in her words: "[Thank you, Mister Long.]"

His red lips were pressed together, mind starting to close in on her, focus. "[Unfortunately, in this business, one must follow elegant dictum of the otherwise crude game of poker.]"

"Oh?"

"[Trust everyone, but cut the cards.]"

She glanced back at Big Circle. There was no sympathy there. Indeed, the fear was creeping into his eyes, as well. "[Stop that!]" he yelled. The men fighting stopped. Watched what was going down.

Mister Long's fingers dipped into his sleeve and withdrew, slowly, a pin shining between thumb and forefinger.

"[What is it?]" asked Ly.

"[Oh, just a little thing I have been working on. It checks for missing time in one's memory feed. Analyses the time that is there and checks for inconsistencies.]"

Ly looked at Big Circle. "[I'm telling the truth, honey.]"

There was a slapping sound, sudden and hard, and the point of view spun and blacked. When she came to, she had a close view of the whorls of the fauxwood floor.

Off-vision, someone was yelling: "[...lying bitch. Everyone can see it.]"

Ly pushed herself up from the floor. Long and Big Circle were standing over her. Big Circle's face twisted uglier by his rage, Mister Long looking down as though she were a specimen waiting for his microscope.

Long said: "[Sit her in the ring if you would, Big Circle, while I assess her stream.]"

"[Good idea,]" replied the boss, red-faced. "Powell."

"Oh no, too tough for me," said Powell in his distinct sing-song voice, off-vision. "Only you can take her, big man, boss man."

"[Do as you're told!]"

"Hush now, little big man, strutting on the stage, remember all who own you. Hush."

Big Circle's face went a deep red, and he did what most men do in such a situation: kicked the woman already on the ground. He lashed out and there was the sound, unmistakable, of a shoe hitting flesh, like a hard, wet slap. Ly cried out, then cried, softly. The vision was of the floor as she was dragged across it. "[Help me,]" she whispered.

Lin bit her lip.

They checked her stream. Whatever the tech Mister Long designed, it was very good. It found anomalies almost immediately, pinpointing the moments after Ly had been knocked from the bike. Mnemonic tech of a standard beyond anything she'd ever seen before. A minute later, no more, Long hissed: "[There's someone riding on her feed.]"

Ly was looking at Big Circle.

"[That you, Bao? You like to watch, old man? I'll give you a show. I'll give you something to watch. You two,]" he said, to the two large fighters in the ring. And he told them what to do to Ly. She screamed as he said the words, her vision frantic.

Lin forced herself to watch until it ended.

"Fuckchops."

"Yes, Miz Vu?"

"I'm going to take a four-drop of ice-seven."

"Wonderful."

"I want to make the last hour or so hazy. Get that shit I just watched out of my head."

"An excellent idea, Miz Vu. Though ice-seven is not considered an effective agent in this regard. I would recommend Neothebaine to block the formation of natural memory completely."

"Oh no. I want to remember just enough."

"For what, Miz Vu?"

"Enough to know which cunt I'm going to fucken murder."

"Indeed."

"But I want the memory stream of me watching Blue Point's message wiped. Stop it where I turn out the lights."

"It will be done."

Lin breathed out, rubbing her forehead with the back of her hand. She took out the gold-glowing vial.

39

☆

Lin was woken from her drug-induced sleep by a bleeping from her neural implant. Driving into her dream state, a violence, pulling apart the tendrils of a deep comfort. A single red dot flashed, on-retina.

Personal channel. Only four gang members had access. She looked at the message.

Nanh.

The name bate-abated, green-hued.

12:31 am.

She groaned: "*Jesus Christ*," pushed herself off the couch, fumbled around the darkened room lit only by the neon wash of the city, and poured and drank a long drink of water.

She opened the message:

I'll be at parking lot seven off Bạch Đằng. I'm leaving for Sài Gòn. I forgive you, sexy. Come to me, so I can give you a goodbye to remember.

Sleep and drug groggy, she sat on one of the high stools by the kitchen bench and read over the message again, glass of water in her hand. Bull must have set it all up.

She dragged on her bomber jacket, made sure the revolver was loaded, slipped it into her pocket. Lin stretched, realising she hadn't eaten since breakfast the previous day. Her stomach reminded her, anyway, twisting in protest at its neglect.

Lin opened her front door and peeked out. Mosquito Brother was sitting on a wooden chair in the corridor, reading a flexiscreen, his face lit up by the soft green.

He started. "Oh. [Elder sister.]"

"Where's Bull?"

"[Asleep.]"

She stepped out, closing the door behind her. "I'm going for a walk."

He stood. "Okay."

"Alone."

One of his eyes looked at her feet, the other, droop-eyelid, at a point somewhere on the floor. "[I have to go with you, elder sister.]"

"No."

"[Bao's orders.]"

Lin swore to herself, ran a hand through her hair.

She turned and stalked down the corridor, throwing a *come on* over her shoulder.

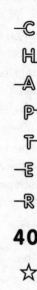

CHAPTER

40

☆

She drove Mosquito Brother's glimmer scooter. He rode pillion.

A Chinese military checkpoint awaited them at the edge of the Old Quarter. Hard-eyed soldiers ran a retina scan of them both. Lin was unworried. Their travel credentials inside Hà Nội were perfect, supplied by Bao's tubby Chinese officer friend, Zhu. Still, those manning the checkpoint dragged it out, made it clear who was in charge. A squad of twenty, spread around sandbags, the outdoor furnishings for a war. Armoured vests, helmets, automatic weapons, body cameras linked to overwatch drones above. An armoured personnel carrier stood sentinel at the roadblock, its turret-mounted heavy machine gun locked on any who approached. Sort of gun that punched a hole the size of a fist entering a car, left one the size of a basketball exiting.

When they left the checkpoint, the world transformed. The roads widened, filled with cars rather than scooters. Glimmer cars, or hydrocell, or Tesla-Sinopec electric. Shining, sleek, and new. Outside the Old Quarter, they obeyed the traffic rules. Stopped at red lights, indicated when changing lanes, laid off the horns, the sort of bullshit that never happened in the thirty-six streets. The dusk curfew had been lifted the previous year, but any business that wanted to operate beyond midnight had to pay a bribe, so the streets were only half-full.

Lin obeyed the rules, didn't speed or draw attention, just rode steady and enjoyed the wash of night air against her face. Mosquito Brother grasped her hips tightly.

Skyscrapers, smattering of lights still on, rose up either side. Fresh and clean, straight lines of gleaming steel and glass. Clean air, no food stalls frying, no biodiesel exhausts, no overflowing sewerage pipes. They passed under an elevated bus, its legs spread like a flying fox astride the roadway, its sixteen wheels in the channels either side of the lanes, stopping periodically to let its passengers exit at elevated walkways while traffic whooshed by underneath.

Many of the buildings were neon-topped with the brand of a state-owned enterprise. One a hologram, living colour and movement, three-storeys high of an apple-cheeked girl clad in a red dress, her black hair in bunches and her chin poised in her hands. She mouthed the words and they appeared below in giant script: *The Chinese Dream is my Dream*.

They rode through the new world in silence. Its clean air and order and shining progress. Harmony and obedience and bowed necks, heavy with the weight of surrender.

The meeting point was at the banks of the Red River, past one of the old bridges. Blasted by bombers into mounds of shattered concrete and shards of metal, now rusting. Lin assumed Nanh had a ride on a stealth junk. Low riding, narrow, wrapped in displacement cloth, ferry her down the river. Maybe.

They coasted into a dirt parking lot. Thinly lit by two solar-battery street lamps. Two cars in the lot, darkened, quiet. Lin stopped the bike in the middle of the space, throwing up a cloud of dust. She propped the scooter and removed her helmet. Dust settling. In the silence she could hear the sharp cries of the geckos, the hum of cars in the distance. She hung the helmet from the handlebar. Mosquito Brother got off, she didn't.

"Don't go far," she said.

"[Do you see something, elder sister?]"

"No." She saw nothing. Felt nothing. Just the steady grind of paranoia in the cogs of her mind. She put her hand in her jacket pocket, the grip of the gun soothing her.

The minutes passed. She smoked a cigarette while Mosquito Brother drew lines in the dirt with the tip of his shoe. Her stomach gnawed, she felt a little light-headed.

She swore.

"[What's wrong, elder sister?]"

"Hungry."

He hesitated. "[I-I know a place, near Hoàn Kiêm Lake. Good ramen. It opens after midnight.]"

"Take me there, after. I'll buy you dinner."

He said: "[Yes,]" and she could hear the smile in his answer.

A whisper of footfalls, Lin's head shot around, and Nanh was there. At the edge of the low lights. Tall, slender, long hair tied back. Blue jeans tight leather jacket and Lin felt a buzz of lust, below her belt, in her fingertips.

Lin smiled, but it didn't last long. Nanh wasn't smiling back. She had a different expression on her face. Nanh walked towards her, favouring one leg. Her girlfriend stopped fifteen feet away. Lin had to strain to hear her when she said, in Vietnamese: "[I have to leave my city, Silent One.]"

Lin pursed her lips. "Yeah." She ran a hand through her hair, pushing it back from her brow. "I'm sorry."

"[My city, my job, this.]" She gestured angrily at her leg.

"Yeah."

"[I can't work in good bars. Lucky to be a cheap whore.]"

"I can give you money."

"[I don't want it.]"

"Babe," said Lin, "I never meant to—"

Nanh closed the distance between them, and Lin held her breath as the woman leaned in. The soft brush of cheek on cheek, the smell of lavender and gin. Intoxicating. Lin closed her eyes, the woman's breath against her ear.

"[I've already been paid.]"

Lin frowned. Nanh's eyes flashed bitter and she gave Lin the look, the one she reserved for particularly stupid and vulgar marks at the bar when they turned their leering faces away from her. Contempt, for them being so easy to exploit, and getting so little in return. Giving it to Lin, raw, right to her face.

Nanh turned and limped away quickly, and as she did, footfalls, heavier, out of the darkness. For all her training and reflexes, Lin just sat on the bike and stared dully at the woman's back, brain failing to compute. Her lover's back proud with contempt as she walked away. For good.

Lin stared until instinct, subterranean, rose up onto her hands, her feet. She gunned the scooter, whirled it in a half-circle kicking up dirt, her helmet flying from the handlebars. She held an arm out for Mosquito Brother and he swung onto the seat, clasping her waist, as she shot the bike at the dirt exit ramp. Too late she saw the darkened car near the entrance lurch out.

Lin braked, jumping as the front wheel collided with the side of the car. She tucked into a forward roll over the bonnet, shoulder banging against the hood, and came up, revolver in hand.

She fired three shots, *boom boom boom*, three holes punched through the passenger side window, liquid spray in the interior. Movement out behind the car, shadows separating from the darkness near the river, forming themselves into men, running across the car park.

Groaning, behind her, she whirled to see Mosquito Brother pushing himself to his feet, a bloody gash on his forehead.

"Down!" she yelled, moving, hitting him with her shoulder as the words left her mouth, driving him down to the ground with her as machine-gun fire split the night.

They crawled, down in the dirt, into the darkness, fear instinct pushing them, driving them on. Bullets whirred overhead. Lin popped up on one knee, shoulder pressed against the trunk of a tree, and fired three shots into one of the living shadows. The shadow fell and her gun said *click click click*.

She swore, rolling again on the ground, behind the tree, onwards, into a narrow concrete ditch, inch-deep water soaking knees and elbows. Mosquito Brother was there, only his eyes visible, shining in the darkness. She puffed: "Got a gun?"

Another sheen to match his eyes, held out to her; she grasped it, the cool hard metal a comfortable weight in her hand. Her combat vision finally caught up with her situation, adjusting to the dark, letting the world lighten and lose its colour, monochrome, colours leached away. The car, thirty metres away, was silent and still, the glimmer bike, crumpled where it had flipped and landed. The car park behind, shadows left and right, riverfront shrubbery, thick unkempt grass. A dirt road on their right running back to the real road another fifty metres behind them.

Crouching, behind the car, men with guns, semi-automatic. Movement either side, in the darkness, more gangsters, too many.

Lin breathed.

One-handed, she clicked the safety on the gun. A .45. Classic model, black steel.

"Come on," she whispered, pulling at Mosquito Brother's arm. Crouching low, they ran back towards the road.

Immediately the gunfire started up again, *bullets whizzing in the air, the Viet Cong, chasing them down. Everywhere in this place, implacable, relentless.*

She dived and rolled, finding a place behind the exposed roots of a large tree. The black-clad figures flittered in the shadows, all around. There were too many of them, and there was no way out. No way out of this hard and relentless war, this heat, this protracted torture of the soul.

I breathed. Sometimes the Viet Cong would take prisoners. They were the most valuable item, after all, in dealing with the Americans. Just one soldier could buy the freedom of twenty comrades rotting in a South Vietnamese prison. I swallowed, and slowly raised my hands in the air.

A man pulled at me: a skinny man, Viet Cong with a drooping eye. On instinct I grabbed him by the collar, shoving the barrel of the gun into his throat. His good eye went wide and he turned his face. "[No, big sister, it's me.]"

My finger twitched on the trigger. Something wasn't right, something pressed down on my mind and—

Lin gritted her teeth, angry noise forming in the base of her throat. The game, that stupid game. Mosquito Brother had fear in his eyes as she held his arm and pulled herself from the ground. She kept pulling at him, forcing him to move. Lin pumped her legs as they hit a slope, the earth around her feet chewed up by bullets. Her breathing ragged, she glanced back over her shoulder to see a face lit up by orange gunfire. Hard-eyed man, firing up at them as they staggered up onto the road. Suddenly, light everywhere, making her wince as her combat visuals adjusted; she and Mosquito Brother bathed in light as a car hummed by.

They ran across the six lanes – a second car blaring its horn as it swerved around them – and rolled onto the bitumen on the other side, behind a parked older model electric. Lin leaned against it, both hands on the .45, and shot the first face that showed itself over the shoulder of the other side of the road.

BOOM.

The head jerked back, haloed by pink mist; Lin smiled, grimly.

She was lit up by headlights again, as a car drove back from the dirt road and straight across the six lanes of traffic, right at Lin. A second car braked heavily to avoid the collision, tyres screaming, Lin grabbed Mosquito Brother by the shoulder and pulled him towards the building behind them. He was sluggish, she yelled: "Move!" as she fired his .45 at the approaching car.

Two shots shattered the windshield and it drove on, hitting the car between itself and Lin, spinning it out of the way as Lin dragged her comrade and slammed through the doors under a flashing green neon sign, staggering into a dimly lit foyer.

A woman shining with an inner light – a hologram – rose behind a black reception desk like an apparition, her finger raised, scolding—

—as the pursuit car drove itself through the glass and metal façade, ear-splitting, as Lin and Mosquito Brother fell across a table and onto the tiled floor.

Lin rose to one knee, pistol ready, trying to breathe. The space after the crash was silent, save the tinkling of glass as it fell and hit the ground, and the distant *throb throb throb* of music and wail of a poorly pitched voice.

Lin realised, distantly, that they were in a karaoke joint. There'd be floors of rooms, above, synthetic leather seats, drunken Chinese soldiers and Vietnamese businessmen, watching each other belt out old tunes; for a moment, each the lead singer and star of their own life story.

Stairs, leading up to the rooms and floors above, were just behind her. Hologram red Chinese lanterns hung from the ceiling. The red lines of the illusion filled the room with its muted light, reflected in the mirrors lining the walls.

The image of the receptionist had frozen, her arms crossed, head morphed into ideograms in Mandarin and Vietnamese script, flashing in blue: THE POLICE HAVE BEEN NOTIFIED

Lin pulled at Mosquito Brother again, but he was even more sluggish this time. Body flopping backwards.

"Come on, fuck, come—"

Then she saw it. One whole side of his shirt, soaked in blood. His eyes shone as he looked at her. "[Go, elder sister,]" he whispered. "[Go.]"

Seconds, for all this to happen. To see the room, then the blood. She heard the car doors click open and turned, a warrior's roar at the back of her throat, firing three bullets into the man exiting on her side and the rest of the clip through the windshield into the driver, struggling with his seat belt.

A third gangster, opposite rear side, sprawled from the vehicle and Lin's roar came again as she moved, juiced up on the combat chemicals being pumped into her system: adrenalin and good old-fashioned methamphetamine. She front-flipped, full three-sixty, just one hand touching the hood of the car, landing on the other side. A man, black leather jacket, was crouched there; he raised his gun as she heel-kicked his face, the man's head snapping, the blow running deep through her bones right to her hip, and he flopped back, stilled.

She yanked open the passenger door, no one else in the car save the driver, head lolled back, vacant eyes on the ceiling.

"Run rabbit, fight rabbit, kill rabbit, run."

She whirled and he was there. The white giant. Stepping through the shattered frontage. The foot-long handle of his greatsword visible over one shoulder, combat vest gleaming dull in the low light, eyes concerned as he looked down on her. His feet ground the glass to dust as he walked.

She pointed the .45 at his head. It said *click*.

Lin swore.

"Break you, snap you, take you down, rabbit bones are brittle bones." Passaic Powell said it all with a light voice.

Lin breathed.

The foyer was a cramped space for a fight. The car to her right, reception desk to her left, the breadth of her outstretched arms. Powell was three metres in front. Behind her, the stairs and Mosquito Brother lying at the bottom of them, his breathing ragged, wet. Lin bent slowly and picked up a slender metal pipe at her feet. Snapped off something in the collision, two feet long, one edge ripped jagged. Satisfying heft.

She said: "Your poetry sucks."

"Rabbit bones broken, used to pick my teeth. Crickily-crack, crack-crick."

"Doesn't even fucking rhyme."

His eyes gleamed; they came together.

She surprised him, moving faster and cleaner than the first time. He kicked, she swerved and struck his leg with the pipe, spun fluid, a back kick to his groin, spinning again, pipe vertical, into his head.

Still fast, too fast, he pulled his head back, the jagged pipe tip tearing a jagged line across his cheek. Lin kept moving, flowing, driving whatever small advantage she had. Spinning again, he blocked with his forearm and the force of the blow ran right up her arm and she slide-stepped back.

A regular man would be down by now. Arm broken, balls pancakes.

Passaic Powell just cricked his neck, left and right, and raised his fists. Blood flowing down his cheek, purple welt on his right forearm.

They came together again.

Defence this time, as he jab / jab / right / jab / heel kick / side-kicked. On the last she stepped in and hammered his knee with the pipe; he grunted, first time she'd heard him react and she back-spun at his face.

Lin cried out in pain as her fist hit his forearm, the pipe clanging to the ground. She swerved again, Powell closing the distance, swinging, his other fist airing past her cheek, shattering the car window. She pushed-kicked his midriff to force him away, get some distance, and she may as well have been kicking a sandbag. He responded with the same kick as hers and she leapt into the air as something shattered underneath her, landing just in time to catch a reverse blow across her chest, backfist, slamming her sideways into the car.

She dropped to the smooth hard tiles, fighting for air.

Gasping, the room coming into focus.

The reception desk shattered, splinters of pale wood showing under the black paint. Red lantern above Powell's head, bathing his face with a neon demon glow. But the giant's expression was not demonic. No. He looked down at her as a parent would a child with a scraped knee.

His lips moved, but another's voice said, in Mandarin: "[You were warned.]" The voice modulator, shining on Powell's throat.

Lin lay on her back, something sharp pressing through her jacket, digging into the small of her back.

"[The wrong side of history. You people just don't understand your place.]" Then: "[Kill her, Powell.]"

The giant raised his foot, the black sole looking down at her, eager to imprint her face with its pattern.

Until Powell's face was covered by hands, fingers pressing into his eye sockets. Mosquito Brother's eyes, just visible over the giant's shoulder. Droop eye and good eye shining, knuckles white. Powell grunted, raised leg wavered back down, bracing him against the floor.

Lin twisted, pulling the pipe out from behind her back.

Powell, eyes clenched together, fumbled at the hands digging into his face.

Lin, double-handed, rammed the pipe down through the top of the giant's foot.

Passaic Powell roared, the kind of noise that would make a lesser fighter than Lin freeze in shock, and yanked violently at Mosquito Brother, hurling him over the car and in the same motion, coming back with the *dadao* in his hands. The blade shone, at least six feet long, curved, widening as it curved, the end of it as wide as Lin's head.

She rolled under the car, rolled-rolled as the slam-screech of metal on metal reverberated and she popped up on one knee, the other side of the car, as it bowed in on itself. She wasn't good enough not to freeze for that moment as the car parted under the second blow, orange sparks flying, and as Powell hurled the back end of it up and over, one-handed, looking for her, finding her mad heathen hate in his eyes.

She leapt up, hands backwards, every chemical in her body real and manufactured screaming, and she grasped the balustrade of the stairs above her as Powell's blade arced into the space she'd just left. Pulled herself up, landing on her feet and move-moving, up the flight. Metal twisted and snapped underneath her and the whole stairwell shifted, her shoulder bouncing against the wall and still she moved, the stairwell shuddering as the giant tried to cut the thick metal struts out from under it.

She ran and ran and ran, fear and shame pressing on her chest and temples, leaving a mad giant, and the man who'd saved her, in the ruined threshold of a karaoke joint far below.

CHAPTER 41

They picked her up three blocks from the karaoke joint.

She winced, hand on her ribs, back seat of the glimmer car. Bao Nguyen with her, compact machine gun on his lap, two armed men up front, necks snapping left and right, the vehicle on auto-drive. Another car following, two scooters weaving out ahead.

"[Mosquito Brother is gone,]" said Bao.

She closed her eyes against the lights of the city.

"[This death is on you, Silent One.]"

Still she kept her eyes closed. Her hand moved from her broken ribs to the crumpled soft pack of cigarettes in her inside pocket. Propping one in her mouth, she felt for, but could not find, a lighter.

"[I tell you not to leave the Old Quarter, you leave it. I tell you to forget the whore from the Seventeen Cowboys. Yet you remember her, hard.]"

He didn't speak it angry, which was worse.

"[How did Mosquito Brother die?]"

She winced against the image, playing on repeat in her mind's eye. That last glance down at his body, as the giant chopped through a car with a fucking sword, as she fled, in terror. Mosquito Brother, droop eye looking at her, good eye on the ceiling above. His chest facing the opposite direction. Neck twisted impossibly; shot, broken, discarded.

"Bravely," she replied.

A flicking sound, metal on metal, and Lin opened her eyes. Bao held a square steel lighter; she lit her cigarette on the blue flame, inhaled the smoke deep into her lungs. She welcomed the cloud of black poison tar, wishing the punishment.

"[We need his body back,]" said Bao. Not looking at her, anymore, his face towards the window. Perhaps not talking to her, either.

"We won't get it," said Lin. Then left the rest unsaid. That they'd take his body for the memory pin, tear the cochlear implant from his head, and give it to the Macau Syndicate. That the Green Dragon would most likely take his organs, sell them off. That the husk of his body, dumped on some nameless back street, would be seized with eager hands late at night and sold to a reprocessing plant, to be mulched and bagged and sold as fertiliser.

"[A death away from home, in the streets, is a bad death. We need to recover his bones. Otherwise his spirit will live in this karaoke bar. Dying the same death over and over.]"

Eyes heavy, Lin looked over, unsure whether he was being serious. He lit a cigarette for himself.

"[I will request his bones,]" he said, picking a stray strand of tobacco from his bottom lip. "[I will request his bones, so we can return them to his mother in Vĩnh Quang, where he may find peace with his ancestors.]"

Lin hadn't known Mosquito Brother had a mother. She hadn't known anything about the boy at all, other than he brought her food. Brought her anything she requested, dashed off to do her bidding. Let his good eye linger on her, when he thought she wasn't looking.

Idolised her, she knew deep down, she knew, and that he'd die for her as well. She wasn't surprised, at his sacrifice. Just surprised at her own anger about it. As though his loyalty were a weakness. Because his loyalty was weakness. Distance. Always distance.

"He…" she started, and stopped to draw on her cigarette. Her mouth forming a sentiment she hadn't wanted expressed.

Bao turned back to her.

"He saved my life."

"[Mosquito Brother's death is yours to atone, Lin,]" he said. And as he spoke it wasn't accusatory or in anger. Just matter-of-fact.

"How?"

"[You will kill the man who killed Mosquito Brother.]"

She nodded; Bao turned away. She wasn't nodding in agreement. Just nodding to stop Bao looking at her. She settled back into her seat, into the hum of the engine, the dull pain in her chest. Pushing down on the sentiments she didn't want to look at, her cheeks burning, her throat thick.

Ice-seven to smooth it over, to keep emotion at a safe distance. To glide over memory, like a frozen pond, distorted shapes trapped underneath the surface as she passed over, unrecognisable. Ice-seven to bring to her the eternal present, where body buzz and mind shine are the only concerns. No history, no country, no family, no blood debts.

She ran her thumb across her bottom lip. The cityscape glided by her window, unseen.

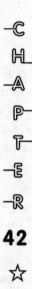

They walked through the headquarters of the Bình Xuyên. The men and women inside stood as they passed. Stood for Bao, glared at Lin. No rowdiness as they entered, no drinking games. Bottles of good rice whiskey sat on the low tables, the air thick with cigarette smoke. Faces smoothed in their anger, closing themselves off to her, like they did for outsiders.

After she and Bao had settled in his office, drinks and cigarettes running, she said: "They blame me."

He looked at her for longer than necessary. "[Mosquito Brother was well-liked.]"

Bao seemed closed to her as well. He took a woven bamboo container from his drawer, slid out a flexiscreen and unfurled it. Subvocalised a command.

A three-dimensional image flickered into life above the flexiscreen. A street scene, Old Quarter, evening. Down one sidewalk moved a white man, thick-set, suit, baseball cap. Lin narrowed her eyes. Herbert Molayson, limping, shoulders hunched, eyes on the ground, cap a non sequitur. But definitely Herbert.

"Where was this? When?"

"[Yesterday. Outside the safe house. Watch.]"

She watched. Herbert walked out of view as the city continued its frenetic dance, indifferent. It was like that for thirty seconds, and Lin was about to ask what he was getting at when she saw herself in the playback, running from the opposite direction, crossing the street. Forcing a scooter to swerve. Down into the darkness of an alley, at the end of which the worn concrete stairs led up to the safe house.

The moving pictures flicked out of existence, clearing the space between her and Bao.

"Can you go back to the start?" she asked.

"[No one else comes out. No one goes in.]"

She raised an eyebrow. "Then how?"

"[Perhaps this Englishman is not all he appears.]"

Lin paused to get his meaning, then shook her head. "Yeah. Nah. That man wouldn't know how to kill himself with a grenade and detailed instructions, let alone rip another man's head off and leave it on the kitchen bench."

Bao sipped his brandy, made a noise in the back of his throat, noncommittal.

"The man I fought today, Passaic Powell. He could do it."

Bao waited.

"Maybe Herbert escaped while they were working on Blue Point and Snakehead. The attackers went out the window."

"[Maybe.]"

"Yeah." Lin sighed a cloud of smoke. "Doesn't seem likely."

"[No.]"

"These pieces don't fit together." She thought it over. "What if…"

"[What if?]" repeated Bao.

"What if Herbert had some sort of martial arts training downloaded, into his other personality. Into Hermann."

"[No,]" said Bao, without hesitation.

"No?"

"[The will and the act, Lin. The physical capacity for violence does not equate to the ability to inflict it. A European dillettante with a clean criminal record does not suddenly start tearing men's spinal columns from their bodies, whether or not they've had some memory edits and an unwanted personality upload. These edits cannot change who we are at our core, cannot make sudden murderers out of suburban housewives. If this were true, China could simply build an army of cold-blooded, remorseless killers and send them down here to do their mean and endless work. If it were true, China could simply round up Vietnamese civilians and turn them, one by one, into fiercely loyal supporters of Beijing. No. Violence as we saw in the safe house was by a person committed to the art of violence. The call of blood magic lies in the true heart of the killer. This was not Herbert Molayson.]"

He was right. What Bao said was right. Her eyes felt heavy, her mind starting to drift.

Smoked curled up from his cigarette. "[It's late,]" he said.

Her timestamp read: 3:10 am. It reminded her how hungry she was. Then reminded her she was meant to be eating with Mosquito Brother. She stopped thinking about food.

"[You look bad, Silent One.]"

"Cheers."

"[I saw such a look, in other places. Those men and women disappeared soon after, into the jungle.]"

"I'm not fucking going anywhere."

"[Other times they died. Suicide charge, blood words in their mouth.]"

Lin ran a hand through her hair, uncomfortable. Some part of her shining at the idea. "I just need some sleep, Bao."

"[This will not be happening for some time.]"

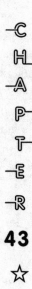

CHAPTER 43 ☆

The master would share a small bottle of sake with Lin before each fight. She wasn't sure if it was ceremonial, a warrior's tradition. Maybe he just liked sake. He wasn't big on explanation.

Cross-legged, low, real wood table between them. Polished, smooth. A flat bamboo serving tray, square. Two traditional ceramic cups (ochoko), and matching flask (tokkuri). Two-handed, the master would pour her sake; two-handed, she would pour his. His ceramic cup marked with the symbol for the dragon, hers with the carp.

Normally he would remain silent. Content to close his eyes and savour the drink as he sipped it, watch her as she poured. It was the only time he'd smile, even if only slightly. Off the mats, he almost gave the appearance of being human. Just a middle-aged Japanese man who liked a quiet drink. Not the sociopath who made her kick a bamboo trunk until her shins bled.

Sometimes he would talk.

It was the sake before their forty-fifth fight. This time he talked. Upbeat, she supposed, after thrashing Lin two fights in a row. In the two fights since she'd pinned his foot to the floor he'd been ruthless. For their forty-third fight he'd selected halberds. Ponderous, heavy, awkward weapons. The least suited to Lin's style. He knocked her unconscious with the flat of the heavy blade within the first twenty seconds.

She'd woken, screaming, to a broken kneecap.

For their forty-fourth fight he'd given her a baseball bat, himself a crowbar. Weapons of the street, he said, before promptly breaking both her arms.

Lin Thi Vu was tired of losing. She'd gotten fast, had upgrades to make her faster, but she'd never be faster than the shihan. And he'd always be stronger. She thought it over, in traction, after the crowbar fight. Came to a conclusion. If she was going to win, she'd have to use the one thing she was better at.

So she took the tokkuri in both hands. Her master was talking about the weapons hung on the wall of the small room. A samurai sword, gleaming. A longspear, red tassels below the blade, the shaft snapped in half. A Western-style broadsword, its edges blunted, rust-pitted. And an AK-47, long thin bayonet affixed, the stock scratched and battered.

A long time before, he'd told her the weapons were from his four great battles. She'd asked whether it was more noble to avoid war. Not because she believed, but because it sounded like the ancient wisdom bullshit she'd heard in movies.

He responded by hitting her with a bamboo switch and telling her not to be so stupid.

He said the four fights had made him. Forged him. The only greatness was in war. The only moments in life with true meaning, when the soul was stripped bare, were on the battlefield.

Her master was talking about the weapons, because Lin had asked him. She'd heard the story of the samurai sword, now she asked for the story of the spear.

"[The Two Battles of the Broken Spear,]" he said, glancing up at the wall. His fights all seemed to have elaborate titles. The samurai sword was 'Dosaku's Masterpiece'. The Western sword was 'Encounter on the Eastern Perimeter, at Dusk'. The machine gun, 'Sixteen Soldiers at Danghu'.

The moment he glanced up at the spear was the moment she struck. The ice-three tablet, wedged gently between the ring and little fingers of her left hand, dropped into his ochoko with the sake, dissolving instantly.

Yeah.

Lin had to play to her strengths. She'd learned it in the working-class town she grew up in, against tough kids, bigger kids, for whom violence was part of their cosmology, a way to define and measure the world. What it dealt to them, and what they could deal back before they were broken. She learned it on the hard slick stones of the thirty-six streets. Against the thugs and the desperate and the war-ravaged who'd already lost it all.

Lin knew what she had to do.

She had to be the bigger cunt.

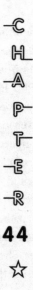

CHAPTER 44 ☆

Lin was awoken by priority message three hours later. 6:13 am, according to her timestamp. Lying deep in her couch, boots still on her feet, orange dawn breaking through the slats. She stared at the ceiling.

Torn away from her dreams, deep dreams of sun-white beaches. Fading now, with those sensations, of the rough comfort of sand between her toes, sun-bitten skin, the sea-music of waves crashing against long pure expanses of white.

Calmed as the dream drifted out beyond the edge of her mind's peripheral. Tranquil within those few moments, of a morning, in the anonymity of amnesia. Those few moments when a person can forget who they are and every problem they've accumulated. Before the world comes rushing in, a kind of peace. Before her boots hit the floor, a solace in ignorance of the self.

Her boots hit the floor.

She thought about Ly. She thought about Mosquito Brother. She opened the message.

Bao: The Englishman has been sighted. Serviced apartments on Trần Phú. Pick him up. Take him to the clubhouse. Get the answers.

She stood, dizzy with hunger and exhaustion. Felt around for the ice-seven vial, found it, held it up to the light. Empty. She popped the lid and tongued it anyway, a faint bitterness of the drug, but that was all. No body rush. Half a cup of water left in the tower; she wet her parched lips. As she did she caught sight of herself in the mirror. Purple lines under her eyes, face drawn. Her skin pale, unhealthy pale. Her shoulders looked small, with no jacket on. A small sick girl. She put her bomber jacket on and ran her hands through her hair, pulling her fingers through the tangles. She stood in front of it, full length, and watched herself pour and drink three shots of sake, all that was left in the bottle.

"Mosquito Brother's dead."

Barry hopped around on his perch behind her, in the mirror.

"I know you sang for him."

The songbird turned on his perch, looked out the window, and watched the failing rain.

Lin put her shaking hand to her lips, her chin, her heart.

"*Fuck.*"

Her other hand let the empty bottle drop to the floor.

She got a ride over in her regular cab. Bull Neck Bui was waiting out the front of the apartments, sheltered from the morning drizzle by a canvas awning. Bull said nothing, not even a nod, his face smooth as she exited the cab and stood next to him. The two gangsters with him, a man and a woman, hard young faces, were vaguely familiar; she didn't know their names. Probably runners pulled into action by Bao, now it all had started.

Lin asked Bull: "He alone?"

"[No. A girl is with him.]"

"One of ours?"

"[Close enough.]"

Lin looked up and down the street. Quiet, this early, just before the storm of people rose up to occupy. The morning air was muggy, roads slick with last night's rains. A woman rode past on a bicycle, speaker blaring with the weather the forecast, with reports of Chinese gains along the fronts on Jammu and Kashmir in India and Quảng Ngãi in Vietnam.

Lin signalled the two young gangsters to wait in the black-and-white tiled foyer. Carefully she went up to the room with Bull. Mosquito Brother's .45 in her hand, fresh magazine, spare in her pocket. Bull had a sawn-off double-barrel shotgun, useful if they were suddenly attacked by an elephant.

They soft-footed down the corridor. Well, Lin did anyway, Bull scuffed his feet, breathing heavy; Lin gritted her teeth in frustration. They stopped outside the door on the second floor, she raised a finger at Bull, stilled him, so she could listen.

Only one sound she could make out. Didn't need enhanced senses either, to catch it.

"[Is that snoring?]" asked Bull.

Lin nodded and kicked in the door. Following through to a one-kneed crouch, marking the terrain inside with the barrel of her gun. Modern, cream faux leather furnishings, cleansteel kitchen, hardwood dry bar, one other door leading from the room. A huge tai screen on one wall; on another a large oil painting of old-school European women in ancient clothes, one or both breasts exposed, fat naked baby angels fluttering around their heads.

The snoring continued.

Lin pointed at the bedroom door with her chin, Bull aimed his shotgun at it.

Lin looked over items spread across the kitchen bench. Yellow-tinted glasses, a pack of cigarettes, a small clear vial marked 'clozapine', a silver cylinder of hi-end spray-on prophylactic, a fat roll of yuan, and two small, ivory-handled, double-barrelled pistols. Lin picked each up, eyebrow raised, feeling the weight, snapping both to see if they were loaded, sniffing for the residue of a recent firing. She slipped the pistols into the pocket of her jacket.

Lin eased herself over to the bedroom door, turned the knob and pushed it open, gently. Bull raised the shotgun to his shoulder.

A woman sat in a chair, next to the bed, watching herself in the mirror as she brushed her long, pink hair. Naked from the waist up, creamy smooth skin, went by the name All City Do. Hooker, thirty-six streets, rich clients only, protected by the Bình Xuyên. The only payment required from her was information on her clients, whenever asked, in every detail.

Lying face-up on the bed was Herbert Molayson, arms akimbo, mouth wide. Fast asleep. He was wearing a crumpled suit, slightly too small for him. Sock on one foot, the other one bare.

All City Do looked at Lin, in the reflection of the mirror, and smiled, sultry. Lin, starving, exhausted, strung out, still got a buzz from the glance. Didn't show it though, jerking her head at the door instead, indicating for the escort to leave. All City Do gave a little pout at the rejection, and took her time running the brush through her hair once more, more in rising, casually, to find her clothes, and luxuriantly stretching her arms and back as she pulled a tight black tube top over her small breasts. Facing Lin while she did it all, smiling innocently.

All City Do sauntered past Lin brushing her arm, giving her a little electric thrill at the touch. Behind her back, the escort didn't go straight to the door, but paused to take the roll of hard currency from the kitchen bench.

The apartment door clicked closed. Herbert snored. Bull stood in the bedroom doorway, shotgun over his shoulder, and watched Lin as she sat on the bed, next to the Englishman. Up close, he smelled of cigarettes and the acrid sweat of hard liquor.

She slapped his cheek with the barrel of the .45. He snorted, mumbled, then jerked awake, eyes popping at the intruder.

"Wakey wakey," said Lin. "Hands off snakey."

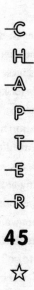

45

"Who the fuck are you?" asked Lin.

Herbert sat at the other side of her desk, in her office back at the clubhouse. Hollow-eyed, still not quite processing where or why he was.

"What?" he said, voice thin.

She regarded him for a moment before chucking her pack of cigarettes in front of him. He stared for ten long seconds, processing the item in front of him, before he nodded to himself and pulled a thin white cigarette from the packet. She signalled him to lean forward, he did; she lit it.

He enjoyed it. Eyes closed. Exhaling a long white cloud of smoke through his nose.

"Like I was saying," said Lin, as she added to his smoke with her own. "The fuck you up to, Bert?"

The confused sheen still hadn't left his eyes. "Bert?"

"You. Herbert Molayson. Dilettante. Louche. Goat-fucker." She pointed at him with her cigarette. "Why are you with a high-end

hooker in the wrong part of town with shit in your hair, a bad suit—"
She clunked the derringers on the table in front of her. "—pistols from
a wild west poker game."

He looked at the guns like they were dead fish she'd just demanded
he gut.

"I don't…" He trailed off.

Shrunken in on himself, shell-shocked, holding on to his cigarette
like a drowning rat to a piece of driftwood. Easy mistake to make,
looking at him.

She sighed. "Hungry?"

He swallowed. "Um. Actually. Yes. I am rather peckish." It occurred
to her that his accent hadn't been present, for a few minutes. She'd
have to go back on-retina and double-check.

"I'm fucken starving," she said, and subvocalised an order to one of
the fetch boys outside. Lin and Herbert smoked cigarettes and waited,
Herbert staring into dead space, his cigarette burning down idle rather
than being smoked. Lin closed her eyes and checked her memory feed,
looked over Herbert's behaviour and words from the morning.

A tap on the door and the fetch boy brought in coffee, two *bánh mìs*
filled with vat-grown beef, and two steaming bowls of phở.

Lin ate with relish, stomach doing a loop-the-loop in pleasure, as
something solid hit it. Herbert ate as though he were as hungry as Lin,
temporarily forgetting he was a space cadet.

"Okay," said Lin, beating on her chest for a moment to force down
the food. She slurped her coffee. "Where were we?"

"I believe," said Herbert, "you were enquiring as to my activities."

"Yeah," said Lin. "I got a theory about that."

"Regale me."

"First thing. Where were you last night, Bert?"

"Well." Herbert cocked his head to one side. "Ah. You know that
is a very good question." He looked back at her. "I am a real shambles
this morning, I must say. Whatever I did do last night must have

been gratuitous, because I can't remember a jolly thing."

"Pull up your memory stream."

Something passed over his features. A glimmer she couldn't quite classify. Then he smiled and said: "Ha. Well, of course. One moment." He leaned back in his chair and closed his eyes.

Lin slid the .45 out her pocket and rested it on her lap, easing the safety with her thumb. Silent, slow.

She sipped her coffee. He opened his eyes, his expression wavered. "It's the damnedest thing. The section is missing." He sucked in a breath through his teeth. "I suppose I could have really misbehaved. Had the drunken prescience to wipe it all, so I had nothing to regret, in the hazy aftermath." He smiled and she didn't believe it.

"I've done that," said Lin. Noncommittal. Coffee in her left hand, her right on the pistol in her lap. "What's your last memory?"

His expression wavered again. "That's hardly here nor there."

"It's here," she said. "And now. So tell me."

He looked at her through bloodshot, shining eyes. "I should never have got messed up with you people."

"*Ha,*" she said, without humour. "Let me see. Unearned wealth inherited via decrepit European aristocracy. Spun it into a business deal with gangsters working for the Chinese military, to enable a war crime on an occupied people." She smoothed her face. "*We people* are the best people you know, *motherfucker.*"

He smiled absently, looked down at his hands. "Hm. Quite." He sighed. "Quite. The last thing I remember, Miz Vu, was one of your genteel colleagues punching me in the stomach, then holding my head against a tile floor while the second man forced a neural jack into my skull." Back at her, hands open. "Then nothing, until this morning. A blank space, where my life should be. I cannot explain it, I cannot fathom it. But there it is."

"There's a saying in poker."

"Edify me."

"Trust everyone, but cut the cards."

"You're not getting into my head again, Miz Vu."

"Gonna happen, old bean. Easy or hard, the manner is up to you."

"Now listen—"

He stopped when she raised the gun from her lap. "Easy or hard, Bert?"

"Ah." He ran a hand through his hair, absently, gaze elsewhere. "Ever turn around, Miz Vu, and wonder how you ended up at this particular juncture in life?"

She paused. "Yeah."

The smoke thickened the air above their heads. Through the window, Lin heard the distant report of gunfire. Silent otherwise, in the room, as Lin watched the Englishman, and he in turned watched the parade of bad choices that was his life.

"All the decisions, all the moments, leading to here and now," he said. "I haven't the faintest idea how I ended up here. Miz Vu. It makes no sense to me at all. The story of my life has no path, no line. There are great spaces where you pretend there used to be someone, but it's not true, there was no one. Do you understand what I'm saying?" He looked to her at the end, like he wanted a real answer, like she possessed a truth.

She gave him a real answer. "Yeah." And then: "I believe you."

"Sorry?"

"When you say your memory stream is blank."

"The tone of your voice does not give me any solace."

"Oh no, we're going to crack open your mind, no matter what I believe."

"Ah."

"I've nearly solved your case, though."

"Oh." A murmur of a smile. "That silly old thing. It's all starting to feel like a sub-plot, isn't it?"

"Yeah. Well. Drink?"

"It's seven in the morning, Miz Vu. Even a louche being like myself has limits."

"I read an article about drinking first thing. It says Bloody Mary is still the classic, respectable start to the day."

"Ah. Well, that could be true."

She pulled a bottle from her desk drawer. "I got bourbon."

He smiled.

She poured each of them a shot. They both let them sit there, amber shimmering in the morning light. She rested her .45 next to her drink.

"So here it is, Herbert: you're not who you think you are."

"No?"

"No. You're Hermann Hebb."

"Oh. Really? Please, do go on," he said, sarcastic tint in his eyes.

"This is what happened: you produce a prototype of the game Fat Victory with Raymond Chang. Celestial Entertainment love the concept. They ask you to come to Hà Nội in order to get a better flavour for the country, make the game more believable."

"Yes," he said, drawing out the word. "This is all true."

"But already they had something else in mind. An idea floated to them by the Chinese military, probably years before: video game as weapon. Now, not everyone can know about this. Not everyone in Celestial, and not everyone in the psych warfare division. Just a handful in each, trying to get noticed, promotions, medals, hand-jobs from the Red Aristocracy. The usual. They get you here because they can control you, control all the flows of information – the great firewall filters everything getting in or out of the freewave, and the Old Quarter is a firewall within a firewall, what with the jamming and the disruption round the clock. They get you here because Hà Nội, right now, is a free-fire zone when it comes to international treaties: nothing is monitored and anything goes."

"Hmm. True."

"Yeah, *but*. I don't quite get the next part, either. There's a piece missing from the puzzle. They decided to keep it in-house: keep the information in a cul-de-sac. Maybe you and Raymond had some proprietary content in there, DNA-encrypted, difficult for them to get out."

"We did."

"Plus they wanted someone with less scruples. My guess is that you, a soft-handed dilettante, and Raymond, an addict of booze and the dice, had too high a moral bar for Chinese counter-insurgency operations."

Herbert looked away from her for the first time. "I... Perhaps there were some conversations, early on, about upping the intensity of the experience. I'm not sure."

"You told me you had exo-mas run over your memory stream. Said they gave you no possible suspects, no clues, about Raymond." He nodded and she continued: "But you didn't say there were large slabs missing."

"There weren't slabs missing."

"Hmm." She smoked, fired the neurons. "Okay, how about this. There's a service we have here, at the Bình Xuyên. Alibi service. Most gangs run 'em. Not uncommon. You come in, we construct an exo-memory that'll pass muster with the cops."

"I imagine, Miz Vu, I would be aware of seeking out memory adjustment."

"Nah, mate. Nah. I'm talking high-end. The sort of crime the crim can't remember doing. Now you got to get in early. Right after. We give 'em some Neothebaine. That tends to wipe out the previous hour. Amnesia. The twenty-four hours before that, pretty rough. More like a dream state. And to really seal in a credible alternate timeline, we take a real memory, something from years past, and loop it through exo-memory.

"So, let me ask you this. When you go back and look at your time in Hà Nội – do you have a set daily routine? Wake up, late breakfast in your room, get high, lunch with Raymond to discuss the program, going over the same ground, lunch becomes dinner, messy, out to a nightclub, big tips to bar girls who flirt outrageously, but never quite put out, then crash in bed at the Metropole, not quite sure how you got home. Rinse, next day, repeat."

Herbert said nothing, rubbing his mouth with his hand, thinking instead of yapping.

"Yeah, something like that. See there's this theory, Bert. You know how they say time flies when you're having fun? It's bullshit. Time flies when you live a life of drudgery. People who feel like they've lived long, full lives, do so because they look back on a range of experiences. Exciting, new, different, rich memories that fill up a life. People stuck in an office job, on the other hand, think back and can't distinguish one day from the next, one year from the next. It all merges into each other. All a blur. The truth is, time flies when you're bored, doing the same shit, day in day out.

"So, when you wanna fake a memory, one that even the dreamer believes, you find a typical day and play it back through their memory. Tweak here and there – can't be a carbon copy – but something that'll blur into all the others, real and imagined."

"But I'm not taking amnesia medication."

"Bullshit. Second time we met, you thought it was the first time we met. One of the symptoms of long-term Neothebaine use and memory wipes is creeping Alzheimer's. Chinese military are half-owners of the Metropole, your drink of choice is grappa, they restock your bar regularly. I reckon you can join those dots."

Herbert downed his bourbon, the shot glass playing a little *rat-a-tat* as he tried to put it back down on the table.

"Mate," said Lin. "I'm only getting started."

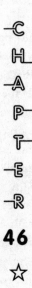

CHAPTER

46

☆

The other door to her office opened; Uncle Bao slipped through. He sat in the corner out of Herbert's line of sight, in shadow, just the tip of his cigarette and the shine of his eyes visible.

"[Continue,]" Bao said, as though he'd been listening. Probably had, the door to his office a thin one.

She poured Herbert another. "So Hermann Hebb starts working for them, full time, your false memory line now filled with experiences they've implanted. You're confused – Hermann's confused – but the pay is great. Hermann's been pulled from the drudgery of some office job they've dreamed up for him, enjoys the new work in an exotic locale. He also possesses more moral flexibility than you. Hermann will do the job until it is done, and after, he disappears."

"Okay, Miz Vu, I see where you're going," said Herbert. "But we're not talking about alibis anymore, we're talking about splitting my personality. You're saying Hermann sat there, thinking he was another person, with a completely different personal history. It doesn't make sense."

"That's the thing. The personal history is the same. You look exactly the same, after all. They would have written his upbringing as pretty much the same as yours, minus the Raymond Chang link. Just a different name... and several years before, they start a new timeline for Hermann – the blurry office drudgery timeline. I guess they threw in some rough experiences, to help provide the moral flexibility they required. But, for the most part, they minimise the differences between you. Then, the dreamed self becomes real. Now he's really working on Fat Victory as Hermann in Vietnam. Now you, Herbert, become the dream: the dreamed timeline of a debauched Englishman in Vietnam. You weren't you, Bert, for weeks, maybe months. Your life was a fiction inserted in memory. As for Hermann: they don't care if he's confused, if he doesn't answer to his name the first time around, if he has these premonitions of another life lived. He's schizophrenic, right? That's not a split personality, as such, but it does mean an inability to know what's real, hearing voices, fucked-up thoughts, hallucinations."

Herbert looked more and more uncomfortable as she talked, first stubbing out his cigarette, then rubbing his hands together, and finally lighting and drawing deep on a fresh one. Bao sat in the corner, unmoved and unmoving.

"This was in your possessions at the hotel." She fished the clear vial of small white pills out of her pocket. "Clozapine. Anti-psychotic medication. Strange coincidence that you and Hermann both have schizophrenia."

"But I don't have schizophrenia."

From behind, Bao said: "[Of course you do not. You have severe brain damage caused by frequent and extensive memory wipes, some of the symptoms of which manifest themselves as schizophrenia. The problem is this: the medication is not actually Clozapine.]"

She looked over at Bao, as did Herbert.

Bao said: "[Medication for PTSD is quite simple. Every time a former soldier has a flashback, and wakes up with nightmare images from the war still fresh in his mind, he takes something called a zeta-blocker. The memories formed at this particular moment are dissolved. The idea is elegant: every time one remembers something from the war, the neural pathways containing that memory light up. The zeta-blocker stops this particular pathway from being used again.]"

"You seem to know a lot about this drug," said Herbert, trying to kill his nerves with words.

Bao continued as though he hadn't heard. "[This is what happens: the doctor tells Hermann to take one of these pills every time he has a flashback, every time he is confused and believes he is someone else. If this is a zeta-blocker, the resurfacing memories are erased. Hermann then relies on his exo-memory to give him the truth about the past, and that truth is constructed by the Chinese. Simple.]"

"Simple," repeated Herbert, as if it was anything but.

"All this ain't unheard of," said Lin. "Some people, whatever reason, want to change their lives. Enough money, they go get plastic surgery and a memory adjustment, and go start themselves a new life."

"But the memories Hermann was wiping, they are my memories – my past."

"Exactly. Been feeling confused lately, Herbert? Forgetful? Friends back home asking why you've been out of contact for so long?"

The Englishman ran a hand through his hair. The product in it made it smooth back in place. His hair now half-slicked, half hanging down in limp ringlets.

"Another thing I reckon."

"It's getting to the point, Miz Vu, where I'm not sure I want to hear the next revelation."

"Well you're gonna. In a second. But first. Tell me: you augmented? Physically?"

"Well," said Herbert. "Of course. I have implants. Shoulders, hips, knees, not unusual for a man of my age."

"Chinese?"

"My dear, what's the point of being rich if you don't get the best of everything? Of course they're Chinese. And, yes, before I left for Hanoi, I also had my ribcage fused, and a nano-cleanse to knock a few years off my organs, make sure I was fit and sturdy when entering a war zone."

"So you're strong. Probably strong enough to rip a man's head from his body."

"Well I… Well I wouldn't know."

Lin and Bao stayed silent. Herbert shifted in his seat, sucked on his cigarette until it hit filter.

Finally, Lin said: "Take another drink, Bert."

He didn't argue, just looked resigned, and downed the bourbon. Coughing a little as he reset the glass.

"I'm going to send you a picture now. Two of our colleagues, shot and beaten to death. Both gut shot with a pistol, kinda like this one." Lin picked up one of the derringers, levelled it at Herbert. "You were the only one in the room, the only one to go in or out. Three storeys up, it makes no sense that someone scampered up the wall outside, tore Snakehead and Blue Point to shreds, then scampered down again. Did all that, but left you intact. They came to my apartment, chopped up my girlfriend; led us into an ambush; they make no bones about who they are. They're not going for subtlety. Fucken ninja attacks on safe houses? No. No, Herbert, the only available answer is that you did it. You did it and you don't remember. These people have put a psychopath into your head."

She lit a new cigarette.

"Now Bao here doesn't agree. He doesn't reckon a mild-mannered goat-fucker like you can turn around and tear a man's head from his body. But I'm starting to think otherwise. Haven't quite figured at the how, as yet, but you know: Occam's Razor, and all that. The thing is, Bert, I'm a betting woman. I'd bet your alter ego, Hermann, is a lot more dangerous than we've been led to believe. Raymond Chang was gut shot, again with a weapon much like this. I'd bet it was this gun, and you killed him."

"No," said Herbert. Sharply, his bloodshot eyes flashing. "Raymond was my best friend."

"Yeah," she said, voice softer now. "Yeah. This is one of the pieces that doesn't quite fit. Why create a second person to kill Raymond, when it would be far easier to do it themselves. Anything can happen in these thirty-six streets; some foreigner who's overindulged, winds up dead – ain't nobody here bat an eyelid at that."

"Precisely," said Herbert, grasping onto the thought line. "Precisely."

"Yet, when we test the bullets inside our boys, I reckon they'll match this gun." She let it lie flat in her hand now, morning light catching the ivory of the handle, the clean steel of the barrels. Brightest thing in the room, the centre-point. "So someone has done it to you, Herbert, even if I don't know why yet. The same people are fucking us over."

Something changed in Herbert. A ripple in his consciousness, and his reflection changed. He ran a hand through his hair again and now the lot was slicked back, straightened in his chair and suddenly she could see how big his shoulders were. His voice came out rough: "Yeah? What now?"

"[You killed two of our men,]" said Bao, simply. Silence followed the statement. Lin placed her hand on the .45, lying on the desk.

"You going to kill me?" asked Herbert. Not pleading, not fearful. Resigned, like he was airing a knowledge he'd had since they bundled him into the car that morning.

Lin, not knowing the answer, waited for Bao.

"[No,]" said Bao. "[If it is true you're a straw dog, made by the memory gods. No.]"

Herbert breathed out, but the tension stayed on his shoulders.

"[But.]" Bao paused, eyes on Herbert's back. Herbert in turn watching Lin, as though her face would tell him what Bao would say next. "[You will pay. Compensation to the families of both men, and compensation to us. We will find the truth, the shape of it all. And not via some technician. No. We shall bring an Omissioner in, the best one. He will lay out all your timelines and hang them on the wall so I can look at them. Then I will name the price.]"

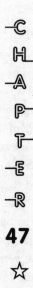

CHAPTER

47

☆

They left Herbert Molayson chained up in Lin's office, watched over by a sullen, peanut-eating gangster – Moustache Pham – who wouldn't say a word to the Englishman. Pham nodded, smiling, when Bao told him to act the mean, taciturn guard. Gangsters loved to role play.

A very civilised chaining, as these things go. Just his ankles clamped with titanium-nanocarbon alloy cuffs, looped through a shackle of the same drilled into the floor. Enough to keep Herbert stationary, Chinese endo-implants or no.

They departed in a black hydrocell, armoured, and drove over to the edge of the thirty-six streets, to the far end of Hoàn Kiêm Lake. One car ahead of them, another behind. All the men strapped heavy. Bao handed her a spideriron vest. She shucked off her jacket and the shoulder holster with the .45, slipped the thin black vest over her singlet. It had the weight and look of thick silk, though more rigid. She thumbed a silver pip at the hem; the vest moulded itself to her proportions.

When Lin asked him where they were going, Bao said: "[*To make a fair exchange.*]"

Bao and the two men in the front ignored her as they edged past the lake. In the centre of it a tiny island with the turtle tower – a small rotting concrete structure set in lush green reeds, isolated in the middle of the lake. The lake had a sword legend – because everyone loves a good sword legend. The one here was kinda like The Lady of the Lake and King Arthur, except the lady in this case was a giant golden turtle, and the Arthur was the Emperor Lê Lợi, and he gave his magical sword to the turtle, rather than the other way around. He gave the sword back because he'd finished fighting the Ming Chinese Empire, and didn't need it anymore.

Bit premature, that Lê Lợi.

They turned down a narrow alley, about the width of a car, traffic left behind. The alley opened out into a courtyard at the centre of an abandoned government building. Bombed government building, to be more precise. The white stone around its hollow windows was blackened, like the mascara on a hooker. The three Bình Xuyên vehicles parked at the near end of the parking space; twenty metres away were two dark cars, like theirs, regular gangster issue. Surrounding them, more gangsters, posing. Black shirts, sunglasses, guns and dragon tattoos on show.

Lin didn't take much notice of these mean-street adornments. What she noticed was a long, eight-windowed glimmersine. Looking at it, Lin recalled Ly mentioning the same, the one the white giant got into after he'd made his first visit to Lin. She swallowed, memory flicker at the c-cast. A dead-eyed man called Long, Ly's voice cracking with terror. Lin breathed out slowly through clamped teeth.

On cue the back door popped open and Passaic Powell exited. Size thirteen feet crunching the gravel, the pommel of his sword gleaming, cream homburg perched on the back of his head. He left the door open and stepped to one side.

Lin and Bao stepped out of their vehicle as well. Overcast, the air thick with heat and the threat of rain. Bao had his compact machine gun slung over his shoulder. They stood, side by side, facing Powell. He did his usual circus freak / serial killer act, smiling, weirdly, kindly, at Lin. Whoever else was in the limo stayed there.

Bao signalled Bull Neck Bui, standing next to one of the other cars. He nodded at Bao and popped the boot. Reached in and pulled out a body. Lin raised an eyebrow. She didn't recognise the man, but his tattoos marked him as a Green Dragon. His throat had been slashed. His neck and chest covered in blood caked brown, wearing only underpants, stained too with old blood. Another two bodies were pulled, much like the first. Bull piled them on top of each other, crude, arms and legs at odd angles, and dragged all three with seeming ease across the space. He dumped them halfway, and waited.

Opposite, a Green Dragon woman with a black t-shit and large shoulders walked across the space carrying an iron box, two feet wide by one foot deep. She dropped it onto the ground, next to the bodies, the *crunch* of metal echoing against the walls. Bull and the woman eyed each other, talked, disagreed. Tight-faced, the woman opened the box and walked away.

Bull bent down next to it, pulling what looked like a silver pen from his pocket, poked at something in the box.

"What's happening?" Lin whispered.

"DNA [test,]" replied Bao.

Ah, she said to herself. Mosquito Brother's remains.

Bull Neck Bui looked over at Bao and nodded, fractionally.

"[It's him,]" said Bao.

"What now?" asked Lin.

Bao gestured at the open limousine door, across the way. "[As you would say, Silent One: now we go talk to this motherfucker.]"

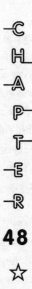

Passaic Powell clicked the car door closed behind him. In the dark, cool interior were just the four of them, two by two, facing each other. Four that counted, anyway. Big Circle, gold teeth glittering in the low light, was there, on the bench seat along one side, glass of booze in his hand, ice clinking as he drank. His demeanour was distant, out-of-sync with the reality around him, like he wasn't even aware there were other people in the vehicle. He knew he wasn't part of this. Appearances had to be kept. That's all.

An uncomfortable memory rose in Lin's mind when she recognised the boss. But she pushed it back down, submerged it, quieting her thoughts while he remained a silent bystander. The four that really mattered watched each other. The American giant, leaning so his head wouldn't hit the roof, huge hands on his knees, nova grenade necklace resting gently against his combat vest. Eyes, kindly, on Lin.

Next to him was a man with short cropped hair, stiff bearing, an old-fashioned three-button dark brown suit with a wide collar. His eyes were dark, depthless, both hands on the iron head of a cane. His skin was young and soft, in stark contrast to his scars. His scars looked like his skin was being eaten by infection, angry purple, creeping out from his collar up his neck, a couple inches out the sleeve over his left hand. Scars that shifted as Lin look at them, disgust rising in her throat; slight ripples, something moving under his skin. He had a strange odour, ripe, unable to be smothered by the smell of his aftershave. A cocktail of aromas that thickened the air, made Lin gag.

Lin pulled a soft pack of cigarettes from her pocket, tapped one out.

Powell said: "No no, little rabbit, not that, not here."

"Oh hey," said Lin. "It's the Cro-Magnon Dr Seuss."

Passaic shifted.

She eyed the big man. "How's the foot, dickhead?"

"My foot, kitty-cat, will be on your skull, soon, snap-crack."

"Must feel weird, working for a Chinese motherfucker who looks like an ice-whore dying from a rare case of purple syphilis."

Passaic shifted again, forward, hands curling, half fists. The rotting man held up a hand. "[Let the straw dog yip,]" he said, in Mandarin. "[All the vanquished have are words. This one here, was betrayed by her woman, and led another soldier to his death. No judgement, no vision – failure heaped on failure.]" He looked at Bao. "[A perfect choice for the Bình Xuyên's second in command.]"

The big man eased back into his seat. Lin smoothed her face and lit her cigarette, relieved to have the sting of smoke dull her smell. Smoothed her face also to hide her realisation: this was the man who spoke through the modulator at Powell's throat. Who'd ordered Nanh hobbled, and Lin dead.

Bao remained silent throughout, watching, waiting. The rotting man kept both hands on the handle of the cane as he spoke, its metal head – a snake head, on second glance – gleaming in the low light.

"[I am Colonel Peng,]" he said, voice scratchy, steady. "[The representative of the Macau Syndicate here, in the Southern Province of Jiaozhi. All this you will know by now.]" Hand still on the cane, he pointed his index finger. "[You are Bao Nguyen. Real name Bao Dang, formally of the Twenty-Seventh scout brigade. Lieutenant Colonel, brigade commander. You deserted after the battle of Khe Sanh, one of only seven survivors. You lived for three years, an animal among animals, in the mountains. Our intelligence estimates you made over fifty kills in that time, including at least ten of your own people, whom you claimed to be traitors. You ate many of your kills.]"

Lin darted a look at Bao. His face gave away nothing. His only response was to tap out his own cigarette as well, and light up.

The colonel said to himself: "[Yet these same savages resent the Middle Kingdom and its civilising mission.]"

The ice in Big Circle's glass clinked. Bao waited.

"[I did not see final days of the great victory we had in Khe Sanh. But I will be at this minor one in the thirty-six streets. We will scatter the Bình Xuyên to the wind. We will take the head of the English puppet you have hidden away.]"

"[How long before you die?]" asked Bao, voice even.

The colonel's hand tightened on the head of his cane.

"[Five years,] continued Bao, "[perhaps, before your flesh sloughs from your limbs. Leaving behind just your bones, white and clean. I negotiate with the dead.]"

"[Yet you cannot defeat even the dead. Yet you will lose this negotiation, as you have lost this battle, as you lost the war.]"

"[The war goes on twenty years later, Colonel. Each year your generals say this will soon be over. Yet each year you fill trains with silver caskets wrapped in Chinese flags and send them home.]"

The colonel's black, depthless eyes shone as they looked over Bao. "[You speak of the other war. It is strange that you fill your mouth with the words of a patriot. Yet you are a hoodlum who condemns patriotic countrymen in exchange for a lucrative square of real estate in an occupied city.]"

Bao was silent.

The colonel said: "[But those times are past.]" His eyes flicked over Lin. "[Your disobedient whore ended them. Now we will negotiate the terms of the surrender of the Bình Xuyên.]"

"We'll never fucking surrender," spat Lin.

The colonel smiled, as did Powell. The former hollow, the latter with sadness.

Peng said: "[The terms: the Bình Xuyên is to leave the thirty-six streets, handing over your operations to the Green Dragon. To me, you will hand over the Englishman, and the names of all the Việt Minh dogs in your territory. You drip feed them to the military command here, one by one. No more. You will give me all the rebels, all those who give comfort and aid to our enemy. Every name, every family. All this, turned over to me, immediately.]"

Lin looked again at Bao, sharply. Still his face gave nothing away, leaning back into the headrest, smoke gathering around him. He did not return Lin's look. Finally, he said: "[Agreed.]"

"*What?*" Lin clenched her fists.

"[But,]" Bao said, "[we require one month to deconstruct our operations. My men, women, and their families shall remain unmolested for this time.]"

"[You have forty-eight hours.]"

Bao regarded the burning end of his cigarette. "[In that time, I cannot do as you wish. I cannot get all the names of insurgents. Nor can I liquidate my resources, and pay off the members of the Bình Xuyên, sufficient to enable them to leave and take their families with them.]"

"[I don't care.]"

Bao took his time inhaling-exhaling as he watched Peng. "[This is what I can do for you in forty-eight hours. I can pack a stolen armoured personnel carrier with hexogene-spliced C-6. I can have this vehicle ram its way into the Metropole car park, on the western side, under the section where senior Chinese military personnel are quartered. At the moment there are two generals in residence, six others close to this rank. It will take down the entire wing of this hotel.]" He paused, looking Peng over. "[Or perhaps this hotel will be the Hilton, or the Intercontinental, or the Pearl. One of these places where you parasites dwell.]" Bao exhaled smoke through his nose, eyes still on the colonel. "[We have a saying here in Vietnam: better a lean peace than a fat victory. You will win a war against us, Colonel. Of course you will. But we will make you pay, inch by bloody inch. I offer you an alternative: exactly what you want, but in a period of time slightly longer than you'd hoped. I offer you a lean peace. But this is not enough for you. No. Still you want the war. Just say the word, Peng, and your wish will be granted.]"

Peng made to speak, black eyes finally showing a tic of emotion, when Bao stopped him with his voice: "[The final thing I can give in the next forty-eight hours is this: an on-retina of this meeting, transmitted to the Chinese command. Allow them to know that the franchise kingpin of their criminal enterprise here in Northern Vietnam placed his ego over harmony in an occupied city.]"

Peng's knuckles were white on the iron snake head. "[You have one week.]"

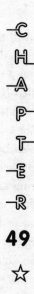

"You gave him the Old Quarter." Lin was angry, not bothering to hide it. Facing Bao, back seat of the car, stuck in traffic halfway along Hoàn Kiêm. The front seats had been rotated to face the rear as the car auto-drove back to the clubhouse. The only one with them was Bull Neck Bui, spideriron vest still on, an AK-47 across his knees.

"[I lent it to him,]" replied Bao.

"*Gave him*. Everything he wanted."

"[This is war, Silent One. I am responsible for my soldiers. I will not sacrifice them for my feelings.]"

"What is the point of having soldiers if your only move is surrender?"

Bao was facing Bull. Something passed between them, which Lin couldn't read.

"[Fighting a war against a superior opponent, one cannot go on the attack,]" said Bao, as though he were reciting a common wisdom. "[We were in a truce, which is the best a weaker force can hope for.

We must move to the natural condition, which is retreat. We will retreat, gather our strength, until we can again force a truce. Once we force a truce, we will again build our strength until we can take the offensive.]"

"Who is that? Sun Tzu?"

"Che Guevara."

"Well, we're not fighting a war, Bao. We're just fighting for a vulnerable customer-base desperate for loans; for a slice of the fights; for drugs and hookers. If we don't have these things to supply, we're not even a gang."

Bao said nothing, his mind already somewhere else, his cigarette burning down. On the seat opposite was the iron box with Mosquito Brother's bones. Paid for with the corpses of three Green Dragons. Lin stared at it with tired eyes. Through the bullet-proof windows, muffled horns of scooters. Fat drops of rain struck the vehicle, the first of a coming storm. White noise, rising in the car as the rain intensified. She looked out over Hoàn Kiêm Lake, waters rising to meet the rain. Strumming with it.

She sighed. "Will it hold for a week?"

Bao, also watching the rain, said: "[This is the only important question. No. Likely no. A day is all it should take, to pay out the men, clear out the Old Quarter. All I wanted to buy was one day.]"

"I got to go." Lin popped the door, the sounds of the world outside rushed in, along with the smell of rain.

Bull leaned forward, as though he was going to join her. Bao said: "[Now is not the time to be storming off like a child denied their way.]"

"It's not that," snapped Lin. Then, calmer: "I have to see my family. I take it I'm leaving Hà Nội with you?"

He nodded.

"I meant to see them today, anyway. It's my—my sister will want to see me. May as well say goodbye, while I'm at it." She glanced over at Bull. "Alone."

"[Good,]" said Bao. He exchanged a look with the other man, who settled back into his seat. "[We'll leave a car out front. Come back to the clubhouse straight after. No drug-fuelled frolics. No revenge quests.]"

Lin smiled, self-deprecating. "Mate. When have I ever done a stupid thing like that?"

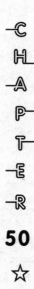

50

"Well, well, well. Cat. Dragged. In." Phuong stood, arms crossed, eyebrow raised.

Lin, inside the doorway, accepted a towel from her mother with a nod. Dried her hair, her neck. Phuong looked pleased with herself; Kylie just looked pleased, eyes lit up, hands twisting nervously. "It's pissing down," said Lin, as a way of not saying anything at all.

"Hmm," said her sister, walking over. "Give me that jacket." Lin did, Phuong eyed her chest. "Nice tits."

"Jesus, Phuong." Lin smiled, despite herself, and gripped her soaked singlet in both hands, squeezing out some of the excess water.

"Oh, honey," said Kylie. "Let me get you a dry shirt."

Lin made to say no, but she'd already bustled off out of the room, eager to be doing something other than trying to think of conversation.

Lin folded her arms. "What?"

Phuong mirrored her twin. "Just smiling at my sister."

"Don't make this any harder."

"I'm just smiling."

"No you're not."

"You know," said Phuong, uncurling her arms. "For a hoodlum, you're really fucken sensitive."

Lin put the towel over her shoulders, one hand gripping each end. "Good to see you too." She shucked off her boots and walked into the kitchen. "Any Larue in this place?"

Phuong followed her. "No. But check this out." She reached up into a cupboard and pulled down a bottle of sake with a green and white label. Lin grabbed it from her. "Ah. Fuck yeah. You really do care."

"I didn't buy it, idiot. It was Mum."

Kylie came back in time for the last two sentences. She blushed and Lin closed her eyes, for a moment, annoyed at her instincts. Suppressing them, she said: "It's great sake, Kylie."

She retrieved a glass from the cupboard and poured herself a drink. Took the clean white t-shirt offered by the older woman, peeling off her black singlet and replacing it. The cotton soft and comfortable on her skin. Music played from speakers hidden somewhere in the kitchen. Old pop ballad, from back in Australia.

"Something smells good," said Lin.

"Real roast lamb," replied Phuong.

"Holy shit."

"Well," said Kylie. "It's a special occasion."

"Where's my drink, bitch," said Phuong, looking at the glass in Lin's hand. Lin passed her that one, and grabbed a second one down from the shelf.

"Special occasion?" asked Lin, as she made sure to pour herself a bigger sake than the one she'd given Phuong, as her sister watched.

Kylie raised an eyebrow at her.

"If you've forgotten I'll honestly slap you," said Phuong.

"Forgot what?" asked Lin, smile quirking at the corner of her mouth.

Phuong grunted and turned to her mother, asked her a question about the lunch. There wasn't much space in the kitchen, the three of them all within arm's reach. Lin sipped her sake, listening to Phuong as she raised the cost of the lamb with Kylie, and Kylie insisting it was fine, and Phuong erecting an eyebrow and saying she knew how hard it was to get a one-time meat licence. And so on and then skipping to other topics, strands of conversation already started in other parts of their lives, outside Lin's. The connection between the two women open and natural, their words a ritual of affection.

The music played in the background and Lin poured herself another sake, happy to be in a space where words didn't contain threats, or demands, or jagged transactions. Words instead, of warmth and affection, like a touch on the upper arm from a friend.

"Before you get drunk," said Phuong, and clinked her glass down on the bench. She walked out of the kitchen, retrieved a long, polished wooden box from a side table, and handed it to Lin.

"Happy birthday, bitch."

The box had heft. "You remembered."

"Just open it, smart arse."

Lin set it on the kitchen bench next to the sake. Popped the small brass clasps, and hinged it open.

Lin breathed in sharply. No sarcasm. Not a shred.

She pulled out the weapons, one in each hand. Blades twelve inches long, slight curve, single-edged, blood channel. Cured black leather grip, hilt and pommel gleaming chrome. The edge shimmering, nano-sharpened, the blade itself a nano-steel alloy.

"Jesus. They're beautiful."

Phuong and her mother laughed.

"What?"

"You're so fucking weird, Lin," said her sister.

Lin was too impressed with the present to be pissed. Instead, she pulled the scabbards from the box and strapped the tanto to each hip. Back straight, facing the two women, hands on hilts. "How do I look?"

"Suits you."

"Wonderful, honey."

"Well?" Phuong asked Lin.

"Well what?"

"I know you haven't forgotten, bitch. Where's mine?"

Lin shrugged an *okay* and went and fished it out of the large pocket of her jacket. Unwrapped the spideriron sheath. The faded cover showed a long dusty road, tall flame trees running along its side. In the distance, a woman in an *áo dài* and conical bamboo hat carrying a basket. *The Sorrow of War*, in faded white lettering.

"Oh, come on," said Phuong. "You carry that with you everywhere."

"I know," replied Lin.

Phuong's wry smile faded. "Oh."

Lin ran her fingertips over the cover. "No one talks about the war," she said. She hesitated, pressing her lips together.

"Go on," Phuong prompted.

Fingertips still tracing the cover, she said: "War is everything. The DNA of this country is threaded with violence. This embedded memory, some fucking loop, dragging the country back in on itself, every generation." She looked at her sister. "I'm not good with fitting in, I know that. It's not just because I'm a cunt. I just—I just don't understand this stuff. I don't get it. I don't get this country." Her eyes flicked over to Kylie. "I didn't get Australia, either. The first time I understood anything about Vietnam it was this book. It's old, but it's true, you know?" She held it out to Phuong.

Her sister reached out, held both Lin's hands and the book.

"Lin," she said, her eyes soft. "The truth is, it's mainly because you're a cunt."

Lin laughed, despite herself, and slapped her sister's hands. "Oh, fuck off."

Phuong smiled, warm. "But I love this, babe. Thank you."

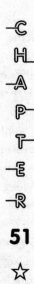

CHAPTER
51
☆

"Fuck this is good," said Lin, between mouthfuls of roast lamb.

"Thanks, honey," Kylie replied.

"She's right," said Phuong. "It's like an angel came in my mouth."

Lin laughed.

Kylie furrowed her brow. "Phuong. But yes. It is pretty bloody good."

They sat around the small fauxwood dining table. Plates laden with roast meat and vegetables, tall glasses of beer, and some expensive Australian whiskey Kylie had been saving. Lin was on to her third glass. It went down smooth at first, then afterburn, fifteen seconds later.

Lin burped, hitting her chest with her fist.

"Honestly, I don't know why you're not married yet," said Phuong.

"Shut up."

"What's brought this on?" asked Phuong.

"What?"

"Acting like a member of the human race." Phuong was smiling, but there was something behind it. "Barely, anyway."

Kylie's eyes flicked from her daughter, back to her hands.

Lin turned her glass of whiskey on the tabletop. Thought about Mosquito Brother, rag doll neck, droop eye staring. She thought about Nanh, hustler, stranger with a Judas kiss. She thought about eternal white beaches, in another reality, and the strong arms that carried her. "Nothing."

Phuong raised an eyebrow. "Nothing?"

Lin sighed. "I've got to go away."

The vibe around the table ebbed.

"Go away, like as in prison?" asked Phuong.

Lin laughed without humour. "Ha. No. As in away from Hà Nội."

"How long, Lin?" asked Kylie, edge in her voice.

"I don't know. Don't give me that look, Phuong, I don't." She sighed. "It's not safe, for my people. It might be years."

Kylie squeezed her hands together, as she always did in times like this. Phuong leaned back in her chair, arms crossed, eyebrows disapproving.

"It's better for you both, this way," said Lin.

"This isn't about us," said Phuong.

"It *is*." Lin smoothed her face. Pushed back down on the feeling trying to get to the surface.

"You know the people I run with. This enclave they carved out here, it could never last."

Phuong and Kylie waited.

"I've got to go away," she repeated. "I came here to tell you. To…"

Phuong leaned forward, eyes twinkling. "Oh, I wanna hear *this*."

Lin finished her drink. Her voice thick with the burn. "To set things right."

Phuong mugged a surprised face. "Oh? Really? What sort of things, for example?"

"Shut up, Phuong."

Kylie put a hand on Lin's arm. Lin resisted the urge to flinch. "Just try not to be away for too long, okay."

Lin took a deep breath, aware of the pressure on her chest, that it had been there most of the afternoon. Pressing right down on her heart.

She stood. "I gotta take a piss."

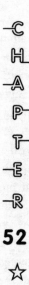

CHAPTER 52

☆

Lin looked at herself in the mirror. Bags under her eyes, ice-addict sheen in her gaze, in the shake of her fingertips. Washed up at the age of twenty-five. She smiled at herself, bitter. A splinter in her soul and part of her wanted it never to leave.

She placed her hands on the white ceramic basin and bowed her head. The main part of her. Pain was addictive, she'd been told, by a gambler. Skinny, wrinkled scarred skin, a veteran. Educated though, former officer perhaps, now a debtor to the Bình Xuyên. "[Pain is heroin," he'd told her. "Psychic, physical, uses the same pathways in the brain. If the pain is sustained, over time, this changes the body chemistry. It becomes addictive, pain becomes the natural condition. Coursing through your body, a shield, to block out the world.]"

It was his way of telling her he couldn't pay. It was his way of saying after he did pay, he'd lose it all again, and the Silent One would have to return, iron bar slapping the palm of her hand.

"Heroin is for pussies," Lin had replied, and broken his kneecaps. He screamed and cried and grinned up at her, from the gutter, when she was done. She'd broken eye contact and walked away, uncomfortable, the feeling of his gaze on her spine.

Lin Thi Vu looked back at the mirror. Reached out for it, to touch it, when someone knocked at the front door. It took her a moment to register the noise. That was all they needed.

Lin spun away from the sink, yanking open the bathroom door. At that precise moment, a name appeared on-retina **Bao Nguyen**, bate-abating red. Two steps into the corridor, hands on the hilts of the tanto, when a cylinder spun across her vision.

Doorway view of the lounge room.

Phuong, the novel Lin had given her in her hands, turning slowly towards the front of the apartment.

Bouncing and landing at her sister's feet, the steel cylinder flashed, caught by a rare shaft of sunlight. A nova grenade.

Phuong, soft-silhouetted by the sun, raising a hand, like she was trying to surrender—

—and the light came, incandescent, whiter hotter than the sun; Lin throwing her arm up, clenching her eyes, the light pouring through her eyelids, the light seeping into her skin her bones, the light seeping into her scream.

PART THREE
Neon Gods

The story of my life doesn't exist. Does not exist.
There's never any center to it. No path, no line.
There are great spaces where you pretend there used to be someone,
but it's not true, there was no one.

– Marguerite Duras, *The Lover*

CHAPTER

53

☆

It was their forty-fifth fight.

Beforehand, he told her of the Two Battles of the Broken Spear. Cross-legged, the other side of the low table, his sake held perfectly steady in his hand. Lin eyed it, willing him to down the drink.

He said: "[It was fifteen years ago. Chinese sanctions were beginning to hurt, and many countries had turned their face from Japan, out of fear. But the country was still peaceful, back then, the Japanese people united. I lived above my dojo with my wife, in a nice clean apartment. We had no children, that I remember.

"[My school, in appearance, was very much like the one we have here. I had many students, a high standing in the community. I lived a life of contentment, in karate, and with my family. This did not last, because such things can never last. I was visited by the Yakuza – the Yamaguchi-gumi clan – during class. There were four of these men. They spoke roughly, nor did they remove their shoes. My students were very

angry; I told them to stand aside, to hold their anger, while inside, mine rose. It was the incivility of these men, these Yakuza, that struck me the most. My reaction to this was the source of my first error, which flowed on to the two battles to follow.]"

He told his story with an even voice, eyes flat. The kind of eyes that betrayed not one strong feeling on any subject, because there were no strong feelings left to be had.

"[I told my students to restrain their anger, but I did not hold mine. I was prideful. The Yakuza told me I was to train their men for free, as payment. This town was under their protection, they said, the government no longer had the resources. The police, the fire department, the ration bureau, all undermanned and corrupt.]"

He paused to down his sake. Placed it on the table; she refilled it. Concentrating on holding her hands steady, fearful he'd use some kind of transcendental voodoo to detect the drug. But he wasn't looking at her, he was somewhere else, watching the story in his mind. He picked the cup up again and held it as before.

"[I did not listen to these men. I just gripped the red-tasselled longspear in my hand and stared at their shoes, on my tatami mat. They showed no fear, nor respect, and they did it all in front of my students. I later discovered the one who did all the talking was a second-lieutenant. He had a large square head, fat from arrogance and endless rice bowls. He smoked a cigarette and jabbed his finger in my face.

"[One moment, his finger was in my face, the next moment, I'd snapped it in a direction it was never meant to face. Then I put down his three companions. The longspear was a training spear, its tip blunted. I used it to break their arms, or ribs, or knees. The lieutenant swore he'd kill me. Said he'd burn my dojo to the ground, kill every student in the room, and kill my family. I broke his mouth with the flat of the spear, and had the students dump the men in the alleyway.]"

The master's eyes returned to Lin. "[This was my second mistake. What should I have done?]"

"Killed them all," she replied. "Pulled their pins. Dumped them in the car they drove to your dojo. Driven the car into the ocean on an isolated stretch of land. Then denied they ever came, when more men came. Probably wouldn't have fooled them. But better than a half-measure."

Her master nodded at her and downed his sake. She poured him another, double-handed.

He continued: "[They came back that night, to my apartment, of course. The second-lieutenant and a dozen men, all with guns. They kicked in my door. They broke the children's toys under their feet, knocked down my wife and held her up by the hair, screaming.]"

The master said it all without emotion. Like he was retelling the main scenes of a movie he'd watched, many years before.

"[I had been praying at my kamidana, and emerged to this scene. I had my samurai sword. It was little use against twelve men with guns. Worse still, with these men was the boss. I don't recall his name, only that his neck and his spine were tough. It took me three blows to separate his head from his body.

"[At the time, there was much fear in my heart. This is a weakness every warrior submits to when they take on a family and home. These things can be used by enemies to dilute the potency of one's martial prowess, they can cloud one's decision-making. The boss had my spear, the training spear, in his hands. He explained the things he was going to do to my wife, monstrous things, while I would be forced to watch. She stopped struggling as she listened to him speak, her face smeared with tears, too fearful anymore to even struggle.

"[She was quite young. Younger than me. Despite this, it was what you would call a love match. I don't remember her name, or how we came to be. All I know is the unforgivable selfishness of my decision to accept such a happiness.]"

"How— Why don't you know her name?" Lin asked.

His eyes came back to her again. "[I don't remember her because I had it wiped. Sentimentality, loss, regret, have no place in a warrior's mind. Memory is a chain that binds us to an eternal past. Memory is a flaw that stills our hand at the killing strike.]"

"But you remember her death – and your love."

"[Of course. The fight is the seed, the fight is the universe. The beginning and the end. I watched the battle, over and over, learning from it. To watch and to understand, I require the knowledge of my weaknesses at an intellectual level. In order to win.

"[Revenge, of course, was necessary. Not as an emotional response, as some claim it to always be. Rather, as an assertion of one's place in the cosmos, as a warrior. Vengeance helps to mould oneself into the perfect weapon. Vengeance focusses one's intent.

"[It is a delicate balance. Too much weighs one down, becomes baggage. Instead of reflecting on the martial art, one reflects on a different life: one as a husband, or a father, or a friend. Curating the memory is another art, that of the Omissioners. The one that adjusted me advised of the need to remember enough of the love I shared with my wife, so as to never make that mistake again.]"

He made to put down his tokkuri, the ceramic rat-at-tatting on the tabletop. A sheen in his eyes. The drug, ice-three, was not a popular one. Almost impossible to find on the street. The only effect it had was to multiply the potency of alcohol. Most people believed there were better ways to spend a high, than projectile vomiting and hours of missing time.

The master continued, his words starting to slur, running into each other. "[My love marked her for death. Selfish.]"

He sighed, brought himself back to the moment.

"[Finally, I made the correct decision. I attacked without hesitation. Three men I had struck down before the rest even reacted. The third man, death impulse in his trigger finger, raked the room with machine-gun fire, dead before he hit the ground.

"[More men fell, gunned down by a dead man, and I moved in close to the boss to deliver the death stroke. When I did, he revealed how he had become a boss. Overcoming the surprise of my assault, he *blocked my strike, the longspear breaking into two. He used both parts as weapons to counter-attack. He had been classically trained, the shape of his offensive quite beautiful. We were close and fast, so the other men could not fire their weapons. They drew blades, instead, to slash at me if our fight flowed into their reach.*

"[I had been struck twice this way, in the back. Once more by the boss, my front teeth broken. He was injured as well, a long gash on his arm, and so the fight found a space as we gasped for breath and faced each other, as we weighed the distances, as the instinct of the artist found pattern-counter-pattern to unfurl. It was then I saw my wife had been shot through the forehead by a stray bullet. The long stare of hers, I decided, was on me.

"[I looked around at the enemy. Still the boss, still five others remained, moving closer. It was then I made another correct decision. One that would ensure my victory. I turned and dove through the second-storey window. Then I ran, and ran.]"

Lin drank her own sake. "But. You said you cut his head off?"

"[Yes. Two years later, after I had prepared myself completely. It was my last act before leaving Japan. By that time the memory adjustment had taken away all unnecessary emotion, slid most of the events from my mind. But I made sure to tell the Omissioner I wanted to retain the knowledge of revenge. I had to make penance for my failure to think clearly, and thus my failure on the field of battle. The only thing that matters in life is to defeat every opponent.]" His glazed eyes, stutter-mouth pointed at Lin. "[S-sometimes battles may be lost. These are vital learning experiences. And to live—to live is never truly a defeat. If you are alive, your opponent has made an error. All that matters is to defeat every enemy.]"

Lin said nothing. There was nothing to say, when looking into the abyss of his beliefs.

The master pushed himself to his feet, unsteady. This confused him, momentarily looking down at his legs. Then he said: "[Now, we will fight.]"

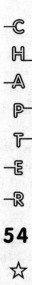

CHAPTER

54

☆

Bao Nguyen watched as Lin Thi Vu disappeared into the rain, her back bent against the storm, against the weight she always carried in her mind.

"You should tell her the truth, Uncle," said Bull Neck Bui, opposite, watching his former commander. "She deserves it."

Bao watched the smoke rise from the tip of his cigarette. "No one gets what they deserve in this country."

Bull, his large hands resting on the AK-47 on his lap, shook his head. "We're sending her to the jungle. It's time."

The traffic eased and the car nudged its way ahead. Bao watched the outlines of cars and beings against the neon, moving through the rain. He'd take the concrete jungle any time, over the rugged mountains, the thick unforgiving green in the valleys, the blasted Marscape of the plains. Here there was food. Just a bowl of rice, and his sunflower seeds. All his mind and body could handle, after the body horror of malnutrition and its desperate remedies. Bull had the opposite reaction. He ate everything when they got back, like starvation was right around the corner. He revelled in gluttony, treating every meal like a man's last before the firing squad.

Bao glanced at the iron box on the seat next to his former sergeant. Bull never spoke of the ghosts, either. He never said anything of how they sat there, at the corners of one's vision, watching. How they attached themselves. Reminding, reminding.

The car eased to a halt outside the clubhouse. Bao said: "Take the bones to our courier. Have them sent to Mosquito Brother's mother. Send money as well."

Bull nodded.

"The preparations?" ask Bao.

"We'll be ready," said Bull. He slapped his hand against the stock of his gun. "Just like old times."

"The old times were not so successful, Sergeant."

"Yeah," said Bull. "Shit leadership, in my opinion."

Bao looked over his sergeant. His powerful chest and neck. The thick fingers resting gently on his weapon. How he smiled with old knowledge at his former colonel.

"You have been spending too much time with the Australian, Sergeant."

"Well," Bull replied, smile fading. "I guess that's the plan, Uncle."

CHAPTER

55

☆

Bao Nguyen walked through the main floor of the headquarters. The floor was swept clean. Two of his soldiers were playing Vietnamese Chess, another four were playing dice. It was quiet, save the clacking of the dice.

Their eyes turned to him, expectantly. He said nothing, instead pressing a finger to his cochlear implant and subvocalising a password and series of commands. On-retina appeared the words every Bình Xuyên would see:

Withdraw to cell gathering points. Full weapons and hard currency. Wait for orders.

He went through the door to Lin's office. Herbert Molayson looked up as Bao entered, his face pale, a thin sheen of sweat on his skin. "[Ah, Mister Nguyen.]" The chains on his ankles clinked as he rose from his seat.

Bao said nothing. He moved over to the table where Herbert's guns lay, and slipped them into his pocket. He pointed the barrel of the type-

17 machine gun at the Englishman. Keeping one hand on the grip, with his other Bao slid the keys from his pocket and tossed them to Herbert.

"Just the floor chain," he said. "Keep your ankles shackled."

Herbert made to object, but after eyeing the gun and the man holding it, he sighed and did as he was told. Bao pointed at the door. Herbert hobbled over to it and out into the main room. With a look from Bao, the gangsters there gathered their weapons. Bao paused, mid-step, as images popped up, unasked, on-retina.

Nano-cam vision, at the bottom corner of his on-retina, showed the space outside the faded blue steel door of the clubhouse. Two men, not recognised by the system, were attaching something to the door and backing away quickly.

Bao had half turned, yelling "*Down!*" when the steel door of the headquarters blew inwards. Blinded, the force of the blast lifting him up, for a moment he felt suspended in mid-air, overwhelmed by the light and the sensation of floating, and then the moment passed and he was flying faster and faster, brighter and brighter until his head struck something hard.

"[Wake up, princess.]"

Bao groaned, then gasped as something struck his face, hard and sharp. His eyes flickered open, sight sound and smell rushing in. Smoke, and screams, and gunfire, and Herbert's face above him, blood covering one side, a half-mask of red. His face was twisted beyond recognition, a snarl.

"[Better. Now, darling. You're a smart little bastard,]" Herbert said, in a voice not his own. "[I'm sure you have another way out of this shithole.]"

Bao's English was fairly good, the product of years of private conversation with Lin. Good enough that he noticed that Herbert's accent had flattened, smothering the upper-class inflection.

Herbert picked him up as though he were made of straw, iron grip on his upper arms, and pulled Bao so he was sitting upright against his office wall. The Englishman rifled Bao's pockets.

Bao groaned again, tried to stop him, but Herbert slapped him. The sting jerked his mind back into the room. Smoke seeped under the closed door of Lin's office. Bullet holes were tattooed on the wall and door, more smoke seeping through them. Sub-machine guns barked in the next room, a shotgun too, *BOOM BOOM*.

Bao said: "Heat signatures," and faced the wall. Outlines popped up, shifting red-purple-orange forms. It didn't take long to figure out who was who, and what direction they were facing. Two Bình Xuyên remained, kneeling and firing just outside his door, while the other end of the room was alive with shifting outlines, pouring into the room, twenty – twenty-five at least.

Bao picked up his machine gun, lying between his legs. Herbert jumped to one side as Bao thumbed the dial to full auto and sprayed the room through the wall. Controlled bursts. *Bratatat, bratatat, bratatat.*

Outlines fell, replaced by more, shifting purple-red-orange outlines of legs and bodies, a twenty-headed gangster-monster, firing its guns.

Bao flattened himself as the reply came, the *boom* of shotgun and *bratatat* of sub-machine gun. Plaster exploded inwards over the room, glass shattered, bullets *whined* on metal. Bao crawl-crawled, his teeth gritted, and pushed open the door connecting to his office with the stock of the type-17. Yells and smoke from outside, the firestorm ebbing, heavy breathing next to him and Herbert was there, chin on the floor, double-barrel pistol in his hand, sweat and blood on his face.

With a mad grin, teeth shining, the Englishman said: "[Playing my fucking tune.]"

Bao turned over onto his back, feet facing the direction of the main room, and fired. No controlled burst this time, just full clip, raking across the room war scream forming at the back of his teeth, blood fire thrumming, coursing through his being and spat out through the barrel, war rage transmuted into howling metal—

—until the gun said *clicka clicka*, and silence fell with the plaster dust.

Herbert roared: "[That's the spirit!]"

Finger to his cochlear implant, chest rising and falling fast, Bao whispered the command phrase. There was a grind of metal on metal and the filing cabinet shifted forward. Bao crawled over to it and had his hand on the edge of the metal manhole when the door to his office burst open. His machine gun was pressed at an awkward angle against the ground; he just had enough time to look over his shoulder at a sweat-slicked gangster pointing a repeater shotgun at his face—

BOOM.

—the gangster's skull disintegrated into a spray of blood and brain, and Herbert was there, wrestling with the second man to enter the room. The Englishman hammer-punched him overhand with the butt of his pistol, the gangster's Uzi clattered to the ground. The man's face was bloodied, head lolling like a rag doll, as Herbert used the man's body to jam the door to the office closed.

Herbert stepped back and the gangster – wearing a spideriron vest and heavily tattooed shoulders – by some neural instinct, stayed on his feet, swaying. Herbert pointed his derringer and shot the man in the groin, the *BOOM* in the closed space of the room starting Bao moving again, swinging his legs into the manhole, lowering himself to chest level as the room erupted, brick matter spewing over the walls and the desk, the second gangster's head disappearing in red mist.

Bao dropped, rolled, and pushed himself upright. He was in a gloomy narrow brick corridor running along the back wall of the apartment block, built for precisely this purpose. Small ventilation shafts at the top of the corridor no more than a foot wide let the light slant in, the beams highlighting the motes of plaster Bao had brought down with him.

The Englishman, no longer Herbert, now a grunting swearing killer, landed and rolled. His hand against the wall, like Bao, he gave his optics a moment to adjust, raise the ambient light level, let him see where he was. The Englishman glanced down, holding his right arm out, furrowed with a bullet line – not deep, but bloody enough.

"[I fucking love this city,]" the man said, eyes shining in the gloom.

Bao whispered a command, and the filing cabinet above scraped back into place. He turned and jogged down the corridor. The big man swore and followed.

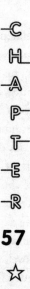

Passaic Powell entered the smouldering apartment. Two men in front, two behind in the corridor, two downstairs. On-retina, a green light blipped on, bottom-right-hand corner. The colonel was riding on his feed. Powell swallowed his distaste, the crawl of his skin at the knowledge someone else was under it, and looked around at what had been wrought.

A crater in the floor, still glowing, sides perfectly smooth, opened up a hole to the apartment below. Orange metal slag, dripping. The curtains opposite him flickered with flames. The rest of the space blackened, smouldering, smoke drifting out the shattered apartment windows. The space smelled foul, like sulphur and roasted meat. The heat made the men with him wince and shield their faces.

The house was playing the same part of an old pop song, over and over, caught in a loop. Garbled words then, '*Fly like a bird through the,*' then garbled again.

Belatedly, the sprinklers overhead sprang into action, dousing the space in a fine mist. Charcoaled objects crunched under his feet as he walked over to the bodies, water pitter-pattered on his homburg, dripped from the tip of his nose. One of the other men bent over the bodies, husks with arms up in defensive postures, fingers noses extremities burned away completely. The gangster poked at the bodies with a silver DNA pen. Skinny, gang tattoos, ghetto strut: Powell considered the sound the man's ankles would make, should he break them, *snick-snick*. No more strut, oh no, hobble-step.

The man said to Powell, "DNA [test confirmed. Ninety-nine point nine-nine. It's the bitch.]"

Powell raised a finger. "Hush, puppy. A better warrior has fallen, far better, hush hush."

The gangster swallowed his retort and eased himself away from the husk.

"Leave, puppy, one and two, *pad pad pad*, out the door."

The men left.

Powell knelt by the body of Lin Thi Vu. "Little rabbit, should have run, your bones are ashes. Drip-drop, the world weeps, drip-drip. Little rabbit, goodbye."

He leaned forward and placed a long, lingering kiss on the forehead of the dead warrior. His lips coated, tingling, with the still-hot ash.

He whispered, at the place where her ear once was. "Here's your rhyme, Rabbit."

"And so the veil falls
Revealing walls
Of cavernous halls
Valhalla calls."

As he leaned back, hands on his knees, he noticed a shimmer among the ashes. He slid it from the body, water running from it in a black trickle. Peeling back the spideriron jacket, he saw a book. He flipped back the jacket to protect it from the water, and ran his hand over it, gently.

"[What are you doing?]" asked a voice in Mandarin, displeased. Metallic, from the voice modulator. Powell's fingers twitched at the pain that shot through his throat, same as every time the colonel spoke through him. "[The English host and Bao escaped, get to the Old Quarter and manage.]"

Powell stood, slipping the book into a large pocket in his combat vest. As he left the ruins the song stopped, and the only sound that remained was the *hiss* as the water touched the corpses.

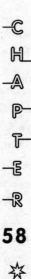

Phuong and Lin quick-stepped over the hot white sand, Lin swearing, Phuong laughing. They found a shady spot, lush green trees overhanging a narrow sand walkway at the edge of the beach.

"We should have brought our sandals," said Lin.

"Everything in this country is hot hot hot," said Phuong. "Especially the boys."

Lin rolled her eyes. "Mum should have warned us."

"She did warn us. You were sulking, headphones on, watching your dumb movies."

"They're not dumb."

"Hey-yah!" said Phuong, making an exaggerated martial arts pose.

Lin whacked her on the shoulder with the palm of her hand. They both smiled, both looked up the beach. It went for as far as they could see, pure white sand, crystal blue ocean, the curl of surf rolling up the long beach. No clouds overhead, sun low on the horizon, but hot, still hot. They slapped at sand flies and sweated.

A black dot in the distance. Mum with a parasol, picnic basket, huge towels, an e-reader. Don't go too far *she'd said, as she settled in with the book. They agreed and promptly went too far, screeching as they ran through inch-deep water that rushed up the beach after break of wave, trying to push each other into the deeper part, squealing as they threw cool globs of wet sand in each other's hair. Next thing they knew, Mum had become a black dot in a shimmering heat haze.*

"I wish we'd come here earlier," said Phuong.

"It sucks," replied Lin.

"What? It's awesome."

"Everyone here stares at us."

Phuong ran her hands along the sides of her body. "That's because I'm sexy." She, like Lin, was wearing a one-piece swimsuit. Hers purple, Lin's blue. Unlike Lin, Phuong's chest was already starting to come in; puberty, like everything else, coming to her quicker and easier. Lin pursed her lips and looked away, out at the ocean. She'd first seen it the day before, Mum finally saving enough for a train-trip and week at the coast. Mum couldn't afford the place during school holidays, but the girls made solemn faces and assured her they could afford to miss some school.

When she first set her eyes on the ocean her heart clenched, at its vastness, at its indifference. She felt a tightening in her chest again, now.

Voices and rough laughter came from down the path. Lin's chest clenched at that, as well. Boys sauntered into view, beach towels over shoulders, quieting when they saw the girls there. The first boy tall, long limbs, tanned skin, iconic Australian, nodded at them. Or at Phuong, to be precise. Clean white teeth, sun-bleached hair, freckles. With him two more boys, the second that looked like the younger brother of the first, the third solid, dark-haired, an angry tilt to his mouth, instantly glaring at Lin and Phuong.

The stocky one said, "It's the fucken Chinese invasion."

"We're Vietnamese!" retorted Lin, angrily.

"We're Australian, actually," said Phuong.

The stocky boy shouldered past the tall one, stood in front of Phuong. "You look Chinese."

The tall boy said, "They sound pretty Australian to me. Come on Simon, it'll be too hot to swim soon."

The angry one jerked his shoulder away from the tall boy's hand.

"My dad was a volunteer at Taipei," he said. "Fucken Chinese killed him."

"Simon," said the tall boy, warning-sympathetic tone, like he'd heard the story before.

"Shut up, Rob." Simon jabbed a finger at Phuong. "They're probably spies, like the ones they caught up in Sydney."

"I'm twelve," said Phuong, eyebrow raised.

"Doesn't matter!"

"Young Chinese spies, twelve," said Phuong, hands on hips, wiggling like Marilyn Monroe. "Invade Australian beach, seduce innocent Australian boys, overthrow government."

The next part happened quickly: the tall boy Rob, laughed, as did his younger brother. Phuong smiled at them, broadly, genuine. Simon got angry and pushed Phuong, who stumbled back and plomped down on her butt.

And Lin, silent, fists clenched through the whole exchange, finally exploded, running full tilt into the boy. Not quite sure of the attack she was trying to make, but fortuitously stumbling in the sand, pitching forward, the top of her head hitting his face. An ugly crunching sound; a tangle of limbs in the sand under the shade, Phuong and Rob pulling them apart.

The boy, holding his bloody nose, struggled to get at Lin. Rob threw Simon back down into the sand. "Enough! They're not the bloody enemy, mate. Think yer old man would want you fighting girls?"

Simon looked up at him, eyes wet and furious. But he stayed down.

Rob turned to Phuong. "Sorry."

Phuong took his offered hand and allowed him to help her up. She smiled and said, "It's okay. Thank you."

Lin stood to one side, pushing herself to her feet, ignored completely.

"Not easy, without an old man," said Rob.

"Seriously." Phuong tilted her head, smile fading. "I do understand. It's okay."

Rob helped his friend up, who death-stared at Lin, but otherwise allowed himself to be pushed along the path by the taller boy.

They walked down, out onto the sand, and the tension in Lin's chest ebbed.

Until Rob turned and said, "Wanna hang out with us?"

And Phuong, before Lin could respond, said, "Great!" and skipped down the sand after them.

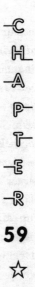

CHAPTER

59

☆

Dull throbbing pain, cotton wool thoughts. Lin Thi Vu groaned and tried to see where she was, but her eyes were stuck together. After some effort, just one popped open.

The first thing she saw was Bao Nguyen leaning over her, cigarette dangling from his lips.

Then the strangest thing happened. He smiled. Leaned away, stamped out his smoke in a nearby ashtray. He said: "[Get the nurse,]" softly, at someone nearby, and hovered over her again, going to touch her forehead, then withdrawing his hands, uncertain. "*Little sister,*" he said, in English. "*Can you hear me?*"

Lin assumed it was a dream. Dry lips, peeling away top from bottom, as she made to speak. She moved her head away from his hand. "I'm not fucken deaf," she said. Tried to, anyway, but all that came from her lips was a hoarse: "*Fuck*".

Bao shook his head, evidently pleased by her response. Up closer,

317

he was blurred, like he'd gone out of focus.

She looked around the room, her vision clearing. White walls, bleeping equipment, no windows, sterile steel surfaces. Water, on the side table. She reached for it, suddenly aware of how parched she was. Her head spun with the effort and she closed her eyes, sucking in air through her teeth. She couldn't even raise her arm from the bed. All she could move were her eyes. Moved them to see one arm, resting on top of white sheets, encased in a translucent cast. The skin underneath fever red.

"Water," she croaked. Her strength fading already, the room spinning.

"[Here,]" said Bao. He held a glass to her lips, gently easing her head up off the pillow.

Before she drank, an image blink-flashed into her mind. She asked: "Phuong?"

Bao, out of focus, said nothing, tipping the cup, making her drink instead. She tried to drink deeply; he said: "[Not too much.]"

She coughed the water, pain racking her chest, until the room become a blur of colour, and of sound, of sheets rasping against skin, a unified blur, and then darkness.

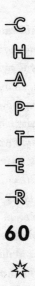

CHAPTER 60

✴

They pushed into the small hotel room, relieved at the cool within. Phuong and Lin flopped down on one of the twin beds. Kylie removed her hat and placed it on the table next to the door, sighing with relief.

"You girls were away a long time. Have fun?"

Phuong and Lin lay face to face, body postures mirrored. Lin frowning at her sister, Phuong smiling, her thoughts far away.

"Girls?" asked Kylie.

"Phuong kissed a boy," said Lin.

"Lin!" exclaimed Phuong, now frowning as well.

Kylie put a hand on her hip. "Phuong?"

The twins looked over at her, sat up together, arms around their knees. Kylie was wearing a one-piece, as well. Round hips, shapely.

Phuong said, "He was tall and handsome."

Kylie raised her eyebrows. "And?"

"His name is Rob. He tasted like the ocean."

Kylie said, "Hmmm," her eyes a little distant. "Sounds dreamy."

"He showed me how to body surf. He has strong arms."

Kylie sighed. "Maybe I should start dating again."

Lin, mouth screwed tighter as the conversation went on, said, "You're not angry?"

Kylie looked a little taken aback. "Honey. You girls are becoming women. I want you to meet nice boys."

"Rob's brother liked you," said Phuong. "You could have kissed him."

"Gross. Boys are gross."

"Not all," said Kylie. "Just most of them. You'll find a nice one, one day."

"Never!"

"Maybe a girl," said Phuong, nudging her sister's shoulder with her own.

"Shut up." Lin was red-faced now, mouth a tight line.

Kylie watched the exchange, her head tilted a little. "Hmm. Well. Either way, avoid the bastards, hold on to the ones that taste like the ocean." She winked at Phuong, who giggled.

"Now," said Kylie. "I'm hungry. Hot chips for lunch?"

Phuong jumped off the bed. "Yeah! Let me come with you!"

"Of course. Lin?"

Lin Lashley flopped back on the bed, eyes on the ceiling. She grunted.

"Okay," said Kylie, unflustered. "Watch a movie, if you want. We'll be back soon."

Lin said nothing, eyes fixed on the ceiling as they grabbed their towels and left.

The twins crashed out early that night. Exhausted by the sun and the excitement. Lin dreamed, but her mind went tic-tic, tic-tic, like always. In the demi-monde, someone trying to pull her down into the vast, fathomless ocean. Trying to scream, but unable, pressure building on her chest as she was pulled, down and down and down. Her eyes blinking open, fear still in her throat for three-four seconds until she realised it was her sister's arm, flung out, hugging her close.

"You okay, honey?" Kylie was looking over at her. Face lit by *the backwash of light from her e-reader, soft, like a dream. Lin said nothing.*

Kylie put down her book and soft-footed over. She crouched down on Lin's side of the bed. "You were whimpering. Bad dreams?" Kylie's hard fingers softly brushing Lin's cheek. "Honey."

Lin turned her face, moved by the gentle hand. Looking at Kylie's face, the resentments faded. The tight ball of thought, coalescing in her mind, dissipated.

"Sometimes," Lin whispered.

"Yes?"

"I dreamed I was drowning."

"Oh. It's your first time here." Kylie ran a hand through her hair. "The ocean can be a scary place."

"Yeah. No. I've had this dream before. Keep having it."

"Oh." The woman was silent, thinking, as she rested her hand on her daughter's head. "I'm sleepy, honey. Want to sleep with me?"

"Yes."

Kylie picked up her daughter, careful not to disturb Phuong, picked her up easily, with strong arms. Lin, close enough to the dream world to forget the girl she always pretended to be, nestled her head into her mother's chest.

Kylie sang the lullaby she always sang when Lin was little, just arrived; the song she'd sung every night to put her whimpering daughter to sleep. Kylie's voice was clear and soft. The lullaby an old rock ballad called Flame Trees, about a town that never changed.

Kylie made small laps of the room, walking slowly, singing about the town and about lost love. Lin tightened her embrace.

As Lin had grown older she'd realised it wasn't really about love. No not at all. Flame Trees was about the impossibility of return. About changing so much you were no longer recognisable, even to yourself.

But she didn't care at the moment. All Lin cared about was the body memory of warmth and belonging and trust.

Kylie laid her down on the bed, pulled the sheet up to her chest. The woman's voice carried the rest of the song and Lin drifted on the waves of the sound and the love that held it.

Her eyes were heavy as it came to an end. It was a comfort, this song, this woman. The dark urgencies that whispered to Lin quieted.

"This is your country, honey," her mother whispered. "It will always be your country." She placed a hand over Lin's heart. "I'll never leave you, no matter what happens. You'll always have a mother, always. I'll never abandon you, not like... I'll never abandon you."

"Promise?"

"Promise."

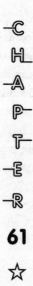

61

When Lin opened her eyes the second time, Bao was still there. Legs crossed, ankle resting on knee, looking down at a flexiscreen on his lap. Smoke trailed from the cigarette in his hand. His usually full, wavy hair tousled, lank, his face pale, bags under his eyes.

"Phuong is dead."

He looked up at her. Tired glazed eyes taking a moment to focus on her and her question. "[Yes.]"

"And Kylie."

"[Yes.]"

Lin Thi Vu looked at the ceiling. White paint bubbled with moisture. Silence, bar the subdued beeping of medical equipment. The crackle of tobacco as Bao sucked on his cigarette. She felt light as air. Free of her body, somehow.

"Remember we discussed the X-37?"

"[Yes.]"

"I want it."

Bao hesitated. Lin considered her arguments. The threats and the pleading she could use, to get it. But finally Bao said: "*Yes,*" and it sounded like a resignation.

"I want to see the Omissioner as well. I want this shit out of my head."

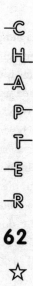

CHAPTER

62

☆

The surgeon was Vietnamese. Young, lean, didn't blink much. He told her the implications of the operation, matter-of-factly.

"[The X-37 Changhe Infiltration Endoskeleton was never approved for battlefield use because of its side effects. It causes acute strain on the joints, even if all the joints are prosthetic. This results in severe arthritis, especially after frequent use. The X-37 increases the risk of heart attack. Embolism, stroke, certain cancers – these all become more likely. These side effects are manageable with correct medication or elective transplants. The financial cost of mitigating the side effects is extremely high. These problems are not the primary reason it was declined for widespread military use. The main reason – and one that cannot be corrected – is premature ageing.]"

Next to him on a stainless-steel tray was the X-37. Didn't look like much. A small sphere the size of a marble, metal, colour of burnished copper. Out of it, myriad strands, three feet long and not much wider than a hair, clear, catching the light and glimmering a rainbow hue.

He indicated the system with a curt gesture, "[At rest, your reflexes will be significantly improved, your gross motor skills calibrated and perfected. It will operate continuously; resting mode should take no more than five years from your expected life span.]"

"[Why?]" asked Bao.

"[Hyper-metabolism,]" replied the doctor. "[Bad for the heart.]"

"And battle mode?" asked Lin.

"[In full battle mode, you will exchange approximately one month of your life for each minute of operation.]"

Bao shook his head, gently, to himself.

The doctor looked to Lin for a reaction, so she said: "Right. Anything else?"

"[I've outlined the major implications.]"

"Yeah, well. Better get started."

The young man looked at her. Really looked at her, for the first time. "[Bao says you are doing this for the Việt Minh.]"

Lin nearly said *does he now?* But the doctor's eyes had taken on a fervour she'd seen, often, when locals had had too much to drink, and conversation turned to the occupation. She shrugged. "Sure."

"[You are Australian?]"

"I'm not anything."

"[You are a hero, for making this sacrifice.]"

"I just want to kill some motherfuckers that need killing."

The doctor smiled without mirth. "[And you will.]"

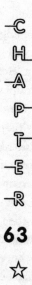

The facility was underground. Bao told her they were still in Hà Nội, outside the Old Quarter, but didn't elaborate. She didn't press him further because she didn't care. Her focus was getting well after the procedure. They'd moved her from the room with a shit-tonne of monitors, to a room with slightly fewer, and a couple of plants. They gave her some shots to speed her recovery, nanomeds normally reserved for high-ranking Chinese military, to strengthen her body in preparation for surgery.

Her injuries were severe. Burns to at least fifty per cent of her body. She'd lost an eye. The woman looking back at her in the mirror was a stranger. Red, blistered skin smeared in shining ointment, and that was the best of it. The worst was the translucent cast, growing new skin. Right arm up to the shoulder; half of her head, like the Phantom of the Opera, but see-through, so her horror remained visible.

They'd given her an eye transplant immediately. Top-of-the-line, some enterprising worker in a Chinese prosthetics plant somewhere, nimble fingers. Hadn't been personalised to her; the iris factory red. Red eye black eye, staring back, displaced objects in a displaced person. Her broken nose had been reset; she'd asked them to make it look different, said she needed a new identity now Lin Thi Vu had died. The doctor had left the kink in the bridge of her nose. Just a little thing, but that, plus the bald head, the ominous eye colour she'd decided to keep, made her look like a different woman.

No drink, no drugs, the Vietnamese doctor had said, sternly. Only the pain medication he'd prescribed. On the small table near her bottle of sake and a dropper of ice-seven. She gave the neck of the bottle four drops, then took a long swig. Watching herself as she did so. Radiant glow flowing through her, dulling the pain in her limbs-knees-shoulders. Her sternum, especially. That's where the unit had been implanted, the squid-like fibre tentacles programmed to grow throughout her body, wire themselves to her nervous system. Keyhole surgery by a steel-limbed machine, while the doctor stood by and watched. He said: "[You won't feel anything,]" and pressed a button. Less than three blinks and she'd gone out under the anaesthetic.

She felt it. When she woke, an itch she couldn't fucking scratch, down deep inside, as though in her bones, as the X-37 adjusted itself to her system. Stinging, fierce, every few minutes. Reminded her of a bluebottle sting she'd had, both thighs, a little girl at the beach wailing in agony, burning, until Kylie had put her in a hot bath.

The red eye looked back at her. A fortune. A fucking fortune, Bao had spent on her. Shihan, the system, the recovery. No one else would get what she had. No sense to it, she swallowed her shame with another swig of the bottle.

Black-eye red-eye staring back at her. Trying to gel the doppelgänger in the mirror with the woman, here, living in her skin. Two strangers.

She took another drink. No buzz from the alcohol, the glow of the ice-seven already fading. Annoyed, she put the bottle down.

Fragments of memory, from the attack. She hadn't re-watched it via her memory feed. But the splinters worked themselves deeper, made her recall things she wanted submerged.

…Phuong, bathed in an aura of light, a terrible scream forming on her lips…

…dragging herself into the bathroom, up into the bath…

…section of skin sloughing off, her remaining eye wide, raw horror as part of her forearm separates and slaps against the white ceramic…

…oh god when they pulled the orangutan fur back it looked like a slender man with ulcerous skin, and the Mosquito Brother's good eye moved in its orbit wildly…

…black, fading in and out, medical alerts pulsing on-retina, a scroll of medical information Lin couldn't follow, the voices of men, in the apartment. Every fragment of her focussed on the pain, the feeling of being burned alive – and it took everything not to scream, biting into her good arm instead, whimpering, blood in her mouth; whatever tears within her evaporated in the blast. She tried to turn on the water, blipping blindly at the control panel, mashing the buttons. Biting deeper into her arm in frustration, then the sprinklers started, soaking her clothes, blessed cool on her face, her arms…

The door to her suite opened and Bao walked in. He was looking at the bottle on the table when he asked: "[Ready?]"

Lin picked up a conical bamboo hat sitting next to it and placed it gingerly on her head. It covered the cast, the red ragged burns, left only the bottom half of her face showing. She eased on a long-sleeved peasant smock. A poor woman in a crowd: anonymous.

"Ready."

"[Are you sure about this?]" he asked, his voice quiet.

"Bao."

"[I know.]" He nodded, to himself. "[I know.]"

He held the door and followed her from the room.

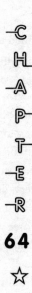

CHAPTER

64

☆

Bao Nguyen drove them out to the burial site in an old hydrocell after midnight. Battered, the auto-drive not working, the vehicle was inconspicuous. The precaution likely unnecessary. He was confident the gravesite would be safe. No one had figured the connection between Lin and Phuong – not the gangsters on one side, or the mourners on the other. Long ago he'd paid to have their immigration records wiped. An easy thing to do given the surfeit of Vietnamese mid-level bureaucrats looking for good cigarettes, or a silk dress for the wife, or some relief from a gambling debt. Still, paranoia is an ally, in an occupied land. So he drove that shitty car carefully, slowly, along dirt roads, through paddy field and marshland on the outskirts of the city.

Bao looked over at the young woman. Her face, part-hidden under the hat, was smoothed. Hidden again by the blast damage, the blistered and melted skin. Multiple masks, old ones she'd worn for so long, pretending for so long, she'd become the thing she'd pretended to be. A fearful young woman now inhabiting the role of fearless gangster.

He eased the car to a halt, tyres crunching in the dirt. No other cars nearby, only lights in the distance, some small peasant homes clustered at the edge of the fields. He popped the door and exited; Lin did the same. It was silent out in the stifling night, save for the sharp cries of the geckos, the play of the wind over the rice fields.

They stood together before the narrow road, winding into the cemetery. Lin seemed hesitant. She asked, in English: "[How long ago was the funeral?]"

"Three weeks now."

"[You were there,]" she said. Not a question.

"Yes."

"[I want to see it.]"

"Little sister. I don't—"

"[I want,]" she said, voice tight, "[to see. My sister's and Kylie's funeral.]"

Bao put a finger to his cochlear implant. "I'll send it over. My point of view."

They saw two worlds. The day a doppelgänger of the night, the same location, though a different place entirely. Down the river of the past, a place that would never again be, superimposed on the eternal present. Ghosts moved through the darkness, through the daylight. Bao closed his eyes. The hard light of the day broke against the back of his eyelids. The sky was clear blue, breathless. It'd been many months since he'd seen a cloudless sky, like that day. The heat suffocating, the sun white.

His cochlear implant directed him over to his point in the middle of the funeral procession, where he'd walked with the mourners, three weeks before.

The procession was long. They'd assume he was another war widower, paying respects to Phuong with so many others. Bao, a harmless old man, in about the middle of the line. Men and women like him, wearing their age across their shoulders, on their brows, the age that accrued to those outliving a wife, a husband, a child.

The crowd wore white tunics of mourning, and conical bamboo hats. Plodding in silence, through a raised dirt path between reeds bleached white by heat. Funeral banners fluttered above the heads of the cortège that advanced, cloaked in a swirling cloud of red dust. Two altars carried on the backs of mourners, one with the picture of Phuong, the other of Kylie. Bao had never been to a joint funeral, but he'd heard the gentle whispers of the bereaved earlier, saying the Chinese husband had insisted on it.

Bao could see Xin Huan, Phuong's widower, up ahead. Huan wore a white suit, his head was bare. The man once had strong features: an imperial jawline, broad shoulders. Bao could see none of those now. Just a soul who didn't know where it was anymore, face red with heat and grief and loss. Walking backwards, in front of the procession, as was the custom. Lost and alone and desperate in his isolation.

A monk was next, at the head of the crowd, swathed in orange robes. Near him, men and women who could not have been relatives, as Phuong had none that anyone could locate. No white faces from Australia, either, had come to see Kylie. There was no one here to contact them, who knew of her relations. A sad and foolish woman, dying in this foreign land, for a war that was not hers.

Then the altars, then two black hearses, rolling silently. Behind them the long remainder of the mourners, winding back through the fields, shoes shuffling the dust, white apparitions in a heat that made them shimmer.

Two women near the front ran past Huan and rolled in the dust, wailing. White clothes stained red with the dirt. Sobs passed through the crowd, a ripple of grief.

"[What are they doing?]" asked Lin. Her voice thin.

Bao started. Words, from a shadow walking next to him, a shadow from the future, travelling back to the past, to witness.

"*They are opening the road to death, so their spirits are not lost.*" He whispered the words, some part of his mind still in the past, worried the ghosts around him would hear, thinking him insane.

The procession reached the graves and gathered around them. Bao found a place where he could see it all, past the shoulders of a group of women. Huan was opposite, not looking at the holes in the ground, his chest rising and falling visibly, straining, as he tried to look at something out over the horizon. At some alternate world, some denial of the two corpses being lowered by rope into the cool earth, near his feet. Bao felt a fragment of emotion, one finger pressing on his chest, to look at the man's grief. He blinked and thought of Khe Sanh instead, and the corpses piled like fish washed ashore after the waters are poisoned. Heaped atop each other, pale skin glistening in the rain and—

He blinked again. The pressure on his chest eased. He looked across at the Chinese officer with dead eyes.

The monk stepped forward and his voice, though quiet, rang clear in the silence of that place:

"Those who had many friends and relatives but
died lonely
Mandarins in exile
Those who died on the battlefield
Students who died on the way back from exams
Those who were buried hurriedly with no coffin
and no clothing
Those who died at sea under thunderstorms
Merchants
Those from foreign lands unable to return
Those who died with a shoulder hardened by too
many bamboo poles carried on it
Prostitutes
Innocent souls who died in prison

All spirits in the jungle, in the stream, in the
shadows, beneath a bridge, outside a pagoda, in
the market, in an empty rice field, on a sand dune
You are cold and you are fearful
You move together, young ones holding the old
We offer you this rice gruel and fruit nectar
Do not fear
Come and receive our offering
We pray for you, we pray."

The monk stepped back, one hand holding his orange robes out of the dust. The red lacquer coffins were lowered into the earth. There was a shifting sudden movement, near the graves, and two Chinese officers Bao had not seen before that moment appeared next to Huan, their hands on his upper arms. Huan's eyes fluttered, his body swayed, his skin pallid. But he said nothing, still shed no tears, as the men led him away.

The other mourners followed, slowly.

Lin's ghost remained. It stepped across the grave, to the other side, near where Huan had stood in that other world. She pulled her bamboo hat from her head and let it fall to the earth. Slowly, she sank to her knees, and Bao opened his eyes...

The past blinked away like tears, and he was left alone with the girl. The moon let him see her face, the shine of the burn, the shine of something else in her eyes, for a moment looking to the horizon, like Huan.

Her eyes tracked down to the graves and she stilled. Bao said nothing. The lizards cried out. He waited for her, the heat of the night making the sweat bead on his forehead. He wet his lip, to tell her it was time to leave this place when—

—a great sob came from the girl's chest. Her lips parted, though she wanted to say something, but the only language she had was grief. Tears welled in her eyes and Bao felt the pressure on his heart again, never having seen this girl cry.

"*Phuong.*" The voice that came from her was not hers. It was a broken thing, filled with pain.

Bao swallowed, the pressure on his chest increasing, and took a step towards her. He stopped himself as she bent forward, her hands grasping at the dirt. Taking handfuls of it.

"[Mum,]" she said quietly, and she leaned forward, pressing her face into the ground. She sobbed, waves of her grief breaking and flowing out through the shudder of her back, through the wails she mouthed into the earth. Choking on the pain, on the dirt *sig sig sig*, and her moan, her moan *aaaaaaaaaaaa*, that entered his bones and left an ache that remained for days.

"[Mummy.]"

Bao covered his mouth with the back of his hand. Lin raised herself to her knees again, her face a mask of red dirt. Tear tracks already forming in it. She looked up at the sky.

"[*Mummy!*]"

Bao Nguyen bit into the back of his hand, his heart quietly breaking, as Lin Thi Vu ate of tears, and red dust, and sorrow.

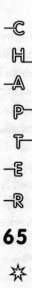

CHAPTER 65

Three years later men in suits had knocked at the door. Inexpensive suits, sweating in the sun, dead-eyed as they spoke. Officious in the way they held their data-screens, proprietorial in the way they stalked around the small home. The worst sort of bureaucrat: the immigration official. Outside, in the street, a police car idled.

Kylie asked if they wanted coffee or tea, they said no thank you, and sat at the kitchen table without asking.

Kylie sat with them, hands twisting in her apron. Phuong as well, hands folded, staring at the men. Lin, in the doorway, watching unnoticed.

A few moments of quiet while the men prepared their words, and Kylie waited for them to be spoken. Cars droned in the distance, their budgie trill-trilled in the next room.

"There's no easy way to say this," said one. Older, clearly the senior of the two, dandruff on his shoulders.

Kylie waited, lips pressed together, too scared to speak, to prompt his next sentence.

He said it anyway. "The refugee application for," he paused and looked down at his screen, "Lin Lashley and Phuong Lashley has been rejected."

Kylie seemed unsurprised. Though some dark expectation had been realised. She held her chin up. "I'll appeal."

"You've exhausted all your appeals." He looked at the screen again. "This is the last, from the refugee review tribunal." Then he looked at her and said, "It has been twelve years."

"I'm aware," Kylie said, through gritted teeth.

"There was never any documentation provided for the claimants, no birth certificates."

"They were from an orphanage."

"We are very sorry."

"Are you?"

"I beg your pardon?"

Kylie folded her arms. "Are you sorry?"

"Well, it's out of our hands."

"I asked you a question, mate. Are. You. Sorry?"

The younger man looked uncomfortable, shifting in his seat. The mask of tired indifference fell from the face of the older man. He focussed on Kylie for the first time. "Your wards have grown up here, with full access to education and health services. You've worked the system better than most."

Kylie slapped him. The wet slap of skin, loud in the room. Sprang up in her chair, leaned across the table, and full-palmed him up the side of his head. Lin's eyes widened, she'd never seen Kylie lift a hand against another, never heard her raise her voice, save for when she was barracking for Australia in the cricket.

For a moment Kylie looked about as shocked as the official did, hand coming up to his cheek. "Wards?! They are my daughters!" She stepped around the table and slapped him again. "Come in here like this." SLAP.

"In my house." SLAP. "My house!" She screamed at the man as she struck him, the other bureaucrat trying to hold her arms. Something deep inside Kylie had torn loose. Her soul, raging, throwing itself against the walls of her being. Phuong pulled at her mother, face red, eyes wet, hugging-restraining her mother, trying to. The screen door banging open and two police officers rushing in, crowd-control voices, yelling at her to BE CALM and STEP BACK.

Finally, Phuong pulled her mother away and Kylie leaned back against the kitchen sink, grasping at it like she was trying to hold herself up. Red-faced, she screamed, "Out of my house! Get out of my house, you animals!"

One of the police officers, grey moustache, uncharacteristic, gave her a mercy. "Alright, then," he said, hand on the chest of the immigration official. "You've delivered the judgement, as required. Thank you, sir." He moved his hand to indicate the door.

The official, hand still to his face, his bottom lip split, bleeding, said indignantly, "She assaulted me."

"Yes, sir."

"Arrest her."

"These are tense situations, sir. You need to exit the premises so we can defuse the situation."

"I—"

"Sir," the cop said, crowd-control tone returning to his voice.

The immigration official dropped his hand from his face, held his head up. "I will be pressing charges, officer."

"Yes, sir. Now." Again, he indicated the door. The official glared at Kylie, and left the house, younger man in tow.

Something passed between the two cops; the younger man nodded and followed the officials.

The cop looked at Kylie. "I'm Sergeant Dunning, Miz Lashley."

Kylie was trying to hold it together. Hugging Phuong, her daughter's cheek pressed against her chest. Lin, still half-hidden, watched as Kylie looked at the cop. Plaintive. Bottom lip trembling. Looking at the officer like a drowning woman does a boat on the horizon.

The cop wet his lips, moustache moving up down. Thinking, hand resting on his belt. "You'll get two weeks. You're entitled to it. I'll talk to the agent. You won't need to worry about charges." He sighed. "But you need to come to terms with this, for the sake of your daughters."

"I can't—" Kylie started, stopping herself, voice shaking.

The cop removed his hat, placed it under his arm. Easier to see his age, like that, the lines on his face, the grey in his hair.

"We're doing this every day. It's the law now." He cleared his throat, shifted on his feet. "My son-in-law was deported last month. It is—" He sighed again, moustache moving as he worked his lips. A hundred things left unsaid. Instead, he said, "There are no exemptions, Miz Lashley." He placed his hat back atop his head, nodded at Phuong, and left.

The screen door rattled shut.

Kylie sat back against the sink and wept, ragged, her shoulders shaking. Phuong hugged her, and told her it was okay. Lin watched from the doorway. She'd never seen her mother cry.

Kylie looked up at Lin, eyes water-blurred, finally realising she was there. Phuong too, crying with her mother. Lin backed away until the doorframe took them out of her sight. Turned and ran through the back door so the sounds of their fear were gone from her ears. Ran, under the burning sun, until the pounding of her shoes on sun-baked asphalt, and the pitch of her breathing hard in her ears, filled her mind.

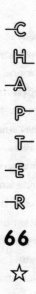

CHAPTER

66

☆

Lin Thi Vu glided, now. Every moment smooth, crisp, precise. Her body out in space, limbs in place, before her mind even realised it. She hadn't even arced up the system yet, tried the dial on ten, but when she moved she felt sinuous, strong, unfettered: a panther, a predator, a warrior, a god.

She glided through the front room of the bar, Le Samourai, second floor of a towering apartment complex in Yên Hoà district. Nine million people in nine square kilometres, skyscrapers choking the sky, the most densely populated place on earth. Not a bad place to hide. A holo-greeter at the doorway. European woman, purple mini-skirt, prodigious bust, welcoming, flirting in Vietnamese. Dark interior, room for thirty, the landscape of a dense cityscape painted along one wall, holotype three-dimensional in blues and purples and reds. Cigarette smoke, jarring K-pop playing over the speaker system, and circular red neon set into the roof giving the space the subdued, foreboding light of the demi-monde. Female bartender, precise eyebrows, nodded at Lin when she entered.

Around ten men and women in three groups in the bar. Bare shoulders, beer, muted conversation over card games; all Bình Xuyên. Two of the groups were like that, no different from the other; the third was not a group, just a man, crumpled white suit; a big man, hair slicked back, fat cigar in his mouth, watching cricket on a tai screen down one end of the bar. Herbert – or, to be precise, the Englishman formerly known as Herbert – chomped on his cigar, glancing at her through his yellow-tinted glasses as she entered, and quickly returned his attention to the cricket.

Lin hesitated, considered talking to him, then decided to deal with the main issue first. She walked up the stairs behind the bar.

The office above was basic: brown fauxwood desk and chairs, sandbags lined against the outside wall, up to the level of the window. The smell of cigarettes. Bull Neck Bui, near corner, drinking a bottle of beer. A cooling unit near his feet, magazine clips and grenades piled next to it. Bao, at the desk, half-bottle of brandy, smoke haze, eyes shining as she closed the door behind her.

Lin said nothing, took a chair, and pulled out her cigarettes.

"[Looked in on your bird from time to time,]" said Bull. "[Barry's fine.]"

Lin paused for a moment before lighting her cigarette. "Appreciated, Bull."

He nodded.

"[You said you wanted certain modifications to your memory,]" said Bao.

The presence of Bull, behind her, made Lin hesitate. She lit her cigarette. "This why I'm here?"

"[Everything needs to be in place.]" He prompted her: "[So?]"

"I want to be—to be unencumbered when I fight."

He waited.

"No more addictions – booze and the drugs. They are a weakness."
Bao nodded.

"This game, Fat Victory, in my head. I want it out."

"[Of course.]"

"I'm sick of drinking Larue beer."

Bao shook his head. "[They did not miss the opportunity to slip product placements for a Chinese-owned brewery.]" He sipped his brandy, looking her over. "[This is fine. We have an excellent Omissioner working for us. The best. This procedure takes a few hours, and these things you wish to change, will change.]" Bao gestured with his cigarette. "[We can wait until this procedure is done, for your wounds to heal. It is good, for a period, to let the Green Dragon think they have won their battle, and for Colonel Peng to believe all his loose ends dead or driven out. This quiet is our ally. But only so much. Too long and our funds dry up, the community loses faith, and idle men drift away. At some point we are no longer a gang anymore, just barflies nursing a grievance, telling each other fairy tales about revenge. Eventually the memory fades, of their wrongs, and of who we are.]"

"There's more," said Lin. "I want to be—to be streamlined."

Bao stilled, watching her with twinkling eyes. "My master," she continued. "He had the parts of his life removed, certain traumatic experiences, so he could focus on his art. His life mission."

"[Certain traumatic experiences,]" Bao repeated, tongue rolling over the vagueness of the statement.

Lin took a deep breath. "Family. Friends. Extraneous material."

"[Your master,]" said Bao. "[Was a mad man.]"

"He was the greatest fighter I knew."

"*Was*," Bao replied, curtly. He took a breath and cracked his sunflower seeds, popping them into his mouth. His concern evident, to Lin. His careful gaze now rapid, flicking back to her. "[You are not a machine, Silent One. Human beings cannot simply be *streamlined*.]"

"Bullshit," she replied. "Happens to Chinese troops every day."

"[Not what you are asking for, it does not. This thing you want is a butcher's work, and the people I hire are not butchers. The people for this work are such like the creators of Fat Victory. Mad scientists making monsters.]"

Lin sensed concern, a softness, in Bao since the burial. She didn't like it. "Monsters," she said, eyebrow raised in disdain. "Monsters." She indicated the window with her chin. The forest of skyscrapers. Pyres of smoke in the distance.

"The monsters are winning, in case you haven't noticed. The fuck we doing here, if not to drive these people out?"

"[Not like this,]" was all he said.

She made to retort, but he held up his hand, eyes hard. "[Enough. This discussion is over. You have the X-37. You are the most lethal warrior in this city.]"

Lin stubbed her cigarette out. "That's not enough."

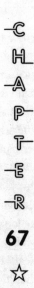

67

☆

Lin demanded and received a bottle of sake at the bar. An idea forming in her mind, she glided over to where Hermann Hebb was sitting, still watching the cricket.

"Why are you here?" she asked.

Hermann didn't even look up at her when he answered: "Fuck off. Not interested."

Lin clenched her jaw. He thought she was a hooker. "Herbert. Hermann. It's Lin."

His eyes flicked back to her face and paused there. He grunted. "Oh. You. Your head is a fucking horror show."

"Cheers."

Eyes back on the screen, he said: "Now shut it. Third innings at Leeds."

"You in the gang now?"

"Your boss says I owe." Hermann shrugged. "So I owe. I can't leave, anyway. The other guy – Herbert – passport's been cancelled. He's wanted by the cops. No ship'll sail with me on it. So," he said, waving his cigar at the screen. "Cricket and booze. Until the big man names his price, or sells my pieces to the black market." He didn't look at her as he said it all. If he wanted to put out the impression he didn't give a shit about any of it, it was a convincing one.

"The other guy. He ever gonna come back?"

Hermann looked at her, bloodshot eyes, like always, but now with the veil of violence. Like so many men she met on these streets, hard and shiny, assessing every person they met as prey.

"He's gone," he said.

She looked over him, his ragged tough guy insouciance. "But this isn't real."

"Real." He smiled without humour. "No one's fucking real, darling. You should know that better than anyone."

She said nothing.

They watched the cricket. Lin tuned in her implant, listened to the commentary, let it wash over her. She finished her sake, poured another, smoked another cigarette. Couldn't concentrate on the game. Kept glancing at the score and promptly forgetting it. She swore under her breath and blipped off the sound.

"Herbert. Hermann."

He didn't look at her. "Shut it. Cricket."

"Listen, dickhead: want to earn your pass with Bao?"

Hermann's eyes drifted over to her, his body shifted. He put a finger to his implant, likely turning off the commentators as well. He waited.

When she didn't speak straight away, he said: "Being forced to look at your melted fucking head should be the payment."

Lin clenched her jaw. Her head wasn't melted, as such. The skin growth had worked. It was just that the new, pink skin over her scalp and part of the right side of her face didn't match the colour of the old skin. It would take a few months to even out, the doctor told her.

"Says the fat old English bastard."

"What's *your* pass with the boss man?" he asked.

"What?"

"Well. You got a man killed over some whore. The boys here have been talking about it, a good fellow, they say. So: you paying off your debt with those fat lips?"

A blur of movement and her blade was out, at Hermann's throat. "I will kill you." He hadn't moved, hadn't had time to. One hand on the table, fingers on his glass of grappa, the other hand holding his cigar resting on his thigh.

Only his eyes moved. "Well don't just fucking yap about it." He moved his chin up, exposed his throat fully.

Lin breathed out and sat back down, blade first pointed at Hermann, then sheathed, fast, silently. "The man," she said, "who did this to you – Long?"

Hermann puffed on his cigar. "Yeah?"

"Know where he is?"

He said nothing, glowered instead.

"I've got a deal for you, mate. Square your tab with the Bình Xuyên."

"Well," he said, settling into his chair. "Don't tell me half a story."

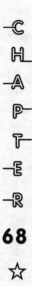

CHAPTER

68

☆

She should have been drunk. Two bottles of sake, working through her third, six or seven drops of ice-seven along the way. But the body buzz, the mind high were fleeting, the amnesiac oblivion out of reach. All her memories were intact, racing, repeating.

The fucking X-37 was working perfectly. One of the many unintended benefits, her liver processed everything like a motherfucker. Alcohol was poison, drugs were poison, and Lin Thi Vu was poison-proof.

So the flash-bang imprint on her memory, over and over – Phuong, turning, mouth parting as though to speak, arm rising as though to ward, frozen in the moment when the light hit – this was never dulled.

Lin threw the bottle across the room, white glass shattering on the window opposite.

Her mind was not poison-proof. Not yet.

She was in a suite, couple of floors above Le Samourai. Probably luxury, she hadn't turned the lights on to see. Just sat on the couch, looking out over the city. A film of sake now, running down the glass, distorting the view and the worlds between the shining straight lines of the skyscrapers. The neon of the bars, the holo-billboards of the corporations, shining beacons of the profit motive, radiant and glorious.

Lin breathed, thinking over her conversation with Hermann. He'd left the bar straight after; she hadn't heard from him since.

On-retina, a message pulsed from Bao. She said: "Open message."

At the other place, across the street. Now. You need to hear this.

Lin ran a hand over her head. Hair growing, spikey now, half an inch long. She sighed and grabbed her jacket.

"The fuck is he doing here?"

Lin stopped in the doorway of a well-appointed suite with Bao and a Chinese military official. Lieutenant Zhu, the tubby, smiling small-talker and venal bribe-taker. Here he was, one building over from their new headquarters, deep into the couch, legs spread, exposing his minimal khaki crotch.

Bao blew a cloud of smoke into the air. Lieutenant Zhu downed his drink, eyes sparkling. In his other hand a cigarette. No brown envelope, that she could see.

Bao said: "[Our friend has some information. Valuable information.]"

Lin floated over to them, thinking of all the ways she could put a blade in the tubby man's body. Took a wooden chair and sat two metres from them both. She pulled out her soft pack of cigarettes, lit one, and took a deep drag. That still hit her, a little, stung her lungs, made her feel something.

Bao said: "Zhu?"

"[Yes,]" the other man agreed, and put down his empty shot glass. Bao refilled it while the Chinese officer spoke in Mandarin. "[Two days from now, there will be a contest. A martial arts contest, in Lotte tower.]"

Lin waited, listening for boots outside the door, for the whine of drones, the *dubadubadubaduba* of helicopter blades.

Zhu smiled and toasted: "*Chúc sức khỏe*," before downing his rice whiskey. The man's levity was starting to grate.

"[A man,]" the Chinese officer continued, "[I believe you know quite well, is fighting in the main event. Passaic Powell.]"

Lin smoked, listening now.

"[Colonel Peng is one of the guests of honour. He will be joined by many of his close contacts in the Chinese military, who, like him, enjoy wagering vast amounts on the bouts.]"

"Lin?" Bao said. "[Thoughts?]"

Lin blew smoke in the direction of Zhu. "This is what I think. I think this is a trap. This Chinese snake is leading you, me, and all your men, into a firing squad. I think I should cut him open like a pig, leave him here, let him spend the last few minutes of his life trying to put his intestines back in his stomach. That's what I think."

Bao said nothing, gave nothing away. He just looked over at Zhu.

Zhu smiled, his line of emotion unconnected to Lin's words. "[Yes. I understand. I am part of the invading force, after all. My family is as well, I should add. My son was in the Nanjing special forces unit – they were called the 'Flying Dragons'. My wife works in the bureau of cultural adjustment, war division.]" He rested his hands on his knees. "[Do you know how this conflict started, Lin? It's so long ago, many do not remember.]"

"This a fucken history class?" asked Lin.

"[First was the assassination of the president here, thought by many in this country to be a puppet of Beijing, giving particular concessions to Chinese businesses. Second was the trade sanctions we imposed after the assassination. Third was our provocation in the Gulf of Tonkin, when we sunk several Vietnamese fishing trawlers we claimed came into our waters – desperate, no doubt, for fish given the precarious state of the Vietnamese economy.]"

"Fuck. It is a history class."

"[Lastly, were the mass protests in Vietnamese streets, and the subsequent burning down of many Chinese businesses. So, our regime took what they said was the sad but necessary action of invasion, in order to punish our disrespectful younger brother in the south. Not many remember this now, it has all become all twisted, in the last twenty years. But that, more or less, was the truth of it.]"

Lin smoked, indifferent, but Bao seemed to be waiting for her to respond. She sighed. "Right. So it was ego and greed, and the hurt feelings of some rich motherfuckers. Same bullshit, all over."

"[No. Of course not.]" Zhu slapped a small hand against his wide belly, thinking. "[You see, young lady, these events of history are never so easily reducible. It was one thing, that led to another thing, then to another. It was an aggressive foreign policy, bad judgement in Beijing, and in Hà Nội, and on the bridges of those vessels in the Tonkin. It was hurt feelings, it was a history of conflict between two neighbours. It was China, a great nation that saved the world from climate change, being disrespected by its younger brother, Vietnam. It was,]" he paused, glittering eyes on her, "[rich motherfuckers, and their egos, and their greed.

"[I am here, in this room, for many reasons, young woman. Just like you, I'm not sure why. And I think if you chart the series of events back to here, to this place, where you are talking about the assassination of a Chinese colonel during a martial arts contest, you would not be able to tell me, to explain this path. I don't understand mine. You see, my only son, the one I mentioned. He died, in Đồng Hới. This was eight years ago. He died because of a line on a twelve-hundred-year-old map that said Jiaozhi, and the reckless strategy of a general who wanted to enforce this line. Maybe my son froze in fear, when the fighting started. Or maybe he charged the enemy guns to save his fellow soldiers. Maybe he was shot in the back by a comrade who had mistaken him for an enemy. Or maybe he died for none of those things. I can't trace that path of cause and effect. There is no truth I can rely on anymore, that is not manufactured. But I do know he died in this country, not his own. Far from his own. He died in a country that has fought, and beaten, every empire, from every era in history. I know he died before he was twenty years old, for a war not even the smartest official can explain, for reasons not even the stoutest patriot is allowed to know. My beautiful son.]"

Zhu stopped talking, his gleaming eyes shifting away from Lin. He looked at the next whiskey, poured by Bao; he didn't touch it. "[I don't want us to win this war, and I don't want us to lose this war. I just want it to be finished. I'm a corrupt official who cares for nothing, who believes in nothing. Those like me grow in number, every day. But there are others who would have us fight this war forever, by any means necessary, at any cost. Colonel Peng is one of those true believers. He is a zealot.]"

Zhu, face quiet, hands on his knees, looked at her and she believed. "[This is why he must be stopped,]" he said. "[Men like him will let this war rage for nine hundred years. They will send fifty million of our sons to die. They will never blink.]"

Lin's eyes flicked over to Bao, back to Zhu.

"Okay," she said. "Tell me about this fight."

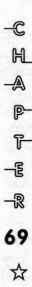
Lin had the furniture removed from the main room of her suite. Spacious, equivalent to twenty mats. She did her Karate, then Taekwondo, then Kendo forms, months since she'd done any of them. Working her new physicality, the feel of it through each punch, kick, spin, leap.

Her body knew what it was doing. Perfect and fluid and responsive. The only thing lagging was her mind, her willingness to accept her new speed and precision. She felt outside of herself, as she trained, watching on, as a lithe young woman flowed and blurred *strike / counterstrike / block.*

Her trance was broken by a knock on the door of the suite, heavy, *bam bam bam.*

Lin stopped, chest heaving, and glided over to the kitchen bench where she'd left her pair of tanto blades. On-retina, her vision adjusted, showing the outlines of two people behind the doors.

"Yeah?"

"Hey. Phantom of the Opera – let us in."

Fuckchops whispered: "Voice match, Herbert Molayson."

"Who's the other?"

"Unclear. There is no visual feed outside this room. Infrared suggest the second person is unconscious."

"Open the door," she said, moving to the back of the space. Ready to jump, move, strike.

The door popped open. Hermann entered the room, breathing heavy, and threw a body down on the floor. Hermann was sweating, hair clinging to his forehead. Blood spray on the shoulder of his jacket, dried brown.

He looked around the room, seeking her and finding her. "Right," he said, indicating the man on the ground. "Debt fucking paid."

The person shifted, groaned, rolled onto their back. Chinese. Wearing a white, stiff-collared silk shirt that accentuated his lithe frame. Blood stains marred the material, and his bottom lip. He was wearing white foundation, like a geisha, his skin seemingly without imperfection. His eyes ranged around the room, dizzy, before finally settling on Lin. He raised himself to a sitting position, straightened his shirt, touched his lips with his fingertips. Rubbed the blood between them, let his tongue dart out, and taste of it.

He took his time about it all. Unperturbed. Beaten, dragged out of whatever hole he was hiding in, dumped in a bare apartment by a British thug, watched over by a sweat-slicked Vietnamese woman, blade in each hand. Unperturbed.

His dark hair mussed by the passage, he smoothed it back with his hand, and pushed himself to his feet. He looked at Lin. "[And what may I do for you?]"

She couldn't guess his age. He could be twenty-five, but Lin felt he was closer to fifty. His eyes were black, shiny, incurious.

"I think if we broke your knees," said Lin, "we'd wipe that dead cow look from your face."

He tilted his head. "[That accent. There was another woman, with just the same.]"

"You'll figure it out eventually." Lin picked up a white towel from the kitchen bench, wiped the sweat from her face, and slung it over her shoulders. She floated over to the thin man. Up close she realised it wasn't just blood on his lips, it was lipstick. "Red is your colour," she said. "And boy I'm going to make it your fucking colour today."

He bowed a *thank you*, no trace of sarcasm. No trace of anything, in his eyes.

"We done, darling?" asked Hermann.

"Not even close."

He bared his teeth. "We had a deal. I give you the skinny bitch, you turn the fucking bomb off in my head."

"He gives me what I want, is the deal."

"Fuck that."

"[A nano-charge in your cochlear implant, I take it?]" asked Mister Long. "[To retain your obedience?]"

"Shut up, motherfucker," hissed Hermann, through clenched teeth.

Lin raised an eyebrow. "You want to get out of here, Hermann? Then help me get what I want out of this prick. Should be right down your alley."

Hermann clenched his jaw; in that moment of silence, Long said: "[You are Lin Thi Vu. Your face changed, your body altered, but you are the same woman hired by Herbert Molayson, you're the bug that the colonel decided to take to with a sledgehammer. Your death verified by a DNA test, administered by a man incapable of lying. And yet here you stand.]"

"Pretty smart, for a painted cadaver," she said. "Well. Half-smart, anyway. Still haven't figured how I'm standing here." She gestured at him with her chin. "And you are Mister Long, Omissioner. A memory artist. The only one capable of creating the brain-fuck inside

Fat Victory, the only one in this picture who could have messed so completely with the mind of Herbert Molayson."

She looked over at Hermann. "You want out, mate? Then let's solve this fucken case once and for all."

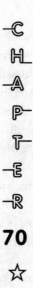

70

"[Yes,]" said Long. "[I divided the personality of Herbert Molayson into two. Colonel Peng wanted the psychological impact of Fat Victory enhanced, Herbert Molayson and his partner Raymond Chang demurred. Weaponising the game went beyond their moral code, however opaque that was.]"

"Pussies," grunted Hermann.

"[Indeed,]" said Long.

They'd moved three seats to the centre of the bare fauxwood floor of the suite. Lin sat facing Mister Long. Hermann sat behind, wearing his tinted yellow glasses, smoking a cigar. Long had managed to remain calm, through everything. Treating the experience as if he were exchanging chitchat while waiting for a manicure.

To one side were the windows, looking out over the city. Oceans of people passed, in the spaces between the neon and the street light. Towers of steel and glass, lighted windows, a universe in each one. People living out their lives, side by side, yet so far from each other. In Lin's line of sight was the holo-billboard of the girl in a red dress, twirling it, smiling, mouthing the words: *The Chinese Dream is my Dream.*

"And by creating Hermann," said Lin, "you also created someone who could be erased. No leaks of information, and a plausible deniability, if it ever came to a complaint from ASEAN, or India."

"[Partly true, though perhaps the least important element.]" He took a long breath, as though the idea of having to explain complexity to thugs was distasteful. "[The other part was this: I needed an avatar. Herbert Molayson was a gifted storyteller, Raymond Chang more than capable of developing the game mechanics. But I needed someone in whom I could join the programming knowledge I do not possess with the mnemonic realignment only I am capable of seeding in the mind. This was Hermann Hebb. This was the crucial third element that made Fat Victory truly remarkable.]"

"Right," said Lin. "But what about this bloke?" she asked, indicating the man sitting behind Long. "I get why you wanted someone to do your programming work. But why turn him into a killer?"

"[He closed the loop. The creator of Fat Victory is killed by the creator of Fat Victory, and the creator of Fat Victory returns to England, unaware.]"

"Sounds clever," said Lin. "But I don't think that's the big story."

Long waited, precise eyebrow raised.

"It's a nice line. Elegant. Like your makeup and your clothes. But I got this feeling, Long, that a tiny black heart beats beneath it all. I got this sense, behind the conspiracies of war and crimes of perfect circular logic, there's a cunt, malicious. You see, I reckon I can think up an easier solution to the problem of Raymond Chang, and I can think it between breaths. A druggie, for instance, paid to murder Chang. Then when he's done, you give the junkie an OD and *he's* done. *There's* elegance, mate. Not this convoluted game you've insisted on playing."

Hermann's cigar, moving as he chewed on it, now stilled as he listened to Lin, then waited for the reply.

No ripples on the surface of his emotion, Long replied: "[You have something of a point, of course. I was curious, and I did derive a certain professional pleasure from the division of Herbert into a second personality, and then in exploring how far I push that from the original. But please do not assume decisions of great importance will be influenced by a whim of my nature. What I was doing was experimental. Over the last few years, various Omissioners have pioneered changes in the minds of select individuals: memories wiped or altered, motivations tweaked, personality traits filed down, others sharpened, others again created. These types of procedures are complex, but achievable for Omissioners of sufficient talent. What I did – divide the personality, drive it from the self, and then return it to the original form – this was revolutionary.]" The shine in the eyes of Long was an indication, finally, he was feeling something. "[And it was successful. There were, certainly, some unintended consequences. But the experiment was a success. Now I can move on to the next phase.]"

"Unintended consequences?" repeated Lin. She shook a cigarette out from her soft pack, eyes on Long. "Like Herbert's alter ego emerging, deciding he liked it outside, and subsuming the original personality." She lit her cigarette and blew a cloud of smoke towards Long. "Then hunting down his creator, slapping him around, and kidnapping him?"

Mister Long made a small irritated gesture, as though waving away the trivial. "[Bugs that can be corrected. The move I made with Herbert had two purposes, thus had the result of being powerful. Risky, yet powerful.]" He paused, looking at Lin, really looking, and asked: "[Have you ever played Go, Miz Vu?]"

"I don't have time for fucken games."

"[No, Miz Vu? Dice? Poker?]"

Lin said: "Just tell your fucken story."

Long nodded and continued, unperturbed. "[In Go, as in other tactical games, defence and attack in the same move is the most powerful: threatening the enemy position while reinforcing one's own. The creation of Hermann Hebb was bold, several moves simultaneously. Attacking the Vietnamese, while protecting the origins of the attack.]"

"Jesus. You needed a fucken analogy to say that?"

"[Being designed as particularly amoral,]" continued Long, unflustered, "[Hermann Hebb soon became resentful against Herbert Molayson, whom he thought was taking too large a share of the profits.]" Long allowed himself a smile, corners of his red lips twitching. "[I will admit to some pride at this. A separation so completely perfect, even the subject did not realise. I further planted the notion that Raymond – deep in debt to the Green Dragon – was about to sell Hermann out.]"

"For?"

"[He killed someone on their turf.]"

"He did? Who?"

"[Oh.]" Again, the hand wave. "[Trivial. A prostitute. Gang property. But this aside, the experiment was perfect.]"

"Perfect," repeated Lin. "You fucking psycho."

Long acted as if she hadn't spoken. Hermann clenched his fists, knuckles cracking.

"But how?" asked Lin. "How did you push him so far?"

"[A prison sentence,]" said Long, matter-of-factly. "[Three years of trauma, of the routine depredations faced by a soft man in a hard environment.]"

Lin felt Hermann shift beside her and she put out her hand. "Not yet," she said.

"[You should thank me,]" said Long, to Hermann. "[I liberated you from your soft and banal existence. I freed you from the bondage of natural memory. Now you are strong, Hermann Hebb. Now you have agency. And all it took was the figment of some unpleasant experiences.]"

A chair screeched, fell, and Hermann was on his feet, violent growl at the back of his throat but Lin was there, first. She placed the fingers of her left hand on his chest, the index finger of her right raised like she was trying to hypnotise. "If you want that thing out of your head, and to get out of this city alive: not yet."

Hermann's eyes moved from Long, to her finger, to her eyes. Nothing else moved, but Lin could feel the moment pass. The tension ebb.

Lin settled back on her chair, Hermann remained standing.

"That's not original," she said to Long. "Anyone can download that experience into some poor sod. If it were that easy everyone would be doing it."

"[I am not *anyone*,]" hissed Long. "[As you keep failing to realise.]"

"Nah," said Hermann, still standing. "You're the monster that put three years of beatings and rape into my head."

Long ignored him. Lin realised that Long wanted to talk, wanted the chance to revel in his dark achievements. Probably wasn't allowed to say a damn word to anyone, in normal circumstances. But now, he said it all: "[Hermann Hebb implemented the protocols I needed, then he killed Chang, and then everything reverted to the original: Herbert. Next time it will be a simple matter of tweaking the host so they do not become determined to solve a crime that they themselves committed. I underestimated Herbert's connection to Chang.]"

"You'll always make that mistake," said Lin.

"[How so?]"

"You're a sociopath. You can't connect. That's why you're so calm right now, when you know I'd be happy to put your head on a pike, and that Hermann here would do far worse."

"[You misinterpret the logic I've applied to this situation, Miz Vu. In the game of Go, one must be prepared to cut one's losses, immediately. Not one stone should be wasted chasing a formation that is already lost. I have many options. The most prominent being ransom by your gang, for which you would receive a weighty sum. I could work for your gang, which I would be willing to do – my only condition being the ability to continue my own work. You could kill me, of course. You could take my formation from the board. But there is a larger game here, and your leader, Bao Nguyen, is a man known for seeing the bigger picture. It is unlikely he would throw away a valuable resource out of personal distaste. There are numerous plays still available to me.]"

Lin smoked and watched him. Hermann crushed the stub of his cigar underfoot and went looking in the kitchen for something, presumably alcohol.

"Bao doesn't know you're here, mate. Even if he did, I don't reckon he'd be so logical with a fucken war criminal."

Long raised a single, precise eyebrow. "[War criminal.]"

"Fat Victory."

"[Oh, is that the label you are giving it? Fat Victory was an experiment, a grander, much more vital one than that of Herbert Molayson. The purpose of the game was to restore social order and moral propriety in an age of growing political and social anarchy.]" Long ran a hand over his legs, smoothing the fabric. "[This war is a tragic misallocation of resources. Men and women, killed in the millions. Economic disruption to the entire region. Environmental degradation to swaths of arable land that should be growing food for China. Oceans that should be doing the same. The psychosphere disrupted as peoples all around the Earth question the nature of Chinese rule, undermining the mandate of heaven. Harmony is impossible while minds roil with chaos. We only seek to calm these turbulent oceans. Fat Victory was a path towards this noble goal.]" His empty eyes flicked over her. "[Strange you should take such a line of attack. You don't strike me as one particularly married to ethics.]"

"And you fucked up Fat Victory like you fucked Herbert."

Mister Long allowed himself a smile. Nothing in his eyes matched it, just the hard sheen of contempt. "[You understand so little. Your mind fixated on minutia. Of course it did not succeed. Not yet. But here's the thing, Miz Vu: if I solve the riddle of Fat Victory – and I will – I solve the riddle of how to rule the world. Think: I attempted to make an occupied people believe the occupation was natural, historically inevitable, and even desirable. *And I very nearly succeeded.* This is bigger than some marginal war on this thin strip of rebelliousness you call Vietnam.]"

"Should kill this fucker." Hermann stood behind Mister Long, glass of booze in his hand. "He's a fanatic."

Lin finally got round to lighting another cigarette. She leaned back in her chair and took a drag. Hermann was right. Dead right. Long was a fanatic, and would never stop, driving towards this fever dream in his mind's eye. Problem was, she needed the fanatic to do something for her first.

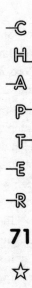

CHAPTER
71
☆

"[I can't do the memory wipe today, not if you're going to fight tonight,]" said Long.

"The fuck not?" asked Lin.

"[There is always some fogginess and distraction after a wipe, in particular as extensive as you wish me to perform.]" He raised a finger to stop a further objection. "[But I can map the memories to be erased, and program a tetrapin to wipe them at a later time. You will not need an Omissioner.]"

It was just her and Long in the room. The *Kandel-Yu* looked like little more than a reclining chair of the type you'd see in a dentist's, and a neon green halo above the headrest that belonged in a science fiction film. There was a tai screen connected to it all, a padded chair where Long was sitting.

A black-market lab the Bình Xuyên used for mnemonic services – alibis, wipes, the usual.

"So?" She indicated the chair, eyebrow raised.

"[You know how this works?]"

"More or less."

"[But you have had natural memory wiped?]"

"Just seen it done to others."

"[Interesting.]" Lin found herself watching the man's red lips as he talked. "[I don't think I've ever met anyone, criminal or military, who has not required some information expunged.]"

"Yeah, well. I'm making up for lost time."

"[Quite so,]" he said, his indifference moving him on without a bump. "[The procedure is straight-forward. Memories are mapped as they are remembered.]" He indicated the screen in front of him with a flick of his eyes. "[The simple act of recall will show which synapses are forged with the relevant memory. I will instruct you to remember specific things, those events will be mapped, synapse by synapse, and later dissolved. It is better if the memory is wiped in that particular moment, but so long as you do not sleep the wipe will be fully effective.]"

"Why?"

"[Because memories are not stable, and the pathways they take in our mind renew themselves. Every time you recall an event from the past, it is layered with the experiences of your life in between, creating a new synaptic pathway. Sleep is crucial in this equation, as it constitutes the period when we consolidate memories, where our brain prioritises and makes sense of what we have seen on the day, and how this relates to what came before, and in turn how this relates to our self-image. No memory is independent; it is built upon a lifetime of memories.

"[What I will do, Miz Vu, is sever the chain. To your past, to the things that plague your dreams, that make you question and make you doubt. I have done this many times, for warriors such as yourself – it is the correct course of action. It focusses the mind, removes the extraneous. You want your family and the country you grew up in removed, yes?]"

Lin nodded, some part of her not wishing to vocalise it again.

"[This is quite a lot. But such wipes are not unknown. I cannot eliminate Australia completely. Twelve years is too great a period. However, I can reduce it to nothing more than two or three short holidays, to a hot, flyblown wasteland at the end of the Earth among the poor white trash of Asia. A place you will have no desire to return to.]"

He narrowed his eyes. "[You have an objection?]"

"No," said Lin, quickly. "No."

He whispered at the screen, red lips glistening. Ideograms streamed down the green-glowing screen. Attention back on Lin, he said: "[Family, too, are something of a nuisance. They are hard to eradicate completely.]"

"Yeah," said Lin. "On that. I want to remember how they died, so I can avenge it."

"Ah," said Long. "[Excellent. A flat, objective understanding of the need to revenge, without any of the associated emotion. Yes, I will be able to adjust your memories to this end. You will dream of their deaths, often.]"

"And the rest?"

"[The unwanted memories will fade. However, you will need alternate memories programmed – more combat training, a different childhood – so your timeline makes sense to you, consciously and otherwise. While you will be aware you have received a significant adjustment, it will come to the point – months or years from now – where you cannot tell the difference between what is real and what is programmed. You will dream yourself into a new reality. As Hermann has so quickly come to understand: real or unreal makes no difference, as either is of equal power in manufacturing the person you are.]"

Lin ran a thumb over her bottom lip, looking at the chair.

"[This really isn't as dramatic as society would have you believe, Miz Vu.]"

"If you fuck with me," said Lin, eyes still on the chair. "If there's something in my head that shouldn't be there. If there's an accident, and your scissor slips and trims the wrong thing. Accident, by design, whatever, I will run your mind through Fat Victory for weeks, until you are little more than a drooling, screaming vegetable." She looked over at Long, who gave her no satisfaction in the way of a reaction. "Bao will be eager, I reckon, to have someone review your handiwork, to catch an error or oversight."

Not even a glimmer of a reaction in his dead eyes. "[It is a simple mapping exercise, Miz Vu, easily verified. Within it, all I can promise is perfection. A clean and coherent foundation for all your hate. Now please, lie down.]"

She did. He settled the neon halo down over her head; not touching, but she could feel the warmth from its glow, on her forehead.

Long said: "[Now. Think about your mother.]"

"Ah. You mean when I was growing up in—"

"[Don't speak please, Miz Vu. I have precisely zero desire to hear of your life experiences. It bears no relevance to this procedure. This part of mapping is quite elegant: you recall the memory, your synaptic activity is recorded, and an otherwise inscrutable process in the vast universe of your mind is revealed.

"[Now: think about your mother.]"

Lin took a deep breath, and closed her eyes.

After a pause, Long said: "[Good. Now think about your sister.]"

…

"[Good. Try to recall the first memory of your mother.]"

…

"[The first memory of your sister.]"

…

"[Remember now the worst fight you ever had with your sister.]"

Lin swallowed. Mister Long was behind her; he couldn't see her face. His voice a metronome.

"[Please, Miz Vu, the worst fight you had with your sister. Hmm. Good.]"

...

"[Your best memory of your sister.]"

...

"[A time your mother made you cry.]"

...

"[A time you saw your mother cry.]"

...

"[Your first memory of Australia.]"

...

"[Your last memory of Australia.]"

...

"[Your mother's birthday.]"

...

"[The last present you gave your mother.]"

...

"[The first present you can remember your mother giving you.]"

...

"[The favourite meal your mother cooked.]"

...

"[An Australian activity you enjoyed doing.]"

...

"[An Australian activity you enjoyed watching.]"

...

"[Remember now, your mother putting you to bed when you were little.]"

Unbidden, a tear rolled down Lin's cheek.

"[Good. A time your mother made you laugh.]"

...

"[Take a deep breath, Miz Vu. We have several hours to go. Good. Now. A way your sister could always make you laugh.]"

...

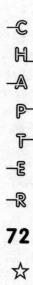

CHAPTER

72

☆

Lin Thi Vu waited on the street corner with All City Do. The escort had her long, pale pink hair in braids. Lipstick matching her hair, short shorts that showcased her creamy smooth skin, a pale blue latex bustier, long clear plastic rain jacket over it all, against the rain. Despite everything, Lin found her eyes wandering back to the woman.

All City Do smiled, sultry, when she caught her looking. Lin pursed her lips and looked away. Lin slipped on sunglasses, aviators, inner relief at being able to hide her red eye. She felt self-conscious in the tight faux leather pants, skin-tight. A matching, black leather sleeveless top, long steel zip all the way down the front. Dressed like a fetish stereotype from a porn feed. She wore a conical bamboo hat, red-painted, keeping the rain, and the eyes, from her face.

"[Stop blushing,]" said All City. "[You look great.]"

"I'm not blushing," hissed Lin. But she calmed herself, smoothed her face. Her body responded immediately, presumably, because

All City Do said: "Better. You'd make a perfect hooker."

Lin said nothing, watched the traffic instead, easing past. Slicing through the rain, coloured neon of the bars and shopfronts reflected in the puddles on the road. Lin felt wired, alert, the X-37 gave her a kind of natural high, a hyper-awareness like the ice-seven. Unlike the seven, though, it didn't dull her memory, didn't help her skate over the surface of everything; that was a different problem, with a different remedy.

"[I'm tempted to say no to the money,]" said Do. "[Exchange it for an evening with you instead.]"

"Shut up," said Lin. "Watch the road."

All City Do gave a little pout at the rejection, and did as she'd been paid to do. Waving away the vehicles that slowed for the duo. Eyes out for the prize, along the road bordering the thirty-six streets, a favourite one for johns trawling for street pussy.

Lin saw it first, thumbed her implant, subvocalised an order.

Ten seconds later, a taxi ran into the back of a scooter, sending the rider sprawling. A slow-motion crash, like most in this part of town, bumps and bruises secondary to the spectacle of the various parties to the incident yelling at each other, remonstrating, demanding the account of witnesses in the crowd. This one was no different, and the glimmersine was forced to stop behind it.

The solar particle coating of the vehicle scintillated, reflecting the city lights in spectrum from its surface. Like the reward at the end of the rainbow. Oh, and what a reward.

All City Do sauntered past Lin, grabbing her hand as she did so; despite herself, she felt a little electric thrill at the touch of the woman. Pulled Lin along, strutting, taking her time as she approached the limo; Lin tried to match, letting her hips roll and her body responded, perfect, like a panther on a catwalk.

The tinted window rolled down and a voice said, raspy, faint: "[You'll suck my cock and be finished before the traffic clears.]"

"[Well,]" said Do, hand on her hip, sweet smile on her lips. "[Only because you asked so nicely. Three thousand.]"

The door opened.

"[Wait,]" said Do. "[We're a double act.]"

"[I'm not paying double.]"

"[The price is all-inclusive.]"

A grunt, which Do took for assent, as she smiled a smile hotter than a Hà Nội summer night, and ducked into the limo. Lin followed.

The smell hit her as she entered the vehicle – rotten, like a corpse, smothered with the perfume of aftershave. Lin swallowed her disgust and eased her way in, keeping her head low, face obscured by the hat and sunglasses. The colonel looked the same as before: short cropped hair, stiff bearing, old-fashioned three-button dark brown suit with a wide collar. His dark eyes depthless, both hands on the iron snake head of a cane, vertical. His skin was young, in contrast to those hideous wounds. Angry purple on his neck, his left hand, shifting, something moving under his skin.

Opposite on a bench seat, two men, sunglasses, black suits. Auto-drive limo, the only people inside: the two guards, Peng, and the women. The men had their pistols holstered under their jackets. Not even resting in their laps. Fucking amateurs.

All City Do, snuggling in on the near side of Peng, pointed up at the roof of the limo. "[Can you turn off the security system.]" As she talked she was already working the man's fly, expertly, hand slipped in. The smell, if anything increased and Lin averted her eyes, instead focussing on the two men opposite. She made a place for herself on the other side of the colonel, moving in close to him, playing the part.

Colonel Peng grunted. "[Why?]"

"[Well, because prostitution is illegal, *big* boy. Your comrades have been known to use security feeds against my sisters and brothers. But…]" her hand, still inside his pants, started moving faster, "[I know you wouldn't do that to me.]"

One of the guards opposite said: "[*Sir,*]" in a warning tone.

Colonel Peng, not listening, cleared his throat. "[Internal-only, limousine security, deactivate.]"

A small red light on the ceiling blinked off.

And that's all it took. Lin blurred from the seat, right fist into the throat of the first guard, spin, elbow into the throat of the second. Adam's apples, both perfect blows, Lin finishing sitting between the two, her heart screaming, Colonel Peng and All City Do looking at her, eyes wide, before Do caught herself and jabbed a needle into Peng's throat. A one-shot needle, in the palm of her hand, neo-gamma-choline. His body paralysed, mind fully conscious.

One of the guards had collapsed, a hollow thump as he hit the floor of the limo, death spasm, and he was done. The second had slid from the seat to his knees, both hands on his throat, ugly animal sounds coming from his mouth. Lin shifted and kicked him in the temple. He dropped, soundless. She moved, jacking into the control slot of her cochlear implant, a gleaming fibre-optic thread connected to a second jack. She pointed the silver jack, like a miniature pistol, subvocalised the command and a jolt of electricity lanced out, hitting Peng's smooth steel implant. Two-three seconds, and his control pin slid out. She grabbed it with thumb and forefinger, pulled and tossed it, and jacked hers in instead.

She did all of it – killed the two guards, overrode the lock on Peng's control pin, and inserted her puppet jack – just as Do was withdrawing the needle she'd just used on the man.

Lin eased herself into the seat opposite them both. Her heart still screamed at her, but her mind did the opposite. Cool, diamond sharp, every twitch every sound in the enclosed space, she knew it, instantly. The two men on the floor, hearts stopped, dead, the colonel's shock turned to paralysis turned to eyes gleaming in his head, fear.

Do, lips parted slightly, blushing, as she looked at Lin.

"[You were a blur,]" said Do.

Lin pressed a finger to her cochlear implant and said: "Sync."

All City Do leaned back luxuriantly in her seat.

Lin ignored her, reading the report that came up on-retina, data falling down in front of her eyes.

"He didn't have time to send out an alarm." She looked up at All City Do. She put a finger to her implant and said: "Limousine, stop, open the passenger door," and as she spoke, the colonel moved his lips and the words were his words, his voice, in Mandarin.

The window opened, a fetch boy on a scooter passed a small green backpack to Lin, worked his throttle, and shot off into the rain. Lin unzipped the backpack, pulled out her tanto, strapped them to her hips. She unzipped and shrugged off the ridiculous leather top, All City Do's eyes flicked over her as she did so. The colonel didn't blink. Didn't see. Just a wide-eyed terror, eyes in the distance, his body rigid.

Lin pulled on a spideriron vest, thin, like semi-rigid silk, body hugging, a black singlet over that.

"You need to move," said Lin. "My link with this motherfucker won't last long. The shot you gave him should last a couple of hours, but it could be less. You need to get to the meeting place."

All City Do moistened her lips, gathering herself. "Zoi zoi zoi." She moved to the door, but stopped herself, looking back over her shoulder at Lin. "[After all this is done, there'll be a spare room waiting for you in Sài Gòn, sweet lips.]" She smiled. "[Well, maybe not a whole room. But there'll be a space in my bed.]"

Lin thought about it. No more than two seconds, but she really thought about it. When Lin said nothing, Do just shrugged, sultry smile back on her lips, and stepped out into the rain. She walked away, hips swaying, one last show for Lin, before disappearing into the steaming city night.

Lin sighed, put a finger to the implant and said: "Close the door. Take me to Lotte tower," but the words came from Peng's mouth, and so the vehicle moved.

Lin took light blue medical gloves from the bag she'd been handed, snapped them on, and fished out the final object. It looked like plasticine, oily, with a small translucent monitor embedded in it. C-6 with a hexogene core. Breakfast of champions. "Bomb number five," said Lin.

Words, English, scrolled left to right on the plastic slip. **Yes, Ms Vu.**

"After I leave the vehicle, the limo is going to drive to a cemetery inside a field of dead reeds. Ninety minutes from here."

Yes, Ms Vu.

"When you arrive, and if no civilians are within your blast radius, I want you to blow this fucking vehicle."

Sky high, Ms Vu, sky high.

Through a force of will, Peng managed to move his eyeballs until they were on Lin, still unblinking, still terror-wide.

Lin smiled at the colonel. She continued: "Now, if at any time, it looks like Peng is going to get out of this vehicle, someone is going to rescue him, just blow this motherfucker up. I don't care who's around."

With pleasure, Ms Vu.

She pressed the explosives into the ceiling, sticking it there, screen facing downwards, pulsing red.

Lin Thi Vu leaned back into the soft leather of the bench seat, head resting against it, arms along the back. "So, Colonel," she said. "There's going to be a last-minute change to the main event."

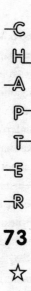

CHAPTER

73

☆

Lin stepped out of the limo, relieved at the clean, rain-soaked air, breathing it down deep into her lungs. She watched the limo depart, then turned her head and spat into the street in its wake, getting the taste of decay out of her mouth.

It didn't take a genius to see something big was happening at Lotte tower. They'd driven through a roadblock policed by three armoured personnel carriers with turret-mounted heavy machine guns, a platoon of soldiers watching the traffic in the rain. Looking up at the sky as they'd passed through, Lin had seen the glint of drones among the dark clouds, dozens of them circling.

At the entrance was another sleek armoured personnel carrier. Black-and-rusty brown armour – ceramite and layered nano alloys, turret rotating slowly. She walked past it, bored soldiers watching her do so, eyes on the tanto bouncing at her hips, unimpressed.

The tower itself was sixty-seven storeys, gleaming blue steel and glass.

Not the tallest, but certainly one of the oldest of the tall skyscrapers, Korean-made when such a thing was still considered reliable. The world's embassies at its feet, a favoured meeting place among the high-ranking officers and the soft-handed diplomats who kowtowed to them.

Lin walked through the sliding double doors, over red carpet, and under a sniffer arch: blue neon hiding the advanced tech inside. It picked up traces of explosives, primer in bullets; anything anyone could shoot or blow up. Lin let out a long, slow breath as she approached the security counter in front of a bank of gleaming elevators, trying to release the building tension inside.

Chinese soldier, a hard-faced woman with a white beret / red uniform Lin didn't recognise watched her approach. A dozen others dressed like her around the entrance. The spread of neo-Confucianism in China had resulted in them removing all women from front-line duties in Vietnam. But you'd still see them around, time to time, in specialist roles.

Whoever the squad in the red uniforms were, they held themselves like professionals. Alert, heads on a swivel, top-shelf arms and armour. There was no way Lin was getting out of here, after it was done. Not via these elevators, not past tanks and a platoon of men. No matter how fast she was, the tanks would have auto-targetters, and Lin wasn't faster than a bullet.

She hesitated, just a stutter-step.

The woman barked: "[Stop.]" She placed her hand on the holster of her pistol. "[You are armed.]"

Behind her, the other guards casually brought their weapons to bear.

Lin raised her hands, slowly. "*I'm in the bout*," she said, in Vietnamese.

"[Sunglasses, jacket, hat, weapons.]"

Lin did so. The woman looked her up and down, then off to the side, checking something on-retina.

"[Red-Eyed Phu?]"

"*Yes.*"

The woman held up a thin green translucent card. "[Press your thumb.]"

Lin did. The card could have been mistaken for a piece of plastic, but it blipped, soft glowing green, after a few seconds, and Chinese ideograms ran down it. The guard read it, looked up at Lin, read the card again. Trying to make her sweat.

But Lin had already seen it. She was in.

"[You're late.]"

"*Traffic.*"

"[You're in the wrong weight class.]"

"*I'm Vietnamese. We're used to beating bigger opponents.*"

The woman set her mouth and Lin walked past the red-uniformed guards. All eyes on her, as she stood in front of the smooth steel doors of the lift. Her metal reflection looked back. A lean young woman, a blade on each hip, red-eye black-eye, staring back at her fixedly.

The elevator went only to the sixty-fifth floor. To get to the roof, she had to go through a second security check. Thirty elevators at the first bank at ground level, only one at the second. A perfect choke point. No. She wasn't going to get back through here.

The last two floors, breath in out, in out, slowly. Evening her pulse, eyes closed. Her body hummed, as it was meant to. Her mind did not. It screamed, throat wide, as it had for the last few days, as it would for the next few minutes.

She ran her thumb across her lips.

The doors opened.

Red-Eyed Phu was swallowed by the roar of the crowd.

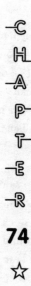

CHAPTER

74

☆

The problem with blowing up luxury hotels in Vietnam, thought Bao, is that everyone expected you to try. The Hyatt-Aman near Tây Hồ Lake expected it more than anyone else. The most expensive and exclusive, reserved for the Red Aristocracy, the crème of the military, visiting Hengdian movie stars, and K-pop singers.

Sniffers good for two hundred metres, could detect explosives bigger than a pinhead. Anti-missile systems, good for ten kilometres, pick up and shoot warheads out of the air ninety-nine times out of a hundred. Blast walls like a citadel. Imperial Overwatch drones circling above, glinting, and red-uniformed guards on patrol inside and out of the complex. For half a kilometre around, all the apartment blocks, houses, restaurants had been bought up, now lived in by military or left empty.

Bao Nguyen and Bull Neck Bui watched via a repurposed drone, outside of the sniffer radius, hovering over the waters of Tây Hồ, its telephoto lens on the front gates of the hotel.

"Lot of material in this," said Bull. He sat next to Bao Nguyen, smoke trailing from his cigarette, face lit by the green backwash of the screen.

"All of our material," replied Bao.

"Yeah."

"We've hidden our power for a long time," said Bao.

Bull grunted.

"If we don't use it tonight, we'll never use it."

His sergeant replied: "Don't think Sun Tzu ever said that. Or Guevara."

Bao said nothing, eyes flicking to the time on-retina: **10:29 pm**. His shoulders rigid with tension, he breathed, concentrated on the feel of the stock of the machine gun under his hands.

Around them, men and women shifted in the darkness, marked by the orange points of light from their cigarettes. Heavy-soled boots scrapped on the rough plascrete floor, sub-machine guns cocked, heavy *clack-clack*. Silence, otherwise, as they waited. Many were veterans, the rest blooded by the thirty-six streets – no illusions, any of them, of what could happen next, or of the price they'd have to pay.

10:30 pm

Bao put a finger to the smooth cool steel of his neural implant. "Begin."

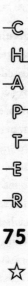
The first wave of electro-magnetic pulses started half a kilometre out, at the edge of the surveillance loop for the Imperial Overwatch drones.

Captain Sun Fei placed his teacup carefully on the table edge. "They can't be."

The captain stood behind six men, sitting up in the control room, a converted suite on the thirty-fourth floor of the Hyatt-Aman. The seven were arranged in a circle, looking in on a holo-emitter, two metres in diameter. In the centre of the layout was the hotel, in full living colour, green points circling slowly above marking drone locations, red for troops on the ground, blue for armoured vehicles. There were three generals currently in the hotel, including the head of the Jiaozhi reunification campaign, General Cao, on R & R from the 17th parallel.

As such, there were a lot of red, green, and blue points on the topographic display, much more than necessary. Sun Fei's job was considered one of the easier ones, a six-star life while heading up the defences of a target no one had either the resources or the stupidity to attack. At the officers' club they teased him: safe and comfortable postings almost unheard of in this war. Teased him gently, given the circumstances.

Sun Fei winced as he moved, still not used to the prosthetic leg, still not used to *not knowing* how he lost it. He'd been standing at the open door of an attack ship, swooping down low over the jungle dawn, wind in his hair, hollow *thump thump thump* of the missiles as they fired out from under the body of the craft. Trying to find the calm reserve that came with three years of hard action, but instead thinking about his wife, and new child, a stranger to him. His eyes down on the jungle when a blinding flash of light—

Waking up a week later, with a new leg, a new spleen, the old memories of the action wiped clean, and a Meritorious Service Medal, second class, on his chest.

One of the operators, a private who looked like he should be in high school, said, "Sir. The sniffers have something."

Sun Fei said, "Let me see it," his voice flat.

The operator said, "C-6. Closing fast," as the visual display set above the holo-emitter showed a white van weaving through traffic.

At the perimeter of the topographic map, a yellow dot blipped into life. Fei glanced up at the windows opposite, overlooking the shoreline of Tây Hồ Lake, favoured by expatriates. Behind it, a raised road built on an old dyke led right past the Hyatt-Aman. The van came from this direction.

"It's approaching the roadblock." The young man looked up at Fei. "The sniffers detect hexogene, as well."

Fei's jawline tightened. He placed a finger to his cochlear-glyph implant. "Message: Lieutenant Li Zhang. The hotel is under terrorist attack. Remove the generals to the bunker."

A several-second pause then a voice in his ear said, "Really?" The man on the end, friend from the club, sounded nonplussed.

"Hexogene spliced with C-6," said Fei. "Incoming. There will be more than one."

"Will do, Captain." The voice still didn't sound convinced, probably more concerned by disturbing General Cao – who always retired early to bed – than a van packed with explosives.

On screen, the white van made it to the roadblock one kilometre out, sandbags and a squad – twenty men and two support drones. The vehicle weaved through the sandbags, Chinese soldiers waving their hands, followed by the orange flash of small-arms fire, then blinding white, the display polarising for several seconds.

The blast windows opposite lit up, and Fei put a hand up to shield his eyes. A roar followed, rattling ceramic cups on tabletops.

The display vision above returned, showing a blackened crater, an armoured car on its side, twisted and smoking, and the checkpoint sandbags obliterated. Through the windows opposite, Sun Fei could see fires blazing in the distance, a point of light in darkened surrounds, nearby streetlights knocked out, flattened.

On the display, the number of green dots – drones – was dropping sharply. The Việt Minh were throwing drones – captured and repurposed with EMPs – more than Fei had ever seen in a single attack. Pressure began to build in his stomach. He said, "Watch for another."

"There's another," replied the young operator.

A garbage truck. Same road, hurtling. The traffic dissipated, some cars already abandoned. Locals familiar with the routine. Though not here. Not in this place. The truck looked like it had sheets of metal welded over the windshield, the engine block. Possibly remote driven, but not necessarily.

"Are the guns readied?"

"Yes, sir," said a second operator.

"Target that vehicle."

Atop the roof of the hotel were four Type-9 autocannons: AI-controlled, human confirmation required, depleted uranium rounds, five thousand per minute, one-point-five-kilometre range. They could chew up an armoured vehicle and spit it out, in between breaths.

On screen, tracers flashed out and down at the truck. Rending the road, the earth around it, then the vehicle, the windscreen then bumper torn away, smoke, fire, *BOOOOM*.

The second blast shook the windows again, a teacup shattered on the fauxwood floor. The screen above blinked out, Sun Fei found himself gripping the back of the chair in front of him. He straightened his uniform and pointed at the screen above the display. "Get that back up now."

One of the operators, eyes already closed, working on-retina with his hands, like a conductor of an invisible orchestra. "Underway, sir."

Sun Fei grabbed binoculars off the kitchen bench and moved to the floor-to-ceiling windows. The truck had made it only a hundred metres further than the van. No casualties in the second blast, Chinese or civilian – just a section of road destroyed, now shattered asphalt and dirt.

The sinking feeling in Fei's stomach remained. He tracked back down the road, until he saw it. He murmured, "*My heaven.*"

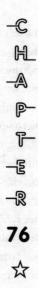

An armoured personnel carrier, Chinese make, turret-mounted machine gun, was hammering down the same road. The binoculars read the speed at 68 km/hour.

"Are the autocannons online?" Sun Fei asked, voice tight.

There was a scrabbling sound behind him.

"Are they online?"

"Sir. We were on the outer range of an EMP. The AI is unresponsive."

Sun Fei turned, pointed at the young operator. "Use manual targeting. Stop that vehicle." He placed a finger to his implant. "Message: checkpoint four. Armoured vehicle approaching. Chinese model 117. Việt Minh controlling it, repeat Việt Minh terrorists controlling incoming vehicle. Intercept before it reaches the hotel. Out." He drew a breath. "Message: Hà Nội Defence Command. Hotel Hyatt-Aman under heavy attack. Send reinforcements."

Colours flickered behind him. He turned, the topographic display was back on. The APC, on screen above, had slowed, negotiating its way around the second blast site; on the display below, the green dots had all but disappeared. Two red dots – APCs of the same make as the one approaching – were moving away from the hotel, towards the yellow dot.

On the display above, the retaining wall behind the APC shattered, dust filling the air, as the APC lurched forward and away.

Sun Fei walked to the man operating the autocannon. Sweat was on the man's brow, eyes clenched tightly closed; on screen, the tracers were spraying all over the screen. Fei put a hand on the man's shoulder. "Breathe, Private."

The firing stopped for a few moments. When it restarted it was closer, hitting, spotlight on the turret shattering, a square section of armour exploding upwards, but the guns tracked behind again and Fei could feel the tension in the man.

"Breathe."

Again, clumps of brick, of earth, of road flying up in the air, an explosion in the tracks, links jagging and cartwheeling away from the front of the vehicle as it drove over them. It veered off the road into shopfronts located below the dyke, obscured from the cameras.

Fei thought it had crashed but infrared kicked in and caught up with it, wreckage of café fronts – chairs tables signs – flying into the air, before it angled back into the dyke rampart and made it back up to the road, earth spraying. Weaving all over the place, sideswiping an abandoned car, crushing a scooter.

"Four hundred metres out," said one of the men.

The APC was lit up by the headlights of an approaching vehicle, another APC, theirs, trying to hit it but the terrorist vehicle was still swerving, trying to regain control—

Impact – orange sparks flying metal-on-metal, but then they'd passed each other, only a brief touch and the incoming kept coming.

"Three hundred metres."

The tracer fire started in again and either the man had got his eye in, or the auto-targeting was back online. The rear of the APC exploded in flames, smoke billowing. Sun Fei could hear the rumble of the vehicle through the blast windows now.

"Two hundred metres."

A second Chinese-manned armoured vehicle had stopped sideways on the road, edging to intercept the wild arc of the oncoming vehicle. Everyone in the control room felt the collision in the soles of their boots.

An operator turned to him and said, "I think—"

The blast threw Sun Fei off his feet. He flung his arm up over his eyes, against the stinging light.

He coughed, ears ringing. Pushed himself up slowly to his knees, his feet. A fine layer of white dust fell from him as he rose. The other men were picking themselves up from the floor as well; the blast windows, opposite, had a single giant crack from top to bottom. The display – holo-topography and visual feed above it – was dead.

Sun Fei found the binoculars and moved back to the windows, surveyed the damage. The men talked to each other behind him, quiet, relieved. He scanned and found the large crater, surrounded by twisted metal. Sun estimated the last blast was at least twice the size of the two before.

The feeling in his stomach hadn't gone. A pressing nausea, just below his heart. He wiped the back of his hand against his mouth, put the binoculars back to his eyes.

"Oh my god." The binoculars bounced once on the floor.

He pressed a finger behind his ear. "Message: Lieutenant Li Zhang. Is the general in the bunker?"

"Yes, Captain."

"Incoming. Seal the doors."

A long pause. "Yes, Captain. Goodbye."

"Message: Mei Lien."

A green dot pulsed on-retina, indicating that the call was being made. Behind him, the men had started talking, loudly, perhaps to him; he wasn't listening. Someone picked up the binoculars at his feet, stood nearby, breathing heavily. The man gasped, swore. The last Sun Fei heard from him were the soles of his shoes as he ran across the suite and out the door.

Captain Sun Fei did not notice.

A sleek, Chinese Type-199 battle tank, shaped like a fat arrowhead. Black-and-rusty brown armour. The barrel was missing from the turret; Sun Fei supposed it had been stolen from a repair depot, sometime during the war. A fast tank, a hard tank, closing in on the Hotel Hyatt-Aman at one hundred kilometres an hour.

The green dot pulsed. Sun Fei closed his eyes, his jaw tight.

The last of the men, hesitating no more than a few seconds, followed the others out and Sun Fei was alone.

On-retina, a woman appeared, young, skin like jade, hair tied up, no makeup. She looked happy. Big smile on her face. "Sun!" The smile faded. "What is it? What—"

"Is Ai there?"

"No. No she's at her nan's today. You know that, Sun."

"I love you, Mei Lien."

"Sun." A worry line formed on his wife's brow. The point just between her eyes. If he'd done something wrong, if there was something on her mind, and she didn't want to speak it he'd know, from that little crease in her perfect, perfect skin.

"Sun," she said, "are you crying?"

"Is— Is Ai there, I need to, I need…"

"Sun. I told you that already. Darling. What is wrong?"

"I could've. I should've—"

White light bloomed through his eyelids. White heat consumed him.

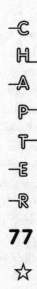

At 10:34 they finally had movement. The alert appearing on-retina, sent by the scout up top.

Colonel Bao Nguyen stood, locked and loaded his Type-17 compact automatic. He'd taken it from the body of a Chinese special forces sapper ten years earlier. Sergeant Bull hefted his AK-47; the rest of the squad shuffled, watched, waited for orders.

Bao subvocalised, *Wait for my signal*, and moved to the front of the room. He nodded to the man on the door, who thumbed the lock and eased it open. Fluorescent light split the darkness, motes of dust dancing in the beam. Beyond was the front room of a house that held a small café. Long-time associates of the Bình Xuyên, quiet, dependable, and situated directly opposite a local bar called The Bad Sleep Well. The bar served as the headquarters of the Green Dragon. It had a steady stream of clientele, though only gang members, local police on the take, and, more recently, a scattering of Chinese military, were allowed.

Three men sitting at a low plastic table, singlets rolled up to expose their bellies to the night air, drinking beer, went wide-eyed as Bao Nguyen walked out the back of the shop. The three were Green Dragon grunts, tasked with watching the street in front of the bar.

Bao said: "As the call," and pulled the trigger.

Bratatat, bratatat.

Glasses of beer exploded, chunks flew up from the plastic table, and the men died.

A moment, just one-two seconds of silence, and the roar began.

Three heavy machine guns, brought in piece by piece and assembled three floors above, opened up. Men and women armed and armoured beneath peasant clothes poured past Colonel Nguyen from the room behind and the apartments on either side of it.

The Bad Sleep Well was a modern two-storey bar: balcony, glass, clean steel edges, glowing blue neon sign. A line of expensive cars out front: Tesla Europas, Sinopec glimmer bikes, Wuling sedans. The bar's glass was armoured, the walls woven with spideriron. It didn't matter. The heavy machine guns up top were usually turret-mounted, stolen from the docks at Hội An. Their shells shattered the glass, tore chunks out of the walls; the people on the balcony were taken apart, limbs and torsos exploding, dead before they hit the ground.

Bao moved with his men and women, firing as he did so. At least forty of them in the street now, Sergeant Bull roaring at them, urging them forward, directing firing positions, grabbing a man who'd slipped by the collar and hauling him up, pushing him out to the street.

The fusillade tore up the façade of the bar, sparks spewing out of the damaged sign, ricochets flashing on metal; *bratatat* and *boom* thundering in Bao's ears. The double doors of the bar had snapped shut, security protocols kicking in, gleaming steel bollards shooting up along the sidewalk, six feet high. Designed to stop a ram raid; not much use against a squad on foot.

Bao, move-moving, stasis was death, across the bitumen. He subvocalised an order.

Above, the heavy machine guns responded, pouring everything into the front doors. Bao could feel the impact of the shells in his teeth, the heavy doors buckling, smoke pouring from the impact points, buckling, the left snapping in half; Bao leaning against a bollard now, using it as cover, still firing; Sergeant Bull barking orders. A man ran up to the doors and hurled a grenade into the interior, his arm at the top of its arc when the bullet struck him, he did a pirouette and fell at the base of the doors, but the damage was done, smoke pouring from inside the bar now, two more men at the breach firing wildly into the interior.

Bull Neck Bui, full-throated roar, rammed his shoulder into the wrecked door knocking it inwards, men and women following, black peasant clothes hiding spideriron vests, conical bamboo hats with a light armoured lining, no fucking illusions, not one of them, charging in after Sergeant Bull, and Colonel Bao Nguyen joined them.

Bao's eyes were alight as his troops swarmed the place, high-end furnishings ablaze or punctured with bullet holes, subdued purple lighting. The place now a fever dream of his hate, bodies sprawled and shattered and crawling and screaming, men and women rushing up the stairs, following the sergeant, and Colonel Bao, eyes ablaze teeth gritted saw a man rising up, the Green Dragon boss Big Circle, mouth agape the glint of his gold tooth, hands open in surrender, blood staining his whole right side and Bao Nguyen gunned him down. No hesitation.

His eyes ablaze, swinging the barrel of his weapon around the room, sporadic fire from up above, the men and women near him, already the grim satisfaction showing in their eyes.

Bao Nguyen lowered his gun and breathed. Mind fire ebbing.

"So the echo."

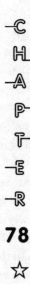

CHAPTER 78 ☆

Lin Thi Vu stood in the arena. A wide space, twenty metres by twenty, bare white spotlights, blinding. Slick and smooth fauxwood, she noted, no fighting surface had been laid to absorb the impact of falling bodies. A chest-high glass railing surrounded the ring. Hadn't bothered to modify that, either. Perhaps in the hope a fighter would shatter it, fall, wind flapping at his hair for sixty-seven storeys, while those above roared and placed their next bets.

They must have been disappointed; the railing was still intact.

The rain was thin, the air thick with heat. Sweat mingling with the water, running down her spine, her bare shoulders. So high, up here, rough winds running over her short hair, keening sounds as it rushed through the steel and glass at the top of the tower. High above the metropolis, spread out to the horizon, on all sides, thirty million souls. High enough so thin clouds gathered at the top of the tower. In the distance, dark thunderheads could be seen over the horizon, roiling with lightning.

Behind her was a purpose-built grandstand, covered from the rain by translucent material, water retardant. Large tai screens, set either side of the grandstand, running three-dimensional replays of the previous fight. Slow motion, skull fractured, blood splatter, fist raised, triumphant.

Her eyes had danced over the audience as she'd walked up blood-slicked steps. Perhaps a hundred people jammed in there, cheering, gesturing at each other, downing expensive whiskey or beer or glowing cocktails. Seated in the gloom, in contrast to the bright white lights of the ring. Still, she noted many officers in uniform, mainly Chinese, though a couple of Vietnamese officers in the mix. Plus the usual set of wealthy in their tailor-made suits and real silk dresses. A few young girlfriend and boyfriend types, on the arm of someone older and powerful, laughing or looking seductive, as the moment required.

She pursed her lips. *Oh well*, she told herself. *Can't be helped.*

The crowd had whispered, some even laughed, as she entered. But she was beyond that now, beyond herself, somewhere behind her own right shoulder, watching.

The fight space, the crowd, the wind up high, taken in at a glance, factored in to her fight plan, and submerged. The one thing that truly mattered was standing right in front of her.

Passaic Powell, combat vest tight over his titanic chest, giant *dadao* strapped to his back. Shoulders and biceps slick with rain, breathing slow, patient. Black combat pants with large pockets, rain beading and sliding from them. Feet bare, like Lin's – she'd been made to remove her boots on entry.

It took Powell a few moments to come out of his head space, to look down on her. Right away his eyes narrowed, his head tilted to one side.

He seemed about to say something when the announcer bellowed, in Mandarin:

"[A big reward, today, for you all. Colonel Peng, decorated hero of the Jiaozhi Reunification Campaign. Former commander of the Southern Blade special forces, former commissar of the cultural alignment program, and now Vice President of Celestial Entertainment.]" (*Smattering of applause.*)

"[Colonel Peng has generously provided *two* fighters from his stable for the main event. The first contestant, you know. A savage fighter from the former United States of America. An artist of the broken limb, a savant of the shattered spine, the blood-soaked ring. He is undefeated after fourteen fights. Eight fatalities, six knockouts. The barbaric, the brave, Passaic Powell.]"

Enthusiastic applause erupted in response, but Powell didn't acknowledge it. Just kept looking at Lin with those soft, concerned, curious eyes.

"[The second fighter you will not know, as Colonel Peng has chosen to keep her shrouded in mystery.]" (*Murmurs from the crowd.*) "[We know she is a young Vietnamese woman who fights with a tanto in each hand, a *Japanese* weapon.]" (*Boos, hisses.*) "[We know this is her first fight. And we know her name: Red-Eyed Phu!]"

Boos for the most part, some scattered applause. The announcement and response felt distant, like the fight was on a screen in another room of a bar, background noise.

DING DING DING, rang the speakers and a large display behind Powell blinked into life, red neon: 3:00, blink, 2:59, blink, 2:58

Passaic Powell didn't move. "Little rabbit, on a wall up high, who are you, little rabbit, little girl?"

Lin drew her blades slowly, took up position, one arm horizontal, one arm vertical and slightly bent, tips of both blades pointed at Powell.

Still, he did not move. "A phoenix, not the rabbit? No no, pitter-patter, the rain on your ashes, drip-drip, I saw the tears, knew why it cried."

Lin moved. Powell did too, finally, faster than anyone she'd seen. He even managed to raise one hand to his face as she passed, whir / blur / whir.

Stopped, turned, other side of the arena, and faced him, Powell staggered, belatedly; the raucous crowd quieted, seeing the blood stream down his shoulder. The nova grenade around his neck glittered, swinging in the white light.

Lin watched it all, everything in slow motion, contempt rising in her at the ease of it. The heat rising in her chest as well, and, on-retina, a red glow at the edges bate-abating. A small script appeared, bottom-right-hand corner:

X-37 activated.

Heart rate: orange.

An outline of her body underneath, green, showing no injuries.

Powell stepped once, the seconds trickled down, to Lin it felt like five minutes had passed.

She blurred again as Powell went for his *dadao* and he grunted this time, deep wounds bone deep, high up on his rib cage under his arm, her blade jarring ever so slightly as it struck endoskeleton. She stopped and turned again, kept the pose this time. The crowd was silent now. The only sound the wind through the structure, as though howling for the pain the white giant was feeling. Howling metal, and the wash of the rain across the arena, the grandstand, wind pushing it along.

Powell recovered his stance and had the mighty sword out, two-handed, water gleaming along its edge.

Lin spun, charged, again, and Powell did about all he could; timed a huge swing, perfectly, scooping out the space around him in a wide arc and it would have split Lin in two, belly button, had she not flipped and soared her blade dancing out, then she hit the wood and flipped again, turning and sliding along the slick surface.

Powell growled deep in his throat. Blood tricked down his forehead. Neat bloody part along his scalp.

The fight timer ticked: 2:27, 2:26

Her on-retina clock said: 10:28 pm

Too fast. Everything needed to slow down.

Powell obliged.

He roared, real noise for the first time coming from his throat, as he swung the heavy *dadao* down, shattered a section of the floorboards either side of him, and backed towards the edge of the ring. Left and right, deep swings with a blade that widened to near a foot at its tip. Smashing the boards, splintering shattering; Lin hung back and let him do it. As a final touch he turned and took out two sections of the glass-panelled railing behind in a single blow, showering the space with broken glass. He turned to her when he was done, breathing heavy, gentle smile forming on his lips, red blood line an inch wide down the centre of his face – forehead-nose-chin.

The arena floor surrounding Powell, two metres wide, was broken, shards of fauxwood sticking out at random angles; his feet wide on a section of unbroken floor, listing. At his back, the wind beckoned, gravity called.

10:29 pm

The fight clock said: 1:42, 1:41

Behind Lin, the crowd, murmurs rising, impatient.

The heat rose in her chest, burning, and the readout said: Heart rate: red. In her little green outline, a red spot bate-abated in the middle of the chest. The X-37 had about a minute's running time before it shut down, and an hour before it could be used again. More than this wasn't a question of premature ageing, rather of her heart exploding inside her chest cavity.

So she danced forward, in between jagged scars of wood, feinting, Powell swinging his huge blade around, Lin dodging it easily. She took her last few precious seconds to lay deep wounds on Powell's arms, forearm, inside wrists, so when she was done it looked like he was wearing red gloves up to each elbow.

10:30 pm and the first explosion hit. The shockwave diverted the crowd's attention, a plume of smoke rising in the distance, over the other side of the lake. There was a collective, *Oooh*, and even Lin glanced past Powell's back, to see what her side had wrought.

Two things happened. One, the X-37 wound back her body function from the superhuman.

Two, the big man was on her and all she had time to do was backflip over his blade and backflip again at the second swing, he lashed out with his foot as she danced backwards, flicking her shoulder, staggering her.

She slid / hopped / slid a little, but stayed clear of the hundred pounds of metal he waved around as though it were no heavier than a switch of bamboo.

His bleeding had stopped. Six blows, bone deep; most men would be laid out needing a transfusion, or dead. Dismay crept into her chest. The big man was a little pale, maybe, but otherwise full-focussed.

10:31 pm

0:45, 0:44

Her heart screamed in her chest, *ba-dup ba-dup ba-dup.*

"Kitty-cat, it's you, fast thing too fast, must hurt, little rabbit."

She semi-circled left and right, Powell moved back across the listing broken space of damaged floorboards until his back foot was only a few inches from the ledge.

0:37, 0:36

"Come follow, little rabbit—"

The second explosion lit up the silhouette of the big man, shutting him the fuck up, his outline black against a brief dawn across the lake, smoke billowing into the sky. Lotte tower rattled, the *Ooohs* of the last blast now something else, a worried murmuring, a shuffling of feet. Above, some of the drones broke away, streaking towards the explosion, metal hides reflecting the hard light of the arena.

And Lin felt tired, her limbs heavy. She turned her head, projectile vomited, and reset her fighting stance. The system required some down time after use, apparently. Lips stinging from the vomit, dizziness creeping in.

"Careful of your fire, little phoenix, crackle-crackle oh how the fire consumes. Careful now, as I thread you on my spit."

He hefted his sword at the last words and set his legs apart, stance firm, and Lin thought *fuck this*. One more blast and there'd be panic and her opportunity would pass. She wiped the rain from her face, spittle from her lips, and charged.

She was tired, but she was an instrument, perfect, of will. She was the will and the act. The language and the pen.

Feint high / Powell swung / down she slid, feet first, sliding on her back across the slick floor jagged long splinter snapping off in her thigh, but momentum and will carried her to the point between his legs.

On through, over the precipice, four feet out into the void her slide arrested as both her blades entered the point between his thigh and groin; Lin twisting, momentum whiplashing her legs out in the space beyond, but Powell, the giant with a titanium alloy endoskeleton, three hundred kilograms minimum, moved about as far as a granite statue.

Unmoving, grunting, standing at the edge, legs still apart, he still hadn't moved an inch; she left one of the blades in his groin and used the other to swing, back around, spinning in the air again and twisting, landing, perfect, the blade at his throat. All one long smooth motion, like art, each move flowing into the next, like it were choreographed, preordained.

Powell's *dadao* clattered to the ground. His arms and hands shaking, exhausted finally, dropping to his side. He looked out into space, and said:

"*Cattle die*
Kinsmen die
All men are mortal
Words of praise
Will never perish
Nor a noble name."

"No one will remember your name," she whispered. The wind whipped at them, his large frame swayed. "Bodies fall like rain in this country. Drops in the river of an eternal war. This—" Her blade bit deep. "—is for my sister."

Her other hand flicked out to his chest, touched the thing there. She turned to face the crowd, all of them looking down at her, silent, mouths parted, as Powell dropped forward to his knees.

Lin had a hand on the nova grenade around his neck. She pulled as he fell. It came apart from the chain with a *snick* and *fizz*. She hurled the grenade into the audience as the bell *DING DING DINGED* for the end of the round. Glittering under the lights, the thin metal tube arced as though in slow motion, and as it landed in the centre of the audience Lin spun again, her back pressed against Passaic Powell's. The dead titan her shield and her saviour.

She pushed her eyes into the crook of her elbow as the light blazed, as the air was sucked from her lungs, as the screams of realisation were silenced, still pressed against him as he fell, as they fell together, sideways, back-to-back.

The heat dissipated. Lin took her arm away from her face. She felt the giant's lungs breathe once more, twice more, three times; they couldn't find a fourth. She put a hand on his side, was about to turn him over, when she saw the pocket in the small of his back. Something that had dug into her, as she pressed against him. Lin slipped her hand into the flap and pulled out a book. Her book, protected by a spideriron cover. *The Sorrow of War*. She turned it in her hands, the cover accentuated by the flames, dancing, twenty metres away.

Her book in her hands, cool paper against her fingertips, she found herself reluctant to look over what she had wrought. She took a long breath.

The centre of the grandstand was slag, orange, superheated, collapsing in on itself. An orange glowing hole in the roof below it, the grandstand around the edges of the blast twisted by the heat, blackened, black lumps of meat smoking and burning still in their seats, some in the space around. Crowd members who'd taken a few steps of agony before the fire consumed.

Red-Eyed Phu, one hand on the shoulder of the thing that was once Passaic Powell, pushed herself to her feet. She subvocalised: *Extraction*.

A few seconds later, the drone circled down and landed in the centre of the arena. The one that had stayed behind while the others responded to an assassination attempt on the head of the southern war. 'Drone' was not a very useful word to describe these things anymore. It could mean a hunter-killer drone ten feet long, so high up it was invisible; it could mean a fly drone buzzing around at knee level, transmitting everything it saw back.

This was an Imperial Overwatch drone. A metre in circumference, perfectly round. Eye in the sky, infrared, ultraviolent, telescopic, you name it. A heavy machine gun slung underneath, two-kilometre range. Watchdog favoured by the elite. Lin had asked Bao: "*How the fuck did you get one?*" He'd thought it over and replied: "[*We'll talk about that afterwards.*]"

Lin stepped onto the smooth convex top of the drone, took a knee.

Fires were burning all around now, eating the edges of the arena, smoke starting to rise from within the glowing hole in the roof, something on the floor below alight. She looked down on it all, red-eye black-eye, from her rage and grief. Hollowed out by both, the ecstasy of revenge moving her limbs her hands, living in her throat, her words, the grunt of blow and counterstrike. But her heart was empty, her eyes felt nothing.

Lin set her hands on the cool steel of the drone. "Extract."

Gently, the drone rose into the air, leaving the heat beneath her, the thin rain trickling down the back of her neck. The drone picked up speed, faster and faster, wet wind washing over her face, the city skimming by below. Further and further below, details distant, fleeting lights in the darkness.

In a translucent glassteel vial in her thigh pocket, a tetrapin. Mister Long's wipe: all she had to do was slot it in, and those things submerged, which she feared to see, would be gone forever. No sleep until it was done, no dreams.

She closed her eyes and felt the perfection of her body, adjusting and readjusting to the sway of the drone as it soared and banked through the sky. Blooming light made her open them again, the vision of a tall sleek hotel across the lake shattering, falling, wrapped in fierce fires.

She laughed and rode the shockwave.

79

Lin entered the office above Le Samourai. Bao Nguyen and Bull Neck Bui were there, glasses full. The bar below deserted, chairs up on tables, lights out, the painted holoscape of the city on the wall the only light.

Bao Nguyen sat behind his desk, smoking a cigarette. Bull Neck Bui clapped her on the back, pressed a glass of whiskey into her hand. "[Those motherfuckers,]" he said, "[reaped their harvest.]"

"Yeah," she said, and drank. The whiskey flavourless, no bite.

Lin set the glass on the table and sat opposite Bao.

"[The Aman is rubble, the Green Dragon shattered, the Fat Victory creators – military and civilian – now ashes, and the Macau Syndicate's point man in Hà Nội a cloud of dust and bone outside a cemetery.]"

"General Cao?"

Bao shrugged with his eyebrows. "[Survived, as expected.]"

"[That would have been a bonus,]" said Bull from behind. "[That son of a dog.]"

"Herbert. Hermann. Two-in-one. You going to let him live?"

Bao took his time smoking, sighed a cloud of smoke. "[During our attack, he deactivated the pinhead charge in his implant. Long must have helped him. They escaped together.]"

"*Fuck*."

"[You left Hermann with Long?]" asked Bull.

"Sure. You had a guy come up and put a bomb in Long's head, as well."

"[Yes,]" said Bao. "[I underestimated the Omissioner. But this is a small matter in the face of this victory.]"

"[We took down hundreds, elder sister,]" added Bull.

Something moved in her when he said *elder sister*. Lin tamped down on it, quick.

"[We were in retreat,]" said Bao. "[Now we are back to stalemate, as Guevara taught us. We need to talk about your role in the war, Silent One.]"

"That woman is dead, Uncle."

"[Quite so. Who is the woman, now, in her place?]"

"I am the thing you trained me to be."

"Ah." Bao looked at her, through the smoke rising from the tip of his cigarette. "[Let me ask you a question: those years of training under the Japanese master, what did you think I was preparing you for?]"

Lin was tired. That was what she was thinking about. Not some secret Bao was dancing around. The X-37 had taken it out of her, she could feel it – the ebb of years in those short moments of perfection. She could feel the weight of the tetrapin too, in her pocket, and its dark promise.

"[Years of training with the finest warrior. This was done not to learn how to collect debts from drug addicts, no, or all the ways one can break a knee.]"

"There was something bigger, I figured. To be tough enough to lead the gang, years away." Her limbs ached, she pushed herself deeper into the chair. "To lead a new concern. In Hội An or Huế. That's what I thought."

"[I was training you to be my replacement. I was training you to win an unwinnable war.]"

"Okay."

"[As leader of the Việt Minh resistance in Hà Nội.]"

He didn't smile. Bull was silent.

"What?"

"[I am not a gangster. This is not a gang. I am a colonel in the Vietnamese military. I never left. After I returned from Khe Sanh, I was ordered to infiltrate Hà Nội and command the Việt Minh resistance. I changed my name, as did Sergeant Bull, we chose ten men and women who had fought alongside us, and we took them to the Old Quarter. We took the name Bình Xuyên, a historical gang formed by military personnel back when the French took their turn in this country's history as its occupier. The Bình Xuyên were ruthless, their allegiances always questionable. It seemed appropriate.]"

He blew out a cloud of smoke, eyes on her, depthless, flat. "[I am a colonel, and this is my war. It will always be my war. It is yours as well, Lin Thi Vu. Today I will give you a commission as captain. You will fight here, resolute, and like your sister your bones will be buried here. This is your country.]"

Deadpan, as he said it all, and Bull still quiet, behind her. She reached for her cigarettes, tapped one out, lit it.

"But," she said, blowing out a cloud of smoke in the pause. "Those rebels we hunted down for the Chinese."

"[Deserters, petty criminals, low-level collaborators. Sometimes we gave them people who played both sides of the fence. Sometimes we would have an Omissioner implant false memories of insurgency for the interrogators to find. Other times we would take people who were informants to one wing of the military, and feed them to a different wing. So vast is the superstructure of the Chinese occupation, some parts may never touch another. Understand this, little sister: we never betrayed loyal Vietnamese. We never handed over a patriot.]"

Her mind was clearing, coming back from her last battle, now in the room, present. "That's why you think there will be a truce. The insurgency maintained order in the thirty-six streets, and when they were displaced all fucking hell broke loose." Bao nodded, she spoke through it: "But Peng knew you. They must know who you are, now. They will wipe you out."

"[No,]" said Bao.

He tamped out his cigarette, took his time lighting another. The smoke was heavy, full bloom under the lights above. Bao's eyes shaded. "[Colonel Peng recognised me because he fought against me. Think, Lin: it made more sense that he come to the head of the Bình Xuyên to help him eliminate Herbert Molayson and Raymond Chang, yes? Why go through the trouble of seeking support from the Green Dragon, when the Bình Xuyên appear to be already collaborating with the Chinese? I think he investigated me as an option to do his bidding, but soon realised I was the same man he fought against so many years before. If he knew who I was and what I went through, then he must have known that I would *never collaborate*.]" Bao's eye shone at the last, but he shut it down, drew on his cigarette. "[Or perhaps it was simple: he wished revenge. It was my men who committed those grievous wounds on him. We sabotaged a stockpile of missiles with nano-virus warheads, right in the centre of his military base. Perhaps this really was just revenge.]" He tapped ash into the bronze ashtray. "[Either way, he told no one of these details, not even his boss in Macau. It was just him and his ambition, searing. He wanted to advance his criminal standing through Fat Victory; he also wanted to protect the military commanders from direct knowledge, so there would be no repercussions. Internally, or internationally. Now they will wish to root out the Việt Minh who launched this brazen attack and disturbed the stable veneer of this occupation.]"

"They'll need local collaborators, who can hand over suspects," said Lin. Bull rose and made to refill her whiskey. She waved away the bottle, Bull looked surprised. "I'm not Vietnamese. I can't lead. Be an officer."

"[Yes,]" said Bao, agreeing. "[It will be very difficult for the Chinese to suspect someone who does not even believe herself to be Vietnamese. Who refuses to speak the language, even though fluent.]"

Lin pursed her lips. "Fluent?"

"[Close to.]" Bao glanced over at Bull. "[Better accent than a southerner, anyway.]"

Bull raised an eyebrow.

Lin said: "But every time I try people laugh."

"[They laugh,]" said Bull, "[because every time you try, your face cracks and turns red. And more. You scare the men, elder sister, all stony-faced and silent. One word out of place and you stomp a man's face into a drain. They laugh because you make them nervous.]"

"But I'm not Vietnamese. I'm not anything."

"[You're a warrior,]" said Bao. "[You're a weapon. You lack people skills—]" Bull grunted at this, Bao ignored him and continued: "[But that is what Sergeant Bull is for, to issue your orders, to police morale, to explain to you what is going on in the minds of your soldiers.]"

It swelled and stirred within her. Sentiment, pride, even connectedness. To this old man and the quiet hate of his obsession. To Bull, loyal sergeant, self-sacrificing friend.

She ran a thumb against her bottom lip. "A week ago I would have accepted this. It may have even made me happy. For a short time. But now I have a different plan."

Smoke gathered around Bao's grey hair. "[Which is?]"

"Take the pin in my pocket, plug it in. Wipe all of the useless sentiments away. Go to Macau, and burn the whole fucken city to the ground."

Bull barked a laugh from behind.

Bao said: "[That is no life, little sister.]"

Lin indicated the room, the booze on the table with her eyes. "This is?"

"[Yes,]" he said, eyes shining. "[Yes.]"

"I am what that master trained me to be. I am his disciple."

"[The master was a madman,]" said Bao. "[He didn't even know his own name.]"

"He was the greatest warrior I've ever known."

"[You beat him.]"

"Did I?"

Bao, who had leaned further forward in his chair during the exchange, eased himself back again. He took a deep breath, considering the top of his cigarette, the young woman in front of him.

"[Vietnam has always had a problem with memory,]" he said, finally. "[The purpose of Fat Victory was to exploit this, twist it and twist it further. The Chinese want us to be a country so turned in on itself, so patently false, that we ourselves do not believe it anymore. They want us, in essence, to be a country without memory.]" His cigarette crackled as he drew on it. "[But this is beside the point. The point is history. At the end of what is called the Second World War, Ho Chi Minh was asked by the United Nations whether he wanted Northern Vietnam administered by the French, or by the Chinese. He answered immediately: *the French*. Later, when one of his men asked him why he made the decision so easily, he answered: *Better to sniff French shit for a while than to eat Chinese dung for the rest of our lives*.]"

"Oh. Yeah? Because the French were weak?"

"[Because, Lin, the Chinese occupied these lands for nine hundred years. We became a southern province called Jiaozhi. The French, the Americans, they were gone in the blink of an eye. Vietnam is the only colony the Chinese ever lost. Tibet, Mongolia, then later Hong Kong, and finally Taiwan were returned. You see, Lin, China is the only civilisation worth worrying about. The only serious empire, that has stood the test of time. The Romans lasted fourteen hundred years. The Khmer six hundred. The British four hundred. The Americans a hundred, at most. China has been an empire since before the birth of their Christ. They will be an empire until Christ's second coming.

"[But not here, not in Vietnam. We are history's exception. Yet our rebelliousness came at a price. The heaviest imaginable. The horrors of all these wars are hard for a people to face. Our history threatens to swallow us in its darkness. It is a buried giant we dare not awaken. So we try to forget. We tried to forget the American War, so long ago, even as we try to forget the Chinese War, here in our midst. Dramas on c-cast trot out the tired old tropes of virtuous, stoic Vietnamese fighters battling perfidious oppressors, while novels portraying the genuine horrors of the conflict like *The Sorrow of War* remain unread. The monstrosity of what was done to our people – the industrial-scale murder, the deployment of technologies which reap grotesque distortions upon bodies and mind and nature itself – hidden, denied, wiped, forgotten.

"[So on the one hand we have Vietnam, expert in suppressing trauma and feeling, and on the other we have our invaders, China, the artisans of amnesia. Whole swaths of their history rewritten to suit the politics of the present day. Forgetting parts of their history undesirable, remembering anew historical precedents that never happened. Two countries, in symbiosis, forgetting and remembering immanent to the identity of each.]"

It was quiet in the room. Save the crackle of cigarettes, and strands of traffic noise seeping in from somewhere far away. Bao motioned at the windows.

"[Most of the main streets in our cities are named after heroes who fought the Chinese: Hai Bà Trưng, the sisters who led a rebellion two thousand years ago; Ngô Quyền, who freed the country from Chinese occupation a thousand years ago; Trần Hưng Đạo, who defeated the Mongols; Lê Lợi, who defeated the Ming; and Quang Trung, who defeated the Qing. Yet no one remembers what these names signify anymore. Not officially.

"[So we suppress the traumas of previous centuries, as we suppress the trauma of this day. But here we all worship the spirit of our ancestors in every home. The past is never suppressed, not totally. The act of forgetting is both mechanical and natural. We can erase and alter records. We can also erase and alter memory feeds, to bring them into line with the history China wishes us to have. But the final act of forgetting is the most audacious and most necessary. We have to *choose* to do it. We must sleepwalk into an eternal present, without a past to guide us, without a dream of future to lead us. Only then will we be conquered. Without memory we lose the vitality of our resistance, Lin. We lose the strength given to us, transmitted from our past.]"

He gestured at her with the fingers holding his cigarette. "[And this is what you wish to bring upon yourself.]"

"Yes," she said, without pause.

"[Yes?]"

"I am not a people, Uncle. I am not an idea. I am a weapon. To be the perfect weapon, I need only to conquer myself. But I will still dream. I will dream of the death of my sister and of Kylie, every night, and every day I will bring about vengeance."

"[That is no life. That is a torment. You will be as a spectre, wandering and lost.]"

Lin was silent; Bao waited, eyes gleaming. She finished her drink while Bao waited and Bull, behind her, retained his uncharacteristic silence. "My master knew, didn't he? That you were Việt Minh."

Bao paused at the change in track. His eyes flicked over to Bull, then back to her. "[He suspected.]"

"That's why."

"[Yes. This is why.]"

Her fingers twitched at the memory.

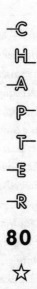

CHAPTER

80

☆

In their forty-fifth fight, the master stumbled as they walked out onto the mats. He grunted, to himself, smooth features disturbed by the drug-glaze in his eyes, by his confusion. He ran his hand over his dark, crisp moustache, looking down at the tatami mats, thinking.

Again, Lin was aware of the tightness in her chest, anticipating his realisation, his accusation. Bao, sitting in the corner, waiting, had put away his flexiscreen and now stood, the shine of his eyes and the orange tip of his cigarette visible. What he'd do with the accusation, whether she'd be expelled from the gang.

But her shihan just looked up and said: "Tanto."

She nodded, relieved twice over. The tanto were essentially long daggers. Paired, Japanese, curved blades, speed weapons – easily her most preferred. She picked them from the rack, red leather handles, perfectly balanced, nano-edged blades. Took her position on the mats as shihan took his opposite, tanto in each hand.

They bowed.

Lin pointed at him with one, raised the other over her head. The master raised his chin, pointed both at her, and charged.

And stumbled, fractionally, overbalanced, too much momentum and Lin side-stepped slashed, and turned. The master turned also, feet crossing awkwardly side to side, one hand pressed against his ribs, blood leaking past his fingertips, the handle of his blade.

She came at him, he blocked both her strikes, wild counterstrike, she ducked easily, he whirly-whirled, drip-painting the tatami with his blood. Lin swallowed her guilt and came again, feint high / low strike, both blades biting deep, the master grunting. He didn't go down. Just turned again to face her, one leg trailing, blood stain blossoming along his white gi.

He looked at her, somehow still in his preternatural calm, features unmoved.

"[You would never have beaten me,]" he said. "[I should have anticipated your gambit.]"

She opened her mouth, to answer, to deny, she wasn't sure. But all Lin had time to do was part her lips before the master rushed at her, steel flashing, and she stepped back and the blades rang out muscle memory driving her strike / counterstrike.

And when it was over, the master was lying on the tatami, both hands pressed against his stomach, trying to hold in his intestines. He closed his eyes, opened them, controlling his breathing, eyes on the ceiling above.

Lin flinched, belatedly, face stinging, and put the back of her hand to it. Her cheekbone, cut open.

Bao walked from the shadows, cigarette in one hand, the other in the pocket of his trousers. He took a long drag as he looked down at the master, blew a slow cloud into the air. Her heart hammered inside her chest as she struggled to catch her breath. Otherwise it was silent in the space. The master didn't groan or take shallow breaths. Just lay there, like he was having an afternoon repose, looking at the clouds.

"We should get him into the medical centre," said Lin.

Bao looked at her like he hadn't heard. He said: "[Violence is the language of the streets, little sister. You are an instrument of that violence. You are the pen, and you are the calligrapher. Of course, to be a calligrapher worthy of that name takes years of practice under a master. More than the strokes and forms, one must understand the history, the moment, and the meaning of what you do and write. Now you have developed the correct memories in your muscles, and the knowledge of how to use them, I will teach you the rest. I will teach you the history and the meaning of the thirty-six streets.]"

Lin glanced down at the master, lips parted, but Bao continued, intense, unperturbed.

"[Violence is an art, Lin. And unlike scribbles on a piece of paper, violence is the only art worth knowing. Knowing: how to bend a man, how to break one. Knowing: how much to bloody an enemy, until that enemy makes the decisions you wish them to make. Violence as negotiation, violence as proposal and counter-proposal, violence as a language, universal and complete.

"[It is an art that exists only in the act. Knowing: never to shrink from a violent act, never to waver. Knowing: each moment in this world requires either an act of violence or the promise of it. You must be both instrument and master, both the will and the act.

"[It is said that power flows from the barrel of a gun. This is true. But only if you are willing to pull the trigger. The gun and the will, the will and the act. Violence is the only art worth knowing, Lin Thi Vu, because power is the only abstraction worth possessing. Everything else flows from this. Civilisation, culture, nation, all of it.]"

Lin looked from him and his speech, back to the master, lying on the floor. If he was listening to Bao, he gave no indication of it.

Through the haze of his smoke, Bao said: "[More.]"

Lin pressed her lips together. The pool of blood around the master was growing. As it was, he'd be in the medical bay for a week, maybe more. She tightened her jaw, reversed the blade, yelling: "Hey-yah," as she struck downwards. The master's nose crunched underneath the pommel. At first she thought she'd knocked him out. But he opened his eyes, again, bloodshot, and looked straight at her.

"[More,]" said Bao Nguyen.

Lin looked up at Bao, gestured at the master with her tanto. "He's done."

"[More.]"

Bao's gaze didn't waver, and finally she felt his intent, creeping up her spine.

"He's done," she said, softly.

"[More.]"

She looked down again at the Japanese warrior. His eyes met hers, blood on his lips, and his gaze tracked back to the roof and stayed there. Waiting.

Lin Thi Vu reversed her blade and knelt by the man. Her knee soaked by his pooling blood.

She whispered: "The will and the act," and thrust her blade into his heart.

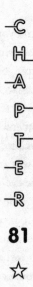
"I'm leaving, Uncle," she said. "For Macau, and I want you to give me a visa."

Bao said nothing, so Bull spoke up. "[Impossible, Lin, to get you there now, even for us. Listen. You won, elder sister. You cut the throats of these dogs. Listen,]" he said again, plaintive. Lin turned to face him, give him that at least. Bull's large hands were on his knees, as he leaned forward and spoke. "[These streets are your home. These motherfuckers, what they did to your mother and to Phuong, they do this every day. To families, to the sons and daughters of Vietnam. My wife. If revenge is the only thing that moves you anymore, be moved by their plight.]"

"No," she said, her throat thick.

He opened his mouth to say more, but she turned to face Bao. "You gave me my identity. Now I embrace it."

Bao's eyes shone. "[You are talking about annihilating yourself. No. I just wanted to prepare you, little sister, for the horrors to come.]"

"And you did. You wanted me to become accustomed to pain. My own, and that of others. You wanted me to no longer view my body as sacred, because someone who no longer believes in the sanctity of the human body is capable of doing anything to the bodies of others. Were you trying to make me a veteran, Bao? Were you trying to make me understand your horrors? Perhaps, perhaps not. Maybe you don't even realise it yourself.

"I was an orphan, Uncle. I was abandoned by my own mother, and no one ever even told me why. This makes a person worth nothing. I wasn't even worth an *explanation*. Now I have been orphaned twice. It hurts to be an orphan, it hurts more than any pain you can imagine. I tried to avoid that pain my whole life. But I've been hurt so many times I can't feel anymore. I can't feel a thing. I don't care about my heart, and you made it so I don't care about my body."

He made to speak and she said: "No. This isn't a criticism, Bao. I thank you, for this. I'm free of all my pain. Well: almost free. My shihan showed me the final path."

"Lin," he said, voice breaking. She swallowed. It was the first time she had seen him show any real emotion, outside of hate.

"My sister and Kylie will not rest. Their ghosts will walk these streets."

"[You avenged them.]"

"Did Peng give the order?"

"[Yes. You know this.]"

"No. I mean the order to develop Fat Victory and trial it on the Vietnamese."

"Lin—"

"The whole story is bigger than Peng, than Long, than us."

"[You are as my daughter.]" Tears welled in Bao's eyes. "[You belong here, with your family. We love you.]"

Lin felt her throat thicken again. She stood. Stood to do something to stop her hesitation, to break her rising emotion. She cleared her throat. "Yeah. Well. Maybe I saw you as a father, Bao. I don't know for sure. You see, I never had one to compare you against. There was a man once, who came close. But I put a blade in that man's heart, and watched him die.

"Maybe I wanted this place to be home. But I never knew one of those either, never knew one year to the next whether my country wanted me, or just wanted me to go away. But I do know love." Her voice caught. She breathed out and started again, voice even. "I love my sister and my—" She made herself breathe. "—I loved Phuong and now she's gone. All I have left in the world, anymore, is to win every fight. All that matters is the next fight, the one after, the one after that. And on until I have killed every last motherfucker that took away the better part of myself."

She wanted to say more, to get it all out, but she felt the pressure growing in her chest and instead whirled and walked from the room.

That was the last time she saw them. Faces sad and disbelieving, fading away in the smoke and shadow.

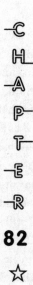

CHAPTER

82

☆

Lin's blades whirred into her hands, one raised above her head, ready to hurl. A man was in her chair, facing the door, his features in shadow. Her senses reached out automatically, all around her, checking for footsteps behind, breathing in the next room.

There was none of that, no one else. Her eyes adjusted to the gloom quickly and she realised she knew the man, sitting in her seat, in her apartment, drinking her sake.

She lowered her blades, shut the door with her foot.

"Xin Huan," she said, her voice cold.

Phuong's husband, face and shoulders slumped, bottle of sake in his hand. He was wearing his uniform, crumpled, the collar stained. His impressive jawline set at an angle that made it a parody of strength, crippled by grief.

"Lin?" he asked, unsure.

"Lin is gone," she said.

He stared at her for a long time. "[No. Yes. You've changed your face. But it is you.]"

Lin slotted her blades at her hips, ran a hand through her short hair, thinking. Xin watched her as she breathed out, took two ceramic cups from the kitchen, set them on the coffee table in front of him, and poured both to the brim. He seemed surprised as she pulled the bottle from his hand, as though he couldn't remember how it got there. There wasn't much left.

Lin sat opposite the Chinese captain and raised her cup, waiting until he had fumbled for his, and drank, before she downed hers as well.

"[I still see her in you. I still see her.]" His eyes were wet.

"There's nothing of Phuong in me," she replied, quietly.

He said nothing at this, his mind not in the same space as his body.

"That's why you came," she said. "You wanted to see my sister again."

Xin looked at her, tearing his gaze away from some dark pocket universe of his grief. He nodded, eyes still wet, lips pressed together.

Lin closed her eyes, letting out a long breath. Too much, to look at this broken man. Not wishing to see the same darkness he saw. The slight press of the tetrapin, in her pocket, reminded her of its presence.

"There's something you can do," she said. "For Phuong."

His head tilted towards her. "[Yes?]"

She thought back to the end of her conversation with Bao. "You can help me get to Macau."

"[What is in Macau?]"

"Revenge."

He blinked a couple of times, eyes on her, and pushed himself upright in his seat. "[Revenge,]" he repeated.

"On the people responsible for Phuong's death. Those right at the top. It leads back to Macau."

"Oh," he said. Not much changed in his face, his hands still on the armrest. They sat in silence; the building did not. It was never silent. The sound of footfalls or conversation carried through the

424

walls, from the corridor, other rooms. Pipes banging, the wash of rain against the window, laughter. A building living and breathing and moving with the people in it, pressed up against each other's lives, their meals their squabbles their tragedies. Gossiping with each other, jealous of each other's successes, mourning each other's losses, together. All except the woman on the third floor, who never spoke, who hid her face and her words, out in the middle of the night, haunting the building like a pale spectre.

Xin Huan broke her trance, his trance, feeling for something in the breast pocket of his uniform. He pulled out a rigid rectangle of translucent plastic.

"[Your gangster friends will never be able to get you out of the country legally,]" he said. "[For that you need someone with real power.]"

"Yeah? Who would that be?"

"[A bureaucrat.]"

She smiled, tired. After midnight. Later. Not able to sleep, not yet.

"[What name are you going to travel under?]"

She shrugged. "Doesn't make a difference."

"[No. But still you need one.]"

"Linh Phu, then."

His eyes moved from her to the wafer-thin rectangle between his thumb and forefinger. He whispered into it, his lips close; it glowed softly in reply.

"[Closer,]" he said to Lin. "[Come closer.]"

She pulled herself from her chair, limbs aching, and moved over to him. He passed her the rectangle and said: "[Hold this in front of your eye for five seconds. Don't blink.]"

She did and the thin material blipped, happily.

Xin held his hand out, she passed it back to him.

"[You have your visa, Linh Phu.]"

She hesitated.

"[It's done,]" he said. "[You can travel there freely. So go, weave your blood magic.]"

"I will," she replied.

He roused himself from the couch. Xin Huan was tall, nearly a head bigger than she. He looked into her eyes, close, searching. Lin felt something stir in her then, though she could not name it. Perhaps he did too, but it did not matter. He wouldn't find what he was searching for. He'd never find it.

The tall officer moved his attention to some other place. Moved past her, the material of his jacket brushing her shoulder, and left her life without another word.

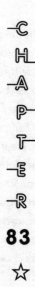

CHAPTER

83

☆

...I sit dizzied, shocked by the barbarous excitement of reliving close combat with bayonets and rifle butts. My heart beats rapidly as I stare at the dark corners of the room where ghost-soldiers emerge, shredded with gaping wounds.

My life seems little different from that of a sampan pushed upstream towards the past. The future lied to us, there long ago in the past. There is no new life, no new era, nor is it hope for a beautiful future that now drives me on, but rather the opposite. The hope is contained in a beautiful prewar past.

The tragedies of the war years have bequeathed to my soul the spiritual strength that allows me to escape the infinite present. The little trust and will to live that remains stems not from illusions but from the power of my recall...

Linh closed the pages, placed the novel on the coffee table. She took the pin from the slender glass tube, the magic that would give her only the infinite present, refine her powers of recall so only one motivation remained. It shone in the palm of her hand, in the new dawn light slanting through the windows. No longer trapped in a past of endless white beaches, of arms wrapped around her as she whimpered sleepless, holding her with fierce and fathomless love. A woman's tender voice singing Flame Trees to her, while her sister slept nearby, deeply and at peace. Trapped in an illusion of belonging, calling to her from the past.

She slotted the tetrapin into her cochlear implant.

Linh Phu rose, picking up the small backpack as she did so. Express cruise, third class cabin, leaving Hạ Long Bay just after lunchtime. She had an early train to catch down to the coast. Tired, but she would sleep on the ship. Sleep and wake, born again.

She clicked open the door to Barry's cage. "You're free."

The bird looked at the open door, but stayed on its perch.

"You gonna give me a song before I go, Barry? Last chance."

The bird turned its head, one black shining eye regarding her for a few moments.

"Don't worry. I won't remember it. Won't remember you."

He fluffed the feathers at his throat. Lin leaned forward.

But Barry simply hopped back to the other side of the cage and looked out the window. A little yellow sentinel, watching the day as it passed.

The door to her apartment open, Lin left the book behind and all the other things she had gathered in her years. Down to the street and thick humid air, enveloping her.

Linh walked the thirty-six streets one more time.

The early-morning hawkers called out as she passed them. The traffic washed by, the people a stream that parted around her. Kids yelled and ran up and down the sidewalk. The smell of fish sauce and sewer and fried chili and the blare of scooter horns filled the early-morning air. Bicycles fitted with small speaker systems rode past, blaring exhortations to report dissidents, not to park on the sidewalk, to not use car and bike horns.

Thick black electrical wires ran overhead, dozens bundled together, legal and illegal, twisted around trees and poles like some noxious invasive species. She eased her way past a gnarled, five-foot-tall woman carrying a bamboo pole across her shoulders, laden with fruit, haggling with another woman over the price. Past the families cooking their breakfasts on the sidewalk, pots over solar stoves, laughing with their neighbours.

The city pressed in on all her senses, the noise like a second skin. Down these streets, past crumbling Buddhist temples sandwiched between handbag stores, past the cafés with their strong sweet condensed milk coffees.

An eternal city, ancient yet ageless, refusing to change as the world outside grew brighter, and shinier, and taller, conjured and raised by the spells of the neon gods. Not the thirty-six streets, never this place, caught in a pocket of time, querulous, refusing to change, to submit, to be anything other than what it always was.

Linh paused. Up ahead, a woman walked towards her, by her, passed by. A woman with a genuine smile on her face, broad, as she took in the city, exchanged banter with the street sellers. Jeans, leather jacket, full hips, alive. Phuong, her sister, walking towards her, arms almost touching, right past without saying a word to Linh, without seeing her. Linh turned, looked back down the street.

The doppelgänger was gone into thin air, the crowds, the city.

Linh felt a weight on her chest and so she turned back the way she was headed. Back down through the streets. The heart of Hà Nội, beating mad and proud and wild. These thirty-six streets would outlive her, outlive the occupation, outlive the meanness and calamity of time.

The pressure on her chest stayed. The ache. It didn't matter.

Soon she would sleep. In her dreams, she would leave this land and its ghosts behind. She would dream of a terrible future and make it come to pass. No longer bound by the illusions of the past, no longer part of these eternal streets.

Linh Phu made her path into the infinite, sublime present. Beyond happiness. Beyond sorrow.

About the author

T.R. Napper is a multi-award-winning science fiction author. His short stories have appeared in *Asimov's*, *Interzone*, *The Magazine of Fantasy & Science Fiction*, and numerous others, and been translated into Hebrew, German, French, and Vietnamese. He received a creative writing doctorate for his thesis: *Noir, Cyberpunk, and Asian Modernity*.

Before turning to writing, T. R. Napper was a diplomat and aid worker, delivering humanitarian programs in Southeast Asia for a decade. During this period, he received a commendation from the Government of Laos for his work with the poor. He also was a resident of the Old Quarter in Ha Noi for several years, the setting for *36 Streets*.

These days he has returned to his home country of Australia, where he works as a Dungeon Master, running campaigns for young people with autism for a local charity.

Acknowledgements

My agent, John Jarrold, and the editor of Titan Books, George Sandison, who took a chance on this novel when no one else would. Bao Ninh, whose novel changed the way I understood Vietnam, even as I lived there. Duc Qui Nguyen, rebel poet, for the whisky. Kim Huynh, for your affirmation.

Fellow bogan, Kaaron, for the wine. Louise, for reading it. Jen, for the conversation, when this was all being done. Adrian, for making that other project happen, which in turned helped lead to this one. Richard Morgan, a cyberpunk savant, for his enthusiastic support of an unknown author.

Most of all my partner, Sarah, who was there for me all the way, good times and bad, lockdowns and free. Thanks babe. My sons: Willem, mischievous prince and pocket tsunami; Robert, Minecraft pro, my best friend and companion every day on the streets of Hanoi. None of this matters, without you three.

THE RIG
by Roger Levy

Humanity has spread across the depths of space but is connected by AfterLife – a vote made by every member of humanity on the worth of a life. Bale, a disillusioned policeman on the planet Bleak, is brutally attacked, leading writer Razer on to a story spanning centuries of corruption. On Gehenna, the last religious planet, a hyperintelligent boy, Alef, meets psychopath Pellonhorc and so begins a rivalry and friendship to last an epoch.

"Roger Levy is SF's best kept secret, and *The Rig* is a tour de force: a darkly brilliant epic of life, death and huge drilling platforms. Read it and discover what you've been missing." Adam Roberts

"Rich in theme, elegant in execution, full of fire and purpose... a space-operatic plot of dazzling intricacy and dizzying scope." James Lovegrove

"A welcome return from a thoughtful and gifted writer." Gareth L. Powell, author of *Embers of War*

"This is a good, propulsive tale that owes much to Philip K. Dick's underground paranoia fable 'The Penultimate Truth' and is at times really sadistic." *The Telegraph* on *Icarus*

STARS AND BONES
by Gareth L. Powell

Seventy-five years from today, the human race has been cast from a dying Earth to wander the stars in a vast fleet of arks—each shaped by its inhabitants into a diverse and fascinating new environment, with its own rules and eccentricities.

When her sister disappears while responding to a mysterious alien distress call, Eryn insists on being part of the crew sent to look for her. What she discovers on Candidate-623 is both terrifying and deadly. When the threat follows her back to the fleet and people start dying, she is tasked with seeking out a legendary recluse who may just hold the key to humanity's survival.

"Gareth Powell drops you into the action from the first page and then Just. Keeps. Going. This is a pro at the top of his game." John Scalzi

"A headlong, visceral plunge into a future equal parts fascinating and terrifying." Adrian Tchaikovsky

"A gripping, fast-paced space opera that poses the unique question: what if instead of saving humanity, aliens decided to save the Earth?" Stina Leicht, author of *Persephone Station*

"A grand scale adventure packed with fun banter, snappy prose, and masterful science." Essa Hansen, author of *Nophek Gloss*

TITANBOOKS.COM